SUMMARY

He's the most dangerous male she's ever met...

All witch and part succubus, savvy businesswoman Raina runs an
old-fashioned bordello out of a historic Southern plantation home.
Because of her abilities, the demons under Raina's protection can feed
off the sexual energy of their clients without killing them—definitely a
good thing for repeat business.

But when Dark Guardian Mikhael Roman tracks a rogue incubus
to her doorstep, everything is at risk. Raina will enter a dangerous
match of wits with him to achieve their mutual goals—only to
discover that the reluctant attraction between her and Mikhael is the
most hazardous game of all...

[NOTE: *Arcane Madame* was originally released under the title *In
the Company of Witches*.]

ARCANE MADAME

An Arcane Shot Series Novel

JOEY W. HILL

Arcane Madame

Formerly Titled: In the Company of Witches

An Arcane Shot Series Novel - Book #2

Copyright © 2012 - 2018 Joey W. Hill

Cover design by W. Scott Hill

Original publication 2012 by the Penguin Group, Penguin Group (USA) Inc. 375 Hudson Street, New York, New York 10014, USA

SWP Digital & Print Edition publication April 2018 by Story Witch Press, 452 Mattamushkeet Dr., Little River, South Carolina 29566, USA

The following material contains graphic sexual content meant for mature readers. Reader discretion is advised.

Digital ISBN: 978-1-942122-73-9

Print ISBN: 978-1-951544-19-5

ACKNOWLEDGMENTS

It's always amazing, the types of information you need when you write a story about characters who have an array of skills, experiences or even hobbies the author knows nothing about. I'm therefore exceedingly glad I have a wonderful network of friends with far more diverse interests than this author, who rarely sees the light of day beyond the glow of her computer screen.

My deepest thanks to Arwen, who, through her Tarot by Arwen site, was kind enough to provide a comprehensive tarot reading on my hero that revealed an amazing side to Mikhael, as well as created a great scene opportunity to open Raina's heart to him further.

On that same note, I also thank Bernie, the father of my childhood friend. He intrigued me with his enthusiasm for model trains, such that they found their way into this book in an unexpected way—and tempted me to buy a train myself! My additional thanks to him for reviewing that portion of the story to ensure I didn't make any faux pas related to this delightful hobby.

Last but not least, my thanks to Ted, my brother, for soldiering through a chapter of romance (written by his sister—ugh!) to help tweak my understanding of poker.

As always, any errors are entirely my own. My thanks to everyone who added to this story to make it the best journey possible for the readers.

CHAPTER ONE

Something was coming. Damn it all to hell and back.

Every time she planned an evening for herself, the Underworld had to vomit out some kind of trouble. A hundred million places it could go, but no, it oozed right to the doorstep of her bordello.

"All I wanted was a cup of tea, *People* magazine and a movie." Raina cast an irritated eye toward the heavens. "What? You don't get enough Me time, so I can't have any, either?"

Yeah, pissing off the Goddess right before trouble arrived was a winning plan. The wind picked up, bringing a wealth of messages with it. Nothing clear except one thing—danger. Stepping to the edge of the porch, Raina saw heat lightning flash, heard the distant rumble of thunder. A gust blew across her velvet skirt, rippling it against her legs.

"*Whaaatsuuup?*"

At the deep man's voice, she flicked a glance toward Cathair. The raven was perched on the porch swing. His weight was settled low, so with the flex of his claws and the help of the rising wind, the swing maintained a steady rhythm.

"Not sure yet. Be still for now."

His usual response to that command was an impudent composition of the most obnoxious sounds in his repertoire. Discordant screeches, hoarse coughing sounds, and a peppering of vulgar words

1

strung together in a creative way. But, sensing what she was sensing, her familiar stayed silent, his head cocked, bright eyes sharp.

Moving down the wooden steps, she listened to the resonances coming through the weathered planking. Not clear enough. She descended to the stone walkway and stepped onto the grass alongside it, a cold cushion for her toes. Instantly, a shiver went up into her soul. Power. Lots of it.

Whatever was coming, it was coming fast, through the forest.

The winding drive to the Queen Anne–style house was about a mile long, all of it through thick wood and marsh. Ancient oaks draped with Spanish moss lined the road like gray-bearded, gnarled wizards, the great ancients of times past. The energy running through those trees now was electric, crackling static, radios gone haywire.

Might be good to get a head start on this one. She shrugged her shoulders, cracked her neck. Let her hair loose, so it blew down her back. Dropping to a squat, she slapped one palm flat on the earth, drawing energy. The other she thrust to the sky, pulling light from the moon and the air stream scudding the clouds across the dark firmament. When her gaze went to the center fountain, its waters rippled as if her hand had swept across it, a disruption of its flow. Nerve endings tingled along her spine, her palms heating from the elemental charge.

As she straightened, her eyes narrowed. The driveway appeared to be moving. Snakes, coming out of the foliage. About a dozen of them, copperheads, black snakes, a rattler. A blink later, two alligators followed. In the coastal South, a reptile pedestrian crossing wasn't unusual. Those coming up the driveway to indulge in the dark delights her bordello had to offer would slow their vehicles until the animal passed. But seeing a mass exodus of snakes, in the company of alligators, was not the norm. Whatever was coming was not headed in her direction for the pleasures the house had to offer—it was coming for the sanctuary it provided.

Walking down the lawn, she passed the Sweet Dreams welcome sign, positioned before the center fountain. Glittering water poured over the smooth, sculpted lines of a naked man and woman embracing in erotic bliss. Over the sound of that, she heard the rushing beat of Cathair's wings as the raven took flight. Glancing up, she saw him pass across the yellow crescent moon, then do a loop. She braced herself out of habit as he landed on her shoulder, but he folded his wings with minimal mussing of her hair, underscoring the seriousness of the situation.

"Be ready to move," she said, low. "I wouldn't want to ruffle your feathers."

He hunkered down like a soldier settling into a foxhole. She almost smiled, but then she was hit full blast.

Panic, desperation. Air... She struggled to work through the images tumbling through her mind. Blood, death. Pain. She was in the head of something running for its life. A male, gasping for air as he ran through the swamp. Trying to escape.

She focused, parsing his emotional responses from her own, steadied. He was coming from the southwest side of her property. However, he wasn't her main concern. She extended her senses, pushing past him. What was following him? That was the true threat. She didn't identify it right away, but she caught a magical whiff of something strong, deadly...male. Something that had every intention of catching up to the fugitive and using lethal means to get what he wanted from him.

Automatically, she reinforced the wards on her house. Inside, those she protected stirred, feeling the danger, so she sent them a compulsion to stay where they were. It was Sunday evening, the only day of the week they slept at night. The Bible was a good practical handbook, all said and done.

Sex demons stayed on a better keel when they observed a day of rest.

Plus, they'd only be in the way. Ironically, most succubi and incubi were lethal in a sexual encounter, but less than useless in a fight. A macabre twist on the whole *lover not a fighter* adage.

Another blast of fear hit her like an ocean wave. The prey was running, scrambling, using every ounce of self-preservation to get to her. His testicles were shrunk up into his body. If what was behind him caught up, death would be the least of his worries.

Unfortunately, what pursued him was closing the gap, and suddenly it was a direct ping on her radar. A crimson dot moving calm, steady...cold.

Oh, shit. A Dark Guardian.

Fuck. Her lips drew back in a snarl. She loved her quiet Sundays, the fact she had very few roles to play. She'd sit on the tower balcony, listen to her music and feed Cathair bits of biscotti. She'd already picked out her movie for the night. *Titanic*, because she'd seen it a hundred times and loved it even more each time. Now Leonardo and Kate's beautiful scene at the prow of a doomed ship was going to have to wait because a damn Dark Guardian was making an unplanned visit.

That just pissed her off.

Sifting the power she'd drawn from the elements, she spun it up fast and sharp, like revving a street racer before the light change. Since it was going to be a shitty night, she might as well come out fighting. The fugitive was one of her brethren, an incubus. Though she was only half sex demon, she was all witch. The Guardian wasn't going to get him, even if she had to use her dead body to stop him.

There. The frightened male broke out of the forest. He was swift, as their kind could be, flashing over the ground. However, as fast as he was, she already knew he wasn't going to make it.

"Duck," she shouted, raising her hands. *"Do it, now!"*

Fortunately, he wasn't too panicked to listen. He dropped.

Her power crackled past his head like a horizontal lightning blast. Twenty yards behind him, just inside the forest line, that volley hit a force field. She had herself braced for impact, but it still felt like she'd slammed her fists against a brick wall, shock and pain reverberating through every joint and bone from fingertips to collarbone. Cathair let out a shriek and took off.

The backwash of her power glittered along the full scope of the Guardian's protective shield, about fifty feet wide and at least that high. *Holy Goddess.*

Never mind. She might not have hurt him, but she'd slowed him down. The incubus hadn't needed further instruction. As soon as she'd loosed her power, he'd been moving toward her like a veteran marine, his pelvis glued to the earth and his strong arms and legs pumping like a crab's. The whites of his eyes were prominent as a cue ball, lips drawn back in a rictus of fear, his body soaked in sweat.

She shot another barrage over his head, buying him more time, but this time the Guardian answered. The incubus cringed to a halt as red flame arced through the sky and speared the ground at her feet, billowing out searing heat. Seeing it coming, she slammed down a

4

protection on herself and the sex demon, just in time. Only that kept her from being flung back up on the porch. Even so, the charge rang through her legs, making her sway, but she locked her knees, held fast.

"Get over here," she snarled at the incubus as she suppressed the fire with an air-sucking counter-spell. Lifting his head from beneath his hands, he shot forward in that same low-level crawl.

"Damn it." Some of the flame had squeezed through a crack in the protection and the fluttering hem of her dress had caught fire. She doused it, scowling at the scorched edge. She'd have to shorten it, and she liked that hem, nearly two hundred inches around, so it flowed just right when she moved. *Asshole Guardian.*

The incubus collapsed behind her. He was wheezing like a hunting dog who'd gotten too carried away with a scent and overtaxed his lungs. Or gotten lost from his clod-headed owner and nearly starved in the swamp. She'd nursed a few of those stressed beasts when they stumbled into her driveway. Found them nice homes and didn't lose a bit of sleep over the whereabouts of the owner. There was plenty of need and reason to kill in the world if you had the itch for blood and the balls to do it. Blasphemy to be doing it for sport.

Keeping the canine theme in mind, she glanced at the incubus. "Stay," she ordered. "I can't protect you if you move away from me. Nod if you understand."

She asked for the confirmation, because his almond-shaped eyes were half-wild. He wasn't like the incubi and succubi who lived in her establishment. Nor even one of those who'd learned to live unnoticed on the fringes of human society. Though he had the shape of a man, everything else about him told her he lived as a deadly scavenger, an opportunistic feeder who'd never known or learned better. She was all too familiar with the story. What hunted him probably held the usual philosophy toward her kind. Exterminate them.

The old, bitter rage turned over inside her, but she pushed it back. She'd need her wits about her, because it was about to become that kind of fight. The Guardian had only fired the one volley, and that told her he'd been checking to see if she'd turn tail and scamper back into the house. Yeah, that'd be a cold day in hell.

She waited, because she certainly wasn't going to him. The small fires scattered across the lawn were starting to ebb, though she concentrated more bursts of oxygen deprivation magic on them to

5

finish the job. If he'd damaged her landscaping, particularly the delicate clematis vine on the nearby trellises, she was going to have his ass for dinner.

Maybe he'd called it off, headed to a Starbucks for an overpriced coffee, chalking it up to a bad business. And she'd get that *People* magazine fantasy tonight. Sure.

The incubus stirred, started to speak. "No," she ordered. "Be quiet until Mommy and Daddy finish our custody fight."

Her dry humor went right over his pretty head. Definitely a scrounger. Even though his type could be vicious and savage, she had pity for him. She'd take the straightforward challenge of vicious and savage over the subtle quagmire of cultured and deadly any day. The latter was coming toward her now.

As the Dark Guardian emerged from the forest, she caught a glimpse of his wings. She had to admit, that was kind of a thrill. Not many got a chance to see their wings. For one thing, much of their wet-work was done at the dead of night, and the wings were black. Not glossy black like Cathair's, but the deep ash of cemetery statuary at midnight on a moonless night, where the shadows seemed to collect in the hollows, offering a mere glimpse of the eerie silhouette. She noted the texture was more bat than bird. Sinister looking. The ragged edges made her think of the black sails on a pirate ship, loaded with cold-eyed criminals armed with wicked daggers to slit their victim's throats.

The fact the wings were out suggested he'd had to exert himself to stay in the race. The incubus cowering behind her had some game. Didn't mean he was clever. Incurring the wrath of a Dark Guardian was a low check on the IQ scale.

As the Guardian strode toward her, the wings tucked in and vanished, leaving her looking at something altogether different. She told herself she wasn't impressed. As the madam of a bordello, she was well aware a man's outer beauty had nothing to do with whatever lay inside his soul. Appearances only offered clues to a man's bankroll. A normal man, that is. What she was seeing was pure illusion, unless they had a fabulous gentlemen's store in the Underworld.

His clothes were custom tailored. Black slacks, white shirt, black suit coat. What every discerning, fashion-conscious man wore to a hard chase through a Southern swamp. Not a speck of mud or a drop of sweat evident. Not even a spiderweb caught in his dark hair, which was cut short but had an array of strands across a broad forehead, teasing a woman's fingers to touch it.

As he shifted in and out of the moonlight, his brown eyes became black, then brown again. His cruel face was precisely chiseled, as beautiful as Creation could make it. Cruel things were always beautiful. That was the way it worked; otherwise he couldn't get close enough to *be* cruel.

He could break anything he wanted, destroy anything he desired. Destruction was not new to him. Actually, it was no more than breathing. She knew it, because she knew him, indirectly. By reputation versus face-to-face meeting.

Mikhael Roman, Dark Guardian of the Underworld, and the hugely inadvisable former hookup of her good friend Ruby. Ruby was keeping better company these days, with the wizard and Light Guardian Derek Stormwind, the polar white to this guy's dark. Raina would never admit that was a good change, because there was no sense in letting Derek know she liked him. Reciprocal affection would be distasteful to them both. A shared love of Ruby was enough, thank you.

A Dark Guardian was essentially a cop, just like Derek, and Raina had never had a good relationship with authority. Neither Heaven nor the Underworld favored her decision to open a bordello with creatures who sucked life out of mortals through sexual touch. Hers didn't do that, thanks to her special abilities, but it didn't mean anyone approved. If she ever relaxed her enchantments and her incubi and succubi unleashed the fatal side of their nature, Derek would be the first on her doorstep to take her down. It was his job, nothing personal. She understood it, the way he understood she had to dislike him on principle.

She didn't really give a rat's ass what any of them thought, but she had learned to be diplomatic enough about her disdain to be left alone. Unfortunately, standing between a Dark Guardian and his prey was likely to destroy that already thin civilized façade.

Ruby had described Mikhael as "distracting", in a bad boy way. Actually, her exact quote was: *"He's the bad boy of all bad boys. Rhett Butler lumped in with Sawyer from* Lost, *Alex from* Grey's Anatomy—first and second season, *Mickey Rourke from* 9 ½ Weeks, *and Nicholas Cage from*

Valley Girl"—the best part of that '80s movie, they both agreed. *"Oh, and Antonio Banderas doing the tango in* Take the Lead. *That sexy part where you see the cross tattooed on his arm, a weird mix of the sacred and profane."*

As she watched him approach, Raina agreed, enough that she wondered if Mikhael also had some incubus blood. Though he was built much bigger than most incubus males, the sinuous muscle and broad shoulders, as well as the way he moved, the intensity of his eyes, flex of his hands, were all designed to make a woman think of sex. When he finished his stroll across her lawn, he might try to dismember the incubus or do something equally nefarious to her, yet all she could think about were tangled sheets, those muscles slick under her palms, his body moving upon her.

Ruby had been pretty obsessed with him for a while, and she could see why.

She wouldn't fall under the same spell as Ruby, though, because sex didn't matter. It could be strong, passionate, overwhelming, but in the end, it was a moment balanced against the whole-rest-of-your-life kind of shit. So she set it aside and focused on what did matter—whether she was going to have to kick his ass. On her home turf, she was unbeatable. Most of the time.

"Dark Guardian." She nodded. "Fancy seeing you all the way out here on a Sunday night. We're closed. If you come back tomorrow night, perhaps we can meet your needs."

Mikhael glanced at the incubus cowering behind her. "He took something of Lucifer's. Lucifer wants it back."

You dumb bastard. Raina looked down at the creature, who was staring at Mikhael as if he held a death notice in hand. Except for his drop-dead sex appeal, Mikhael looked as emotionally invested as a bored collection agent who regularly de-limbed individuals.

"I'm sorry," she said. "We didn't get around to names. You are?"

Shifting his terrified gaze up to her, the incubus blinked in surprise, probably at her pleasant tone. "R-Reginald."

"A fake name will do right now." She nodded. Spoke succinctly and slow. "Reginald, you've taken one of Lucifer's toys. They're very possessive of their toys in the Underworld. If you have his toy, you need to give it back, because it's not nice to take other people's toys. Do you have the toy?"

8

"N-No, I don't have it."

"I see." She looked at Mikhael. "Seems we have a conundrum. He has sanctuary here. Until I can get to the bottom of this, maybe you can just go away. Give me your cell number and I'll text you."

Mikhael pivoted, made a gesture. That minuscule movement had the incubus whimpering, quailing into a smaller ball behind her. However, Mikhael's head tilt said he wanted her to step toward him for a semi-private word. There was command in that motion, which annoyed her, more because something in her responded to it than the fact he did it. She drew closer with an arched brow that said she recognized the command and was unimpressed by it. Her protections on the incubus remained firmly in place.

Because of her shorter stature, close proximity required that she tilt her head to stare into the Dark Guardian's face, which was an advantage she wouldn't give him. Instead she looked past his shoulder, staring at the woods, waiting for what he had to say. He bent his head, the heat of his breath stirring against her ear.

"I will incinerate him where he lies, witch. I will also do the same to you, your house and everyone in it, before you have the chance to cast your next spell. Is he worth that to you?"

His low tone wasn't for the incubus's benefit, she was sure. His concentrated intensity was enough to command attention without him ever having to raise his voice. Ruby had said he had a prominent Russian accent. It wasn't that pronounced now, suggesting it had been exaggerated for the role he'd played with her, a gunrunner, but it wasn't false. It was still there, a faint hint that gave his speech a rhythmic cadence intriguing in the deep timbre. She shifted her gaze up to his, locked. "You can huff and puff all you want, big bad wolf. This house isn't blowing down."

"You think I'm bluffing?"

"No, I think you're testing. If you'd intended to do such a thing, you'd have already done it. Regardless, I won't be your doormat. If you want to slaughter us for your information, you go right ahead."

His face was so close to hers, it brushed those tempting strands of hair along his forehead against her brow. Her protection allowed that simple penetration, but it was almost as ground-rocking as a face punch. His gaze dropped with interested speculation to her mouth. She suppressed the flutter in her throat, the need to swallow.

Something in the dark eyes flickered. "All right, Raina. What would you propose?"

"You know my name." That was unexpected, but then she knew his, didn't she? They probably had the same source of information.

"Dark Guardians know everyone's name."

"How lovely. You never have that awkward moment at parties where you can't put a name to a familiar face."

He didn't blink. "I can read your mind. That's how I know."

"You're lying." She stepped back, a deliberate insertion of space, not a retreat.

He flashed a dangerous smile that wasn't a smile. It was a baring of teeth. "You're calling me a liar?"

"If it rubs your fur the right way, yes. Perhaps even if it rubs it the wrong way. Some cats like that."

His gaze swept over her, a gesture that felt like a full-body stroke. "I'm afraid I'm here to rub *your* fur the wrong way, because I am taking that thing that's behind you."

"Only over my dead body. Are you willing to push it that far?"

"Now who's bluffing?" But he sighed. "Help me find what I need, and then I will be out of your hair, all those wonderful miles of it." As his attention slid over it, she could visualize the two of them naked, his fingers buried in her hair, tugging her scalp as he pulled her to him for another taste of his demanding mouth.

Okay, he might not be an incubus, but his sensual compulsion worked on her, which didn't ever happen. If this was a natural gift, she wanted to figure out how to bottle and sell it for a 50 percent mark up. She quelled her shiver of reaction. "Give him time to calm down, let me discuss his options with him. He's not going anywhere. What he's stolen? Does it jeopardize anyone's life tonight?"

"Unlikely. There are too many of us out there looking for signs of it."

"Fine, then. You can go help them. If he doesn't have it, you're wasting your time being here anyway. I can question him, keep him secure, while you do that."

"He took it, Raina. The question is why and for whom, and where it is now, because it's not with him. You can talk to him, but only while I'm present."

"Then there won't be a lot of talking. There will be gibberish and pissing himself, because you scare him half to death."

"Do you find me scary?" He raised a brow.

She snorted. "In your dreams."

"Yes." He gave her an appraising look. "You do not fear, but you respond well to certain...types of intimidation. Elevated pulse, increased breath. A lovely flush across your skin. Desire often reads like fear."

"Oh, for the love of the gods, Mikhael, you know you have an effect on a woman's body, the same way I have an effect on a man's. It doesn't mean anything more than adding jam to toast."

His gaze lifted to hers. "You know my name."

"Maybe *I* read minds. For real, no faking."

"Ruby described me."

"Yes, bad breath, warts and all."

Goddess, she needed to stop goading him. Every time he got that dangerous glint in his eyes, things went to liquid in her knees and stomach. But now he moved his attention to the incubus.

"How do you know he'll tell you the truth?" he asked.

"I don't know if he will. But I will get the truth from him. That's my particular gift. It's what we do here." A bordello was as much a confessional as a church. Most of her clients thought they checked their souls at her threshold. She knew differently.

Reginald kept his eyes down, fingers dug into the earth so his dirty knuckles were white. He wore only torn jeans, his slim, leanly muscled body scratched and bug bitten from his trek through the swamp.

"All right," the Dark Guardian said. "You can try."

"Wonderful." She offered a sarcastic curtsy that made his eyes narrow. Yet when she knelt to touch Reginald's arm, she let out the relieved sigh she'd been holding. She kept those protections locked down tight, though. She trusted only a couple people and, in the words of Nicholas Cage in *Con Air*, "*One of them is me. The other's not you.*"

"Follow me," she said to the incubus. "Let's talk, then we'll get you a bath and some clean clothes."

CHAPTER TWO

ikhael knew the witch wanted him gone, but that wasn't going to happen. He did agree there was a slim possibility the incubus might be more forthcoming if he were less obtrusive. At least under *her* methods. So he hung back as she took the sex demon through the foyer, toward her main parlor. He sauntered along behind, taking in the polished oak floor, painted beadboard and floral wallpaper of the graceful plantation home. When she walked, she lit wall sconces with an absent wave of her hand. She preferred candlelight to electric, though it appeared the house supplied both.

Erotic artwork lined the hallway, a cornucopia of possibilities. Clients could simply point and say, "I want that position, that fetish, that..." He paused, tilted his head, but the angle change didn't help. Whatever that was. And he considered himself fairly well trained in the erotic arts. He'd ask her later, before he gutted Reginald for the information she wouldn't get. She probably wouldn't want to answer his sex questions after he stained her Persian rugs with incubus excretions. Perhaps she could loan him a plastic tarp from her garden shed.

The large parlor was where the clients warmed up to their à la carte choices with drinks and the chance to view the male and female offerings. To human eyes, her stable comprised mesmerizing men and women in a variety of flavors. To the paranormal world, they were a Fae-demon crossbreed species, a walking death sentence when they coupled with a human. But Raina's powers, the complicated enchant-ments woven over the house, permeating every room, kept that from happening. The witch, who was half succubus herself, had figured out how to let succubi and incubi feed without killing their meal. It was a remarkable accomplishment. One fraught with risk, to her and to those who came here, but she struck him as a woman most comfort-able on the knife edge she'd learned to walk.

When he'd seen her standing over the incubus, he'd expected her to be beautiful and mesmerizing. That went along with the whole succubus thing. She had rich dark hair, grown all the way to her hips in a tempting old-fashioned way, thick and curling. Her hips were generous, and those breasts were worth a nice, long look. Firm and large, not grotesquely out of proportion. The dark green velvet dress clung to her buttocks, enhancing their sway, the brush of her hair across them.

Her body was built for sex. She was quite aware of it on multiple levels—as a succubus, as a witch and a woman. But the way a woman looked didn't enchant him the way it did most males. He could see the underlayer, which distorted the surface. Every soul's true nature was a mix of good and bad, so the physical appearance was an average of the compendium to him.

However, what he saw beneath Raina's surface, behind those exotic green and gold eyes, was complex, unexpected. She embraced her female side fully, no need to put males down to increase her sense of power. He sensed a deep appreciation of males in her makeup, of their strengths and the roles they could play in women's lives. But he also picked up an unusual sense of self-containment to her. A perfect sphere that could repel penetration or incursion. It wasn't so much that she didn't need a man as she wasn't seeking one. A puzzle, because she carried a tremendous capacity for passion and love.

Intriguing, but not his main focus. He'd ponder the rest later, because he was a carnal male who enjoyed his pleasures, but right now, it was all business. He sensed that in her, too, that she didn't mix busi-ness with other things. He appreciated it, even as he perversely wanted to mess with it.

She'd called his bluff about plundering her mind, though it wasn't a complete bluff. He *could* read the surface of a mind, the way he could deduce the color, texture and weight of a flower with a look. Things like a name quivered in the mind's foyer, just behind the skull's fragile shell. To reach more private rooms, he had to dig deeper. A Dark Guardian didn't do that unless he had cause, because a deeper excavation was like scooping out the inside of a melon.

Reginald had given him plenty of cause to do that, but Raina hadn't, and she stood between him and his prey. While he had an urge to dig below the witch's surface, it wasn't to destroy her; at least not that way. He wanted to take her down inside the tightly closed rooms of her mind and soul, let her feel him there in that darkness, overwhelm her. He'd put her on her elbows and knees, a hand on the back of her neck, and plunge into the wet heat of her spread thighs, whispering things that made her uncertain if he was a nightmare or a fantasy, but satisfying her cravings all the same. The desires of a succubus were endless, but she had that side of her tightly leashed. He wondered what would happen if she handed that leash to him.

As he entered the parlor, he chose a chair in a far corner, picking up the day's paper left folded there. Since Raina said Sunday was their day off, this room was probably a communal gathering space when not used for their primary purpose, but the primary purpose had left the strongest imprint. Clients had sat in this chair often, usually with a succubus on their laps. Mikhael had the fleeting mental image of a male sliding a sleeve off a pretty female shoulder, exposing a plump breast. The human had gotten hard against the succubus's soft ass, oblivious as she breathed in the first, appetizing fumes of his sexual energy, her tiny fangs unsheathing to prick the inside of her lip.

It was probably another reason the bordello was so successful. Not only were all the visuals geared to stimulate the appetite, but the energy of what transpired here laid over it as an irresistible ambiance.

Dispelling those images to give him some clear head space, he opened up the local news section. There. Properly unobtrusive. To all appearances, he was reading the newspaper, his ankle balanced on his opposite knee. Though in truth, Reginald seemed more freaked out by him doing that than when he'd been breathing fire down his neck in the swamp.

"Focus on me," Raina said to the creature. She'd guided him to the couch and now sat across from him, reclined on one hip, her elbow propped on the back, her legs folded up beneath her. Her skirt wound snugly around her, emphasizing the lushness of her figure.

The expression she flicked toward Mikhael was cranky, a clear statement. *I told you he'd be like this with you here.*

Tough. He wasn't leaving. He ignored the attitude, kept reading. Unexpected amusement flickered through him when he heard her suppress an irritated sigh. "Your name. The real one."

"I told you. Reginald." The incubus slid closer to her, his fingers overlapping hers on the couch. Like all their kind, he had a handsome form. A surfer's physique, lean and muscled, blond hair to his shoulders, sea green eyes, a sensual mouth. When he leaned forward, Mikhael detected the subtle power arc, the seduction magic, the mortal snare of the sex demon. If affected, the target would lose all memory of anything but pleasure...until they were drained dry. He was about to surge out of the chair, zap the bastard hard enough his brain lit up like a circuit board, but before he could, Reginald let out a sharp, petulant cry. In a blink, he was back on the far end of the couch, eyeing Raina and nursing his hand, which had smoke spiraling off it. The incubus emitted a frightened hiss.

Raina didn't even blink. "Half human doesn't mean vulnerable to our magic," she said. "Your name. Right now."

"Isaac," the incubus spat sullenly. "You could have burned off my fingers."

"It could have been your testicles, so count your blessings. Once you can use your fingers to count again. Isaac," she mused, lacing her fingers and laying her head along the couch back. "It means *he laughs* in Hebrew. Not doing much laughing right now, are you, Isaac?"

"You're just like all of them."

Frost flickered across her gaze, though she didn't move out of that relaxed pose. "No, I'm not. What do you think would have happened if you'd succeeded in your little mind game there?" She tilted her head toward Mikhael without looking at him. "He isn't susceptible to our ways. Plus he has utterly no interest in males. Easy as breathing, he'd empty your brain for what he wants, dispose of your body and then stop at McDonald's for a late-night dollar coffee. He wouldn't waste another thought on you. I'm the only friend you've got. Don't pull that crap again."

Isaac's lip curled, showing fangs, but like the hiss, it was fear, not aggression. There was uncertainty in the sea green gaze. He wasn't sure how to deal with her, Mikhael realized. The creature was used to victims or predators, and everything in his arsenal was geared toward the two castes.

Raina noted the shift as well. In a move Mikhael didn't expect, she unlaced her fingers and reached out, closing her hand over Isaac's. There was true compassion in her gaze, though it didn't dilute the no-nonsense firmness of her chin.

"I know you're not used to trusting anyone," she said. "So I'm not going to tell you to trust me. I know you're not blameless, because your guilt is vibrating off you. But telling your side of the story may improve your situation."

He swallowed, looked toward Mikhael, but she touched his cheek, this time gently. "Just to me," she reminded.

"All right, I stole it." A frustrated expression crossed his face. "I knew how to get in. One of the Underworld gatekeepers, Tara; she likes our kind, and it's okay to be with her. Could feed off her and it didn't hurt her, that was nice. Gets old, killing folks."

Isaac twitched a shoulder, stared at the pattern of the couch, his chin tightening. "They found out about me seeing her, said I had to get past her, get in and take it. Said I could wear her out, make her sleep, so I did. Said if I didn't, they'd come after me. So I took it, gave it to them."

"Who is *they*?"

His eyelids snapped up like popped shades. "Can't tell you that. If I even speak their names, they'll know. They'll put a curse on me. Or vanquish me, and I'll die." Saliva gathered at the corners of his exposed fangs, reflecting undiluted fear.

While Mikhael considered the sex demons a Fae-demon hybrid, no one really knew which species held sway. They had elements of both, demonstrated by Isaac's Dr. Jekyll and Mr. Hyde antics. The Fae considered them a distasteful lower caste, if they accepted them as part of their kind at all, whereas the demon world saw them as weaker beings to use and manipulate, when they could get their hands on them. Their ultimate strength was their ability to kill with seduction, coupled with their elusiveness, their talent at escaping any situation with that disorienting magic of theirs. Very few creatures were immune to it, even Fae and demon kind. It made them excellent assassins...and thieves.

They had indeterminate life spans and, like the Fae or demon kind, it was hard to pinpoint their exact age except as a measure of their power and experience in using it. However, for all his come-hither routine, it was now clear Isaac was barely out of his teens.

Raina laid a hand on his shoulder then, rubbing. Mikhael felt that same power arc from her, only more measured, controlled. She was using it to soothe him. A very experienced succubus could tone her power down, use seduction as a calming effect. It worked on almost any species, including her own. As a result, Isaac's hand turned, his fingers wrapping around her forearm. He moved closer to rub his cheek against her shoulder. Not really sexual, however. It reminded Mikhael of a mother lion and a cub, because he didn't sense that Raina was getting any carnal pleasure from it, or that Isaac was trying to push such an agenda now.

It still bugged him. The male had taken something from the Underworld. He was bad news, tainted and corrupted. Raina walked a lot of fine edges, but he saw neither of those things in her makeup. He therefore wasn't thrilled to see it rubbing up against her. But he held himself back, because he'd given his word to let her take the lead. For now.

"All right," she said, stroking Isaac's hair. She flicked a piece of swamp mud off his shoulder, evaporated it with a quick flutter of fingers before it could hit her floor. "Sit back now. We're going to play twenty questions, narrow things down by the process of elimination. No names. You're using *they* to describe one being, to avoid giving me the gender. Male or female?"

He looked startled that she'd figured that out, but he gave her a grudging nod, a bare whisper. "The scarier one."

"Female, then." She waited for the jerk of his head, confirming it. "Does she have what you stole?"

"I think so. I left it somewhere for her, and when I went back to get it, it was gone. That's where he picked up my trail." He angled his chin at Mikhael. "She was supposed to pay me, and she didn't."

"What was she paying you?"

"Concentrated soul energy. A year's supply of it. She had a way of bottling it."

"And those she took it from?"

He didn't answer, but she stared him down until he looked away. "Humans get their meat in pretty packages in the store. Don't know why we can't, either, if there's a way to let someone else do the hunting and killing."

She closed her eyes. Mikhael wasn't sure why she had that white look around her mouth, but he was sure it wasn't a good thing. "So when will they come looking for you?" she asked at last, opening her eyes.

"I'll be looking for them. They owe me."

That hard note entered her voice again. "Don't bullshit me, Isaac. You'll keep running, because you know you're a loose end. Give us the name."

He shook his head. "I'm not going to be vanquished where I sit."

"They can follow your trail to my property, but they can't penetrate my wards to do a remote kill."

"You don't know that." The scavenger came out in his voice, rough-edged and raw, his eyes getting that white, rolling look again, a calf going up the chute for slaughter. "I ain't never going to get away from her. Not never."

"Easy." She cuddled him close once more. As she eased his head to a resting spot on her breast, she wound her arms around his narrow back to rub. "Easy, now, child. You've had a rough time of it, haven't you? Always running, never trusting, always hungry. You won't be hungry here. I promise you that. You won't have to kill. Maybe once you figure that out, you'll tell me the whole truth."

Tipping up his chin, she met his eyes, letting him see that implacable firmness. "If you want any chance at all, it will be from doing that. But tonight, a bath, some nourishment, and a chance to feel safe."

She shifted her gaze then, met Mikhael's. Her black slip of a brow was lifted in question, waiting for his confirmation. Hers wasn't his preferred method, but Isaac's fear and desperation were real. Even if Mikhael plundered his mind, the information could fragment under the pressure of the incubus's terror. If pieces were all he could get, fine, but a few hours and giving the baby a nap and a bottle might produce more, so he could allow that. There was some urgency involved in what was taken, but as he'd told Raina, whoever took it wasn't going to be using it immediately, unless they were a fool willing to make his job much easier. The Underworld was on full-scale alert, tuned to any sign of it.

So he gave her the answer she wanted. He lifted a shoulder with casual indifference. He could always yank Isaac's ass out of a comfy bed and go back to Plan A. In the meantime, he could hang around, pursue other puzzles. Far more pleasurable ones.

She pushed Isaac back into his own space, not unkindly, and picked up a bell. When a quiet domestic in dark dress and apron appeared, Mikhael knew right off she was a succubus, but in a deliberately understated way, unless one looked closely and saw that mesmerizing tinge of hunger in the eyes, as well as in the sharp teeth the young female hadn't quite learned to hide.

When she saw Mikhael, she underscored her youth by blanching. Raina cleared her throat. "It's okay, Gina. Yes, he's a Dark Guardian, but he means no harm to you."

When Raina's gaze returned to Isaac, it held the warning that the same reassurance didn't necessarily apply to him. "You'll share a room with two of the incubi who work here, Li and Saul. You will behave. Do you understand?" Catching his chin, she dug her nails in enough to make his eyes swivel toward her warily. "You try anything, you won't have to worry about Mikhael. I will gut you like a farm pig. You have my protection, but so do they, and their tenure trumps yours, a hundred times over. Go to bed. That's all you do tonight. Tomorrow we'll talk some more."

Mikhael watched, fascinated, as Isaac rose obediently to his feet. He took a couple steps, then turned, studied her as if she were the most unexpected thing he'd ever seen. Kneeling, he bent and kissed the charred hem of Raina's skirt, keeping his head down until she touched it in obvious benediction.

"Don't mess this up," she said. "You've gotten the luckiest break of your life, even if you don't realize it yet."

The male turned to go but was brought up short as Mikhael shifted. "Hold on a moment."

In a blink, Isaac looked ready to bolt, trampling Gina in the process, but Raina caught his hand. "He gave his word. No harm to you within my home."

Not entirely true, but they were surrounded by swampland. It would be a very short trip to drag Isaac out into it for a more agonizing interrogation method. He sure as hell wouldn't be stroking the incubus's hair or cuddling him against ample breasts. The young man knew it, showed it in his death grip on Raina's hand. Yeah, it was true fear, but calculation as well, playing on her maternal instincts. Except Mikhael could see Raina's maternal instincts were honed with razor-sharp intuition. She managed a houseful of sex demons, after all. That required a pretty iron hand. This kid would need to be set back on his heels a hundred times before he figured that out.

Unfortunately, he wasn't going to live that long.

Isaac let out a frightened yelp. Gina gasped and Raina came to her feet, but by then it was done. The dagger had flashed out, cutting the male's wrist, then Mikhael flipped the weapon and thrust it back into the scabbard hidden beneath his coat. Holding a vial against the cut, he grasped Isaac's forearm in a lock hold. The blood was drawn into the container by its vacuum pressure, saving Raina's rug.

When he had about a tablespoon, he capped it. Gina, efficient sort that she was, had recovered enough to bring a napkin from the wet bar for Isaac's arm. Smart girl, too, because she waited for Raina to motion her forward, her young, uncertain gaze fastened on Mikhael.

Mikhael held the vial up in front of Isaac's deer-in-the-headlights expression as Gina blotted his wound. "Blood calls to itself. Now I don't have to expend the energy hunting you." He met the incubus's resentful gaze. "You step one foot off her property, all bets are off, demon. Your ass is mine. And all your detachable parts, which is pretty much everything."

"I bet you're the first Lucifer calls when it's time to tell bedtime stories to the kids." Throwing an acid look at him, Raina pushed Isaac toward Gina. "Bed. Sleep. We regroup tomorrow. No dismembering tonight. Saul usually leaves the TV on, but he'll be dead to the world, so find something warm and fuzzy to watch. Gina will show you the shower."

She glanced at the succubus, her lips quirking at Gina's frank assessment of their guest. "And scrub you thoroughly. Just keep it down. It's our only day of rest, and we have a busy week ahead."

A completely bemused Isaac let himself be led from the room, but Mikhael noted the way he looked back at both of them. There was cunning in that gaze. Hatred. Fear. None of it boded well.

"He's lying, you know." They'd departed before he said it, but it didn't matter if Isaac heard. He and Raina had both made it clear they didn't trust the blond scavenger any further than they could throw him. He indulged a vision of heaving Isaac with a moderate level of force against one of Raina's ancient oaks and hearing the satisfying crack of bone.

"About portions of it. He did take it for someone, that's indisputable. Someone who scares him shitless. But he's leaving key things out." She sat back down on the couch, resuming her reclined position, her head propped on her forearm on the sofa back. Her hair cascaded down her shoulder, fanned out over her hip, a stray tendril over her breast. She looked like a Waterhouse painting, all soft on the edges, sensual, dreamlike. But her expression was pensive, shrewd. "The gatekeeper. What happened to her?"

"They killed her. Decapitation and immolation, the only way to take out a gatekeeper. She was headless, dumped in the fire pits. The salamanders that play there found her."

The witch nodded. Her gaze drifted to the oil painting over the mantle. A woman, naked and collared, on her knees before a well-dressed man. A man who had kindness as well as command in his touch. There was a fire blazing in the picture, and it seemed Mikhael saw the fire flicker in his peripheral vision when he turned to look at her again.

"How do you make concentrated soul energy?"

The shadow in her face was fleeting, but it left him an unexpectedly strong impression of anguish. "With human children," she said tonelessly. "Under the age of five. It's the purest form. Our kind can live off it for quite a while, but we can't cultivate it ourselves, because harvesting requires sexual arousal, completion. Which is possible with children even at that age, but even our 'despicable' kind has limits. Usually."

He sat down on the sofa in front of her. He laid a hand on her thigh, just above her knee, fingers sliding over the gathered fabric of the skirt. It drew her attention, for certain, but his intent wasn't seduction. He just had the desire to touch, and so he did. "Despicable is your word, Raina. Not mine. A Dark Guardian has no prejudices."

"An equal-opportunity executioner. How liberated. Do you believe he killed the gatekeeper?"

"Do you?"

She shook her head. "He's capable of killing, but not that kind. Not unless his own life is at stake."

21

"Agreed. Whoever sent him to steal the item followed behind to clean up. I think Isaac got a glimpse of Tara, realized he was as good as dead. He ran, hid it, and then ran again. I tracked him to where it was hidden. What took it was old, and strong. A demon for certain, though not enough traces left to determine race. And so here we are."

"She'll track him to tie up loose ends." Those shrewd eyes met his. "Will you protect him?"

"Protection requires trust, Raina. In order to guard someone's back, you have to be able to turn your back on them."

"So you'll let her have him."

"She'll soon have bigger problems than Isaac." Turning his knuckles over, he ran them a few inches down her leg, over her knee, in the folds of the skirt. Her eyes followed the motion. He sensed the heating of her skin, the interested stir of her body, but it was as she'd said. In her profession, the reaction of the body was of no more consequence than the growling of a stomach or dryness of a throat. Just because she felt hunger didn't mean she'd permit herself a full meal.

He was an appetizer man himself. Sampling was far more intriguing than stuffing oneself to a logy state.

"When I catch her," he added, "I'm going to skin her alive in front of him. He was more frightened of her than of me."

She chuckled, humorless. "Male testosterone always rises to the occasion."

He ignored that. "The demon is going to follow his trail here. So I'm staying here tonight."

She shifted her head so she could meet his gaze. They sat on the couch facing each other, his hand on her leg, her not stopping him, her unreadable gaze noting everything. She was as close as a lover, but as far away as a shooting star. Though part succubus, what she radiated was more than the chemical temptation of her species. Perhaps it was the witch element, or the woman herself, but she was also remote, guarded as a queen's diamond. It was a direct challenge to that male testosterone she'd mocked.

She sighed. "I think I prefer your earlier offer of incineration."

"It won't be such a hardship. You are a B and B, after all."

"That's our tax reporting status. You know exactly what we are."

"You have beds and a kitchen. Do you offer a breakfast, or should I go for McDonald's? How did you know I like their coffee?"

"I'm very good at what I do."

He raised his touch to her throat, just a passing caress. Her pulse fluttered, her heart rate increased. An interesting reaction, but not a deal closer. She guarded her desires, because they were dark. She didn't let them rule her.

Of course, he was very good at what *he* did, which meant he'd shatter that rule just to see the pleasurable consequences of those dark cravings. He knew how that lush ass would press against his groin, could imagine her generous breasts filling his hands, the nipples stabbing into his palms as she rubbed a slick sex against him. And begged.

"You have other services that can meet my needs."

Her attention sharpened. "If you're a paying customer. Do Dark Guardians carry a lot of cash?"

"You'll be more interested in what I have to barter."

"Doubtful, but I'm willing to listen." She straightened, putting some distance between them, her thigh sliding away. "It will take one of our more experienced ladies to satisfy you. They don't come cheap." A tight smile flirted on her lips. "Their orgasms are extra, because experiencing a succubus climax is euphoric."

"Hmm. How about a half succubus?"

She blinked once with those thick lashes. "I'm not taking new clients."

"I'm not suggesting it as a client. I can offer you something no one else can."

Raina laughed and rose. When she tossed back her hair with a practiced sweep, he saw the experienced courtesan. One with a jaded underlayer, the first sign of ugliness he'd detected. He'd roused something deep, something cold, hard. "I've never heard that line before," she scoffed.

The cynicism bugged him enough he went for the kill, instead of more games. "When was the last time you unleashed your demon side during sex, Raina?"

She protected the human clients from the fallout from her own staff, but he was certain she couldn't do it for herself. No one's control was good enough to hold the reins on that craving during their own full-on orgasm.

At her startled look, he locked gazes with her. "You can unleash that side with a Dark Guardian. No restraints...except the ones I put on you myself."

~

She hadn't seen that one coming. Having to quell her demon side during sex was like a vampire depriving herself of human blood while it pumped in a fresh fountain within biting distance. It could drive her mad, which was why she took few clients, and those that wanted her to have an orgasm...well, while she enjoyed all her clients, the pleasure she showed stopped short of that, even if they believed otherwise.

It wasn't as awful as it sounded. She fed the succubus side by taking small portions of the sexual energy that nourished the other residents in the house, catching stray bits. It made her like a dog eating scraps under the table, but it worked. With her self-discipline and that occasional meal, it kept the libido in check, her faculties balanced. She pleasured herself, under controlled circumstances. The joy of electronics. If the orgasm was too strong, she zapped the house's old circuitry, but Li would kindly trip the breakers for her.

Yes, it wasn't ideal. And seeing something like Mikhael close-up, feeling his hand on her thigh like a trail of fire that led right between her legs, could stir it all up, but she knew how to control it.

He wasn't done uncovering her secrets, however. "I'd also ask how long it's been since you've unleashed your true nature, your true desires...separate from your succubus side." Those dark eyes swept over her. "But I already know the answer to that one."

Things swirled up in her breast, those cravings she kept locked down, always. He was too clever for his own good. The chance to indulge the succubus side alone was an offer almost too painful to resist. Adding the other...that got into some emotional territory, and she sure as hell wasn't going there with a Dark Guardian, no matter how intuitive he was.

Sex didn't matter, she reminded herself. Pushing herself away from the personal side of it, it was worth considering, a purely practical arrangement. She could turn the tables, get more control over the situation.

Her intuition said *hell no*. It pricked her pride, but her sanity was more important than her pride. "Thank you for the kind offer, but no. Pick one of the others, or make use of that strong knife hand of yours to jerk off. The hand's cheaper."

His lips curved humorlessly. She held fast before the intent gaze, not giving a damn what he did or didn't see. The answer was still no.

"What if your consent would save the lives of those you protect?"

Her lips twisted. "You'd blackmail me to have sex with you?"

"No. But if you think you're doing it for them, then perhaps you'd do it for yourself."

She tightened her jaw to hold on to the scathing retort. "I've given you your options," she said coolly.

He rose. "I'll take the bed solo. For now. A room with a TV is preferable. I don't sleep much."

She wasn't surprised; the battle-readiness switch he kept on continuous low hum didn't suggest he was the drowsy type. "Third bedroom on the right, second floor. If you change your mind, ring the bell in the room. Catalina will arrange things according to your liking. She's the most suitable for your tastes."

He lifted a brow. "Familiar with my tastes, are you?"

"It's my job."

She'd risen from the couch; now he stepped closer to her. "Then you already know she's not the most suitable for them."

He was sending a strong message with that one. He knew what she wanted, on a lot of different levels. She gave herself credit for not even blinking. "That sounds like a personal problem. Use the bell if you change your mind about Catalina."

"I won't. If you change yours, you don't need to ring a bell. I'll come to you. Good night for now, Raina."

Said the spider to the fly, she thought. He gave her a surprisingly elegant old-world bow, where his eyes never left hers. Then he turned away. While his departure relieved her of his far too intense stare, it didn't dispel the things he'd uncovered with that offer. She wasn't going to be sleeping much tonight, either.

CHAPTER THREE

*R*aina climbed the stairs to her room. It was in the widow's peak, complete with balcony, the best gravitational point to spin and reinforce enchantments on the house as needed. Her tea carafe was still on the warmer, the *People* magazine on the wedding-ring quilt bedspread. Candles flickered from the breeze coming through the cracked French doors. Opening them wide, she let in the moist night air, her enchantments warding off the swamp mosquitoes. Hearing the rush of wings, she lifted her arm so Cathair had a landing perch. As the male's talons gripped her arm, he made his rasping sound, flapping his wings.

"Ow. Cut it out. Some familiar you are. You bugged out like a big, black chicken."

"Bite me, bite me," he chirped at her.

"I'll bite you. I'll cook and chew you up in little pieces." She let him move to his perch. It was where he typically slept, on the threshold between inside and outside. An additional protection for her, and his preferred roosting point.

"Did you find those ingredients I need for the moon ritual?"

He hopped from the perch to a permanent nest he'd built in one of her balcony chairs, ruining it, of course, and plucked out several long strands of foliage, along with two or three wilted florals. A couple dimes rolled out, a silver screw.

"You really need to work on your addiction to shiny things," she

26

commented. Picking up the plants, she examined them with a critical eye, nodded. "Good finds. These will do perfectly."

Despite her teasing, he'd performed as required, as he always did. There'd been no need for him during her interaction with Mikhael, and a good familiar knew when it was best to stay out of the way, let his witch have elbow room. But yanking his chain was one of her little rituals.

Actually, she enjoyed yanking anyone's chain. Mikhael had reminded her of the dangers of that, there at the end. Still, she'd been perversely pleased at the faint flicker of irritation he'd shown when she thwarted his earlier plans.

He thought her too lenient with Isaac. Wrong assumptions could always be used to her advantage. When she'd rebounded that arc of power from Isaac, popped him with it like the snap of a single tail, she'd pulled a tendril of it into herself. Like Mikhael, she'd now know if the incubi left her property. Unlike him, she also had the organic energy of her house to aid her, so she'd get the news bulletin first. Probably not by a wide margin, but that extra minute or two might save Isaac's life, if he was foolish enough to bolt.

She wasn't worried about Mikhael trying to sneak off with him. There was nothing subtle about the Dark Guardian. If he changed his mind about their deal, he'd tell her straight out. Probably because he'd enjoy the fight.

When she glanced in her mirror, she realized she had a feline smile on her face. Yeah, part of her twisted makeup. Mikhael liked to yank chains, too. She thought of a length of chain in his hand, winding around her wrists, twisting over his fingers, a steel tether...

No restraints...except the ones I put on you myself.

She yanked herself away from that door. She didn't discourage fantasies, because they were a much safer outlet than real life, but in this case, the craving was far too close to the surface, and dangerous. Someone who wanted to feed it was in the house.

Your true nature...

She needed a different kind of distraction. Pursing her lips, the smile returned. Time to yank someone else's chain. Dialing Ruby's cell, she glanced at the clock. One in the morning. She shrugged. Time meant little unless client appointments were involved. Since

Ruby traveled with Derek, there was no telling what time zone they were in tonight.

Plus, finding Ruby in bed didn't mean any sleeping was happening, unless it was the postcoital kind, a woman sated and exhausted from a couple hours of sweaty pleasure. Derek was definitely a powerhouse in that area. Maybe because she'd turned Mikhael down, Raina felt an unwelcome twinge at the thought of her friend under Derek, his very substantial cock thrusting into her, catapulting her into climactic ecstasy. *Bitch.*

"What do you want?" The bitch sounded querulous and sleepy, the kind of sleepy that came from being woken at one a.m. Apparently they *were* in the same time zone.

"It's the middle of the night. You could answer with a note of concern."

"Says Peter about the wolf. You always call me at freaking ungodly hours, and it's always absolutely nothing important."

"That's a matter of opinion. But if you feel that way, why do you answer?"

"The wolf did eventually try to eat Peter."

"I can handle any wolf on my own. I think you answer because you're so entertained by what I call you about."

"Yes, I get so bored helping a Light Guardian save the world every other day. Oh, and having mind-blowing sex on the off days."

"Does Derek know you're having mind-blowing sex on the off days? With who?"

Ruby's chuckle made Raina smile. As the tense coil in her lower belly eased a little, she realized she hadn't called to yank Ruby's chain. She'd needed a friend. Mikhael had stirred up some hazardous terrain, whether she admitted it or not.

"All right, what is it, you shrew?"

"It's nothing, really." Raina examined her glossy blood-red nails. Gina had done the manicure, and Raina liked the pair of tiny black triangles projecting from each cuticle like vampire fangs. "I have your old boyfriend Mikhael staying here. Other than pussy, what does he like to eat for breakfast?"

A clatter as something was knocked over, followed by an impressively creative oath. Before Ruby could say anything else, Derek had the phone.

"You want to repeat that?"

"I don't see the need. Just because you can hear what's being said a mile away doesn't mean you should eavesdrop."

"We'll be there in a few minutes." Static was already crackling on the line, because Derek couldn't use cell phones without his magic aura screwing with them. She'd lose him in a moment or two.

"No," Raina said sharply. "You won't. This doesn't concern you, Derek. I'm handling it."

"What exactly does he want?"

"That's between him and me. If I have problems, I'll call Ruby and let her know I need *her* help. Not yours."

She could almost hear Derek grinding his teeth. Music to her ears. "Raina..."

She sighed. He loved her best friend. It was damn annoying. It put a damper on the whole chain-yanking experience. "Honestly, there's no need. I just wanted to pick on Ruby about it. Plus I wanted to give her—and you—a heads-up he's in town, and let you know it has nothing to do with her."

"I wouldn't have worried about that. I trust Ruby."

"I wouldn't trust any woman with a pulse around him. I've seen him. If you get a lull in your save-the-world plans, this would be the perfect time to give her an early birthday gift. Every woman dreams of a threesome with two hot guys, and—"

Click. Raina put the phone down with a saccharine smile. Ruby could thank her for that one later. Once a man's testosterone got poked by that kind of stick, he'd have something to prove. Probably for another couple hours. Lucky bitch.

"*Every* woman dreams of a threesome?"

Holy Mother. She managed, barely, not to spin around and take out the door with a blasting spell. He'd breached the protections on her floor, arrived with no warning at all. While she locked down her reaction to that, it was hard not to react to his appearance. He'd changed clothes. Gone were the shirt and slacks, the polished shoes. He was barefoot, wearing a dark pair of jeans that rode low on his bare hips. He made the most of the look, leaning against the banister to the stairwell, arms crossed.

Gina, an avid reader, had once spent a whole week studying a medical text and teaching them all about male and female anatomy.

Because of that, Raina knew the delicious diagonal lines of a man's lower abdomen that pointed the way to his cock were actually ligaments, the inguinal ligaments. The set of those jeans revealed those ligaments, tapering down from impressive external obliques. Nothing covered his chest except the casually crossed arms, which emphasized the swell of biceps. Everything about him said virile, badass male. If he brought out the wings, she was a goner.

Oh, get a grip. She was around sex all the time. She embraced its many forms, because she was a woman, a witch and a succubus, and all of those incarnations enjoyed earthy pleasures. But she had a line she couldn't cross. It didn't matter that he'd offered her the chance to step over it tonight, unleash her deepest level of sexual energy and have the chance that others did, to be swept away by her release.

Release, surrender... Hazardous, mesmerizing words.

She arched an indifferent brow. "You're trespassing. I didn't invite you here."

He lifted a shoulder. "Trespassing rules? Coming from a woman who regularly flouts authority?"

"I don't flout authority. I just politely ask it to stay the hell out of my business."

His expression was dismissively Slavic. "So...you wouldn't trust any woman with a pulse around me? You have a pulse."

"Don't let it go to your head. Either one of them." She affected a bored look. "Mikhael, as often as you worked Ruby over, I know Dark Guardians have an insatiable libido. We can find you something to fuck, without you sniffing around my bed."

His face closed down, which she found interesting. Ruby had made it clear that feelings weren't involved in her volatile encounters with the Dark Guardian, at least not from his side, but Raina read something different in that reaction.

"You started this business by doing this kind of business, right?" he said curtly. "The hard-to-get routine rings a little false."

Using a sharp tongue on an opponent brought consequences. From someone being casually cruel, who didn't understand certain things about her, she would have dismissed it, treated him with stoic disdain. But he'd already gotten under her skin, gotten too close. Even so, she hadn't expected the return cut to slice so deep. Like a cat, a succubus had a higher metabolism and body temperature, which meant she was always warm. Except now, when the coldness blasted through the cut he'd just made, an arctic freeze that affected her vital organs, swept over her skin, raising all the small hairs.

He straightened, hands dropping to his sides, his brow creasing. "Raina."

She rose from the bed, drew herself up to her full five-two height, knowing that blue sparks were flickering off her skin. If he'd been human, she'd have reined them back, because they were toxic, but now she hoped a few jumped on him like lice and ate him alive.

"I told you you're welcome to use the services of the others here for a reasonable rate. I'm not part of those services. If you're a sick bastard who enjoys rape, you might have the ability to overpower me, but you'll be fucking a corpse, because that's the only way you'll take me down." She'd be damned before she admitted her voice cracked.

Mikhael's reaction wasn't to become more soothing or gentle. Not that she would have expected that from him. But she didn't anticipate his barbed humor transforming into something that filled the room with deadly purpose, his voice the steady steel of an executioner's axe.

"I've hunted those who've committed that crime. By the time I deliver them to Hell, they're begging for the mercy of the fire."

He backed up, began to descend the stairs. When he'd gone several steps, he stopped. It put his head below the level of the landing railing, the straight balusters like the boundary of a cell door.

"One kiss," he said.

"Excuse me?" Still torn between the ice of her reaction and the heat of his reply, she had to clear her throat.

He locked gazes with her. "After one kiss, if you don't want what I have to offer, then we leave it at that. But don't tell me you're not game enough to try the one kiss. You have the courage of a wounded badger."

It was a backhanded compliment, but the unexpected image did pull her back from that intense edge, put her back on her feet. Some-what. She arched a brow. "Daring me to kiss you? Do I look that gullible?"

"No. I think you want what I have to offer, Raina. But you're a smart woman. You're denying yourself, because you know it's dangerous to want things too much. I'm telling you that I'm a safe port. No strings attached, just pleasure."

Safe was not an adjective she'd ever attach to Mikhael Roman, half-naked and slouching with sensual awareness against the wall of her staircase. "I suppose you're offering this out of the goodness of your heart."

"Hell, no," he said mildly. "I'll definitely get something out of it." His attention slid over her lips, making her moisten them in reaction. It resulted in another flare in those dark eyes. They were feeding one another's flames, and in short order the two desires would become one conflagration. Unless she did something to stop her slide down this slippery slope, a headlong plunge into the fire.

"If you're overcome by my kiss, as I've been assured any woman with a pulse will"—he nodded at her phone—"I might get laid. As I said, I don't do a lot of sleeping. Sex passes the time. Good sex passes a lot of time. That's all it is, Raina. I'm not looking for more than that. I'm as curious as you are."

"Have you ever been with a succubus?" She tried to sound offhand, though her heart rate was increasing like a school girl's. Not a usual occurrence for her...not ever.

"No, as a matter of fact."

She gave him an exasperated look. "Then how do you know I *can't* hurt you?"

"The same way I know certain things are too hot to touch. I just know."

But some things were worth the burn. Her slide down this slope was increasing to an out-of-control sledding on her ass.

"Earlier tonight, I could have moved you out of my way," he said. "I didn't."

"You knew I'd fight you. You only hurt a woman if you have no other choice...or if it gives her pleasure."

She really shouldn't have said that, because her voice had thickened over the syllables. His gaze narrowed, watching her manicured nails bite into her palms.

She'd told him she knew what his tastes were, because that was her job. Her succubus nature could ferret out the deepest sexual fantasies and passions a man had. But with experience alone, she'd evaluated plenty of men in her parlor, figuring out from stammering voices or cocky bravado, the subtle shifts of body, the flicker in the eyes, what they sought, what they really wanted. Mikhael had no cocky bravado, no stammer, and he controlled his body language, only revealing what he wanted revealed.

But she'd picked up on it, a strong, recognizable scent, one that called to her uniquely. He was 100 percent sexual Dominant. The number-one reason she needed to shove him down those stairs right now.

What he sought was the complexity of a female who needed restraints, certain levels of pain and endorphin rushes to find pleasure or to heighten it. Even if a woman didn't think she was into that, he could take her into new, thrilling territory, uncovering or nurturing that primal side of her.

In Raina, that side had to be left untouched. No matter what. It was a graveyard, and resurrecting the dead was never advisable.

While she was struggling with herself, his attention had shifted. As if he had all the time in the world, he was now studying her room. She saw him absorbing all the details, the innocuous and less so. Fresh wildflower arrangements, the wedding-ring quilt, the *People* magazine. The stack of DVDs by her flat screen, *Titanic* open on top. There was a picture of her, Ruby and Ramona next to the flowers. It was the only personal photograph.

His nostrils flared, taking in the special blend incense she used for clarity and peaceful rest. The music coming from her player was a soulful Irish ballad, sung by a male with a rough, sexy voice. It always made her think of a warrior, offering a song by the campfire on the eve of battle, when thoughts turned not to the bloodshed ahead, but the woman who might be left behind as the result of it.

He was visibly digesting all of that, but his gaze had moved to the far wall, to one particular picture. She suppressed the immature desire to shift in front of it. Damn it, he shouldn't be here. *Send him away before it's too late, you idiot.*

"You have some exquisite artwork downstairs, but up here, the tone is different. Darker, more personal."

"Hence my private room." Fixing him with a cool gaze, she sat back down on the bed, crossed her legs. They'd left his offer hanging out there, but it wasn't buying her time to marshal defenses. With every moment he was here, in her personal space, she was digging herself a hole, not a protective trench.

He threaded his hands through the balusters, resting his forearms on the floorboards as he shifted his weight to one hip and considered her world through that barricade. She noticed he had chest hair, a dark, silky mat that covered the muscle, that tight arrow down the center ridge of his abdomen. The floor interfered with the rest of the view. Unless she rose on her toes, or came closer.

He might be gathering information about her, but she was doing something similar. Damn succubus blood, which heightened her senses. He had the smell of fire, the good aroma of burning wood and sweet grasses. Her candlelight gave his dark hair a sheen that tempted the stroke of her fingertips through the feathers of it. He had such a strong face, so implacable and ruthless. He'd capture her wrist before he'd let her touch him, she was sure. Would hold it there between them, wait long enough that she knew he held all the reins. That was his power, and what he could give a woman. Turn all control over to him, let him dominate, and he would orchestrate her pleasure beyond her wildest dreams. Though Raina's dreams went further and deeper than most, she had no doubt he could exceed them.

The pulse in her throat now had a matching needy beat between her legs. Even with the breeze coming in from outside, she was getting warmer. Cathair made a warbling noise, then subsided. Recognizing the raven as her familiar, Mikhael gave him a neutral nod, then his gaze shifted back to the solitary charcoal portrait that had caught his attention.

It was a headshot of a woman, drawn from the back. She was visible to her bare shoulder blades. Her long hair was pulled up, her slim hand holding it there. She wore a silver collar, locked. Her other hand rested on it, as if she was wondering at the way wearing it made her feel.

"This has significance to you."

In so many ways. She'd never thought she'd have a picture like that, but she'd found it when she was adding to the bordello gallery. It had caught her, haunted her. She put it off a while, but when she received notification another bidder had put in an offer, she doubled it and bought it out from under him before the auction closed.

"It conveys the beauty and elegance of willing submission," Mikhael mused. "Not someone brutalized into servitude. I expect you have clients who come here for both, to a certain point."

"Yes. It's a common craving, for those willing to acknowledge it."

"For some it's a game. For others, it's like the need for food or air." His gaze shifted from everything in the room to the hub of it all. Her. "It's a road you've closed to yourself."

"When the craving is twisted, exploited, forced, it's different." Then it became something ugly. Staring at him, she understood what he meant about his ability to read the minds of others. It wasn't telepathy, not entirely. Like her, he was in the business of exceptional intuition. But it wasn't an invitation to crawl into her soul. Or her bed.

"You can embrace everything you want to be, Raina. You don't have to trust me as a male, or a Dark Guardian. But you can trust me with that part of you, as a lover."

He said it with a serious sincerity she wanted to doubt but couldn't, because she could read the truth of it from him. He meant it, no sarcasm, no hidden agenda. No strings, right? Sex didn't matter, sex was just sex, even when it turned your soul inside out. That was what made it one of the most devastating of all magics, capable of crippling.

He didn't blink, didn't look away. He waited on her. If she told him to go, he would. But in this solitary room, the top of her personal castle, so many sleeping souls below depending upon her, she could tell he understood what it was to be lonely. To want. To crave. *Goddess.*

She picked up her tea, sipped it. To appear casual, in control. As she set it aside, she rose, aware of the give of her mattress beneath her weight. It made her wonder how it would react to both their weights, her pressed beneath him.

She walked across the room.

CHAPTER FOUR

*H*e straightened, clasping the balusters. He had one foot on an upper step, his body canted at an angle that suggested his readiness to move, to act. The candlelight loved all that power and heated skin. He was an unconditional sexual offering. She could feel that energy expanding, filling the space of her private room, preparing to take it— and her—over.

When she reached the railing, she sank to her knees in front of it, her velvet dress pooling around her. She hadn't changed, so she could still smell the faint charred scent of the hem. His gaze dipped to the expanse of cleavage exposed by the low cut of the fabric, the way it held her breasts, the velvet molded over the nipples. When she'd come up to her bedroom, she'd taken off her bra, sliding it out through the sleeves and tucking the scrap of lace away in her lingerie chest. His attention moved up her neck, back to her face. In this position, she was eye level with him. She curled one set of fingers around the railings, below his, and then his grip shifted, overlapping hers, holding her there.

Reaching through the bars with his other hand, he slid his fingers to her nape, applying firm pressure. Bringing her in. She put her hand through the bars, settling it on his chest. Hard muscle, no give to it, but the silken hair there coaxed a stroking touch. Her nails curled in, digging into his skin, a mute desire to pull him closer, but that feeling quickly became too overwhelming.

Her palm flattened, her arm straightening to hold him at bay. Too intimate, too much.

He eased the pressure on her nape, but tightened his fingers on hers gripping the railing. "Just pleasure," he said. "I'm behind these bars, Raina. Trust yourself. Push your dress to your waist."

Sex felt good. Like candy. She told herself that, even as tremors swept her limbs and desire filled the empty space in her abdomen. When she drew her hand back, he let her other one go, waiting. Pushing the sleeves off her shoulders, she drew the soft brushed fabric down over her bosom. She knew she had great breasts, high and proud, but heavy and eye catching, and they captured his gaze now.

He slid his arm all the way through to circle her waist, hand slipping to the small of her back. She was on her knees, but he brought her forward with simple flexing strength. That power wasn't otherworldly Dark Guardian stuff. He was plain that strong, making her woman's heart trip a little faster as her knees slid a few inches through two of the baluster openings, holding her open.

"There you go," he said, low, as if he were keeping a wild animal calm. Though she was nonplused to be experiencing such behavior from the likes of him, the comparison wasn't entirely wrong. "Put your hands through this opening and this one. All the way to the elbow. Good girl. Now fold them over, holding your forearms at the elbow. Hold them tight." A front boxed position that brought her chest up to the rails. She drew in a breath as his long, capable fingers stroked her breasts, adjusted her so that they were pushed through openings between the balusters as well, her arms locked beneath them. "Beautiful," he said.

Her nipples were pierced, displaying silver rings strung with amethyst and diamonds that brushed the underside of her breasts. He pinched one, tugged on it. Her fingers tightened on her forearms.

"Hold still." Reaching into his jeans pocket, he withdrew two lengths of silver chain. As she watched, her breath shortening, he hooked one of them to a nipple ring, then ran the chain in and out of the railings between and hooked the other, tethering her there. Holding her gaze, he ran the other chain around the back of her neck, double looping it around her throat before fastening it to the baluster directly before her.

They were thin chains, just a symbol of restraint. It was all right, she could break them. She told her thundering heart that. She wasn't going to panic, to act like an inexperienced child with a Dark Guardian. She was tougher than that.

The problem was, something about him made her want to let go, to show the vulnerability she was feeling deep inside. To trust him with her fear. That was an insane thought. This was a mistake. He was too good at this.

"Caught," he said. His touch moved to her back, dipping under the dress bunched at her waist to caress the shallow valley there, then lower, to tease her buttocks.

There was a mirror on the wall behind him. Despite her protections, she also liked seeing the reflection of someone coming up her steps, even if it was someone as innocuous as Catalina bringing her the evening's receipts or Marisa with her tea. Now he shifted, wanting her to see herself. Kneeling in front of the banister rail, tethered by the neck, her breasts pushed through the spacing of the bars, embellished by that delicate silver chain. As she watched, he used his smallest finger, threaded it through one of the nipple rings, slowly pulled on it, increasing the pressure and sending pleasure spearing out from that point into her lower belly.

She bit her lip, saw her eyes go a deeper green-gold as her blood responded. She still had that gateway locked down, but the succubus energy was pushing against it. The scent was starting to perfume the air around her. Undetectable to the human brain but registered by their olfactory system, it ensnared her prey, their arousal only fueling her lust for that energy, to drink it all until the body had no life left.

"Mikhael..."

"I have you. No worries, Raina. No fear."

The Russian accent became more pronounced when he was aroused. He dropped to one knee, replacing his touch on her nipple with his mouth. *Holy Goddess.*

She pushed herself hard against his moist heat, a needy sound breaking from her throat, the power unfurling. His energy would be rich, potent. Overwhelming and dark, and she liked the dark juices, the dark chocolates, the darkest of things.

He cupped her breasts, squeezing them while he suckled and pulled. When he caught the chain in his teeth, he gave it a sharp tug that made her jerk, cry out.

It was only the beginning. Over the next few minutes, she rasped out pleas to several different versions of the Goddess. When she shifted, her arousal was slick against her calves. He moved to the other nipple then. She released her elbows and arched involuntarily, her body snapping back. But his hand was already on her back, biceps flexing to hold her close to the rail so she didn't hurt her nipples. He did it all without a break in rhythm, suckling her.

She wanted to touch. She put her fingers in his hair, the smooth, thick strands. It was like a horse's mane, and she thought of kelpies, magical, deadly creatures.

He lifted his head as her fingertips slid over his temples. The steady gaze that met hers was serious. "Did I give you permission to touch me?"

"No. But I want to."

"Then ask, Raina."

Her throat ached. Though the reassuring warmth of salty tears, of one's humanity—so to speak—was more vital than one realized, at the moment she was glad she was a tearless witch.

"I don't know how to ask."

"Yes, you do." He produced two more lengths of silver chain. He had to be conjuring them, because no male carried pretty jewelry in his pockets unless he had a plan to impress a woman. She didn't think Mikhael expended much effort on impressing women, since he managed to do that well enough without trying, damn the bastard.

He folded her hands back on her forearms, obviously intending to bind her wrists to them. He had his head bent over his task, but when she made a noise he lifted it. Gazing into those dark eyes, so close, she realized this was as intimate and familiar as she'd been with a man in a very long time. Perhaps ever, because this instance was weighted with a lot of different things, the most important one being trust. It only increased the ache, because it was as he said; none of it was about more than this moment. Just the pleasure they could give one another.

It wasn't hard to say the words; they wanted to leap off her tongue. Allowing herself to say them, that was terrifying, a gate she had to push open with enough effort that she stumbled on the first word. "W-Will you let me touch you?"

Her cheeks burned in mortification, and her body jerked as if in protest of her going over that wall. More succubus energy spiraled out, coiling around him like a python. Her adrenaline spiked, but he made a calming murmur, cupping her face, fingers caressing her throat. The gesture made her chin lift despite the hold of the chain around her neck. He caught her, holding her so the strength of his touch restrained her there as he stroked her windpipe with fingers that could crush it without thought.

"You may." The silver chains disappeared back into his pocket, her wrists left unbound. He lowered his head to her breast again, allowing her to do as she would.

Sliding her hands back into his hair, she savored the ability to do so, but she also curved her arms around him, one hand slipping to his nape, then the space between his broad shoulders. She held him to her as he kept pleasuring her breasts, until she was bumping against him rhythmically, pleading for far more than that, incoherent sounds of need as she clutched him.

His arm was around her, too, holding her close. She was twitching on her legs, so aroused, so close to coming. She was drowning now. Those coils of energy had expanded. To anyone with preternatural senses, they were now surrounded by a filmy mist tinged with pale crimson, the hint of blood. That vapor fogged the human mind, an aphrodisiac that took them higher and higher until, even if they realized it, they wouldn't care that their lives were in peril.

That mist caressed Mikhael's bare shoulders, whispered over him. If he had any visible reaction to it, it was to goad her further, taking her up higher, as if he had a mist of his own making.

Giving each nipple ring one last tug with his teeth, he rose, sliding out of her grip. "Put your hands back on your elbows and keep them there."

She didn't think it was possible for her arousal to get any more intense, but the pitch of that low command did the trick. Her sex contracted so hard she shuddered. Moving up the stairs, he towered over her as he came around to where she knelt, vulnerable and captured. Anxiety fluttered, but he squatted next to her, stroking her hair. His mouth was wet from suckling her, and she wanted to touch his lips. He didn't permit her that, but he did release the chains, even slid the gown back up onto her shoulders, covering her aching breasts, the friction of it on her nipples enough to make her sway as he brought her to her feet.

She was the initiator, the aggressor, the strategic planner when it came to lovemaking, because that was her job. It was a job she loved, but it was still a job. He wasn't giving her time to plan or calculate, had actually stolen any need to do so. She just followed her own desires—and his commands—and was lost in it.

Closing his grip on her wrist, he slowly twisted her arm behind her, bringing her into his body fully. His other hand tangled in her hair, his fist tightening in it.

This was different from the hint of mastery from those slender chains. This was full mastery, his strength obviously far greater than hers, and he was going to use it to overpower her, take her where he wanted her.

"No."

"Yes."

She unsheathed her fangs, something she never did, and bit his mouth when he got too close. He pushed her arm up higher, sending pain ricocheting through her shoulder. She let go of him, her eyes flashing, and he nodded. "Now lick it off, nice and gentle."

She did, but she pressed her breasts into his chest at the same time, rubbed herself against his cock with a courtesan's expertise and a woman's raw need. Her mist had an edge now, an edge that kicked the breeze into a sharper wind that swirled through the chamber, rippling the curtains and blowing out several of the candles, increasing the shadows.

"Do your worst, succubus. You can't harm me." Letting go of her arm, he banded both of his around her, lifted and slammed her against the wall. Not hard enough to harm her, but hard enough to under-score his point, make her want him more. He took full command of that kiss, so deep her jaw strained under the assault. She tasted his blood, dug her nails into his back, seeking more of it. If he'd worn a shirt, she would have shredded it as she unleashed her full strength, her nails wicked talons that could lay open flesh like a machete.

She undulated against him. He might have control of her arms and upper body, but a succubus's flexibility was like a serpent's. Working her hips with the precision of a harem dancer, she stroked him with heat that had impressive results, even through the too-thick denim. Pulling her off the wall, he hiked her up against him, and brought her back to the bed.

"Let's slow this down." When she sought to take his mouth again, he restrained her wrists with one hand, settled his other hand on her throat, holding her head down as he took his mouth down her sternum. She writhed but couldn't throw him off. Even now, with the strength of her magic coursing through her, both as witch and succubus, he was much stronger. He slid his body half over hers, had her pinned.

Sexual energy was pulsing off her, building to the intensity of a nuclear threat. If he was wrong, she wouldn't only drain him. She'd leave him a skeleton and send a power surge through the whole house that would blow out every circuit. Probably every transformer within fifty square miles.

He lifted his head, nostrils flaring, eyes registering the power increase. "It's like the smell of your cunt, magnified a hundred times," he growled. "Intoxicating."

Her body rippled at the rough language, her most primal senses responding to it. He wasn't the least bit afraid. His cock was hard, his body revved with lust, absorbed in the pleasures he was taking, but he wasn't lost. His desire wasn't caused by the disorientation of her magic. He was remaining in full command. Desperately—and way too late—she realized his gift to her long-suppressed desires might give him a power over her she could never reclaim.

"Let me go," she rasped.

"No. You want me, you take me on my terms, Raina. Which means you serve my pleasure. And I want you screaming out yours until it rocks this house on its foundation."

He hadn't lowered the neckline of the dress, but he put his mouth over the stiff nipple, breathed on it. As he put his tongue against it, a slow manipulation with the velvet in between, she writhed and writhed. Electricity crackled in the air, lightning through the mist. It was a pyrotechnic show that humans couldn't see. Every sex demon produced a different aura, a different tapestry. An Aurora Borealis to consummate the pleasure, a combination of her magic and the life energy of her victim. She'd often wondered if the human got to glimpse it right before his death. She hoped so, because it was a thing of terrible beauty, one last gift for their unwilling sacrifice.

Then she was swept up in it herself. *"Mikhael."* She'd thrown away a lifetime of restraint on his word alone. He'd been so compelling, and now she was at the point of no return.

"I've got you, baby. You're not going to hurt anyone. I promise. Let go. Let me see you scream."

She shredded her linens, her pillow as he bit down on her nipple, pulling hard on the piercing. Pain speared her amid the pleasure. Then he put his mouth over all of it, soothing and suckling her, the friction of the cloth making her more crazed. He wasn't even inside her, wasn't touching her below the waist at all.

She hadn't been taken over like this in a very, very...well, never. Not like this. She knew all sorts of sexual positions, Tantric methods, fancy maneuvers that would bug out the eyes of the most experienced. But all Mikhael had done was caress her body, lavish her breasts with attention—he was obviously a breast man—and taken control. Simple, uncomplicated gestures, delivered with devastating intent.

When he moved to the other nipple, it was like the sensation magnified another hundred times. She bit back the desire to beg, to plead. By the time he flipped her over onto her stomach, she'd lost that fight entirely.

Putting a hand on her neck, he held her down with that ruthless strength. "Lift your hips up toward me. Show me how much you want me."

Her hips were already doing that, whether she told them to do so or not. He pushed her skirt up.

"No panties. Such a bad, good girl." He cupped her between her legs. A moment later, she screamed as his mouth teased between her legs, his tongue sliding in to explore, to lick, to collect the honey he found there. When he nuzzled her clit, she struggled, cried out, but he was taking his time as she became an incendiary device.

"Let it go, Raina. Pit your energy against mine. *Now*." His tongue thrust in, hard, lapping, swirling, giving her no chance to breathe, to do anything but obey.

She cracked open like an egg, power spilling out in a wash of blinding colors...silver gray, red, flickers of orange-blue flame taking over as it built, then an explosion that surged over them both. Letting her go, he yanked her up to her knees, let her turn. In an instant she was on him, shoving him to his back. As she shredded the jeans, tore them away, she saw blood where her nails gouged him. His hard, beautiful cock rose high and thick over his belly before she covered it with her body. He had her hips, her waist, and though she snarled and fought him, he made her take him slowly. His hand tangled in her hair so he controlled the pace, pushed himself into her. He had a thick organ, and if she'd slammed down on him the way she'd desired, she would have torn herself.

She didn't care, because pain and pleasure were one at this point, but he took that pleasure up beyond what she thought possible as he made her feel every slow, gradual inch, his face savage in his concentration.

When he was thrust in deep, all the way to the hilt, she began to feed.

The energy spiraled up from that joining point, as well as through his skin, through the flickering fire of his eyes. Just like she'd hoped, it was potent and rich. She bathed in it, drank greedily, because it had been so long. Oh, Goddess, it was so fine to let go, to pull that wonderful nectar from his body.

She'd always been a creature of utter control, and yet he'd taken all that away. Her wild gaze flickered to his face, and she saw it *was* okay. His upper body was rigid strength, his expression focused as he funneled their combined energy back to her.

But he wasn't detached. He couldn't be, because that was why the energy nourished a succubus like nothing else. It was his sexual vitality, a powerful soul force, that made her even greedier. He wanted her, was ready to let go his seed, but he held back, either because it fascinated him to watch a sex demon feed, or because he wanted her to savor her meal as long as possible. She didn't know, didn't care, beyond such an internal debate. As she rose and fell with powerful strokes, she gripped him tight. His pupils expanded, then his iris took over the white sclera so his gaze went completely dark. His wings erupted from his back, knocking over things on the side table. She reveled in his passion.

She hadn't thought about the kind of powers he might unleash during such an intimate connection, too absorbed with her own. It was incredibly reckless, because she knew the fatal magics that could be raised during sex. But it was a marvel to behold. Her magic was a female dragon spreading her wings, baring her fangs to swoop in for the strike, countered by a male power, a dark dragon willing to take that strike and turn it into something more.

It wound around her power, wound around her, such that she was captured on his loins. It constricted around her like silken ribbon and barbed wire, absorbing her verve as she built to the final surge, craving the dessert, the sexual energy of his climax.

"You first," he growled. "Your pleasure...first."

It was all pleasure. She would have told him that if she could speak. He reared up, tormenting her nipples with his mouth in a fast, unpredictable rhythm as he pistoned between her legs. A guttural cry came from her lips. "Come for me," he muttered. "Give me that climax, Raina. Do it, now."

Her body simply detonated. Blue sparks coming off her skin, landing on his. She threw back her head, and his hands caught in her hair, holding that extreme arch as he used the position to bite down.

She screamed, the climax taking her over. She formed a wordless plea, *"No..."* but it meant something else, because she didn't ever want to stop. He gripped her buttocks in bruising hands, pushing her into a deeper rhythm that shot her onto another wave.

She sent animal cries out into the night, though the spinning sky was in here, shooting stars, the moon exploding into pearls. She felt the iron restraint he held on his own body, making sure he took her to completion.

Goddess, it was a good thing they both knew this was temporal, because in this moment, she would have done anything for him, died for him...loved him until the end of his days.

She was on the final hill of the wild coaster when he released, sending her up with him again. It was an infusion of undiluted power, his climax total nourishment for her. Despite what she'd already had, it was like drinking after a long, long thirst in the desert. *More, more, more...*

It was the ultimate sexual experience of her life. Even with no emotion involved.

～

As she started to come down, some anxiety came with it, but he had an answer for that as well. He began to lift her free, then, with a gleam in his eye, brought her back down on him deep and hard. A moan broke from her lips as the unexpected move set off aftershocks, more of those blue sparks glittering off her skin. One of them landed on his chest and she watched it burn there against his skin, turn to ash.

She put her hand on his face, his hair. She wanted to wrap her arms around his head, hold him to her heart. Which meant she needed to pull it together, be what she was expected to be. Good thing she had a lot of practice in that respect.

Her fingers curved into his chest as she gave him a feline smile. "That last bit was...diabolical," she said breathlessly.

"Want me to do it again?" He was gazing at her with those eyes that saw too much. She wet her lips, cocked her head, her hair brushing his thighs.

"Do *you* want to do it again?" she asked.

She could see the whites of his eyes again, but the pupils were still large, unfathomable. "No courtesan games, Raina."

"No games," she returned. "I want to know."

I want to hear that you want me. She'd had hundreds of men say it, but what they wanted had nothing to do with her, not really. If he said it, she knew it would mean something different with him.

Putting his hand on the side of her neck, he slid her off his cock, eyes darkening further at her murmur of response. He laid her down on his body, cradling her inside the sprawl of his thighs. When he brought her face up from under his jaw, there was a painfully honest distance between their eyes. "I do. And I will."

But instead of proceeding with that sensual threat, backed by the still substantially firm organ against her hip, he put his mouth on hers. It was a long, lazy trip, and just when she thought she was floating away on the residual energy lingering in the room, he shifted her off him, but only to turn them both.

His body pressed into the angles and curves of hers. She let out a soft sigh as a wash of power swept across her skin, and his wing curved over her. Mikhael was okay with post-coital spooning. Who knew?

The wing was like a bat's, just as she'd suspected, but as he brought it down around her, along with his arm, it provided a warm and safe cocoon.

"Sleep," he murmured against her ear. "Just sleep."

She did, some. But she also remembered what they'd shared, such that as she drifted in and out of a doze, she rubbed her bare bottom against his groin, his hard cock pressed against her cheeks as she teased him in her half-drowsy state. When he stilled her with a hand against her stomach, his fingers trailed the top of her smooth mound, then lower, to play in the residual stickiness, the remains of their release. His seed still marked her. She hadn't considered birth control, since succubi only conceived with humans, and only on blue moons... literally. But Mikhael was extraordinary in many ways. She wondered if she should be worried about conceiving ruthless little bats with solid dark eyes. She pressed a smile against his muscular biceps, caressed his forearm. The man was built like a brick house. No wonder Ruby had been intoxicated with him.

For some reason, she wasn't pleased with that thought, so she pushed it away to notice he was looking at her TV table. He dropped his head to the pillow behind her, puffed a breath on her neck that sent a shiver down her spine. Almost...playful.

"*Titanic*," he said. "Is there any female who doesn't like that movie?"

She tilted her head to look at him. She had a desire to caress his jaw, but she quelled it. "Only the ones without estrogen. Is there any male who doesn't hate it? And why is that, by the way?"

"It's a chick flick on steroids." He made a pained expression. "A male watches a ninety-minute romance with a woman because he anticipates sex as payment for his attention. Ninety minutes is a fair exchange. A three-hour movie, with a tragic ending that leaves the woman sobbing, needing consolation, not sexual pleasure? That's above and beyond the call of duty. He has to be flat-on-his-ass in love with her to put up with that shit."

She elbowed him in the gut, wasn't at all surprised when he caught it before it could make contact. Wrapping his arms closer around her, he nuzzled her neck. It was all so intimate and familiar...so pleasurable, and it was starting to make her uneasy, now that the sex was done. Cuddling was something she'd provide, if the client paid for it. But there was a big difference in sex with a client and this.

"You're thinking too much, Raina," he said. "You can give yourself this, the pleasure with the emotions. It doesn't have to be dissected."

"I don't understand what you want."

"Just this. No more, no less. Go to sleep, or I'll give you a spanking."

Amusement unfurled among all the other less settling emotions. "*That's* supposed to inspire me to sleep?"

His arms tightened. "My mistake. If you go to sleep now, I promise you a spanking later."

She shut her eyes right away, smiling at his snort against her neck. And gave a yelp as he turned her over and gave her a smack right then and there.

Sleep was going to wait.

CHAPTER FIVE

*R*aina woke late. Apparently, her paranormally-sentient house had decided she needed to sleep in. It had adjusted her bed so the early sunlight that normally served as her alarm clock couldn't reach her until midmorning.

The intensity of the previous night seemed surreal. She'd surrendered blatantly to him, to a seductive stranger from the Underworld who'd given her an incredible, over-the-top night. However, today, she might have to kick his ass to keep him from gutting Isaac. Reality could be an energy-sucking bitch. The house was right—she'd need the extra rest to face whatever challenges came her way today.

However, as she struggled free of the tangled sheets, it brought back memories of how creatively he'd tied her up in them. He'd left her the illusion that she could get free, playing at the edge of her darkest fears just as he had with the silver chains, but she'd never had a chance to test either restraint, had she? She could still smell Mikhael on those sheets, had woken up burrowed in them, nesting in that scent.

During one half-drowsy moment, she'd stroked her fingers along his wing. There was a bonelike protrusion, a sharp hook at the widest part. He'd closed his hand over hers, helping her feel the shape of it, protecting her until she figured out it was sharp enough to draw blood, rip flesh.

It gave her an odd feeling, the way he'd prevented her from

coming to harm. "I don't want to mark that soft skin," he'd murmured. "Not unless it's intentional."

Apparently she was going to have to lobotomize herself. Or get moving to get past this. So she got dressed. Did her usual quick meditation to make sure all of her usual protections were in place, a thorough perimeter check she did every day, reaching out to the corners of the property. Cathair arrived on cue, flitting through the window to land on her shoulder, lending his energy and focus as he always did, his body pressed against her.

Isaac was still in the house. So was the Dark Guardian. Hell, she was really off her game. It was past time for Monday brunch. She hadn't formally introduced him to the staff. But she hadn't expected him to be up before she was, not after a night of strenuous fucking. Irritating male.

Since they rested on Sunday, the staff shared a brunch on Monday, a family get-together. Maintaining the house protections took considerable energy, so they were used to her sleeping deep on Sunday night to rebuild her strength, coming in a little later to join them. Not this late, but there was no reason for her to be flustered. Monday was also the day she spent on Craft, reinforcing spell-work and feeling for any weaknesses or cracks in the house protections, using her rejuvenated energy to double-check everything.

That would have to wait, because the possibility of her new brunch guest annihilating one of her staff took higher priority.

When she got to the dining room, Cathair still with her, she saw all dozen of her incubi and succubi were there, intact and gathered at one end of the antique dining table that sat twenty. Isaac was among them. Mikhael was on the corner chair at the other end, eating by himself, reading today's paper. Apparently, he tracked local news.

She subscribed to the paper because her staff liked passing around the comics and reading horoscopes. Or exchanging local news tidbits from the police blotter and front page. She herself nursed the private pleasure of cutting coupons, pestering Li to use them when she sent him and Gina out on supply runs in town. It never hurt to save a dollar.

Given that Gina had spread the news a Dark Guardian was in the house, Raina was surprised to see everyone present, none of them chickening out and staying in their rooms. However, Gina would also have shared Raina's statement that he was a guest and they would not be harmed. Their faith in her judgment, coupled largely with their passion for Monday-morning brunch, had apparently overcome any wariness. It was flattering, but a little disturbing as well, knowing they had that unwavering confidence, even in the face of a Dark Guardian's presence. She hoped she could live up to it.

Nonsense. Of course she could. It irritated her that she allowed herself a moment of doubt. They had a balance in her household. Her spells allowed her staff to feed on the sexual energy of clients without taking their life energy, which was a win-win. The clients were more exhausted afterward than they might be with a human escort, but they also had the sex of their lives, and a desire to return for more. She had only a few rules, but they were nonnegotiable. Her staff knew that if any one of them went outside of her house to feed, therefore resulting in a kill, they were expelled, out the door for good. As Isaac's circumstances starkly demonstrated, most sex demons never found the safety her house offered, the stability and quality of life that existed here.

Monday brunch merely punctuated that fact. Though they didn't live on human food, succubi and incubi had taste buds like anyone else. Eating human food was like eating candy. No nutritional value, but they liked it, and it whetted their appetites for the real nourishment, arriving later in the evening.

Matilda, their cook, was an unflappable black woman who could talk to spirits, and did so quite often. In fact, she preferred to talk to them, such that Raina often found out what Matilda was thinking or demanding only by her loud conversations with the spirits none of them could see. From the first, she ignored any menu Raina told her to prepare, doing what the spirits told her instead. Which had turned out to be fine, since she had a flawless track record for providing the perfect thing for every occasion. She also knew when someone needed a comforting bowl of soup or a steaming hot cup of tea. As such, Raina had decided that, just because she couldn't see Matilda's spirit pals, there was no reason not to defer to their wishes in menu choices. It took meal planning off her to-do list, after all.

Matilda went home each afternoon to her shack, built deep in the swamp on Raina's property. She always left Sweet Dreams before they opened for business. The one time Raina had asked her to stay, to help cater a party event, Matilda had come to a full stop. Banging her wooden spoon on the edge of the chowder pot, she'd turned toward the potato and onion bins, where her spirits apparently preferred to congregate while she cooked.

"Ain't none of us going to stand for all that fornicating," she informed those potatoes and onions. "No, sirree, we won't be anywhere near this house when that nonsense is going on. And we going to put Tabasco sauce on that naughty Luke's unmentionables next time he lets that robe gap open at dinner time to tease old Matilda. He'll be dancing and howling like all you spirits do on All Saints' Night. Just you watch."

She was worth every penny of the exorbitant salary Raina paid to keep her.

Matilda was a perfect mesh for the house itself. Sometimes Raina scheduled a client for one particular playroom, only to discover that door locked when the time came, diverting them to another, more appropriate place. It didn't happen often, for Raina was very good at reading her clients, but she'd learned to respect powers greater than herself to override certain decisions. The house also had its own mind about opening and closing doors and windows, so door locks were fairly useless...unless the house wanted to lock the door. Whether the decisions came from the ghosts that still lingered in the old house or the nature of the magic that saturated it, she and her staff took it in stride.

Today the house apparently wanted the doors to the back garden thrown wide open. It was funneling a pleasant breeze into the dining room by moving the panels in and out in a slow, fanlike motion, like children hanging on to the knobs, rocking the panels back and forth. Mikhael not only seemed unconcerned about that, he also appeared indifferent to the obvious shunning of her staff. Their gazes would dart toward him if he so much as lifted his coffee cup to his lips, but then just as quickly dart away.

When he scraped back his chair, he caused a synchronized jump, like a flock of birds startling, but he paid no attention, turning it to the side so he could put his ankle on his knee, lay an elbow on the table by his plate. Occasionally, he took another bite from a croissant or piece of bacon before he folded back a page. He was wearing his jeans from last night, with a shirt this time. The shirt was carelessly closed, just two buttons in the middle, and his feet were bare, his hair attractively tousled. Positively mouth-watering. And disgustingly effortless.

No woman looked that good without trying. In action movies, when the hero was grungy, bloody and in torn clothes, he looked absolutely edible. Lara Croft, in the same situation, had to have perfect makeup and hair, clothes fitted to best advantage, with just a little stage makeup for the dirt and blood, an artful rip to the tight T-shirt. Otherwise, a woman rolled in the dirt looked like...well, a woman rolled in the dirt.

She didn't even want to get started on men's ability to metabolize food. Her succubi and incubi didn't have any problems in that area, but with her half-human blood, Raina had to be careful not to pack on too many pounds. Eyeing Mikhael with his carb and grease breakfast, Raina concluded women's attraction to men was an involuntary chemical thing, because there were just too many reasons to hate them with a homicidal intensity.

Who and what was a Dark Guardian, really? She knew they served the Underworld for all eternity. They weren't highly favored by Light Guardians like Derek. Dark Guardians were a puzzle to them. Why was there a need for an Underworld legion to ensure the balance of Dark against the Light, when the Dark seemed so prevalent without help? Dark Guardians weren't the PR sort, readily volunteering the reasons for their existence.

But a man was more than what he did for a living, even if he didn't think so. She was in the business of knowing the soul below the surface. Did he truly not mind that no one was sitting with him, or had he gotten so used to being alone in the many years that he'd done what he did, that he didn't think about it anymore?

When he wasn't serving Lucifer's purposes, babysitting an incubus thief, waiting for a female demon to show up at a remote Southern bordello, he might be a big party animal, getting wasted at keg parties and hooking up with trashy women.

Yeah, right.

Coming into the room at last, she passed her people first, transferring Cathair to Li. She touched shoulders, asked how their night was. Despite their bravado, there was some uncertainty about Mikhael's presence, so she calmed the more shy or nervous ones. Her newer staff members were like young cats, hyperalert to threats.

Li was the leader of the group. The oldest at twenty-six, he was the one who would reinforce her reassurances with the others. He was also intuitive enough to discern her night had been a little more entertaining than usual.

The protections on her bedroom tower maintained privacy as well as safety, and Mikhael had reinforced those during their encounter, which meant no sound or evidence should have disturbed the rest of the house. However, physical evidence was hard to hide. Li's handsome Asian eyes sharpened, registering the relaxed movements of a woman well sated. His slim black brows rose, his sensual lips quirking in barely contained curiosity. He would want details as soon as he could corner her. Lots of them.

Not likely. She was still wrapping her own mind around it. The youngest sex demons sat the farthest from Mikhael, the others a buffer between them. Gina was one of the former, sitting next to Marisa. Gina didn't take clients yet, because she was still mastering the basics of working with Raina's protections so the client could have a pleasurable experience without hospitalization or a morgue. Right now, she and Marisa worked as a team and Marisa fed the younger girl from her offerings. Enough male clients wanted a three-way with two beautiful women that Marisa could tutor her at the same time she nourished her.

Isaac sat on the other side of Gina, sandwiched between Luke and Isabella, good choices. Though all of her staff had been with her at least two years, with Li being the longest at six years, Luke had come most recently and could give Isaac the male perspective on his situation. Isabella could make any male, human or incubi, her devoted slave in no time.

The appeal of sex demons in the paid companionship trade was the lack of artifice. They genuinely enjoyed carnality, in all its offerings and varieties, the same way mortals enjoyed a wide array of meals, the different flavors and textures.

She'd trained them to respond appropriately to the emotional reactions of the clients to enhance and deepen the experience for both of them. Because that increased the quality of the nourishment for them, they followed the instruction well. Though it required enormous spell-work to keep those interactions safe, she didn't mind it. While she knew they viewed her as their protector, like a tribal priestess, they also had fun, played together. They were bonded, as close to a family as was possible for their kind.

The way her life had been, she didn't spend a lot of time berating what she couldn't have. She was thankful for the abilities to have what she did. She hadn't waited for those abilities to come to her, either. She'd honed them to what they were now, and she kept working on them, devoting time each week to accumulating more energy and knowledge. Inertia was an indulgence she couldn't afford in her world. Later today, she would find a quiet space to do that spell-work to check for weaknesses, not because anything was amiss, but because she knew the dangers of relaxing her diligence. Isaac's presence meant that there might be a new danger on the horizon besides.

For now, though, she was sleeping with a cop, so she felt like she could take an hour to enjoy brunch. Picking a plate off the sidebar, she chose a few things she liked. Chocolate-dipped strawberries, fresh peach preserves in a fragrant marinade poured over a fluffy biscuit.

Mikhael had pushed out the chair at the head of the table so he could prop his foot on it, resting the paper against his bent knee. His shoes were tucked under the chair, so he'd removed them before putting his feet on the furniture. He had manners, of a sort. It was like watching the lord of a manor make free use of his belongings. Because they were his, he wasn't abusive of them, but he expected certain amounts of accommodating service from them.

Perching on the chair where he had his foot braced, she sat down on his toes, drawing up her feet, smoothing her satin dressing gown so it pooled around her ankles and slid across the arch of his foot, nearly covering it. She considered following the same track with a caress of that ankle, the calf beneath the cuff of the jeans. He'd shaved. Earlier this morning, she'd felt the appealing sandpaper brush of his jaw as he kissed the bumps of her spine. She'd liked that, but she also liked the sharp, clean aristocratic look now.

Vaguely she remembered opening her eyes to see him shaving at her mirror. He'd been using a sharp-bladed knife that looked like it could gut a small mammal, but the sharp edge moved smooth and sure over his face under his steady hand. She thought about doing that for him, sitting naked on the sink, passing that lethal blade near his throat, his eyes tracking her, hands sliding over her hips, up to her breasts...

He continued reading his article without acknowledging her. Not entirely perfect manners after all. Considering the things on her plate, she picked up a juicy blueberry. Flicked it with precision so it hit him square in the forehead.

Or would have, if he hadn't caught it in a movement too fast for her to see. Setting it aside, he lifted his gaze to her. Everything from last night came back when she met that look. Every detail, every touch, every cry that he'd torn from her. She saw where they'd been together, the journey they'd taken, and that he very much intended it would happen again. Perhaps even on this table in the next thirty seconds.

All her body could say was a fervent, almost evangelical *yes. Amen and hallelujah.*

"I wouldn't advise doing that again," he said.

She looked at the dozen blueberries on her plate, then back at him. "It's polite to acknowledge a lady when she comes to the table. Particularly if you shared her bed the night before."

"My apologies. Good morning. How did you sleep?"

She felt the impossible—her cheeks warmed. Now that she'd arrived and they had more confidence to be their usual selves, her staff had increased the volume of their conversation. However, she caught several fascinated stares from those who registered her reaction. It wasn't her fault. The man had sex and sin dripping from every syllable he spoke. "I slept just fine, thank you. And you?"

"The bed was too short. But the company made up for it."

"If you have to inflict your charming personality on us another night, I'm sure we can find you a larger bed. One that you'll have all to yourself." There. She'd made it clear any future interactions were by her invitation only. If he was gone tonight, it wouldn't matter anyhow. Everything back to normal, the way it should be.

He didn't respond to that statement, just took a sip of coffee. He preferred it straight black, and he'd gone for their strongest Colombian blend. The residuals on his plate suggested he was a heavy eater, but not on the sweet side. He went for the salts: bacon, eggs, toast, no preserves. She liked a man who didn't compete with her chocolate cravings.

"Surprised to see Isaac here this morning," he noted.

"Sex demons are pack animals, in a sense. They feel more comfortable in a group, when a group's available. I don't think he's had that for a while."

"Hmm. I meant I was surprised to see him up this early."

"True." She bit into a strawberry. "He had a busy night, fleeing from a homicidal maniac."

"And stealing from the Underworld," Mikhael responded.

"He took it because they threatened him."

"A person has a choice to do wrong or right. He had avenues. He could have told someone."

"Who could he have told? Do you know what it's like to live the life he's led?"

She lowered her voice. Marisa was teaching Isaac how to thumb wrestle, which was creating a wave of giggles at the end of the table, but she didn't want a stray word to catch their attention, or Isaac's. "Most sex demons live on the fringes. Half-wild, and they don't trust anyone. They're hunted by opportunists or those like you, charged to punish them for trying to survive. They have to feed to live."

"Balance in this world depends a great deal on human ignorance. Every preternatural species knows that. Yours respect the boundaries. But even outside these walls, there are plenty of pleasure demons who show discretion and moderation. He's not one of those."

"He's young. He doesn't know any better. He can learn, if given the chance."

Turning a page, Mikhael perused the sports section. The staff paused, confirmed that he wasn't preparing to eat one of them, and returned to their antics.

"Or he's too far gone on it, and a lost cause," Mikhael responded.

Raina blinked. Mikhael wasn't turned toward them, but he'd timed his response to their distracted attention perfectly. It gave her a chilling idea of how good a hunter he was. Patient, never losing focus. He'd notice the bend of one blade of grass in a meadow if a ladybug landed on it.

"You're being sensitive to their anxiety about you. Why?"

"Because I'm charming. You just said so." He flashed his canines, that nonsmile of his that still managed to do strange things to her knees.

"That was sarcasm."

"If they become agitated, they'll interrupt my reading. As well as my brunch."

"I'm interrupting it."

"I don't consider you an interruption. Much." He glanced down at her blueberries, still poised to become projectiles. "Raina, your hope for his rehabilitation is a projection of your experience, not his. He's been marked by dark elements who will continue to use him; if not this female demon, the next one who comes along, and the next one. He's dug himself a hole, and it's a grave. If it's not at my hand, it will be at the hand of another."

"He's not a lost cause." She stared him down. He didn't blink. "He's not harming anyone here, and I can teach him a better way. I'll talk to him again today. He'll be more helpful after having a good night's sleep and spending time with the others."

"I think you've gotten all the information that's going to be useful. The demon that made him steal Lucifer's item is going to come after him to ensure he's not a risk. When she does, I will find out where the stolen object is and deal with that as well. Two birds with one well-aimed volcanic blast that will leave a crater in your front yard."

He nodded to his plate. "Your chef fixes a very good breakfast. My compliments. Even better than McDonald's."

She imagined cramming the blueberries down his throat until he choked. It helped her rein in her temper, channel it into a polite smile. "Monday mornings are the only time we do this, so you'll need to fend for yourself for the very brief time you remain."

"Good to know."

Laying her fingers along the top edge of the newsprint, she impeded his article with her long nails, waited until his dark gaze flicked back up to her face. "Just because we had a good fuck doesn't mean I don't despise you and what you stand for." She kept the frosty curve on her lips. "I've had plenty of mind-blowing sex with despicable men. It's often the only talent they have going for them."

He set aside the paper, folding it. Even though the movement was unhurried, she tensed, sensing something dangerous in the precision with which he did it. "I am not trying to antagonize you, Raina. You can hate the truth because it came out of my mouth, but you don't seem the type to let your emotions overtake your judgment. Since that seems to be the exceptional case here, it suggests I unsettle you more than most of those despicable men."

He leaned forward then, catching a lock of her hair in his fingers. It was a quick move, though done smoothly. The only way to dislodge his grip would be to jerk away, a volatile reaction that would be noticed. But as he wrapped the strand around his hand, drawing her closer to him, she tightened her muscles, resisting him.

"Come here." Though a murmur, it was an undeniable order, a reminder of the mastery he'd exerted over her the night before, and all the complex emotions he'd untangled with it.

As he said, she didn't let her emotions rule her. She wanted to tell him to go fuck himself. But she knew he'd take her hair out by the root. She wasn't dealing with a male who obeyed civilized laws. The words he spoke when his lips were near her temple proved it.

"I have no particular claim on you, Raina. But I have one particular rule. However long I decide to be here, you won't be mentioning other men you've had. If you do, I will be required to drive every one of them out of your head."

She bit down on a gasp. With the shift of his wide shoulders, he was blocking the view of the end of the table. He'd slid his hand beneath her gown, finding her sex with unerring accuracy. The tissues had been so well used in the late hours she was still slippery, even after a morning cleaning. Or perhaps being around him kept her in a state of such readiness. Two of his fingers slid into her, his thumb massaging her clit with slow, expert precision. Her body tightened, spiraled up like a balloon cut loose on a storm front. She dug her nails into the chair arms, squelching the sexual energy that wanted to waft off her like an exotic perfume.

"I will play your game to a point, Raina." His eyes held hers. "But in the end, I set the rules. The more you spit fire at me, the more you'll find how cruel I can be. And I know you crave that roughness." He withdrew his fingers then, brought them to his mouth to taste. "Even better than the crepes," he said in a husky tone.

With that, he returned to his paper and another piece of bacon on his plate. She picked up a croissant, pulled it apart, ate a couple bites as she eyed him. He appeared to be back in his own world again. She threw another blueberry at him. He caught this one as well, but this time she saw his eyes warm with fire and something that resembled amusement. He rolled it back to her with the casual push of a finger, then returned to an analysis of the town's fiscal budget and the question of whether taxes would be raised.

He was the oddest combination of things. Brutally honest in his analysis of Isaac but emotionally detached. Whereas his attitude toward her was fully engaged, not in the least detached. The former gave her hope that if she proved him wrong, he would accept a different theory and back off Isaac. The other kept things in her stomach swirling, and her stomach didn't swirl.

He'd put his foot back up on the edge of her chair, under the fall of her robe. Now his toes found their way to her bare buttock, then farther beneath. His words had made her traitorous body even wetter, and he discovered those secretions now. As she bit her lip in reaction to his firm prodding, those intriguing eyes flickered. "Send them away," he said.

When he'd tethered her to that banister, if he'd taken her while she was bound and helpless, it would have cracked something open in her, good and bad. Yet he'd pulled back, recognized her anxiety, the dangerous edge of emotions playing inside of her. By taking her to the bed instead, it put her a step closer to wanting today what she'd been afraid to want last night. She knew he knew it.

With no encouragement at all, he'd spread her on this table and feast on her. She wanted him to do it, badly enough it scared her. So instead, she gave him a practiced smile, one that could make every cock within a hundred-foot radius harden, even while she promised nothing.

"This is their one meal together. I'll do no such thing. Have you met the rest of my staff?"

After a long, heart-pounding moment, that intent look eased, telling her he'd let her off the hook. For now. "No, they filled their plates and slunk to the opposite end of the table. Which seemed an optimal situation."

"You can hardly blame them, knowing what you are. Most of them came to me half-starved victims, and they've seen others run down by your kind."

"Stories I've heard a thousand times," he said dismissively. "But Marisa likes to watch late-night reruns of *Desperate Housewives*. Li sings AC/DC songs in the shower, and Ana hordes food in her mattress. Saltines, which I thought was an odd choice, because she likes sugar and you have graham crackers in your pantry. But she knows Saul enjoys those with peanut butter. I think they're coping."

Raina felt that coldness return, a fist in her lower abdomen. "Are you mocking me?"

"No." Now there was an edge to his voice, a hint of impatience. "I'm telling you that you don't need to beat a dead horse. Life isn't supposed to be fair, Raina. This is a testing ground, and the choices we make determine whether we have a weak character or a strong one. Your demons have made good choices, and you've helped strengthen them. It's admirable what you've accomplished with them. But all that's obvious."

He set the paper aside once more, crossed his ankle on his knee and hooked a shoulder around the back of the chair, another lazy lord of the manor pose, all the more damnably appealing because of its unconscious authority. When was the last time he'd felt out of place, uncomfortable, embarrassed...nervous?

"What's not so obvious, and therefore intriguing, is you. You're not one of them, because you're a half-breed and a witch. But even if that wasn't the case, a protector is never fully part of the group. It's the price you pay for the responsibility. It's also why you're sitting with me. In the end, you have a greater connection to who and what I am than you do to them. Which is also why you're fencing words with me, rather than spitting in my face and trying to kick me out."

She counted to ten...to twenty. Then leveled her most contemptuous gaze on him and raised her voice. "Everyone? I want to make a formal introduction. This is Mikhael Roman. He'll be staying with us, *very* briefly."

CHAPTER SIX

*H*is gaze narrowed, but she kept her focus on her attentive staff. "I expect you to treat him with courtesy. Our schedule will be the same as always. Isaac will also be with us, though for a less defined amount of time. Trouble is following him. We're going to try to help him with that. The protections on this place have been reinforced by Mikhael's presence here, but if you notice anything unusual, even if it's minor, please bring it to our attention, whichever one of us you can reach the fastest. Understood?" She glanced at Li, waiting until her senior staff member gave her a subtle nod, telling her he'd make sure of it.

Isaac had tensed, as if expecting castigating looks for bringing trouble to their midst. Instead Isabella slid closer to him and Luke put a reassuring hand on his shoulder, caressing his nape. "We all brought trouble with us when we came," Marisa said, her brown eyes crinkling with humor. "Though none of us brought a Dark Guardian, so you get top bragging rights for that one."

She darted a look at Raina, then an even quicker one at Mikhael, to make sure she hadn't caused offense, then she beamed at the incubus. Isaac blinked, unsmiling. He appeared baffled by his surroundings, overwhelmed. For an incubus who'd never learned to trust, being in a place where trust might be possible was more frightening than being chased through the swamp by a Dark Guardian.

It squeezed her heart, but Raina put the emotions in check. Isaac was a far cry from the others at this table. Though they'd come from bad circumstances, almost as dire as Isaac's, they had something missing from Isaac's experience. At some key point in their lives, before they came to her, they'd been exposed to hope, a glimpse of how life could be better. Even more importantly, something in their makeup had allowed them to believe in that vision. Isaac had never had that, or he'd let the opportunity pass him by due to chronic skepticism or some vital weakness in his character. It made her even more determined that Mikhael's prediction for him wouldn't come to pass. If she couldn't save one like him, what hope was there in the world?

"More females than males on your staff," Mikhael noted casually, but she saw his significant look as her staff returned to their conversations, again dividing the room into two distinct sections. She told herself it didn't underscore his point. Mikhael's presence had disrupted the normal order. If he wasn't here, she'd be joining their conversation. Or at least listening amusedly and throwing in her part. Just because he'd embraced the comic-book propaganda about the lone warrior didn't mean she was buying into it. Sounding authoritative on every damn subject didn't mean he really knew everything.

"Do you have trouble keeping the males fed?" he asked. "Your client base in this neck of the woods would be mostly hetero males."

That was true. In fact, she could easily call four of her good-ol'-boy redneck regulars and give them a case of Budweiser to quarter Mikhael on her front lawn with their four-wheel-drive pickup trucks. Dark Guardian blood would make a wonderful fertilizer for her roses.

However, his question appeared to be motivated by sincere curiosity, and no purpose would be served by her snubbing him. Again— emotions *weren't* going to rule her.

"I've increased marketing efforts to encourage female clients, so between that and a handful of openly gay or bi regulars, the males stay suitably fed."

Her monthly tea parties on the back lawn, with her staff doing the serving in tasteful but sexy apparel, had bumped up the female clientele. Women were comfortable in social groups, less inhibited about ogling and flirting with what she had to offer. Particularly when the four males flirted right back with romantic hand kisses and sexy smiles. They also didn't discourage the occasional bold, wandering female hand. The women enjoyed themselves thoroughly, but, more important, the incubi had their fill of appetizers at such events. When stimulated, female sexual energy offered itself in bite-sized pieces.

Many of the women who subsequently came into the house for services had their first experience with one of the succubi, to gain confidence and security. After that, they moved to the males. For all their initial caution about visiting a bordello, women were far less inhibited about crossing gender boundaries than her male clients, likely because they weren't as concerned about being categorized for doing so.

Aside from nourishing her charges and increasing her profit margins, there were practical reasons for increasing the female client base. The more Raina's house was utilized by the women, the more intertwined she was in the community, taking momentum away from those who didn't like having sex-for-hire in their county. Law enforcement was easy to handle. Her energy, carefully disseminated, distracted them from any investigation attempts. She'd had the pleasure of entertaining the sheriff's men on her front porch, offering them her lemonade and encouraging them to bring their wives to one of the coed tea parties.

Her incubi were also fed by the men who weren't openly gay because they hadn't admitted it to themselves, or to the straight friends with whom they came. However, even when the client had a female on his lap, she would note the man's eyes tracking Li's supple form or marking the flex of Saul's powerful physique. When that man went up to his assigned room, she would slip in and ask if he would prefer a male. Inevitably, the truth of his own desires, encouraged by the euphoric vibes of the sex demon energy, would prevail. Her discreet handling of the situation meant he'd come back, again and again.

As she hit those points, Mikhael listened attentively. So much so, she was tempted to discuss more, because she enjoyed her business. However, she noticed most plates were clean at this point.

"Ellen, Aiden, get the table cleared. All of you, go enjoy your day. Doors open at four, so don't wander too far. Isaac, stay here for a moment. Isabella, Luke, you can wait for him in the parlor."

During the meal, while he couldn't hear the discussion she was having with Mikhael, Isaac had studied every shift, every word spoken by the others. He'd made few comments, mostly cautious responses to direct questions. While he'd relaxed a little, as the others left the dining area, he looked pale and tense once again.

Stretching out his powerful frame, Mikhael reached a long arm down the table to snag the comic strips. He put it on the table, studying the *Peanuts* column. The innocuous pose didn't seem to soothe Isaac in the slightest, and Raina didn't blame him. It was like watching a dragon work a crossword puzzle while picking his teeth with the finger bone of his latest virgin victim.

"I expect you have nothing to add to what you told me last night?" she asked the incubus.

His gaze shifted between them. Mikhael didn't look up. He wasn't expecting anything and, in truth, neither was she. She suppressed a sigh as Isaac shook his head.

"I want you to take time today to learn about how we live here. While you're doing that, think very carefully about whether there are things you should have told me that you haven't. I know you have lived by deception, but in this place, honesty is your best chance of survival."

His jaw flexed. He really was a pretty young man. The shower and sleep had brought it out further. Flaxen hair to his shoulders, sea green eyes, straight nose and sensitive mouth. There were no ugly sex demons, but his androgynous look would appeal to her clients, if he chose to join her staff.

Considering the profit possibilities on a parallel track with her concern for his well-being didn't bother her, because she knew which one took precedence. Ramona, her closest friend other than Ruby, had once dubbed her Fagin. Though she preferred Ron Moody's movie depiction of the savvy businessman, Raina didn't dislike the nickname. After all, he had taught the boys marketable skills and gleaned a profit in an environment of thieves and murderers.

"Unless you have questions for me, you can go to Isabella and Luke now. I'll be around today if you wish to speak with me."

With a short, furtive nod, he slunk toward the door, looking like a cunning, abused animal.

"Isaac?" When he halted, she met his uncertain, resentful expression with a steady one of her own. "Every succubus and incubus who crossed this threshold has been told the same thing by me. Self-worth is a gift you give to yourself. No one else can offer it. If you hold yourself cheaply, you'll be treated cheaply. Doesn't matter if that's fair or not. It's not up to the world to rescue you from your poor opinion of yourself. If that poor opinion is deserved, fix it. Each demon here has discovered something in themselves they didn't expect to have. As a result, they've found what they never believed they could. A home. Contentment, brief spots of happiness. A family."

Isaac eyed her suspiciously. "Everything comes with a price."

"Yes, it does. You have to earn that kind of place. I'm not talking about working as one of the companions here. That's your choice. I would make sure you had food regardless, and we'd find other ways for you to earn your keep. An old house always needs hands to keep it up. You earn your spot by pulling your weight honestly, and by not being a scavenger who takes lives indiscriminately. You prove you can be worthy of the trust and friendship of others. It doesn't happen overnight. No one here managed that, and no one would expect it of you. You'd make mistakes, you'd have setbacks. But if it's something you want, you'll find those here willing to help you, to forgive the mistakes and setbacks. Think on that today as well."

He nodded, then slipped out. Mikhael examined the *Scooby-Doo* comic strip. "I will bet you the last croissant that, out of all those well-meaning words, all he heard was, *Blah-blah-blah-blah,* you'll get food, *blah-blah-blah.*"

Picking up the last croissant, Raina took a decisive bite. "I'm *so* turned on by your I-don't-give-a-damn-about-anyone attitude and wiseass cracks. Was it a gradual process, Mikhael, or have you always been a coldhearted bastard?"

As his head rose, the eyes that locked on hers turned cool. She wasn't going to back down from him, though. Not now, not ever. She'd done enough running in her life. Sweet Dreams was her line in the sand. She'd never retreat from that line, even if her ashes were left smoking upon it.

"You've got the sharp-tongued bitch act down," he said quietly. "Yet the facade is thin, isn't it? You're vulnerable, Raina. Almost fragile. You showed me that last night, when you were pleading for release, when you let your fear show."

He pushed the paper aside. "I'm charged to run down your kind when they step out of bounds, beyond what even the Underworld can tolerate. To hunt them effectively, I have to know their stories, inside and out. When I corner them, when I execute them"—his gaze pinned her, and she saw Death there—"those stories come to the surface, much like that tapestry your deadly energy puts forth. In their dying moments, that story is stamped on them. They become a book I have to burn, the story lost forever to anyone but me, because when they reach that point, they have no one.

"You were wise to counsel Isaac the way you did, because it's family that saves a soul. If he turns his back on it too often, he'll be another book on the pyre. My job isn't pity. It's justice, and justice is about balance."

Mikhael stood then, picked up the other half of the croissant she'd left on her plate. "Things don't change. The reasons, the causes, the consequences. The whole world is a cycle and a circle. The songs may romanticize that, but for someone who lives as long as I have, and sees the things I do, it sucks."

Despite the contemporary choice of verb, his age showed in his eyes, an ancient coldness. It swept the whole room, shivering over her skin, making her raise a protection on herself in instinctive defense. Staring at Mikhael, she remembered that Derek was over twelve hundred years old. Even knowing the commitment to Lucifer was all eternity, she hadn't considered that this Dark Guardian could be even older. Which meant he was considerably older than her.

He'd taken a cruel shot at what they'd shared last night, putting a taint on it. But she didn't turn off her radar just because she was knocked back on her heels. She wasn't going to let herself be thrown by his age. She'd also held him in her arms last night, felt things from him, things that connected to this moment. If she was as sure of his facade as he thought he was of hers, she'd say she'd bruised his feelings.

Mikhael Roman had a bone-deep moral code. It might be a code sworn in the dark, against blood and muck, rather than in the light, striking a suit of shining armor, but he was deadly serious about it.

She was used to being able to read men to the bone. While she couldn't yet read Mikhael to that depth, his perspective on this one issue was brutally clear, as his next words proved.

"You've made some sweeping assumptions about me. Let me make some about you. You're absurdly tolerant toward anything resembling an underdog, even if their own choices landed them in that position.

You are closed-minded and intolerant toward those you perceive to be in a position of strength and authority. You risk those you love to help a creature too far gone to be saved, because you choose the ignorant comfort of self-righteousness over full knowledge, which would inform you the world is not us and them. It's just the world, each one of us utterly alone in it."

Okay, she'd been wrong. He did have the ability to trash her radar, under a hailstorm of words that cut. Her fingers were white, pressed into the chair arm, and she expected her face was the same color when his gaze stilled on it. He bit off whatever else he was going to say.

"There's a reason I prefer my own company," he said stiffly. "My apologies. I'll leave you to your breakfast."

Mikhael didn't go as far as he intended. When he went off the side porch, he was heading for the woods, wanting the tranquil darkness of the forest and swamp. Instead, he found himself in her gardens, a tangle of azaleas mixed with flowering vines woven into strategically placed trellises and latticework. Benches and statuary enhanced the design. It encouraged a meandering walk among the beauty of nature, with secluded places for trysts and quiet reflection. He'd probably end up in the swamp anyway, but he took one of those secluded spots, a large bench next to a small fountain and man-made pond, complete with lily pads and a grinning stone frog. Next to the frog was a sculpture of a kneeling fairy, a thin woman with long hair, her delicate hand on the frog's head as she trailed the other fingers in the water, her expression pensive, the tilt of her body attractive, achingly so. The best of nature and beauty together. It reminded him of her.

Fuck, he'd let her get under his skin. That shot at her fragility last night had been unforgivable, particularly when she was still so uncertain about trusting his mastery over her. He'd been too deep inside her last night. She responded to him in a way she hadn't responded to anyone, and he wanted more of that unique gift. He'd just scratched the surface of her response.

There was a vulnerability to a craving like this. His anger didn't get provoked from snide comments and well-orchestrated contempt. But she'd impressed him with what she'd built, and she was endangering it with her stubborn need to save every sex demon that stumbled out of her swamp. She was endangering herself. That mattered to him. Maybe that in itself was unusual, but not as much as the fact that what she thought of *him* mattered.

It was the most absurd feeling he'd had in quite a while. Maybe he needed reconditioning from the Underworld. An oil change or something.

She was clever with words, but a snake-oil salesman or politician had that. She backed her words with herself, with action. He'd walked her property this morning. Her power signature was like her: a bold pen stroke, unflinching, a warning not to mess with what was hers. But the Craft of it was remarkably complex, delicate and exponentially strong, like a spiderweb. She wasn't about brute power; she studied, she learned, she adapted, to the point there were minor modifications of the protection on different terrains, new compilations of spellwork he hadn't seen used before.

In short, she was a damn good witch. Last night, she'd stood toe-to-toe with him on a battlefield and hadn't flinched. In fact, he'd pissed her off, sparking those tempting green-gold eyes to full-out flame. Her courage had faltered not then, but later, in the face of his desire to dominate her as a lover, something she craved but feared, because of the shadows in her soul.

She obviously had a history similar to those she protected. Someone had hurt her, used her, inflicted pain on her. As he'd made clear, he knew every story of brutality and cruelty there was. It was good that there was always somewhere in the world that needed rain, because the Goddess wept daily at what Her creations did to one another.

The shape and color might be different, but it was the same substance. The devil was in those details.

For the first time in a while, he wanted to know the shape and color of that devil, and not because it was an assignment to do so. He told himself it was because he liked a challenge, and her emotional shields were a challenge. Like her perimeter, it would take both a delicate and powerful touch to get through them. That wasn't going to happen unless he could get to the bottom of her soul. But he had an unsettling sense that to learn the shape of her soul, he might have to let her see his. Or that hers might change the shape of his.

He knew the moment she entered the garden. She didn't know when to leave well enough alone. It was a wonder she was still alive, but in his world, she was quite young, mid-thirties. He didn't like the idea of that, her physical fragility. She could be extinguished far more easily than he could. Then he remembered her defense of her home, both with her sharp tongue and her spellwork. He was being typically male. With the clever tongue alone, she could slice most enemies to ribbons.

"I'm sorry," she said, with grace. And sincerity.

It was the last thing he expected her to say. Turning toward her, he found her face pale but serious. "You're right. I made you into a symbol of all the things that have harmed my kind, and bludgeoned you with it, rather than seeing you as you are."

"And what am I?"

As she cocked her head, his eyes followed the fall of her hair along her shoulder. The sweet line of collarbone. "I don't know if I like you or hate you," she answered. "I don't know enough about you to be sure, so any feeling I have about you is transient."

"Fair enough." He wanted to touch her. He didn't usually deny himself such compulsions, but things felt a little...delicate between them. He stretched out his legs. Glanced at the spot next to him, an invitation.

With a smile that was tired, not practiced, which made it more appealing, she came to him. Looking pointedly at the small space left on the bench due to his much larger frame, she moved between his feet and sat down on his thigh, her fingers settling on his shoulder to hold herself there.

Pleased with her decision, he slid an arm around her waist, molding his palm along the line of her hip. Then she put her arms around his neck, drew him to her. Bemused, he capitulated to the pressure, the distinct pleasure of her breasts against his face as she... hugged him.

He hadn't been hugged since... Perhaps he'd never been hugged? That couldn't be right. He was searching his brain for that scrap of information when she drew back, looked at him.

"So if you know the world sucks, why don't you try to change anything?" she demanded.

It damn near made him smile, which he never did. She recovered fast from anger, didn't sulk. At least not in this instance. She could likely do a damn good pout when it suited her purposes.

"Try to change the nature of living beings, their continual struggle between the good and evil in themselves? Try to impact the choices they make to reach the next level of spiritual evolution?" He shook his head. "That's a higher pay grade than me. Sorry."

~

He intrigued her, damn it. Affection was easy for her kind, and the moment had called for a hug. But from the shock on his face, she guessed not a lot of people went around hugging Dark Guardians. He'd recovered, though. That hand on her hip was strong and steady, the idle stroke of his fingers awakening every nerve ending within range.

He was more than she'd expected him to be, but he'd picked up that there was more to her as well. It was an emotional aphrodisiac for any woman, a man's genuine interest in her.

With the male attention span being what it was, the effect would wear off when the next pair of breasts bounced into his field of vision. Of course, the only breasts in his field of vision right now were hers, and they were big enough to take up the full screen. She could enjoy whatever this was, as long as it lasted. Life was short, after all. Well, *her* life was short, compared to his.

"What are you doing today?" When he drew his attention from those breasts, the amused suggestion in his eyes made her smile. "You're not doing me right now," she said decisively. "That's still under negotiation. What's your schedule today?"

"Something you want me to pencil in?"

"You're avoiding the question." She stroked her fingers along the column of his throat. Then trailed down the opening of the shirt, glad he'd only buttoned two buttons.

He closed his hand on hers, his eyes kindled to flame. "You keep doing that, I'll close that negotiation."

"What do you do when you're not doing your job? Para-sailing, Zumba...chess?"

"I do what I did last night. I can do that for a long time. Hours, even."

Well, that certainly gave her toes a curl. He'd kept her hand and his between them, curved around one another. "If I had a clear schedule today, that would be more than tempting. But what I was thinking was—"

"It's here, it's here!" Gina rushed down the garden path, her thick red hair sparkling. "Raina, it came!"

"What came?" Raina rose from Mikhael's knee, moving her hand to his shoulder, still stroking, following his collarbone beneath the shirt's loose hold. What made it even more provocative was it wasn't a deliberate tease. Mikhael could tell she was merely enjoying touching him, like any other visually stimulating thing in her garden. He was going to send Gina away, bend her mistress over that bench, and—

"The *box*," Gina said, as if talking about the Ark of the Covenant. "The box, the box, the box." As the girl chanted it, she caught Raina's hand and pulled her away to spin with her, so wildly she lost her grip and bumped into Mikhael, falling onto his other knee. He steadied her, but Gina was off his leg in a flash, her eyes wide and pulse pounding, like a bird who'd narrowly escaped being caught by a cat. "I'm sorry. I'm really sorry."

"As far as I know, a woman sitting in a Guardian's lap isn't a capital offense in the Underworld," Mikhael commented. "But I can double-check the codex."

Gina's eyes widened farther, her gaze darting to Raina. "You know," the witch said dryly, "it would help if you smiled when you made a joke, Mikhael."

"Oh." Gina blinked, then a tentative smile crossed her face. "Wow. Okay. Raina, the box is here."

"I gathered that."

"The box?" Mikhael asked.

Raina drew Gina to her side and pressed a kiss to her temple, adding to the reassurance. The young woman giggled and wrapped her arms around Raina, squeezing her and giving Mikhael some very pleasant fantasies as she laid her red head on the witch's ample bosom, brushing her cleavage with soft lips.

"Behave," Raina murmured. "About every six months, we order new stuff. Toys, role-playing costumes, jewelry. Supplies."

"It causes a lot of excitement," he noted.

"Well, the staff gets to play with it first. That's the rule. Their own little passion party."

Mikhael lifted a brow. "It's not even lunchtime."

"People have been known to enjoy sex toys before lunchtime. People born in this century."

When Gina tittered, Mikhael gave Raina a look that promised retribution. Like being pulled over his lap right then and there. She gave a little shiver that tightened her nipples more prominently against the satin of that robe. Fuck, he *was* going to take her right here.

Gina didn't help in the slightest. "You like him," she cooed, her hand caressing the full curve outside the satin, teasing across one taut peak. Raina tugged her hair, tsked at her.

"Stop that. Go on in now. We'll come join you in a minute. What *is* this in your hair?"

As Gina straightened, she fluffed the red locks, sending out a cloud of sparkles. Raina put her hands on her hips. "We had a rule about glitter dust. No more. It takes forever to get out of the carpet, and clients don't like taking it back into the real world on their hair and skin."

"It wasn't my fault, it was Ana's. There was some in the top of the box, complimentary, and she sprinkled it on everyone, even Isaac." Gina backpedaled up the path, giving a brilliant, unrepentant smile. "He looked so perplexed by it. Come in soon. This is going to be fun."

"Shake that crap off before you go back in the house," Raina called after her, a scowl on her face. "It smells like a cheap whorehouse, talcum powder and gardenias. I swear, I'm going to snatch Ana bald. No, I'm going to let the cleaning staff do it. I—"

She let out a startled yelp as Mikhael gripped her waist and pulled her back onto his lap. Only this time he spread her thighs with his large hands, draping her legs over his to hold them open that way. When he pulled the robe open, the sun reflected off the pale beauty of her naked body beneath. It might be the garden of a bordello, but it was still a decadent pleasure, revealing her here where anyone could see what he was doing. Cupping her breasts, he captured the distended nipples, making her suck in a breath.

"When I mentioned it wasn't even lunchtime," he said with exaggerated patience, "I meant that your staff has sex professionally all evening."

Raina's head dropped onto his shoulder, a throaty purr coming from her throat. "We live on the sexual energy of others," she managed. "It's like eating. As long as the stomach is empty, food will interest you, no matter the time of day."

He caught her hand when it came toward his shoulder. Gripping that delicate wrist, he guided it back down, his fingers overlapping hers as he took her touch where he wanted it. "Stroke yourself, Raina. Put your fingers inside, then give them back to me. I want to suck your taste off them."

That sexy little shudder again, which was gratifying on so many levels. He didn't think many males made her react without thought, without calculation of their needs, their pleasure. He wanted her focused totally on her pleasure, on his command of her body to serve that end for both of them. She moaned softly as her fingers entered, his own still loosely cupped over her knuckles, so that he was able to push her deeper, slow, easy. "Work your fingers in there. I'm going to spread you out on that dining table later today. Eat your pussy until you come."

"I think I can pencil...that in. Oh, Goddess," she breathed.

"Give them to me," he demanded. She brought the fingers back up to his mouth, and he clasped her wrist, holding her manacled as he licked off that slippery arousal, savored it. When he met her gaze, the gold color had overtaken the green in her eyes, an exotic, feral animal. The heat of her magic pressed on his skin like a warm, wet tropical wave.

"Are you hungry again, Raina?" When his hand clasped her throat, holding her there, the needy plea that vibrated beneath his palm nearly undid him.

Her other hand came up, laid over his on her wrist, and she gave a sinuous little wiggle. In her position, she couldn't get an optimal angle to rub herself against him, so he obligingly brought his legs back together. In a quick move, she twisted under his hold and slid free, a flutter of satin and dark hair that caressed his face.

Scampering a few steps away, she turned back toward him, giving him a brief, glorious glimpse of her body, the aroused nipples, the cleft of her sex, all the pale curves, the lengths of her thighs. Glitter dust was on her breast where Gina had stroked her. He was used to having a strong libido, but she consumed his brain like fire on a dry leaf.

"Yes, I'm hungry." She tossed her hair, retied the garment, but it was still loose enough the curves of her breasts were full crescents. "But I have a party to attend. Maybe later. After all, you were sufficiently adequate last night. I suppose I could invite you for another go."

"Oh, really?"

She laughed, as girlish as Gina, and then gave a shriek as he surged off the bench. She ran back up the path, but she wasn't as fast as the slip of a girl. He caught that womanly body up against the door, turned her to him.

When Raina looked up into his face, expecting the kiss, he slowed it down. Sidled even closer, until by drawing in her breath, she was drawing in his. She wasn't aware of anyone in the room behind the door, or even the birds calling in the garden. Everything disappeared when Mikhael Roman got this close to a woman, filled all her senses.

"You don't want to invite me to do anything, Raina. You want me to do what I want, whether you say yes or no. And I will."

"We'll see." Reaching up, she traced his cheekbone, scraped him with her nail when he turned his head, nipped her wrist. "Do you play cards? That's why I wanted to know about your schedule. Low-stakes poker."

"I usually only play high stakes."

"I'm so shocked to hear that." When she gave him her professional smile, she wasn't surprised to see his jaw tighten. He really didn't like it when she used her practiced charm. Maybe that was why she liked doing it, to yank his chain. But she wasn't going to let him get that upper hand back until her pulse was steadier.

"You have glitter dust on you, too." She used her thumb to rub it off his chin, showed it to him. "I usually play solitaire in the afternoon. It helps me relax, get ready for the evening company, gives me the chance to go over the last minute to-dos in my head. On Monday nights, though, we're usually in pretty good shape. I can handle a more distracting game."

He passed his fingers over his chin, ensuring all the dust was gone. She suppressed a smile as he put a few sparkles back on himself. They'd transferred to his hands when he touched her breast. That thought took her smile, gave her something more important to suppress.

"Unless our demon arrives and requires annihilation, I'll make myself available for a few hands," he said at last. "If you make it interesting for me."

"I'm not known for boring male company." She sniffed. "And when you annihilate that demon, stay out of my rose garden. I assume Lucifer doesn't expense damages?"

"He usually has strings attached to any payment."

"Don't they all?" It made her abruptly sad, and she wasn't sure where the feeling had come from. She was feeling too much around him. When she rotated toward the door, he touched her arm.

"Raina."

She let him turn her back around. Those long, strong fingers stroked her throat as he put his mouth on hers, moist heat he turned into a lingering press of lips before he lifted his head, stared down at her. "Last warning. Stop retreating behind the courtesan routine."

"I was a courtesan," she said evenly. "Before that I was a straight-out whore. For a short time, I was a ten-buck-a-blow teenaged hooker who hung out in alleys, so messed up and hungry for sustenance I left a couple bodies behind. Now I'm a madam. I enjoy men, I enjoy sex. You have a problem with that, you can go fuck yourself. Literally."

CHAPTER SEVEN

*D*amn it all, why had she gone there? Pivoting, she closed her hand on the door latch once more, not at all surprised when he clamped down on it, his body pressed up behind hers, solid and resilient. His mouth brushed the side of her throat, but not in a mean way. It was a devastating caress at the pulse point, his hands settling on her hips to hold her there as his cock, hard and ready, pushed against her ass, making her quiver.

"You were being an arrogant bully," she muttered.

"I am a bully. But I didn't mean to upset you."

She sighed, closed her eyes. "I opened that door, but I really want to close it, okay?"

Waiting on his decision was hard, her fingers closing around one of his at her hip. A moment later, his forefinger slid free, curved over hers. A reprieve. "All right. For now."

"I need to get in there," she said, relieved. "You can come if you like. You might enjoy it."

"Your staff at a passion party? I expect it's like setting a hive of bees loose in a honey shop." He paused though, still holding her. "Watching Gina...she was acting like a child, even when she was touching you. All of them act like that, to some degree."

"You've never noticed that?" She tilted her head back on his shoulder to look at him. When he shook his head, something loosened in her chest. "You've never hunted an immature sex demon."

His puzzled expression confirmed it, and she let out a breath. "All of my demons are like that. They reason and react like twenty-something human adults, but emotionally, they often respond like children. It's an odd mixture, hard to classify, but anyone familiar with sex demons can tell the difference between one who's transitioned to maturity and one who hasn't."

She turned to face him fully. "The box of toys we just received? They'll play with them all morning, and not just in sexual ways. They'll put the vibrators in a glass of water to watch the ripples, they'll dangle the floggers in front of the house cats like balls of string. They're sexual creatures, but their sexuality is very innocent."

"Like a young tiger's ability to kill a toddler during play."

She nodded. "Exactly."

"So how do they become what I've hunted?"

"They've fed and killed enough that they move into a higher, more adult level of thinking, but at a certain maturity level, a sex demon becomes more dangerous, savage. It's harder to keep the energy lust from taking over, eclipsing all morality."

Mikhael's gaze turned to the window, through which she could see the succubi and incubi milling impatiently, waiting for her to arrive. Aiden and Ellen had been making comical faces at them through the window, but seeing his attention, they vanished behind Saul's wide back. He and Li were arm wrestling while Ana tied ribbons around their wrists.

"Is Isaac in limbo?"

Her chin tightened, but she gave him an honest answer. "Teetering on the edge." Not there yet, but close.

"Can it be stopped, for any of them? Doesn't everything grow and mature?"

"It's inevitable, but discipline and experience...they can impact it in a positive direction, with the right influences."

"What I felt last night"—he tugged her closer with the robe tie—"was a fully mature succubus."

"I'm part human and all witch. It helps me manage it." She put her hand back on the door latch, quirked a brow at him as a chorus of strident *Raiiinnnnaaa* calls started up in the room, Cathair adding to the discordant music. "We can talk about this later."

Pushing open the door, she was relieved when he let her slip away.

Her outburst said his presence was taking her down paths she'd abandoned long ago. She knew better than to follow those roads. Having taken those journeys before, she knew exactly where they led.

∼

As Mikhael followed Raina into the main parlor, Cathair was having a grand old time, shredding pink and white tissue, packing material from the shipping container that had transported *the box*. Raina fussed but didn't really stop him, taking a seat on a stool Saul pulled out for her. As she gave them permission to open the box at last, Mikhael slid onto a stool behind her and leaned back against the mahogany and brass trim of a fully stocked bar.

It was like watching a party where all the participants were the birthday guest. They crowded around the box, pulling out a variety of things, shiny objects that kept the raven's bright eyes darting about as he hopped up and down on his perch. Clamps, restraints, a variety of vibrators. Then Luke pulled out an alarming-looking anal probe.

"Awesome. My guys will love this. Especially Mark."

"Luke," Raina said reprovingly. "No names, even among ourselves."

"Yes, ma'am." His eyes twinkled. "But he really will."

"I'm sure." Raina glanced back at Mikhael with amused exasperation. It seemed their enthusiasm had restored her mood. It had startled her, that slip in her composure. What surprised him was how much seeing her rally, regain her good spirits, improved his own mood. Even as he was mulling over what she'd inadvertently revealed to him.

"Would you like to give the anal probe a try, Mikhael?"

He met her devilish gaze. "Only if you bend over."

"You got the nipple jewelry we liked!"

He was sure she said something uncomplimentary to him, but it was lost in the multiple exclamations that followed Catalina's squeal of delight. She and Ana pulled out a thick handful of sparkling chains like Mardi Gras beads. Without hesitation, the females shed their tops and began modeling for one another, treating him and everyone else in the room to a panorama of breasts embellished by a variety of nipple treatments. Ellen put a clamp on one nipple, then ran the chain to a second clamp on Ana's pert nipple. When two more pairs of the other girls did the same, along with one coed partnership of Li and Catalina, they raced each other across the room, like a bizarre three-legged race. Then they crisscrossed them, mixed colors and styles of chains and clamps.

Isaac was staring down at Isabella, bemused as she tugged off his shirt and put a set on him. Seeing his confusion, she laughed and curled her slim hand in the chain, tugging gently to test the pleasure-pain quotient until he kissed her. Smiling against his mouth, she drew him down, rolled over the floor and pinned him, like a couple of puppies.

More things were pulled out of the box. Li chased Gina with the flogger, twirling it over his head like a lasso, threatening to put her over his knee, while Ana and Min experimented with the dual-headed vibrator. They'd stripped off their jeans and the thong panties beneath to get in a Twister-like contortion on the floor, legs scissored together.

A miasma of sex demon energy was soon swirling through the room, such that Cathair was looking a bit dazed.

When Raina took him to the door on her arm and set him aloft, his flight path was a drunken zigzag. She made sure he arrived safely in the branches of one of the live oaks, then left the doors open to the fresh air, mixing with the fragrance of pleasure.

"This is beautiful." Gina went down on her knees next to the half-empty box and pulled out a supple corset collar. "Who ordered this?"

"I did," Marisa said. "It'll look gorgeous with my taffeta." She affected a Southern drawl. "Particularly when I do my Scarlett O'Hara."

"I don't remember Scarlett having a corset collar."

"Scarlett didn't lift her skirts for a dozen guys a night, either." Marisa giggled. "Some modifications make the menfolk happy. Or the womenfolk, as the case may be." She batted her eyes. "Women fantasize about lacing Scarlett into that corset, too."

Laughter went around the room. "Wait, this would look beautiful with Raina's black lace," Gina said. "Oh my God, that would be gorgeous. Raina, try it on. You could use it the nights Marisa wasn't playing Southern belle."

Marisa nodded enthusiastically, brought it over to Raina, holding it up. "Try it on, see what it looks like. You have the most beautiful swan neck."

"In a few minutes," Raina said. "Let's look at the other things first."

"Oh, come on. The fashion show is part of the fun."

"Not now," Raina said, her tone changing. "All right?"

Though Mikhael couldn't see Raina's face, he noted the tension in her shoulders. The flicker on Marisa's face was also telling, as well as the brief pause in the chatter, the exchanged glances. He sensed they'd run up against this in Raina's nature before, but like the house's moods, they didn't always predict where that door would turn up. To her credit, Marisa nodded, pressed Raina's hand, and left the corset collar in her mistress's lap before she retreated.

In a few minutes, they were enraptured by a vibrator the size of a Louisville slugger. He was fairly certain no normal-sized person would sit still to have that shoved up any orifice.

Raina hoped that exchange would go un-noticed, but a consummate hunter noticed everything. While her staff was playing with the enormous dildo, she heard the scrape of the stool as he moved closer. His long-fingered hand slid around her elbow, his chest briefly pressing into her back, his thighs now alongside the outside of hers as he picked up the corset collar from her lap. His breath teased her ear. "Pull your hair to the side."

"I can't. Please...just don't."

"It's all right," he said quietly. "I'm here, we're here, all of them are here. Nothing bad is going to happen. Some part of you wants this. Pull your hair to the side. Obey me."

Before his arrival, if any male tried to command her, even in the most subtle of ways, her back would go up and the unfortunate would get the sharp edge of her temper. But when they came from his lips, those two words had the ability to make her do unthinkable things. That was the problem. Everything with him was different.

That crack he'd opened last night was still there, and getting wider. She couldn't move. Her hands were too cold. But he put his hands under her hair, against her neck. His skin warmed hers. Pushing her hair to the side, he slid his fingers through it, found her nape.

"You do have a neck like a swan. It's beautiful, everything a woman's neck should be. Here we go."

That sexy Russian accent flavored the warning as he fit the collar around her throat, smoothing it. She quivered, vibrated. She wasn't shaking. She wasn't.

"You remember earlier, when I kissed your neck? Putting this over that spot, lacing it to hold it there, to remind you of my marking...I like that idea."

So did she. She wished he'd broken skin with his bite, so she could feel the tenderness under that provocative snugness. As he tightened the laces, testing it to make sure he wasn't constricting her windpipe, it made her keep her chin up. Made her vulnerable and dependent on the Master who owned her, who put it on her.

She knew all the permutations of BDSM. For a woman particularly, its power was in the psychological manipulation. The collar, the restraints...those were mere tools to encourage the mind to accept the submission. She could write helpful fact sheets, "Bondage and You." As he'd pointed out, it was one of the many things offered by her house.

Her relationship to it was far more personal, as she'd just made clear in her ridiculous and irrational reaction to Marisa, prompting Mikhael to push harder. She knew about both sides of the coin, the ugly and not so ugly. But her direct experience, until Mikhael had arrived, was only with the ugly side. The not-so-ugly was just an incoherent yearning behind the darkness. But a Dark Guardian had no fear of darkness. He would stride through it, not let it stop him from giving her what that quivering part of her wanted. Because she knew that, some part of her trusted him to do this. That scared her most of all.

She remained still, but if the turbulence inside her had been translated to movement, she'd have run three laps at a full-out sprint by the time he finished the lacing. He caressed her spine below the collar, and she made a tiny noise as he brushed his lips over her ear. He'd pushed the robe to the points of her shoulders during his task, and she held it loosely clasped over her breasts, her knuckles too tense.

Sophia glanced up. "Gina, look. You're right."

Gina turned with Marisa and the others. Mikhael eased back, but his leg was still alongside her stool, his foot braced on the bottom rung, surrounding her with a sense of ownership. She saw it register in their eyes. In Li's, it was a knowing, somewhat concerned look, making her wonder how much her senior staff member understood about his mistress.

She summoned a faint smile, despite the pressure building in her chest that needed them to look away. To go away. "Well, that cinches it, no pun intended. Marisa, you'll have to order another. This one's mine."

Desperately seeking a distraction, her gaze shifted to Isaac. When the party had escalated into more movement and noise, he'd retreated to the doorway, hanging back and giving himself an escape. It reminded Raina of one of the cats, curious enough to stay where he could see, but ready to bolt all the same. His eyes were on Raina when Min lunged at him playfully from the floor, trying to drag him down to his knees to rejoin the group.

Not expecting it, he leaped back, hitting the doorframe hard enough to knock a few of the pictures off the wall. The glass of one broke as he stumbled, stepping on it. Raina winced. He'd just put his footprint in an original watercolor. His fangs had unsheathed in raw, uncontrolled instinct, cutting his lip. Spinning to hide it, he rammed into Saul.

The other male caught his shoulders, unconcerned, and propelled him back into the room.

"Calm down, dude. The girls aren't that scary. Well, unless they get hold of that giant dildo. Then it's every man for himself."

Isaac twitched in Saul's grip, but Saul was a strong male, large for an incubi, his grip gentle but unshakable. Min dabbed a damp handkerchief on Isaac's lip. "It's all right, silly kitten," she chided in her musical voice. "There's nothing to fear here. Well..." Casting a surreptitious glance toward Mikhael, she dropped to a whisper. "There's *usually* nothing to fear here. But Raina won't let him do anything to you."

Her staff had the situation well in hand, which was good, because she couldn't help them right now. The noise and Isaac's panic had tripped her own to a higher level. Her pulse was pounding beneath that collar and she wanted to claw at it, get it off before it did things to her, made her lose control in five different directions. Images of the past and desires of the present were about to crash like a head-on collision of metal and fire.

She'd shrugged her robe back onto her shoulders, dropped her icy hands back to her lap, but Mikhael's were gliding up and down her upper arms, knuckles grazing the outside of her breasts as he put his mouth to her collarbone, sending fireworks through her bloodstream. He slid closer behind her, those powerful thighs pressing into her hips. When he laid his hands over hers, he was so very warm, curled around her flesh that way. He put his chin on her shoulder, watching what was going on before them, in that casually intimate way a lover would.

She saw the startled glances of the others. It wasn't that men hadn't acted familiar around her when she took the occasional client. It was that he was a Dark Guardian, and not a client.

He hadn't disagreed with Min's statement that Raina would stop him, but she knew why. There was nothing to argue. They both knew she might be able to slow him down, but she couldn't stop a Dark Guardian. Not with power alone.

"What's that thing folded in the bottom of the box?" she asked, forcing her tone to be casual. She wasn't going to freak them out by going to pieces. She could handle this. It was simply a costume piece. It didn't mean anything. She wasn't owned by anyone. Not anymore.

"Cocoon suit. Double awesome!"

Isaac looked perplexed, so Aiden explained, with enthusiasm. "The guest lays down in it, like a sleeping bag. When you inflate it, they're completely immobilized. Let's go test it on Saul, right now."

Saul took off, and they pursued like a lynch mob. A happy, festive lynch mob, the girls topless, wearing nipple clamps that sparkled with glittering jewels, others in bits of costume finery that had also come in the box. Ana was impressively fleet, in the lead despite the fact she wore a new pair of black stilettos that had a silver skull and cross-bones design across the toe. It was a mass exodus of pretty, half-naked bodies, all the appealing parts quivering and bobbing, hair flowing. Isaac was carried along in their midst. The sudden quiet in the parlor was underscored by the thunder of feet up the hallway staircase, the laughter and shrieks that became more muted.

"If they break any of the Wedgwood pieces on the second landing, I'm going to murder the lot of them," she said, her voice unsteady.

"Well, you know what they say about putting away your breakables when you have children."

"Yes. The children should be caged until they learn to behave better." She put her hands up to her throat, but stopped short of touching the collar. She swallowed. "Take this off now."

Instead, he enclosed those nervous, poised hands in his, molded one of her palms over her own throat, let her feel the way the stiff fabric and the lacing defined the swanlike line.

"Whoever he was, he collared you to brutalize you," Mikhael said. "To subjugate you. In true submission, true Mastery, ownership is a protection, a trust, a shelter and a sanctuary. You know this, Raina."

But she didn't. She had the practical knowledge of the way it was supposed to be, could handle it in a professional context. Yet she'd never experienced it so personally, internalized it, such that she could use the knowing to compete with the nightmare experiences of her past.

"You've been here less than a day. You'll be gone in the same amount of time."

"It's not that kind of sanctuary. When you find that feeling, it stays with you, even if you only have the reality of it for that moment."

"A clever way of convincing a woman to give you what you want."

"Hmm." Turning his hands from her now less cold ones, he cupped her breasts, kneading slow, like making bread. Her nipples tightened under the casual rub of his thumbs. She liked having her breasts touched, and he'd noticed. Or more likely, he enjoyed doing it for his own pleasure.

Mikhael could have told her it was both. Watching her get lost in pleasure drove his arousal. The hold of that collar stimulated her, but he'd seen her fear, her borderline panic. She'd held it together with an iron will, refusing to give in to it. Yet her desire to surrender, to submit, was an intoxicating contrast. So in control of her world, of everything she was, yet he could shatter that control with what he could do to her and what he could offer her. He wanted to turn her fear into something entirely different, under the right type of Mastery.

He'd once crossed blades with a master swordswoman. She'd guarded a statesman, a man whose death was required to precipitate other changes. Her control and precision, her focus, had been outstanding. He could have used magic to beat her, and in the end, he'd had to resort to it, but until then it was a complicated dance of footwork, forward, back, sidestepping, staying light, being ready to spring into an opening, spin away from the cut. At a certain point, when the blades were flashing and they were evenly matched, it was as if their respective purposes—his to get past her to kill the man, her to stop him—vanished, and they were immersed in that dance, allied somehow in their conflict.

Winning Raina's submission had the same feel to it. They were locked in a conflict, but it was a conflict that had captured both their interests, enough that they kept circling and engaging, invested in the outcome.

It was time to take the fight down a notch, though. He brought Raina back against his chest, played with the collar's lacings, stroking and turning fear into something else. "You told me they were child-like. That wasn't entirely true."

"What do you mean?" She glanced up at him. A lot was happening in the depths of those green-gold eyes, such that he paused a moment without answering, touching her mouth with his thumb. Her lips parted, her pulse increasing. When he settled his hand fully over her throat, he curved his other palm over her breast so her nipple pressed into his palm. She barely managed a whisper. "Mikhael."

"Don't forget to breathe," he said quietly. He waited until she took a breath, her cheeks flushing in embarrassment, but he kissed her mouth, her eyelids, taking that away before he continued. "Children can be cruel. The way Isaac's fangs unsheathed; he was embarrassed, expecting mockery. Yours didn't do that. They're exceptionally gentle."

"Their synergy together has somewhat to do with it, the environment we've created here. The sanctuary." Her lips twisted, apparently recalling his words. "Their appetites are regularly sated. That helps as well."

He wound a lace around his finger, tightening its hold enough to send a tiny shiver through her. "Or because the spells you've woven to keep their meals from being lethal have an unexpected side effect. You've created a flock of gentle sheep. No aggressive tendencies."

She stiffened, but he wasn't done. "It worries you, how vulnerable they are. Nature intends us to have a certain level of aggression to protect ourselves. Are you working on fixing it?"

She straightened, turned to face him. "If they're too aggressive, you hunt them. Now you're complaining they're too gentle?"

"I'm not complaining about either state." He shook his head. "You do exceptional spell and protection work. You're also very smart. So I expect you've known for a while and have been experimenting with adjustments that will keep some aggression intact while still protecting your clients. A good mother protects her children, but she also knows one of her most important jobs is making sure they can eventually take care of themselves."

"I'm not their mother."

"No. For which I'm eternally grateful. Otherwise, the thoughts I was having when Gina was in your arms would subject me to some Underworld penance."

She pressed her lips against a smile. He could tell she hadn't been quite sure if they were about to have a fight. He made it clear now, rising to his feet and bringing her with him. He stroked her hair back over her shoulder and began unlacing the collar.

"I'm taking this off, not because I wouldn't like to see you wearing it all day for me, but because I don't want you to claim I beat you soundly at cards because you couldn't concentrate."

"I can concentrate just fine with it, on or off." When his fingers stilled, and she realized she'd put herself neatly in that trap, she cleared her throat. "But you should probably take it off so it won't be distracting to you."

"It might at that." Tenderness wasn't something he normally felt, yet he felt it now. Sliding his hand to her waist, he pressed her back against him. She teased him with a far too flexible rotation of her hips, sending his mind in another, safer direction.

"Behave, wench." The collar had left faint red imprints, so he put his mouth on them. When he did, she melted into him. Turning her mouth to his neck, she gave him a touch of her tongue, tasting him, making him want to growl. He settled his hand over where the collar had been, squeezed. It caused a satisfying little breathy sigh from her.

"I don't need a collar to know when I own a woman, Raina. You should keep that in mind."

"If we play for stakes"—she nipped at him—"I may be putting this collar on you. Or you could just concede defeat now."

It made him chuckle with dark pleasure. "I've never lost a battle yet."

"How do I know that's not an exaggeration, a boast? A lie?"

"Because I'm alive."

Her eyes snapped up to his, startled, but he gestured to the box, the froth of tissue paper. "I noticed a nice paddle over there. When I win, I'll use it on you."

"Or maybe I'll use it on you," she noted, a devilish gleam in her eyes. "Since it has a *bad girl* cutout, I think that imprint would look fabulous on your very fine ass."

CHAPTER EIGHT

"*S*o how do you become a Dark Guardian?" Raina shuffled the deck of cards, let him cut it. "Do you spring from the loins of the Underworld, or does Lucifer belch you out after a particularly good meal of fried puppies and newborn babies?"

"Cute." Mikhael leaned back in the chair. They were in the upper level library, which had a balcony overlooking the side garden they'd been in earlier in the day. When they'd entered the room, the house had swung the French doors wide open, letting in the breeze and scent of her roses, as well as the gurgle of two small fountains hidden among the potted plant arrangements on either side of the doors. A card table with two chairs was already by the open archway.

When he said nothing further, she gave him an exasperated look. "You can dig into my head like Indiana Jones raiding a tomb, but I can't ask you anything?"

"That was my plan. But I guess you'll get all pouty if I don't throw you a bone."

She snorted. "Just making conversation. Trust me, you're not that interesting."

"Mmm. So you don't want to know."

He ducked, barely in time to be missed by the book that shot out of the case on a direct line for his head. It stopped short of tumbling to the floor. She returned it to the shelf without a glance, a tiny ripple of power. "The house doesn't like smart-asses."

"That was *not* the house." He gave her a dark look.

She smiled sweetly. "There are a lot of books in here. Some much bigger than that."

"See, I said you'd pout." At her dangerous expression, he relented with a dry chuckle. "My mother was human, a sorceress. My father was nephilim. Child of an angel and a human mother, so I'm one-quarter angel. A mixed breed like you, witch."

She let that pass. "So that's where the wings come from."

"Mine emerged when I reached sexual maturity, but all Dark Guardians are given them when they receive the commission."

"But they're really yours. Not a factory add-on." She dealt their first hand. "Practice rounds while we chat?"

"You're trying to figure out my tells."

She gave him a sanguine smile. "You said you have to accept a commission. So you aren't born into the role."

He grunted, considered his hand. "There's a school for the arcane, a very exclusive school. It takes a class of thirteen students every two decades. You don't apply; you're invited. You attend for thirteen years. Two cards."

She passed them over, took his rejects back into the deck. "It's an initiation into some of the highest levels of magical practice, taught by mages of the Underworld. The school is held there, in its lowest chambers, so it's hot as Hell— literally." He pursed his lips, seemingly unaware of Raina's fascinated attention. "You don't see topside for all of those years. You live, eat and breathe the things they teach."

"The knowledge must be worth a great deal." She could only imagine the skills it had given him. From the brief taste of his magic she'd experienced, it was equaled only by things she'd seen Derek Stormwind do. "Say I wanted to give up sunlight for over a decade and attend. What's the tuition?"

"No women have ever been alumni. That was never explained, but you didn't ask questions there. Or say anything. A vow of silence is part of the requirements." He paused, considering. "Actually, maybe that's why women aren't invited."

She did her very best to leave the embossed imprint of *Moby Dick* on his forehead. He countered, a magical arm wrestling match where the book hovered halfway between the case and her objective. In the brief, exhilarating swirl of energy, she felt him around her in a way that was almost physical, the different pressures and textures of his magic, like the different textures and hardness of his male body. She undercut him by zapping his foot with a short electrical burst, and the book dropped to the floor. He shot her an annoyed look as she levitated it back to the case.

"Cheat."

"You deserved the pain," she said.

"A man is ever punished for the truth. You're giving me crap for cards. I'm going to call for a different dealer."

"Tell me more about the school. The one run by chauvinist pigs." She dealt another hand. "So you didn't speak the whole time you were there? Not even a whisper?"

"If you did, you were gone. Expelled."

She digested that. "But you developed some form of communication with the others. You'd go mad otherwise. Passing notes?"

He snorted. "The youngest of us was five hundred, because human mortality wouldn't have survived the Underworld climate. We'd already done quite a bit of talking in our lives. Some of us too much." He lifted a shoulder. "No writing implements allowed; everything committed to memory. So we became adept at reading hand and face signals, body language."

A skill he'd obviously mastered. She wouldn't be surprised if the mages intended it that way all along. Putting down a pair of threes against his two aces, she gathered in the cards and dealt again. "So what's the tuition cost for the attendee with the appropriate dangly bits?"

That firm mouth quirked. Raina wished she could think of something that would make him smile outright. She'd won a couple chuckles, but nothing that eased those lips into the sexy grin she was sure he'd have.

"At the end of the thirteen years, one student must become a Dark Guardian, forever serving the Underworld. That's the tuition cost for the entire class. On graduation day, you're allowed to speak, but only one word. Yes. To accept the honor."

She stopped, resting her card hand on the edge of the table. "So you were chosen."

"If no one volunteers, the headmaster chooses. I volunteered. I stepped out of the line and said yes."

Her brow furrowed. "Why?"

When he didn't respond right away, just tapped the table, she passed him another card. She couldn't tell if he was going to answer, but she had a feeling he would. He seemed to be studying his hand, but she sensed he was tumbling words, choosing what he would let her know. She did the same whenever she spoke of things that mattered.

"When I started my studies, centuries ago," he said at last, "I aspired to be a Guardian of the Light. That was what all wizards strive toward, unless they're already committed to evil, which is not the same as being committed to Darkness, though most don't realize there's a difference. As time went on, and I was with wizards whose true calling was to serve the Light, it started to feel wrong to me. At the time, though, it was the path that made the most sense for my skills."

"Like a graphic designer deciding to do tech support for Office Depot until Disney or Blizzard come calling."

"Something like that." He nodded. "Then I was chosen to attend the Academy. It nurtured the Darkness in me, and I knew I could serve the Underworld, for the overall good. At least that was my intent. Derek was in my graduating class."

She came to a full stop. "*That's* how you know each other?"

Mikhael shook his head. "We've known each other for a long time. A decade before we were chosen for enrollment, our paths crossed. We'd become friends, of a sort. Given what he does as a Light Guardian, he didn't understand my choice. It doesn't matter. Dark and Light Guardians aren't meant to be drinking buddies. This is what my destiny called me to do, and I chose it."

She flicked the edges of her cards thoughtfully. "I don't know a lot about Dark Guardians. Just the rumors, the results of their work, but I don't think it's easy for a lot of people to understand."

"Being a Dark or Light Guardian...it's like a pendulum. When those who embrace Darkness move too far to the edge, and it's determined that Dark is required to push them back toward the center, toward balance, then I employ the necessary methods to do that."

Meeting his unfathomable eyes, she saw things that chilled the soul, made it curl into itself in the small hours of the night, caught in a web of hopeless desolation. He broke the gaze, and the moment was gone, but she rubbed away gooseflesh on her arms.

"It doesn't help to explain it, trust me," he said quietly. "But understanding isn't necessary. In fact, the lack of comprehension makes the results even more effective." Turning his cards over, he grimaced at the options, folded and slid them back to her. "All jobs have their difficulties, Raina."

"Right." She cleared her throat. "Because a shitty day at the office ranks right up there with using Dark forces to balance the cosmic slate. You aren't drinking buddies with Light Guardians, but what about Dark ones?"

"It's solitary work. And not just because of my uniquely antisocial personality."

"Okay." He had a full house this time, which beat her hand. She didn't deal another set though, putting the cards aside. "Do you have anywhere you call home? The Russian accent...is that home?"

"Not for centuries. It was my mother's country, long before it was the Soviet Union. I learned to use *a* and *the* and rearrange my nouns and verbs in English order some time ago. As well as became fluent in all known languages. Translations spell." He showed cynical amusement. "But I've found the Russian accent to be useful in the human circles I traverse. When I've been handling work in those circles, it affects my accent for a while after the job is done."

He'd been a Russian gunrunner when Ruby had met him, but that had been almost a year before. As if reading her mind on that, Mikhael shrugged. "I could focus and get rid of it, but I suppose it's a reminder of my origins. My version of a home, within myself."

"Because you're never in one place long enough to call it home."

"Yes." He studied her expression. "Derek has a pathological need to save, but I didn't need saving. You've been around me a couple days, Raina. Does anything about me suggest I need your pity?"

"No regrets? No thoughts about what might have happened if you chose another path?"

"Yes." He met her gaze. "But it's not conjecture. I've seen what happens if I don't do what I do. There are other Guardians who've second-guessed themselves or reneged on their oath at a time it was critical they be faithful to it."

It reminded her of how seriously Derek took his oath as a Light

Guardian. She had a feeling neither of them would appreciate the comparison, however.

"What did Isaac take?"

"Are we playing cards or twenty questions?"

She made a face at him, then sobered. "We have privacy here, Mikhael. It might be useful for me to know, to anticipate. I won't share with the rest of my staff, if that's a concern."

"Best not to do so, though the object is useless in the hands of anyone but a highly skilled magic user, like a Guardian. Only a small number of demons could have taken it, and my contacts have eliminated them as possibilities. Which means someone we don't know." Mikhael gave her a long look, then relented. "Isaac stole a soulkeeper for her."

She frowned. "Not sure what that is, but it doesn't sound good."

"It looks like a flute," he said patiently. "With its touch or music, you can tear the soul out of someone's body, capture its energy. The body will serve your will, while the soul itself provides a powerful magic. You can collect innumerable souls in it, and, with the right skills to channel that energy, you're invincible to most opponents."

"Removing a soul is the jurisdiction of the Lady. Or Lucifer."

"A Guardian can do it, but it's a different method, because of our connection to Them. However, the magic user who stole it has to break the body down to near death and pull out the soul the moment before the final gasp, before the body dies and the soul moves into the Lord and Lady's territory."

"The soulkeeper can detect that moment?"

"No, it can't. Which is why it has to be an extremely talented magic user. The soulkeeper is just a refined tool and receptacle for use and storage."

Raina felt a cold twist in her stomach. "Mikhael, a sex demon can detect that moment. We feel it right before it happens. Maybe it doesn't have to be a talented magic user, just one who has the right receptor."

His expression sharpened, considering it. "So the demon may be after Isaac as more than a loose end."

"Yes." She was about to rise, but he caught her wrist. "He's in the house, with the others, protected. It doesn't change anything. Except we might want to put that question point-blank to him to see how he reacts. It will tell us if he knew her plans, but I'm betting he didn't."

"Me, either. He's not the type she'd trust with any element of her strategy."

A pawn. The young incubus was being used, just as Mikhael had said.

As if sensing her change of mood, he pulled her back down to a seated position, put his elbow on the table. She'd pinned her hair back with a barrette, but a shorter piece had come free. As he wrapped it around his fingers, playing with it, he answered her earlier question. "I don't have a home, but I do visit the Underworld to turn in mission-critical information that has to be communicated face-to-face. If you like, I could take you with me sometime."

She blinked. "Sorry. I've had dates in Hell. I wasn't impressed."

He tugged her hair. "There's one particular place I think you'd like."

Saying nothing further than that, he picked up the deck and began to shuffle it with dexterous moves that could be used by dealers in Vegas. Only they didn't have the ability to float the cards from one hand to the other, spinning and cutting them in the air.

"Now you're just showing off."

"A little. You were getting too serious. Your turn to answer some questions. About yourself." He put the deck down between them, the residual energy still sparking off it in a pretty display of purple fire that wafted across the table.

"You're a Dark Guardian, not a priest," she said primly. "A woman's secrets are her treasure to keep."

"And a man's to discover."

"They're none of your business."

"They are, because of the things I plan to do to you tonight." He gave her a heavy-lidded look.

"You're just trying to disrupt my game focus."

"Yeah, and you're already thinking about what I'll do to you." He sobered then, tapped her knuckle where she clasped the cards. "Raina, it will help if I know what happened to you. I won't use the information against you. You know I won't."

"Yes, you will. In ways that I'll want."

She wasn't going to explain why that was bad. It was a woman's prerogative to be this perverse. That cold trepidation was pushing forward. He was doing what he'd been doing all along, drawing forth things she didn't share. If he did break that open in her, let the battle play out once and for all, she might be bonded to him in a way that would mean far more to her than to him. Of course, that would be her little problem, because he wasn't staying, was he?

He put his hand over hers, drawing her eyes up. "Tell me."

She understood why her body wanted to capitulate, but her soul's desire to open to him was more complicated, and probably why she was balking. She hadn't really told anyone, ever. Ramona and Ruby knew some of it, but not the level he was seeking.

Goddess help her, she was going to tell him. Maybe because of what he was, but more likely because of what he'd done to her last night. No one had ever called that from her before.

He wasn't soft, wouldn't reassure her like a child, and that comforted. In fact, she'd be pleased if he was a jerk and simply fucked her brains out afterward, using her and driving her over that cliff edge of pleasure. That way, it wouldn't mean anything. Just a bunch of words, the same way his story about becoming a Dark Guardian was just words. Words about the moment when his life changed irrevocably, making him the mysterious, brooding stranger she saw now. The one who never smiled.

"Incubi and succubi aren't born needing to feed on sexual energy. Thank Goddess. That would be quite disturbing." She gave a grim chuckle. "The transition happens in your teens. Up until then, you're like a normal human child. We have a lot of kinship with the born vampires in that respect. In fact, it's been suggested our blood might be a vampire-demon cross, instead of Fae-demon. Or some of all three. There's no scientific funding for studying the ancestral tree of the energy-sucking genus."

Her short laugh sounded too forced. Rising, she moved to the open doors, focused on the whimsical statue of a frog out by the meditation bench. She'd found it at a junk slash vintage slash antique shop, her favorite type of store.

Crossing her arms across her chest, she rubbed her temple. She needed Gina to redo her nails. She'd chipped one, probably when she'd dug her nails into Mikhael's hard body the night before. "I'm not sure I can do this. Or rather, I'm not sure I should do this. You're not a kind man, Mikhael."

"Are you seeking compassion from me?"

"No." The word was synonymous with pity in her mind. "I don't need it." Recalling his distasteful attitude toward her reaction to his lack of a home gave her a tight feeling. They really were similar, in an off-kilter way. Like two billiards on the same table. Different tracks, different pockets, but same green.

When she heard the scrape of his chair, she tensed. "I really can't handle being touched while I talk about this."

He said nothing, and she turned to find him pushed back in the chair, in that panther predator sprawl of his, dark eyes intent upon her. "Oh. Forgot. Not a kind man."

"Short memory." But there was something in his voice that wasn't...unkind. "You know my nature, my tastes, Raina. You called them the very first night. You want to give me something, I want to take it. I'm not a priest, but when it comes to the information we're given, a sexual Dominant has some very similar qualities."

"Not celibacy, for certain."

"I don't expect either one of us can claim that."

"No." She turned back to the garden. "I was kidnapped when I was ten years old. It was a demon who wanted a succubus as his assassin and personal slave. Taking me at that age, he could groom me before, during and after transition. Since I was half human, he'd calculated, correctly, that the maturation process would not result in a mindless energy lust, but would simply hone the weapon. He wanted a feral nature, but not so much it would impede my intelligence. The night he took me, he killed my mother. She was a powerful witch but didn't see him coming."

He'd killed her in front of Raina. It was the most potent mistake he'd made. Not ever having known love himself, not believing a succubus to be truly capable of it except as a fleeting fancy, he didn't know how long revenge could be nursed in a broken heart.

"I served him for five years, eleven months and three days. He'd enchanted a set of metal cuffs, a collar. He kept them on me so I could never leave him, and my magic had no impact on him. He was smart. Worked the enchantment so I couldn't influence any of his other minions to hurt him. If I tried anything myself, it would rebound on me, three times as strong."

"There's a scar on your thigh. A knife wound."

"Yes." It did dangerous things to a woman when a man noticed things like that during sex. It meant he'd noticed her, not just what he wanted. "I didn't care about living. I just wanted him dead. He liked to have sex with me when his thugs were in the room, liked the way they stared at me. Sometimes he'd tell them to jack off and let me feed off their energy. He got off on that, too. I tried to cut his femoral when he was in a compromising position, but I missed. When he threw me off him, I nearly bled out, but I survived. He changed the spell on the cuffs and collar after that, so I couldn't cause harm to him at all."

"What happened to him?"

He had moved, without her noticing. He wasn't touching her, but he was right behind her, his hand braced on the frame above her head. She glanced up into his face and was caught there. There was a dangerous stillness to Mikhael's expression. She thought it might be the look his prey saw in their last moments. She didn't flinch away from it. If anything, it raised a fierceness in her own breast.

"I killed him." She looked back at the garden. She didn't necessarily want to think about it anymore, but it replayed through her head at least once a day. More, when she was having a bad day. She wasn't sure if that was because the nightmares came back when she was tired, or because she was remembering why even her worst day here was heaven compared to that time in her life.

"There came a day when I'd pretended long and hard enough that he occasionally believed he'd won a modicum of loyalty from me. Devotion." Her lips lifted in a mirthless smile. "One of those momentary lapses in judgment, combined with his greed, gave me my chance. He liked playing human, liked their material things. He liked going into a store as a wealthy client and paying with money he'd 'earned,' rather than using magic to generate it or simply take what he wanted."

She shook her head. "It sounds absurd, doesn't it? I took lives for Elceus, innocent lives. If I didn't, he would starve me until I couldn't stop myself. He sent me after a target, a paid contract. A human one, and the best chance of taking the target out was when he was coming off an airplane. So I had to pass through airport security."

She chuckled, a bitter sound this time. "The cuffs and collar were heavy metal. He took them off to avoid notice. When I'd done what he wanted done, I seduced Elceus, drank all his energy until he was just an empty skin."

It had happened at their rendezvous, the hotel room where she was supposed to report that the job had been done. She'd asked for the collar and cuffs back, had told him she liked wearing them, liked feeling she belonged to him. His eyes had glowed, and she could see exactly what it meant to him. She was another form of wealth. The willing affection of a succubus, a weapon who *wanted* to be in his hands. He'd caressed the enchanted objects, sitting there on the hotel desk, told her to get on her knees.

Beg pretty for them, my love. Use your mouth.

She'd done that, but before he could put them back on her, her sexual energy had coiled around him. He'd taught her to be swift, and very, very good at what she did, after all. "The best part wasn't when he was completely at my mercy. It was the moment he realized that he was trapped, and I was going to kill him. That the sexual pleasure I'd forced upon him was the last thing he was going to feel. His fate was coming toward him and he was helpless to avoid it. It was the sweetest drug I've ever tasted."

For the next six months, she threw up every day, no matter what she ingested. Fortunately, sexual energy was absorbed through the skin and bloodstream, not just the intestinal tract, and it had nourished her human side, somewhat.

The haunted, hollow-eyed look blended well with the urban teen runaway scene, and the clientele seeking her age group weren't that picky, as long as she looked young and was cheap. She'd turned tricks to get her sustenance, and eventually found what she needed to rebuild herself from the ground up.

"So that's it," she said. "The whole story. Or at least as much as I can stomach and hold on to that brunch Matilda cooked. Ready to play cards for real?"

Now he did touch her. She'd changed into day clothes after brunch, her top a cashmere knit that buttoned from a point deep between her cleavage to her waist. The wide neckline, which showed the graceful line of collarbones, had slipped to the right, revealing her bra strap. His touch settled on it, stroking that silken strip. It wasn't even his whole hand, just the four fingertips, the thumb pressing into a neck tendon. It wasn't a gesture of comfort. It was a reminder that he was here. That he had possession of her now. She felt such an over-whelming comfort from that thought, however temporal, it was baffling. And troubling.

"That's why you didn't want to wear the collar."

"It took me awhile before I could even stand the touch of a neck-lace or bracelets." A collar was out of the question...except when those dark cravings rose in her, and she desired them from the right Master. A fantasy. An illusion.

"So, obviously..." she said, and stopped. Taking a breath, she waited until she was sure her voice would be steady, smooth and sultry as it should be. "Motives aren't usually all that complicated, right? Everyone here, I saw a certain something in them. I knew they would seize a chance to live a different life. I won't claim I see that in Isaac. But I don't know the point of no return for a soul. Maybe you do, but I don't want that knowledge. I want to give him the chance to make something of himself, to turn it around. If he can't, he can't."

"I'm not given that knowledge," he said. "I'm not sure even Lucifer or the Goddess Herself knows the depth of the soul. It's probably the most complex magic any of us possess."

She turned then, looking up into his face. "It's a miracle. You don't know everything."

He didn't smile. When he drew a single finger down her face, she willed herself to stay as still as one of her garden statues. It was the only way she'd avoid shattering.

"Don't use sarcasm on me, Raina. It just pisses me off, and you don't want to do that needlessly."

"I don't like how you make me feel," she said. "With you, I want certain things. Things that he did, but different."

"I understand that." She did, too. Mikhael was everything she'd fantasized about, complete with a dangerous, unpredictable edge. "I don't know anything about you, but I want to let you do those things to me. And I don't like that. I really just want you gone."

She had a whole arsenal of persuasive techniques to get a male to do what she wanted. Those techniques were pretty much infallible. So it said something that she was going with brutal honesty, as if she already knew none of that would work on him. As he'd just implied, it would probably make things worse.

"You don't strike me as the type of person who runs, Raina. We've both seen Fate in action. There may be a reason I'm here, beyond Isaac."

"If you go with *Destiny sent me*, I'm going to lose all respect for your seduction techniques." No sarcasm now, proven by the smile she gave him, one she was painfully aware was a little tremulous at the edges. "I really need to do something else now. Let's stop baring our souls and set some interesting stakes for our game."

"All right. I choose strip poker."

CHAPTER NINE

*H*e wasn't kidding, and he made her laugh, lessening some of that hard knot in her gut, even as her heart oddly ached a little more.

"Thank goodness I changed into clothes after brunch. Otherwise I'd only have the robe."

"I should have anticipated that and prevented you from changing. Damn."

She pushed him away. "All right. But if I win, get you down to nothing, you let me tie *you* up, do as I wish. Those are my stakes."

"Why would you want to do that?"

She wouldn't let the shrewd knowledge in that gaze unsettle her. "You like to restrain your lovers, don't you? Make them helpless to the pain and pleasure you offer?" She grazed him with her nails. "I'd like the same pleasure."

"Can you restrain me so I can't get loose?"

Her eyebrow lifted. "I don't know. Can I?"

"If I say yes, I give you an advantage."

"But now I won't trust you if you say no." At his look, she relented. "I don't really know your scope and range, but I guess it's possible, if you don't defend yourself. *If* you submit willingly."

He raised a brow at her taunt. "As your guest, I can accept those terms, but as a Dark Guardian, I have a job to do. You probably can't bind me so I can't get loose, but you could slow me down."

"What if you have my word that any binding will be to take shameless sexual advantage of you? Not for anything connected to Isaac or your role as Dark Guardian. Will you trust me that much?"

"Considering I don't think you're going to win, yes. But let's integrate it into the game. Bondage strip poker."

She blinked. "Excuse me?"

"We mix and match. A winning hand gets the choice of an item of clothing or a restraint. Tying one wrist, an ankle, et cetera. And other assorted parts. Then if there's nothing left to tie or take off, you're at the mercy of the person who's won."

"How will the person look at their cards if they don't have free hands?"

"We'll cross that bridge when we come to it."

"All right," she agreed.

He gave her a searching look. "You're brave enough to risk that?"

"I am."

"I doubt that. You're just confident of your win, which is dangerous, because it aligns the fates against you."

"I don't know about that. Victory goes to the bold, I've always heard. Let's play and see."

"Okay." He nodded. "You've named your stakes. What do I get if I win?"

"The same thing I get." Her brow furrowed. "Me tied up." Though even saying it made butterflies do nosedives in her stomach. She'd better win, or she'd painted herself into a corner she wasn't prepared to be in.

"I intend to have that regardless, win or lose." He gave her that direct look. "So if I win, the stakes have to be something I can't obtain for myself."

Okay, that sent a hard kick through even lower regions, but she covered it with a sultry hip cock. Laying her long-nailed hand on the doorframe just below his, she caressed his palm. "A charming personality?"

At his dour expression, she chuckled. "You don't really want one of those. Okay. If you win, you get your clothes back."

Mikhael closed his fingers over her wrist, holding her there. "Try again."

"Fine." Telling herself she was insane, especially with her pulse tripping beneath his hold, she threw it open. "What would you like the bet to be if you win?"

"Free croissants from Matilda, whenever I stop by, from here forward. Forever."

Her brows rose in surprise. "You'll have to take that up with Matilda and her spirits. She doesn't do anything I say."

"I can work it out. Women respond to me."

She snorted. "If I win, I get you, restrained and naked, at my mercy. And you want *bread?*"

"I'm going to tell Matilda how poorly you value her skills. I've tasted the croissants, and I think those are proportionate stakes. I don't get home-cooked food too often. I want a lifetime supply of free croissants. It seems reasonable."

It was about more than croissants. He was making it clear the stakes would be him becoming a regular visitor to her place. Someone to fence words with, someone who made her feel...the way he made her feel. It wasn't an act of commitment or permanence, anything to make him or her feel hemmed in. But it was...tempting. Far more so than a to-go bag of crescent rolls, no matter how good they were. "Perhaps I'll tell Matilda to give you a meal with those rolls. On occasion."

It must be true that the way to a man's heart was through his stomach. His fingers curved closer over hers, a squeeze that became a clasp, a more intimate link between them.

"You value having me naked, tied up and at your mercy far more highly than I expected."

Arrogant ass. But you have no idea how true that is.

Straightening, she slipped her hand free. "When I win, if my magic can't restrain you, I expect you to be a gentleman and honor the bet. Pretend to be helplessly restrained, like I did with those thin silver chains of yours."

"That was Underworld silver," he said. "It's unbreakable and configured so that only I can break its hold. You would have had to harm yourself or break the balusters. I wouldn't have allowed you to harm yourself. You *were* helpless, Raina." His voice became husky as he held her gaze. "But the moment your mind surrendered to me, you were my slave, with or without the chains."

He had a way of looking at her that was total Bad Guy, but not. He knew how to stroke that part of her, yet twist it as well, like dragging a feather down someone's back, only to have it turn into a poisoned barb. And make the body crave both.

Ducking under his arm to break the contact, and seeking a little space, she sauntered over to the far wall and the music system there. "If it doesn't throw you off your game, I'm going to put on some music."

When he made an assenting noise and headed back toward the table, she let out a breath. She shuffled one of her favorite playlists, buying herself some time before she turned toward the gaming table.

When Mindy McCready's "Ten Thousand Angels" came up, amused despair flashed through her. As Mindy sang about needing a legion of angels to resist the temptation of a sinfully irresistible male, she was staring right at one, taking a seat at the table. It wasn't contrived; it was just the way the damn man moved, all that ripple and flex of power and warrior's grace, with the dangerous profile of a hawk.

He glanced at her, raised a quizzical brow as she schooled her expression into indifference, fast enough she probably looked like she'd swallowed a bug. Sliding into her seat, she picked up the deck. "So if you don't have a home, where do you usually stay when you're not working? Hotels, cottages? Caves?"

He put an ankle on his knee. "It depends on the job I'm assigned, as well as the location. I've stayed at plenty of hotels, but I like forests."

"Do you hang from a tree like a bat? Wrap your wings around you to protect your fancy suits?"

He gave her a look that made her want to take a healthy bite out of him. "Something like that."

She smiled. "I'd like to see that."

"Maybe you will. Two cards." After he picked them up, he spoke again, unexpectedly. "I like trees. I like sleeping in them. It's quiet, and when it's not, what's making noise isn't disruptive. In the ancient forests, I occasionally find a dryad or hamadryad that stayed behind when the Fae separated themselves from this world."

"And she doesn't mind you...nesting in her branches?"

He snapped a rejected card at her nose in reproof. "Crotch would be the obvious crass arboreal term."

"Too crass and obvious." She didn't really want to know about all the women Mikhael had been with. He'd certainly made it clear he didn't want to hear about her liaisons, so she switched topics, noting him tapping his fingers as the tune switched to one of Li's AC/DC favorites, "Highway to Hell." She snickered. Glancing at her, Mikhael tuned in to the irony. His gaze sparked in response.

"Do you know a lot about music?" she asked.

He put his cards down, rapped the table twice with his fist. Then he drew her attention to his other hand, which now held a top-of-the-line player. She chuckled at the subtle theatrics, feeling the short wisp of conjuring energy. "I should introduce you to Ramona. She runs a magic shop. I can get you a top hat and a rabbit."

He laid the music device on the table. "I keep about six thousand songs on this, and I have a library of about fifteen thousand more on a backup drive."

"Where do you keep all this stuff if you have no house?" She shook her head. "Never mind. I've seen Derek pretty much pull a sword out of his ass, so I expect you guys have some weird way of manipulating multidimensional pockets of space. Ruby said you have a Ferrari. You probably keep it folded up in the other pocket."

"Last time I did that, it got an oil leak. Ruined a good jacket."

"Smart ass. Why don't we alternate? I'll play a song, you play a song. I'll learn about the complex male musical culture of beer and boob watching—"

"And I won't lose significant testosterone levels fighting off the effect of continuous sappy chick songs and pretentiously empowered girl bands."

"Fair enough."

Despite her teasing, Mikhael could tell it surprised her that his music was eclectic, but he'd been around long enough to have wide tastes. Wagner, Russ Freeman and Kevin Kern shared storage space with Aerosmith and Foreigner. He was a big fan of the Sinatra music style, but he eschewed those sung by Sinatra himself, too aware of the man's character to enjoy them.

She liked variety, too. Country, classical, Latin rhythms, Celtic instrumentals. In the pop arena, she favored romantic ballads with male vocals that emphasized rough emotion over studio polish.

Since their previous discussion had stirred things up a little more than expected, they'd agreed to one more short practice round. While they did that, she was paying attention to the music he chose, probably to use it as an advantage. He suspected she deliberately lost a couple hands to fathom his poker strategies.

Studying every detail to anticipate a client's wants and needs was innate to her. Everything could be a strategy, even the music she chose. But he preferred to think her deceptively casual scrutiny now had to do with her need to control the situation even as he made her feel more out of control. Their own personally unique dynamic.

"Why don't you hate males?" he asked, when she was reshuffling the deck. It was his turn to do it, but he'd deferred to her, enjoying the graceful slide of her fingers as she turned the cards and positioned them. He always appreciated the female form, but he had to admit he'd rarely been captivated by the way a woman moved her hands. He told himself it was because they were doing their task against the backdrop of her breasts, the tempting cleavage revealed by the cashmere V-neck.

Now though, she looked puzzled. "Because of what Elceus did to you," he prompted. "I'd think you'd have a distrust of the male gender. You don't. Obviously."

"No more than sensible." She gave him a sultry smile. "My father was the one who gave me the sex demon blood. He was an incubus, not like the ones you hunt. He hadn't...transitioned, though he was more seasoned and mature than those you've met here. He was a fair and noble man, strong. He didn't stay with my mother after I was born, because that wasn't in his nature." Her eyes became more flat. "But he tried to get help to rescue me. No one would aid or believe an incubus, no one in authority. When he enlisted the help of more nefarious sources, they sold him out to energy dealers."

The paranormal equivalent of drug dealers, who would kill a sex demon and bottle the blood, because in the supernatural world it provided unparalleled sexual euphoria, a supernatural Viagra. A risky one, since even short-term use could be toxic.

"The protections on my house include a screen that masks the presence of my demons, so it doesn't attract that filth, though if they set one foot across the line, I'd happily stake them out in the yard and let fire ants eat their flesh."

"I wouldn't blame you." He gazed at her. "I'm sorry that no one listened to your father, Raina. He didn't get to the right people. I would have helped him."

"Thank you. I'd like to believe you, so I will." She inclined her head, took a breath. "I was badly treated by Elceus. Not the entire male gender. And the sexual things...it wasn't like rape, though I would rather have starved than feed off him or his carrion. I feed off of sexual energy, so the sex act itself has different connotations for me."

He didn't entirely agree with that assessment, given that she'd suppressed her natural submissive desires because of her experiences at the demon's hands, and it was obvious she harbored a great deal of trepidation about the emotional vulnerability of sex, but he held the thought for now, letting her continue unimpeded.

"I don't paint every zebra with the same stripes." Her eyes sparked. "Plus, regardless of spots, stripes or polka-dots, when it comes to a fight, I prefer rage to fear."

"I've noticed."

"Okay, this hand starts the real game." At his agreeable nod, she started dealing out the cards. It was obvious she wanted to leave the topic behind, so he was surprised when she spoke again, though her gaze didn't leave her hand of cards. "I respect men of noble character, just as I have nothing but disgust for those who lack it."

"Do I dare ask what category I fall into?"

"Does my opinion count?"

He thought that over for a few minutes. "Ultimately, no. But I am curious."

"Is that your roundabout way of saying it *does* matter?" That smile played around her lips.

"I don't say anything roundabout. Wiles and ruses are your area, not mine."

"Honesty actually has a great value in my profession, because the ones without artifice, who are genuinely enthusiastic and caring about their clients, earn the most. But I do think my opinion matters to you."

"All right. It matters." But his tone was so bland, she sniffed.

"Fine. You have a strong code of behavior. You gave me an opportunity with Isaac, rather than summarily killing him, and you've honored the terms of our agreement about that. You've been fair. You're brutally honest, and there's merit to that. So you're a man of character. Whether that character proves good or bad in the end, all depends."

He inclined his head, laid down his cards. "Straight."

She pursed her lips, laid down an ace high flush. "You lose." Letting her gaze rove over him, she paused, deliberated on her choices. "Shirt, please."

Raina kept the faintly amused expression on her lips, but her blood heated as he carelessly slipped the buttons and shrugged out of it, revealing a lot of broad shoulder and gleaming muscle. She lingered on his chest. In the dark hours of the morning, she'd let her fingers trail down that narrowing path of hair, over his muscled abdomen, to the impressive cock.

With the shirt pushed off his shoulders, he unbuttoned the cuffs. It was an appealing look that drew her gaze to the flexing curved lines of his upper arms and chest, a perfect work of carnal art. The man was mouthwatering, no other word for it.

A hard bump, muttered curse and the alarming rattle of china lifted her gaze to the library door. Aiden was bringing in her afternoon tea. He'd taken a look at Mikhael's bared upper body and hit the protruding pocket door with his knee, nearly upsetting the tray. Aiden had a strong appreciation for the male form.

Directing him to set the tea down on a side table, she saw he'd brought Mikhael a selection: a Heineken, a bottled water and a decanter of whiskey. As well as a small bowl of Hershey's cherry chocolate kisses for her. She did love her staff.

Even so, she gave the incubi a stern glance. "Thank you, Aiden. If I have need of anything from anyone, I'll call. Close the doors after you."

He'd obviously figured out what game they were playing, so they'd just ensured there would be a lot of casual wandering through the side garden this afternoon, aka skulking, to report who was winning. In a house all about sex, nothing was really private in that regard.

As Aiden left, she returned to her previous occupation— enjoying the display of male virility in front of her. Only now she could enjoy it with a cherry chocolate melting on her tongue and a sip of chamomile tea.

Mikhael regarded her with amusement. "You saw all of me last night. I wouldn't expect such interest today, especially from one as worldly as yourself."

"I see." Rolling up the red tinfoil ball with its little ribbon tab, she sent it to his side of the table with a flick. "Pot calling the kettle black. I wasn't the one who proposed strip poker."

Amusement fluttered through her as Five's "When the Lights Go Out" was the next music choice on his player. He was the most unexpected male.

He inclined his head, an almost courtly gesture. "My apologies. I assumed females aren't as openly avid in that regard as males."

"Then you were definitely born in a different century, Mikhael. Women are now free to demonstrate as much depravity, decadence and lust as men."

"Good to know."

Mikhael actually had experienced forward women. Drunk, trashy or manipulative females mostly using sex for reasons that weren't about pleasure. She was looking at him as if she wanted to start licking and devouring him like that chocolate. Her interest was clean, reciprocal lust, with a hungry emotional underlayer that captured him.

"We could just skip the game," he offered.

"Oh no. I'm going to beat you fair and square. The stakes are too tempting. Women might feel lust, but we have more self-control."

"I could test that theory."

Raina bet he could shatter it beyond repair. Women had more self-control only because their hearts were often way too involved in their lust. She was dangerously interested in the man himself, when she should keep tunnel vision on those rippling muscles and the *very* nice-sized package under his jeans.

He won the next hand. Sitting back, he gave her his own long, raking appraisal. "Take off your bra."

"I haven't taken off my shirt."

"I get to determine the order, right?"

Shrugging, she wriggled out of it under the cashmere. As she thrust out her breasts to reach behind her and unhook the bra, his heated regard was intense. The cling of the silken yarn showed her nipples in a way she knew was even more provocative than seeing her naked. She covered her own precarious reaction to that by hanging the lacy bra on her chair arm, then dealt the next hand. When he won that one, he wanted her panties.

"Hand them to me. You're not very good at this game, Raina."

She merely lifted a brow, rose. When she did, because of his long legs stretched out next to the table, she was straddling his crossed ankles. Pivoting, she did a shimmy to pull her snug tailored skirt up, hooked the panties and worked them down in a smooth motion, giving him an extremely brief glimpse of her ass and what lay between her thighs. When she turned back around, he was eye level with her breasts.

It reminded her of his mouth there, suckling her, but she knew how to play this game. She liked playing it with him, noting the fire in his dark gaze, and the tighter fit of his jeans. Putting the swatch of silk in his hands, she brushed her fingers across his palm. Stepping back, she settled in her chair, crossing her ankles and sliding her legs to a demure ladylike angle as she picked up the deck.

He lifted the panties to his lips, inhaled her arousal, then draped them over his thigh for safekeeping. He also won the next hand.

"Open the top two buttons of your shirt. Only those two."

He was diabolical. If he'd had her pull off her shirt, it would be like stripping for the bath. Erotic, yes, doing it in front of him, but he was like a master pastry chef, knowing exactly how to stretch things out, making them thinner and thinner, stopping just short of breakage.

"You're good at this." She gave him his due. "Most men aren't."

"I have selfish motives. The more I arouse you, the more you release that sex demon scent of yours. Your skin is flushed, your pulse is rabbiting. It makes me hard as a fucking rock, knowing I can get you this hot."

When his gaze passed over her, it was like they were already in bed, his hands on her. He made her want to take him to bed, take *him* in her bed, over and over.

"I could lift you up against the wall right now," he continued. "Push up your skirt and thrust into you without any interference. Your nipples are erect, and I'd feel that, no padding. Or I'd put your feet on the floor but keep my hand between your legs, my fingers inside you while I pinned you to the wall by the throat. Then I'd suckle your nipples through the cloth until the fabric was wet, and they'd stand out even more than they are now."

She tilted her head so another of her dark curls loosened from its barrette, sliding along her cheek. "This is cashmere. You'd owe me a dry-cleaning bill."

"I'd gladly pay it. Because when it was all over, I'd mark you and your pretty clothes with something other than my mouth."

He thought he almost had her then, had pushed her to the point she'd set aside the cards and let him slam her against the bookshelf as he'd described. Though he saw a fine tremor in her hand, and that scent grew to a maddening musk, she simply dealt another hand and gave him her mysterious smile, though he noted it was tight at the corners.

As they continued to play, her staff found excuses to keep wandering past the open archway of the library. They didn't linger too obviously, because if they did, her eyes would shift to them and they would disappear. But not fast enough.

After she'd opened those top two buttons, Luke was the next one to wander past to get the latest intel on their game. Mikhael cut his gaze toward him before Raina could do it. Whatever Luke saw in his face made the incubus practically vanish into thin air. It quelled any casual wanderers for a good while, with no repeat business from the males, his message delivered loud and clear.

It was a ridiculous reaction. They'd likely all seen Raina naked. Hell, maybe they had sex demon orgies on slow days. He wasn't an overly possessive male. While he was fucking a woman, no one else was, but when he was done, he was done, and she was free to do whatever with whomever. So this was a unique feeling.

Having other males around her—excessively sexually motivated ones—goaded some primitive instincts he was unable to quell, even by mocking himself. *Doesn't matter. You're still thinking of tearing the dick off the next one who walks through that garden.*

She didn't take new clients, but she had a small, exclusive group for whom she was available when they requested her. He'd heard that from her staff. She damn well better not have one while he was here, because he was going to be inside of her every night. Probably mornings and afternoons as well.

He shook himself out of it. Lord and Lady, in a minute he was going to swing from her clematis vine and beat his chest. She was giving him an odd look, so he slouched down in the chair, stretched out his legs even farther to the right of the table, re-hooking his ankles. With a smile oddly more shy than coquettish, she slid her feet out of her heels. He'd noticed she didn't much care for wearing shoes, but then witches could be like that. She was wearing stockings today, but he knew her feet were soft and silky smooth. Last night, he'd put his lips on them more than once, teasing the arches and the tips of the painted toes, caressing the ankles with hands and mouth.

Now she put those soft feet on his thighs, and he found it easy to rest his arm on her ankles, hooking his fingers under the arch of the sole as he stared at the cards, only half seeing them. He'd had easy moments with his one-night lovers, because casual sex came with casual day-after behavior. This was unique, though, this comfortable silence, no hurry to be anywhere or do anything other than be in her company. It didn't even have anything to do with the pending arrival of Isaac's demon.

She won the next hand, probably because of his lack of attention. "The shoes," she said.

He toed off the Italian loafers. Next hand, he gained back ground. He wanted the shirt completely open, framing her breasts. He brushed her hands aside, did it himself, making her keep her hands on the chair arms while he did it. Her breath on his forehead was enough to make him want to lift his attention to the luscious mouth. Instead, once he'd opened the cashmere, arranged it around the sumptuous offering of her naked breasts, he made himself sit back, re-cross his ankles without indulging a single touch, though he could feel her yearning as sharp and potent as his own. He really should have worn slacks, because the denim was starting to cut like a son of a bitch.

"I seem to be winning so far," he noted. "But I think you're holding back."

"Could be. Scared?"

"Petrified," he said, deadpan. "Can't you tell?"

Those full lips curved, and he could vividly imagine them wrapped around his cock, particularly when she moistened them with the tip of her tongue and blinked those mink lashes at him. "Your stoic routine isn't fooling me," she said in that bedroom voice. "You're shaking in your custom-tailored one hundred percent cotton boxer shorts. Which, by the way, I'm looking forward to seeing you strip off."

He didn't gain as much ground over the next hour as he expected. She was a damn deft player, in judgment, bluffing, losing, recouping. However, at last he had her stripped down to stockings. He had his reasons for holding off on the bondage options he'd insisted on integrating. For one thing, her anticipation and trepidation about it just intensified the perfume of that succubi energy. For another, before he started tying her up, he'd wanted her in just those stockings. It tested the hell out of his control, however.

She had her legs crossed, not in modesty, but to display her legs and titillate the imagination as to the treasure between them. Clothed in her stockings and long hair, she carried off being naked with grace and beauty, not vulgar commonality. It made her touchable and untouchable at once. Had she lived centuries before, she would have been a mistress to kings, a geisha in demand by the emperor himself.

He was well aware he lost the next couple hands—and his socks—because of it. Now she was considering her next option, drawing out the tension in her own unique way. Since she was eying the straining denim like a cat contemplating cream, he'd bet he was about to get some relief. At least from the jeans.

"All I want this round is...this." Touching his bare abdomen, she slid her fingers down to the waistband of the jeans. When she hooked beneath it, he held his position, leaned back in the chair, watching those deft fingers slip the top button. She stopped there, though, letting her sharp nails glide over the fly, following his erect length on the outside before she sat back. She opened another chocolate now, sucking on the sweet as she regarded his still confined cock. He imagined spilling the whiskey over her breasts and sucking the bitter taste off her flesh.

"I don't think we talked about touching," he noted.

"It was just along the way."

"You keep staring, you'll be on your back on these cards, and I'll be buried inside that sweet pussy of yours."

"Not likely. It's a challenge to you now. Seeing how crazy we can drive one another."

"How am I doing?"

Those green-gold eyes glittered. "You know exactly how aroused I am, Mikhael."

He tapped his losing hand. "Why the socks before the jeans?" he asked.

She tilted her head, those lips curving. "The sexiest man in the world still looks ridiculous in only a pair of socks. I'd rather have the socks go first, and leave the jeans on until the last possible moment, because jeans on the right body"— her eyes coursed over him—"can be as stimulating as the man beneath, and both should be savored." She arched a brow. "I expect you understand that, as much care as you've taken to slowly unwrap me."

She was right, but there was another reason. He had an end goal, and it relied on precise timing. Despite the feminine power she was demonstrating, he was facing a wild, beautiful creature who'd been damaged when it came to this particular vital treasure in her makeup. He was going to be the first male who enjoyed it the way it was meant to be enjoyed, treating her as she should be treated.

It sharpened his resolve. He won the next hand, and when he did, he left his cards on the table. "Left wrist, tied to the chair."

She was left-handed. He'd chosen the dominant hand deliberately. "I assume you keep restraints, somewhere?"

He saw the brief flash of uncertainty, quickly schooled to that same indifferent look. "In the cabinet, over there. Not conjuring silver chain this time?"

"No. Not this time." Rising, he found nylon rope that would satisfy his purposes. Normally, he would have ordered her to go get the restraints, bring them back and place them in his hands. Her Master's hands. But he knew what was going on beneath the surface of that practiced faint smile she still had glued to her face. She knew he saw through it, but still she kept her shields in place. That touched him, made him do what he did next.

As he'd been searching for the rope, in the corner of his eye he'd seen her move her hand to the chair arm, a little bit of a hesitant jerk to the motion, the fingers tight on the wood. When he returned she'd forced them to relax, forced her body to relax. Meeting her gaze briefly, he wound the rope around her wrist, three, four turns. Then he dropped to one knee, pressed his lips to her knuckles. Her fingers flexed, another sign of uncertainty, and he glanced up at her, his lips still on her hand. There was something raw in her expression, so he turned his cheek, rubbed his five o'clock shadow against her fair skin, tickling her and making her smile, though that bright, unstable look was still there.

"Easy," he murmured.

She took a breath. "This is going to make it difficult to deal."

"You've done all the dealing until now. I can share some of the load."

She pursed her lips. "About time you did something useful."

"I'll see if I can't improve my value to you."

On his next winning hand, he chose a touch, payback for her caress when she'd unbuttoned his jeans. He slid a knuckle down her sternum, the pleasurable valley between those generous breasts. He watched them heave on a quick, shuddering breath. If she'd still worn the bra, one that was front-closing, he would have flicked that fastener, watched the cups ease their hold, the breasts swell outward. He traced the curve, but didn't touch the nipple, no matter how much a temptation the stimulated jut of it was.

"Still want to keep playing?" he asked in a low tone. "Want to quit?"

"Not on your life," she said, though she had to clear her throat first. "I think you're taking more liberties with your touch than I did."

"Damn right."

She sniffed, but a tiny smile bloomed, something almost girlish. He'd like to see that one more often. Though he put 110 percent into every effort, because that was how to be effective, this was immersion for the sake of the moment, instead of the end goal, and that was unique for him.

As he sat back and began to deal again, he was already anticipating having her fully tied, fully helpless. Hearing her scream out multiple climaxes. When he finally thrust into her, he was going to explode. He'd never been so hard in his life.

CHAPTER TEN

Pride goeth before a fall. The biblical reminder should have been tattooed across her ass. That last tempting touch was the end of his winning streak.

She was an expert card hustler, giving her opponent the idea he was winning, giving him confidence—before she basically cleaned his clock. What's more, he knew she wasn't cheating. She was just that damn good. Obviously, she'd played games of chance for quite a while. On her very first winning hand, she chose to have her hand freed.

He was carrying two knives on his person. To underscore how soundly she was beating him, she counted each one as an additional item of clothing, removing those and still leaving the jeans in place. Then she chose the option of winning back her clothing, one frustrating piece at a time. Seeing her don it was almost as provocative as seeing her take it off. Watching her put on the bra in the same order she'd taken it off, working it under the thin shirt, could make a man's mouth water, that lift of curves, the adjustment, the slide of her fingers over herself, visible through the fabric.

Once she had the cups in place, she rose from the chair, presented her back to him, holding the straps in place. "Hook it for me, would you? Third tier."

He slid his hands under the cashmere, noticing how large his hands were, spanning her rib cage, his darker, tanned pigment against her pale, soft flesh. She had a small mole below the bra strap that he caressed. She'd drawn the thick tail of her hair over her shoulder so it was out of his way, exposing her delicate nape. As he rose, he followed the curve of her rib cage and moved his palms forward, under the cups. She tsked at him, though she leaned back, giving him that access.

"You didn't win the hand. Touching is cheating."

"As you wish." He made sure his fingers teased her nipples before he relocated to her back, and was rewarded by a quick jerk of her hips, a rub against his pelvis. Her chuckle had that sexy breathiness to it.

He hooked the bra and was treated to the sight of her adjusting the cups once more, hands sliding over her curves. When she slipped away from him and turned, she'd left the top two buttons of the sweater open, a feast of lace and swelling flesh to drive him to distraction.

She had an endgame in mind as well, and it was obvious she was just as single-minded about it. "Would you like some more whiskey while I'm up?"

"If you're serving me, yes."

Her eyes could glow like emeralds and gold found in a pharaoh's tomb. He took a seat as she moved to the side table, poured a couple fingers of the quality liquor, and then returned, her body a dance of sex.

She leaned over his shoulder, put the drink on the table by the hand he had resting there in a deceptively relaxed pose. She paused long enough that he could get a close up of her cleavage. When she started to straighten, he caught her open collar in two firm fingers. "Raina, you're not playing with one of your trained house cats."

"I surely hope not." She slipped from his grasp. Before she circled back to her side of the table, she indulged herself.

That slipped button and few teeth down on his zipper meant his jeans were low on his hips, so her long nails caressed the upper rise of his ass between that and the waistband. It made him think of being between her legs, her gripping him there as he thrust inside her.

He could end it, just clear the table with one sweep of his arm, take her as hard and rough as he wanted, and she'd love it. Hell, he knew he would. But the way she wove sexual energy into everything she did and said, the way she played the game, it was like watching a master artist. He wanted to keep watching, to see what she did next, to see what straw would make him take her down.

Picking up her cards, she met his gaze. She was as stirred up as he was, and what increased the potency were their competing abilities to channel it, hold back. She was a witch who ran a house of erotic promises. He loved the challenge of taking a woman up higher than she ever thought she could soar. He wanted to take her to the moon and beyond. What's more, he wanted to go with her.

So he made his decision. She might win the next hand, but she'd already won seven consecutive hands. The odds of poker said, no matter how good the player, she would lose a hand eventually, and he didn't want to arrest her forward motion. To get her to trust him, he was going to give her his trust.

He didn't drop any cards, didn't add any. As a result, he lost the next hand with nothing against her pair of twos. He laid his hand down face up, so she saw. Raina's lips pressed together. That curl that teased the corner of her mouth shadowed her gaze as she considered. Then she gathered the cards, pushed them to the side.

"Will you put your hands on the chair arms?" she said quietly.

He complied, curving his fingers over the ornate carved ends. It was a good-sized chair. When he first sat in it, he'd gotten a brief glimpse of its history. Men, perhaps a century or so ago, sitting in it to smoke cigars, swallow the fiery burn of bourbon as they wore dinner-party finery and talked about what Southern gentlemen liked to discuss. She liked things that carried the grace of different times, the civilized veneer. She didn't deny the barbaric side of human nature, but she celebrated those moments when they set that aside and embraced rituals of order and beauty.

She didn't get restraints from the cabinet. Instead, he felt the wave of energy, the conjuring of heat, and glanced down to see a barbed, fiery twisting rope of power curl around his wrist, wrap from his forearm all the way to the elbow. Then it snaked down to his thigh, winding under it and to his ankle, securing it to the chair leg.

Another serpentine length appeared on the left side. As it followed the same track, nipping his skin with licks of heat, tiny pricks as it tightened, he looked back up at her. "I can get out of this, if I choose to do so."

"They would burn, and cut."

"I'm not afraid of pain."

"No, I don't expect that you are." She nodded to the deck of cards. "You lost that last hand deliberately, but the other hands...I won those."

"Yes, you did." He gave her that due. "I haven't ever played cards that badly, except for one night when I was in the Underworld academy with Derek."

"He beat you?"

"Of course not." He was offended even by the thought. "We were both soundly trounced by a pencil-necked, Bill Gates/Harry Potter Asian wizard who looked barely out of grade school, though he was in his sixth century. On every losing hand, you had to take a shot of homemade brew one of us had made out of sulfur and grain alcohol. We were completely shit-faced. So I had an excuse for playing so badly."

"Except you had to drink so much *because* you were losing already." That sexy slip of a brow arched. "How did you stick to the vow of silence if you were drunk?"

"We were very clever. We put a silence spell on each other. We didn't count on an unfortunate side effect. We were also unable to throw up. Having hangover that severe, no ability to vomit? I would not advise."

She laughed as he exaggerated the Russian accent. Truly laughed, which was as intoxicating as everything else about her. "Maybe that's the real reason Derek doesn't like you. I'll bet it was you who came up with the silence spell."

"No. It's the wings. He envies them. He had to settle for his John Wayne meets Merlin gimmick to attract women."

"As much as his dragonskin boots turn me on, the wings *are* a real chick magnet. Or they would be, if they weren't attached to you."

He snorted, but then considered her. "Did it make you feel uncomfortable, Raina, when I bound your one hand?"

"Yes." She gave him a truthful answer, though it took some obvious effort. "Not the binding. But how I felt about you doing it. I wanted you to do it. And much more."

Her honesty alone would have made him test those bonds, but now her eyes slid over him, reflecting. He could feel her power building again. He steeled himself to immobility, but it was difficult, because that rope of power didn't slide only over his chest or throat this time, as he'd anticipated. It crisscrossed his chest, then slid down straight over his groin and underneath him, so when it cinched in, he tensed, feeling the pressure between his balls, against his cock.

She crossed her arms under the magnificent breasts and leaned in to study her work. He was going to take a healthy bite out of her if she got too close, but she stayed just out of reach. "You're right," she said. "You could get free. Most men might soldier through pain to arms, legs, torso, kidneys. But if you threaten to mangle that one vital part…" Her lashes lifted. "I expect you could figure out a spell to free yourself, but that will take time and thought, and I intend to keep you distracted."

He could splinter the chair, but he knew she was counting on him respecting her property. That wasn't a reasonable expectation. He could replace her damn chair for her. "You're not playing very fair," he said.

"I'm playing within the boundaries of the rules. Well"— she lifted a shoulder—"as much as you are. You threw that last hand, so I assumed you were giving me permission to completely bind you." Her gaze shuttered, as if she wasn't comfortable examining why that was. She knew he wasn't the type to voluntarily lose unless bigger stakes were involved. "Are you uncomfortable, being at my mercy?"

"I think we both know me being at your mercy isn't the way it's going to play out."

That flicker in her gaze again, but she said nothing. It didn't matter. It would play out a different way, no matter how much she tried to direct it, because at a certain point, instinct would take over for calculation. She'd *asked* if she could bind him, whereas, if their positions were reversed, he would have ordered it. When it came to her underlying nature and his own, neither of them was going to be denied. There was one predator and one prey in this room, and that prey had an undeniable craving to be run down and captured. He could smell it on her, as strong as an animal in heat, even stronger than her succubi scent. But she was an alpha in her own world, so she wasn't going to go down until he'd earned it.

Rising from the chair, she shifted the table out of the way. She began to take off the clothes she'd won back, all the way to the stockings. Then she moved toward his chair. Placing her foot between his spread thighs, she rolled off one sheer garment, then shifted to do the same with the other. He watched the movement of her breasts, pressing against her lifted thigh, the glimpse of her sex from the spread position. She unclipped her hair, so it draped over her shoulders, sliding along his thigh. Naked, she straightened, trailed her fingers down his chest, creating patterns with her knuckles. She seemed immersed in the way it looked, her fingers against his skin. The fiery flame of the restraints played lovingly over her knuckles, recognizing its mistress.

Men weren't into the savoring when it came to sex. But watching a woman do it, truly enjoy his body when he couldn't touch her, was mesmerizing. She moved to his shoulder, followed his biceps, bent and tasted him there, her fangs pricking his skin.

"Raina." The one word was demand, desire...reverence with a dangerous edge, a desire to pillage the temple as much as worship in it. He had that dichotomy, and when she registered it, as she did now, she trembled, a little quiver over her skin.

She moved behind him, threaded her fingers through his hair, tugged at his scalp. "Did you ever wear it longer than this?"

"No. Too easy for an enemy to grip it."

"Always the warrior." Then she yanked, pulling his head back and trailing her nails over his jugular, leaving scratches along the pumping artery. When she bent to touch her mouth to the skin beneath his ear, his fingers dug into the chair, his muscles rippling against those bindings so he felt the burn of their hold. Despite being solid wood, well made, the chair creaked. He could destroy it if he allowed the power building within his chest to expand. He could blow out the walls of this room with it.

He roped it down, a binding within Raina's bindings, and let out a feral growl as she ran those nails down his chest, tugged his hair there, then scraped his abdomen. Her breasts pressed into his back, and he inhaled her scent. That blue-green-gold field of power was expanding from her as well, that aural mist enclosing them in this moment that belonged only to them.

He muttered an oath as she opened his jeans all the way. Straightening to move her hands down his back, she slid her hands fully into the pants, taking a hard grip on his buttocks, squeezing.

"Goddess, I love your ass," she murmured against his shoulder blade. "Lift up some. The bindings will allow it for a second."

He did, and just as she'd indicated, he had the slack for only the amount of time she needed to shove the denim and the cotton boxers out from under him. Coming back in front of him, she bent and removed them. Because the bindings were magical, the cloth passed right through them. Well, mostly. He noted the smoking burns on the fabric and she shrugged, giving him a teasing look as she dropped them to the side.

Turning, she curled her hair behind an ear and held it there as she bent over the table and considered the music choices on his player. It positioned her bare ass directly in his field of vision, right in between his knees. "Where's that paddle?" he muttered. He'd leave *bad girl* in big bold relief on those quivering cheeks and then kiss away every welt.

She tilted her head so he saw a glimpse of her profile, her coy smile. Then she made her music choice. "You Look So Fine" by Garbage, a gritty song about raw love, with a sultry beat and provocative lyrics.

Facing him once more, she came within the span of his knees, the heat of her body so close. He might be the one tied, but he made sure his gaze was a Master's heated appraisal of what belonged to him. When he reached her thighs, he had to clamp down on that power surge through his muscles again. Honey trickled from the sweet flesh of her labia. Slowly, she pivoted and then folded forward, so now her cunt, glistening with that dew, brought a scent that tested his control further. His growl was back, a lethal sound of need.

She let out a purr of approval, the lioness teasing her mate, and came back up just as slow. Straddling one thigh, she rubbed her sex against him, working her hips in a circular dance, then turned to shimmy in front of him, her breasts so close to his face he made a snap at them. She undulated back, an impressive dip of movement, particularly when she pivoted on her heel and brought her ass back against his fully aroused cock. She treated him to a lap dance so thorough he fought not to come. She stroked, rubbed, teased, and then, when he was a breath away from saying the hell with it and turning the chair to kindling, she turned once more to face him. Her exotic eyes fastened on his face, she sank to her knees, her hair brushing over his cock, teasing his balls, his inner thighs.

She dipped her finger in the pre-cum on the head, used it to lubricate her cleavage, and cupped those large, perfect breasts around his shaft. Working him between them, she reminded him vividly of what it had been like to be inside her. Dipping her chin, she swiped him with her tongue, tasting more of that viscous fluid gathered on the head.

"Raina." He'd had enough, and it was in his voice, in every rigid muscle. Her head lifted, her gaze meeting his. Something became very still between them, him staring down at her between his knees, her looking up. She moistened her lips, and he felt that shift, hungered for what it meant. Her endgame had dovetailed into his, and now he had a feeling, whether intended or not, that was how it was meant to be. He'd never wanted to possess anything the way he wanted to own her.

Her expression, poised between animal hunger and a woman's need, showed her desire for his dominance. She wanted him to prove he could master her, no matter how many bindings she put upon him. It just inflamed him further.

"Take me deep. Stretch those fuckable lips of yours."

A feral light flickered in her gaze, lip curling back from those sharp canines as they unsheathed, became fangs. Though mature succubi didn't drink blood, their dormant fangs became visible when they became agitated...or highly aroused. When she bent her head, he closed his eyes as her mouth sealed over him, sliding down, down, down. She took his full length, something a courtesan would know how to do, but this was more than that. Her grip on the base of his cock flexed with convulsive movements, an emotional reaction, a quivering. He wanted to touch her, hold her, but this moment was key. Mastery wasn't about restraints, it was a tango of two minds, a power exchange. Between two minds like theirs, it had the complexity of a game of chess. He thought of the demon who'd enslaved her, and he wanted to kill the bastard. To win this woman's willing submission...it was one of the most valuable treasures in the heavens, the Underworld, or anywhere in between, and should have been cherished as such.

He sucked in a breath as she scored him with her fangs, and he felt her smile against his cock, the fiendish, sexy bitch. The heat of the bindings was lessening as she focused more of her attention on him and her own desire. Though it took some effort with that devil-blessed mouth working his cock, he began to counter with his own magic, an inexorable push against her bindings that loosened them, and then made them let go, absorbed by his energy such that the color changed to bronze and black flame.

She stilled. Her tongue still caressed him, but the rest of her was tuned in to the fact that barbed energy was now crisscrossing over her back, under her arms...around her throat.

It lifted her chin, brought her off him, tilted her head back to look at him. "Come up here," he said.

She rose as those bindings tightened around her breasts, framing them and constricting them for his pleasure. The rope wound around her throat again and again, forming a wide cuff like the corset collar. By the time she was standing, she was nearly wound up in his magic, and he was free, though sparks of her energy still smoked on his skin, little pinpricks like a kitten's claws he was sure she could turn into the talons of a lion in truth. But her attention was riveted on him, her breath short, waiting.

Too short. She swayed and he caught her waist, flexing his hands to draw her attention from the deep well into which her mind was falling. "Breathe," he ordered. "Stay with me, and breathe. I'm not him, Raina. Say it."

"You're not him," she whispered, her gaze clinging to his face.

"I'm taking you now. I'm not waiting another fucking moment."

Pulling her onto his lap, he guided her thighs around him. When he angled his cock and thrust hard into her, he found her all slippery heat. She moaned, leaning back against his hands, her inner muscles spasming against him. Hell, she was as close to coming as he was. He held her on that point of decision, felt her convulse around him, heard the catch of her breath as she raised her head to stare at him again. Her eyes had gone the green of Ireland, with mere flickers of the gold, those thick mink lashes framing them. She was the most beautiful woman he'd ever seen, inside and out, the dark and light intertwined in a way that would keep him searching all the shadows for centuries to understand her.

She was starting to panic, feeling those bindings coupled to the strength of the climax that would take away all control. "Fuck me," she demanded, but her voice broke. She was warring between what she thought she needed to be and what she truly desired.

In answer, he pulled her off him, despite her struggles, her vicious protest. Turning her around to lay against him, he collared her throat with his hand as held her up against his shoulder. Her feet scrambled for purchase, but he stretched out his legs, pinning them between his calves, so she was lying back against him, legs held closed, dependent on his strength to hold her.

His bindings adjusted to the new position. Shifting his hips, and gripping himself with the other hand, he worked himself inside her again, a difficult angle that didn't make contact with her clit, denying her the pleasure of that friction. He pushed her down on him, hard, kept himself there, moving a hand up to squeeze her breast, pinch a nipple. Then he dropped to stroke her clit, denying her the full thrust of his cock as she squirmed and panted, cursed and called him names.

He kept it up until she ran down and figured it out. "Please," she gasped. "Please."

"That's better. Ask me, Raina. Ask me the right way."

The wet mouth of her sex pulled at him like a vise, her backside quivering against him and breasts pressed against his forearm. Fuck, he was dying here, but he wasn't giving up on what he wanted most.

"Accept me as your Master for this moment, Raina," he said, low. "Do it honestly; let yourself have that. Don't be afraid to do it."

He felt her anguish then, the warring of the past with the present, the fear that rose like a dark tide. It was going to take her over, and they would both lose. They weren't quite there yet. Muttering a quiet curse, he shifted his hold, releasing the magic that held her so the bindings disappeared, flickering away like tongues of flame from a bonfire. Flipping her so fast to a front straddle she gasped, he reentered her in one thrust. When she cried out, he held her there, still and tight, his hand gripping her hair so she stared into his eyes.

"No," he said. "He doesn't come between us. I won't allow him to touch your mind, your heart or your soul when you're with me. Not now, not ever."

She gave a short nod, the only acknowledgment, but it was a significant one, because she obviously wanted to mean it. He was used to terrible things happening to others, because that was his world. He would have killed Elceus for harming her, because Elceus had crossed the line. But here, seeing it so personal in her face, it wasn't about balance. It was about his desire to fucking destroy anything that caused her a moment's pain.

She was on a dangerous edge, and she needed him to keep her from falling off the wrong side. Banding his arm around her waist, he slid his hand from her hair to her nape and brought her down to meet his lips. Hot and demanding, his tongue tangling with hers, driving her mind only to desire. As he began to stroke inside of her, he controlled her movements so she was like a doll in his arms. She could only hang on, make tiny, pleading cries, her wet heat clutching him until his release shot forth. She let go a moment before him, so that he swallowed her cries into his own mouth as his body shuddered.

As he plunged into the pleasure of it, his last thought was that, yes, he'd never been so hard, never been so aroused. But most importantly, he'd never felt so closely bonded with a woman as he did at this precise moment. Not in nearly thirteen hundred years.

That was a serious problem.

So he was really good at sex. It didn't mean unicorns would spring out of his backside and the world would be bathed in rainbows. She told herself that, a reality check, when they were done and she was wondering if she was ever going to breathe normally again.

But he had a way of distorting reality. She'd strained against his magic in those climactic moments, sought pain to spice the pleasure. Now he touched her upper thighs where the energy binding had cut. When he rose, holding her around the waist to steady her, he let her feet touch the ground, then surprised her by dropping to one knee and brushing his mouth over those abraded places, using his tongue like an animal salving a wound. His jaw pressed against her mound, and when he passed over her thigh, he laid gentle kisses on her sex, still convulsing from the shattering climax. She held on to his shoulder, not sure what this was, feeling strange about it, but not able to say anything. Then he rose.

"Do you think there's any bacon left from breakfast?"

It was such a change of paradigm, his face so serious, an odd chuckle bubbled up in her. It made her feel better. She wondered if it was calculated. If it was, he was kinder than she'd given him credit for.

"We can go see," she said. Glancing at the clock, surprised to find it close to three, she added, "The rest of the staff is usually upstairs preparing this time of day." Something she needed to do as well, but not quite yet.

"All right." He pulled on the jeans, no underwear, which was distracting enough. Groping for her clothes, she came up with his shirt and her panties. It seemed fairly natural to slide it on, button a couple buttons. She liked his scent.

He glanced at her, stopped. Coming to her, he buttoned a few more buttons, until the panties were fully covered, since the shirt fell to her knees. She noted he was okay with a couple buttons at the top being open so he could gaze down the front fairly easily.

He looked down at the burn marks across his jeans. "You owe me a new pair of pants."

"When they pay top dollar for that effect on the runways? Not a chance."

He rolled his eyes, looped his arm around her neck and pulled her to him. She braced herself on his chest, wondered as he pressed a kiss to the top of her head. Then he dropped a hand and squeezed her ass hard enough to earn a yelp. "Come on, I'm hungry."

One set of stairs shouldn't do her in, but when she reached the landing, she swayed a bit. She'd fed well last night, hadn't fed off his energy this time, merely twining it around them to launch their coupling to an even more intense level, even though she wasn't sure if that had been at all necessary.

He'd filtered the dangerous aspects of the magic just as he had before, almost as an afterthought, as if it was no active threat to him at all. Did he realize what a gift that was to her? Of course not. Unless he'd experienced years of being unable to release during sex, he couldn't really understand. But he didn't have to understand to make it the best experience she'd ever had. Twice in a row.

Now, though, she was wondering if she should have fed. Her legs were shaky because of the workout.

"Here." He presented his back. "Hop on."

Smiling, she looped her arms around his neck as he bent a knee to lower his height. Catching her legs, he lifted her onto his back with a quick hitch. "For such a badass witch, you're short," he observed as he took the winding staircase with ease. "Though nicely top-heavy."

She snorted. "You can't even feel where your wings come out." She pressed against his back. "Are they magical or anatomical?"

"A little of both. Happily, I can feel your tits with no problem at all."

"Barbarian."

He squeezed her thighs where he held them secure on his hips. Her calves were crossed low over his abdomen.

"Let's go to town tomorrow morning," he said.

"What?" She could think of a couple reasons that was a bad idea, neither of which she was going to share with him. "What about our prisoner?"

"He's not leaving the property with our tracers on him," he said, revealing that he was fully aware she'd marked Isaac as well. "Town's less than six miles away. Demons almost always strike at night, so if she doesn't show tonight, there won't be much to do tomorrow. And I get bored easily. I'm sure you have errands you could do in town."

At the kitchen entrance, he let her down but didn't let her go just yet. Instead, he lifted her hand, brushed his lips across her knuckles, giving her a tantalizing sense of moist heat, then pushed her gently ahead of him into the kitchen. As she'd expected, no one was there this time of day. Matilda had already left for the day. Mikhael pulled a container of bacon out of the fridge with a satisfied grunt. He also brought out the container of chocolate-covered strawberries along with some whipped cream and a half bottle of white wine.

"That whipped cream is the real thing," she said, appreciating his consideration of her own appetites.

"Who says you're getting any?"

She punched him in the side and he ignored her, reaching over her to put the containers on the counter with the wine bottle. Then he put his hands to her waist and boosted her onto the cool marble surface, inserting his body between her thighs as he opened the strawberries. Dipping one into the whipped cream, he offered it, but held the treat out of reach, waiting until she put her hands down, parted her lips so he could feed her from his hand.

When he offered the wine, pulling the cork, she took it straight from the bottle. Holding it to the side, she slid her hand up to his neck and brought him down to share. She flirted with his tongue, giving him the taste of strawberries, wine and cream, and his palm curved around her ass to bring her up against his lower abdomen where he was pressed against the counter.

She drew back, giving him a speculative look. "Where are the kitchen knives?"

His gaze didn't leave her face. "Three feet to the left, behind you, just beyond the range of your reach."

"How many are there?"

"Seven. One's missing."

"Probably in the dishwasher from cutting the fruit for brunch. You never let your guard down."

"Sounds like you don't, either, if you're interrogating me when you should be letting me make you incoherent with lust."

"You blew out my brain cells a little while ago. I'm recuperating."

He passed his fingers over her mouth. "Maintaining the protections on this place. On your staff. It takes a lot from you. That's why you don't leave the property."

She stiffened. *Damn it, Li.* The handsome Asian prick bastard.

"I have everything I need here. My protections help them make me a lot of money."

"Money is a means to an end. It's not the end for you. This house, this property, it's top-notch, graceful, beautiful. Much like its mistress. Quality's important to you, but not the price tag. This place represents safety, a haven, a place you've constructed that belongs to you, a world you've made to control all the variables."

She set aside the wine. When he touched her face, trying to draw it back up to him, she resisted. But he insisted, so she glared up at him.

"This place is your law, your morality," he continued, "because whatever it needs for protection, you provide. Its enemy is your enemy."

Lifting her hand to his lips, he pressed his mouth to her palm, and then to her wrist. "That much is true," she said, mollified a bit. She didn't want him to be an enemy, though she was afraid it was eventually going to end up that way.

"Go to town with me tomorrow," he said, making those distracting nips against her flesh. "I'll reinforce your shielding and power here so you don't have to worry about them."

"I can do that part, if you...shield me."

She couldn't believe she'd said it. His head lifted, eyes studying her. "What do you mean?"

She sighed. "That's why I don't go to town...often. Even without releasing the energy, males...get aggressive, distracted. I can't be in public venues, random gatherings of people, because I can't control every impact. I can protect one or two of my staff when they go into town for supplies, but that's because I do it from here, where my magic is strongest."

He nodded. "All right. You handle the shielding here, I'll protect you, give you a glamour. Or an anti-glamour as the case may be." Amusement flitted through his features as he bent to brush her lips.

She kept her eyes open, staring at him. Just like that. *I'll protect you.* "You weren't like this with Ruby."

Bracing his hands on either side of her hips, he put his mouth to her throat. Raina's pulse tripped, but she gripped his shoulders, pushed at him. He held where he was but spoke against her skin. "No, I wasn't. Because that was different. There was a purpose to what I was doing with Ruby."

"And there's no purpose to this?" Her nails curled into his firm skin.

He raised his face to give her his no-bullshit stare. "Is there a reason you want to talk about your best friend, the one I've fucked? What are you fishing for, Raina?"

"Nothing." She told herself to shut up. When he departed, he would be one more link on a chain, the same way she was for him. To make it more than that was the act of a woman with an unguarded heart, demonstrating the naivety of a moonstruck teenager. Him affecting her that way, responding the way he did now, as if she'd lost her mind, made her pissed off at herself. But also at him.

Sliding from the counter, she tossed her hair back and caressed his chest, teasing a nipple as her fingers came to rest on his rib cage. "As lovely as this has been, I need to start getting ready for tonight. I'll see you after."

He caught her wrist, held her there. "I told you not to play that shit with me."

Then stop playing with me as if I'm something special. She only thought it, though; wasn't stupid enough to say it, to expose herself that much. She didn't blame others for her own shortcomings, and he wasn't at fault for this. That magnetism, the attentiveness that made a woman feel as if she were the center of his world, of course raised long-dead wistful yearnings. She merely needed to detach herself to manage those feelings, but he wasn't willing to let her do that.

Tough. He wasn't calling all the shots here. "I'm not pulling anything on you. If you change your mind and don't want to take me to town, fine. You can go slither under a rock somewhere."

Yanking her hand away, she made it three steps before he caught her, his hands closing on her shoulders. That coldness unfurled within her. "Please, don't," she said. "Give me room to breathe."

"No." His fingers flexed on her, and even that simple touch made her body react. She'd never responded to a male the way she responded to him. No, she couldn't trust that thought. Unleashing her nature during sex was a once-in-a-lifetime experience for her. It was no wonder her emotions were getting involved. He'd be gone in a day or two, and that would be that. Until then, he wanted her stripped bare, laid out to him with no shields. That was his price. He demanded a woman's soul, and she wondered how many he'd collected. She'd no doubt every one of them had handed it over without a fight.

When he turned her around, she struck at him, an arc of power that sizzled between them, close enough to burn them both. She felt the pain of it, then it was gone with a breath of frost across her skin, the same frost he brought to her lips, the cool kiss of snowflakes that became moisture from the heat of their mouths. She made a noise of violent protest, but her fingers clutched his arms, his holding her hard around the waist.

"If you need to breathe, Raina," he said against her mouth, "I'll give you breath."

She closed her eyes as he cradled her face in his hands. She'd met him a blink ago. No one could become the breath in your lungs in that short a time. She would figure out how to handle this. After he'd gone away, never to come back.

He didn't kiss her. He just stayed that close to her mouth, teasing them both. She muttered an oath and closed the distance. When she would have made the kiss rough, insistent, his hands on her face gentled it. His lips eased onto hers, stroking and caressing instead of plundering, until the embrace offered the dreamy delight of the rare Southern snowstorm, the cocooning of the world in hushed winter stillness.

When they finally drew back, she wasn't sure who'd broken the kiss. She opened her eyes, stared into his.

"Let me take you to town tomorrow, Raina. We can go shopping. Get ice cream. See a movie."

She blinked, not sure if he was teasing her or not. But the man dressed well, so he obviously could shop. A Dark Guardian...shopping. Eating ice cream.

"When a Southern gentleman was courting a lady, he used to bring his horse and carriage around to take her to town," she said, buying time.

"Actually, the carriage was more for family outings. He brought a two-seater if there was no chaperone. More intimate. Like a Ferrari versus a minivan."

"I'd like to see someone your size get intimate in a Ferrari." Then she brightened. "Can we fly there? Using your wings?"

"No." He gave her an amused look. "I don't reveal my wings to humans. They react badly."

"Oh, all right, then. I suppose we could take the fabulous sports car. Though that seems kind of boring."

His eyes warmed. "Let me see if I can impress you with some other means of transportation, then."

She lifted a shoulder, turned away. This time he let her go, and she took a deep breath as she moved into the hallway, headed for the staircase. Time to face the reality of her day. Reality, period. But she found herself pausing on the steps, looking back at him. He was leaning in the dining room entranceway, watching her, thoughtfully chewing on a strip of bacon. Shirtless, in jeans and bare feet, hair tousled. Her libido didn't have a prayer.

She shoved it down with a ramrod. "A horse and carriage probably wouldn't have worked out anyway," she said casually. "Horses get too nervous around those with demon blood. Which is a shame. I've always wanted to try riding a horse."

"I expect the broom does get a little uncomfortable. Though you have some nice padding on your ass to protect you."

"You—"

He was gone, retreating back to the kitchen before she could inflict boils on him. Or oozing sores. Instead, he left her standing on the stairs with a smile struggling on her face. But the laughter didn't dispel the worry in her heart. He kept her spinning, unable to find a sure footing. She'd never been in that position with a man, and it was unsettling, exhilarating...terrifying. She kept telling herself he was a roller coaster, one that would come back full circle, leaving her with some pleasant memories. But these feelings, this intensity, this fast? It was also possible she might get launched off an unfinished track, leaving her tumbling through empty space, with the promise of only a hard crash and pain.

What she needed was a safety net. But with every touch, every kiss, he kept taking it away.

CHAPTER ELEVEN

*B*eing Monday, she was able to head to bed close to two thirty a.m., an early night. The evening lineup had been regulars for her staff, and she'd played hostess in the parlor as she usually did. She never saw Mikhael, though she thought she felt his regard once or twice as she flirted and reassured, making sure tonight's all-male guest list had their needs met. She supposed he was checking the perimeter, keeping an eye on Isaac, or doing whatever Dark Guardians did. Watching the latest *Real Housewives of Orange County*, for all she knew.

As she shed her clothes, she noticed his shirt still hanging on her dresser where she'd left it. After a pause and a frisson of amusement with herself, she put it on over bare skin. She liked the way it felt, brushing against her that way. Cathair was gone, probably in the boys' rooms, because they fed him Cheetos while they rehashed their evening and fell asleep in front of the TV. She'd find the dust on his feathers in the morning, or shaken on her curtains when he preened, despite her scolding.

Males. Incorrigible, the whole lot of them.

Curling into her quilts, she shut her eyes. Even without her special chamomile mix that Gina kindly left steaming by her bedside, she was asleep in five minutes.

She knew better than to go to sleep without drinking it, but it had been a good evening. No reason to worry about monsters from the past, but that was when they struck, right? The dream started out wonderfully enough. Mikhael was there, his magnificent body, his scent—probably filtering to her from his shirt—those intense eyes. He was in her bed, pushing her back into the quilts, his hands on her thighs. When he shifted his grip to her wrists, she saw a set of black manacles hanging above her. Manacles wet with her blood, from her struggles when she went mad from the confinement. They were suspended from the top of the narrow metal box in which Elceus hung her like meat when he wanted to prove a point. That he could do whatever the hell he wanted to do to her.

She was a witch. She didn't let her dreams take control of her. "No," she snarled, ripping her hands free. The agony was an echo of what it had been. "You're gone. Dead. You can't keep me trapped here anymore."

She bolted out of the dream. The wind of her agitation swept through her room, dousing the candles, plunging her into full darkness. The French doors to the balcony slammed back, making her leap away from the bed, spinning into a corner to fight whatever came at her.

"Easy."

A flame was struck, and she whirled toward it, fists raised. Mikhael relit one of the candles with that brief spark, sat it back down in its holder. He'd been out on the property. She could smell the salt of the marsh on him, the night air, and there were some pale oleander petals on his shoulders, looking like tiny teardrops thanks to the moonlight.

"You all right?" he asked quietly.

She nodded. Rubbed her forehead, then wrapped her arms around herself, taking comfort in that shirt, the one part of the dream that had stuck. He took a step toward her.

"I rescued myself," she said. "I don't need to be rescued."

"Do I look like the first number on the damsel-in-distress speed dial?"

She saw a lot of things when she looked at him. "You stir things up," she said. It wasn't an accusation. Her mind was just as responsible for resurrecting the bastard in her dreams.

"I can calm them down, too."

She raised her attention back to his face. No, he might not be the first on speed dial. But he'd been here when she woke from her nightmare, when he could have been a hundred other places. She'd never had anyone there when she woke from a nightmare.

Crossing the space of her attic room, she walked into his arms. Goddess, he was warm. Strong.

"Do you ever have nightmares?" she asked against his heartbeat.

"Of course not. It's unmanly to dream about harpies tying you down to eat your privates and skin you alive. Even more unmanly to wake up screaming like a little girl. So, no. Absolutely, no."

Nestling her cheek against that broad chest, she continued to listen to the strong, rhythmic thump of his heart. He bent, lifted her in his arms and took her back to the bed, lying down with her. "Sleep," he murmured. "No more nightmares getting past me."

He didn't ask her for details, didn't make her talk. He probably knew the shape of every nightmare that anyone had ever had. He just held her.

On the rare occasion she had nightmares, she usually didn't sleep the rest of the night. This time, she didn't remember much after two or three minutes in Mikhael's arms. When she woke, sun was streaming in through the open French doors, and there was a note on the pillow next to her.

Our ride arrives at ten. Move that sexy ass or no ice cream for you. Wear something I'll like.

Since he'd promised he'd provide the dampening spell that would keep her from causing four-car pileups in town, and he was a big, bad Dark Guardian, she was happy to test the strength of his spellwork— and his self-control. She donned a pair of snug jeans, low-heeled boots and a pale gold knit top with a rolled off-the-shoulder neckline. The top hugged her curves just like the jeans. The styles were sharp, tailored and classy, but maximized all of her assets so she was guaranteed to cause an erection at a hundred-yard distance. Unless Mikhael did his job, which meant only his cock would be affected. She looked forward to seeing that. Putting emerald and gold studs in her double-pierced ears, she clipped her unruly hair back and donned bangle bracelets that gave her a touch of whimsy. Cathair landed on his perch and regarded her with bright eyes.

"Move your ass, wench," he informed her.

"I'm going to turn his testicles into golf balls and use a five iron on them," she promised herself, giving her familiar a gimlet eye. "You stop encouraging him."

Cathair chirped. She came and stroked his head, bent to let him rub his beak along the corner of her mouth, a quick buss that always made her smile. "The perimeter's reinforced, but stay here, keep an eye on things. Find me if there's trouble."

"Always trouble. Trouble, trouble, trouble. Headed toward trouble."

"With a smile on my face." She flicked a scarf at him as he ruffled his feathers and imitated a sneeze.

When she reached the main floor, she didn't expect to see her staff awake and at the windows. Most were still wearing their pajamas, which suggested one had come down to pilfer a snack and discovered something that sent them all tumbling down here like excited puppies. Even the usually indifferent Matilda was pushed in between Saul and Ana. Luke gave the cook a wide and wary berth.

Glancing over his shoulder, Li gave a low wolf whistle, bringing the others around as well. "Pulling out the whole arsenal, aren't you?"

She tossed her hair with exaggerated sex appeal. "I don't know what you're talking about."

Gina giggled. "He's pulled out his arsenal as well. It's a horse, but not a horse, Raina. There's magic around it. *Fae* magic."

Raina knew her own eyes widened a little bit at that, but she reached for the doorknob. She would not be caught goggling out the window.

Saul gave her a wink. "Remember, you're not impressed at all. Make him work for it."

"Work those jeans as well," Ana advised. "Make him slobber at your feet like a hound."

"You all can go back to bed," she said reprovingly. "I don't want to see any dark circles under your eyes when entertaining tonight."

Still, an almost girlish smile played around her lips as she opened the door. No matter her earlier, darker thoughts, it was hard to resist the drug of infatuation.

God and Goddess, they were right. Mikhael leaned against the old-fashioned hitching post on the front lawn. It was an affectation, except right now he could have put it to functional use. Well, maybe not. Raina didn't think the creature with him would consent to being tethered in any way. The black horse was taller than Mikhael and wide of chest, all rippling, gleaming muscle. The scent of the shore hit her immediately, his origins evidenced by the seaweed and shells tangled in his long mane. The only tack he wore was a short saddle pad cinched in place. As Ana had said, there was an *otherness* to the creature, in the way the crimson eyes appraised her, like human male eyes. When he shifted, she noticed the hooves sparked against the ground, magic escaping from the simple movement.

Everything she knew about magical creatures said she was looking at a kelpie, a creature rumored to shift into a human form to seduce a woman onto his back. Or it could stay in horse form and coax children up there, only to gallop into a body of water and drown them. Hopefully those were vicious rumors put out by anti-kelpie hate groups.

Mikhael's eyes coursed over her. He lingered over thigh and hip, enjoyed an especially long pause on her breasts, then moved up to her throat and face. "Turn," he said.

He was so good at those one-word commands, the ones that made her pulse trip. She gave him an arch look and pivoted, shifting her hips to good effect as she came back around.

"Are you wearing anything under those jeans?"

"A lace thong," she said. "Denim seams chafe."

"You don't dress like you want to go to town," he noted. "I'm thinking of at least ten things that could keep us right here."

"I'm sure most of them are illegal, and you know I strive to be a law-abiding citizen. Besides, these are my going-out clothes. Are you backing out?" The thought was disappointing, almost crushingly so. She wanted to go to town with a lover, flirt and play with him. He'd all but promised, and if she had to get petulant about it, she would.

"Mmm." There was a glint in his eye. "I might have to expand the scope of my spell to cover the things I'll be tempted to do to you in public."

"Think you're a powerful enough sorcerer for that?"

"If I wanted to fuck you senseless on the steps of town hall, the good citizens would be none the wiser. Is that powerful enough for you?" That glint became even more devilish. "Of course, knowing you, you wouldn't mind them catching a glimpse."

She tsked at him. "A gentleman caller doesn't use bad language around a lady."

"No one has ever called me a gentleman. And if we're going to work on manners, I think we'll start on yours." He glanced at the horse. "This is Atlas. Since he's a kelpie, part of your whole energy-sucking clan, your blood won't upset him."

The creature snorted, gave her that appraising look again, only this time Mikhael made a noise, an unmistakable warning. It set off a strange fluttering in her chest to see Mikhael staking his territory against another male. One would think being used as a demon's sex slave during her formative years, turning tricks and then running a bordello, would have completely stamped out her romantic side. But she loved *Titanic* as much as ever.

This was just a day with a casual lover, she reminded herself. But so far it was a really good day. "Aren't kelpies the ones who drown people?"

"He has the day off from that." Taking a handful of mane, Mikhael swung on in one lithe move. "And he owed me a favor."

Atlas gave a snort as if that was only a partial truth, and lifted his feet off the ground, cutting a circle that lashed Mikhael's leg with his tail. It was a pretty display, but also a fairly intimidating one. However, Raina had never backed down from a male in her life. She wasn't going to start now. When Mikhael extended his hand, she approached without hesitation. The warm approval in his eyes made her feel ridiculously pleased.

As Mikhael lifted her up, settling her on his lap, the smell of the ocean became even stronger. She wondered if she would hear its song if she laid her head against Atlas's neck, like listening to a conch shell.

"I admit it," she said. "I'm impressed. Even better than the Ferrari."

"This is the Ferrari, with attitude."

"You seem to like attitude," she teased, sliding her arm beneath his to curve it around his back and hold on. The other hand she placed on his, curled in Atlas's mane. The seaweed and shells were wet. Interesting.

"So it would seem." Putting his arm around her waist, he secured her close to him. "He likes to start out with a bang, but he'll slow down after he feels like he's awed you enough. I won't let you fall."

"Of course you won't." She drank in the energy. For all intents and purposes, she was on a horse. "Can we run? I want to see what it's like to gallop."

Mikhael gave her an intent look, eyes showing his deep pleasure at her enthusiasm. She needed to carry oxygen when he was around.

"You heard the lady, Atlas. Show her what it's like to ride the wind."

~

Atlas took off, a haze of sparks showering off his mane and more jetting from under his hooves, licking her ankles with the after burn. He moved down her drive like nothing in the world could stop him. Mikhael held his seat with strong thighs and kept her close, so she relaxed and moved with the motions of his body and the horse. She let her head fall against his chest, turning her face to the wind. Trusting him, she let go of the mane and his arm, reaching out to it with both hands.

For a moment, she knew just how Rose felt on the prow of *Titanic*.

She laughed into that wind, felt it blow through her clothes, caress her skin. The roar of its passing, the thunder of Atlas's hooves, Mikhael's breath against her temple; it was a rushing symphony and she wanted to twirl in it like a butterfly. When Mikhael called to Atlas to ease up, and they moved into a canter, then a trot, she was grinning like a fool.

"That was incredible," she said. "Can I... Is he okay with being stroked?"

"Most males are."

She made a face at him, aware he was looking at her like a creature he'd never seen before, but she didn't care. Her hair was probably a tangled thicket, and her shirt now had horse hair on it. It didn't matter a bit. She stroked her fingers along Atlas's neck. "Thank you. That was marvelous."

He snorted, sidled into a prancing strut. She bit back a smile. The male animal was always the same, no matter the species. "He obviously speaks our language."

"Kelpies understand all languages, regardless of the origins. Don't know where they got that ability, but they probably pleased a Fae queen somewhere along the line and she gave them that gift. Or it was part of a curse. Fae like to do that. Give a gift that comes with a high cost. They're masters at the balance game themselves, though they're a bit more capricious about it."

"Is he coming into town with us? You'll really have to expand your shield on us then." She tugged on the mane, teasing the kelpie, such that he did some more sidling to delight her.

Mikhael snorted. "Pull my hair, see where it gets you."

She made a grab to do just that and he caught her arm, twisting it behind her back. He did it gently, but with enough strength that it arched her up to him. Taking a biting kiss of her lips, he teased her mouth, stroking her tongue with his until her body quivered. "You're irresistible," he said.

She told herself he was a charming lover, but Mikhael wasn't charming at all. He was honest, which had an appeal all its own. So she touched his face, not sure how to respond. Her, a madam who'd received slews of suggestive compliments.

"He'll drop us off just outside town," Mikhael answered her question. "You'll have to make do with my boring Ferrari for the remainder of the trip. It's not wise to get a kelpie around lots of humans. They start looking like dinner."

"He can eat the librarian. Ramona says she's mean. Though, in all fairness, every time Ramona goes in there, an entire stack gets knocked over, or all the books get re-shelved in the order of Ramona's preference instead of by the library's system."

"Noted." His arm was still around her waist, the other hand on Atlas's mane as the kelpie moved in a reasonably sedate walk. Now that they'd emerged from the woods surrounding her place, they were enjoying the winding road to town, most of which was surrounded by protected marshland. Beyond its expanse, she could see the waterway and the lighthouse on the nearby barrier islands. She liked the open-space look of it. Sometimes she walked this far, within distance of town but not actually there, melting back into the trees for the occasional motorist. Though the road was quiet now, Atlas stayed in the grass right-of-way, preferring the natural road to the paved one.

"I spoke to Isaac this morning. He didn't know anything about the demon's purpose for the soulkeeper, the part he might play in it. He had nothing useful to add."

"You didn't hurt him." When she fixed a fierce eye on him, he gave her breast a pinch that made her yelp and slap at him.

"Tempted, but no." Mikhael frowned. "Underneath the cunning, he's piss-himself terrified. He wants to run, but he knows he's an expendable pawn. So he's here, hopping from one foot to the other, knowing only one thing for sure—she's going to come for him."

Mikhael glanced down at her. "I'd like to put him somewhere else, but he's left us no choice. His track will lead to you first, no matter where I take him from here."

"We'll be fine. I've been protecting this place by myself for a long time."

"You won't be doing it alone right now."

"You probably consider your arrogance a good thing, don't you?"

"It gets you worked up, and I like seeing you worked up. Though being around you is sometimes like plowing a field full of adders."

Now she did smile. "That's an old legend. Wasn't the wizard trying to win the maiden's hand when he did that?"

"Yes, but the maiden didn't symbolize the adders, so that wasn't exactly the purpose of the comparison."

"Keep it up. I'll bribe Matilda to hide vile things in your croissants." She curled her fingers into his shirt, laid her cheek on his chest, feeling the motion of the kelpie beneath them. Mikhael was warm as always, and had that fire-burning smell. In his jeans, boots and untucked shirt, which she was sure hid a weapon or two, he looked like he'd stepped out of a rugged men's magazine, but men with a sense of style. The Ferrari, the tailored, high-quality clothing... Mikhael did like material things, but not to excess. He could have broken the chair yesterday, but he hadn't. She was pretty sure it was because he appreciated the quality of fine things as well.

Or that he'd known how important it was to let her have her way, to build her trust in his mastery of her. That level of perception in a male was discomfiting, enough that she almost wished he'd destroyed the chair.

"Well, fine," she said, not wanting to appear to be giving in to what had obviously been an order. "The longer he's here, the longer he's exposed to a different way of living. Even if he doesn't want to stay, I can find him accommodations elsewhere that are a better situation for him."

He brushed his lips over her hair. "As I said from the beginning, don't get too attached. There's a lot of dark corridors to that little weasel."

"You're condemning him before you know him."

"You don't know him any better than I do. We're both going on gut. As I told you before, your gut is tempered by your personal experiences. Your empathy is influenced by it."

The kelpie came to a halt. Raina saw the black Ferrari parked beneath a live oak on a gravel apron, built there to allow tourists to stop and take pictures of the panoramic view. When Mikhael swung down, she closed her hand in Atlas's mane. "I don't appreciate the patronizing tone."

He put his hand on the horse's nose, stilling him, though Atlas's body quivered. "Don't lash out at me because you don't like where this might be headed for Isaac."

"You could alter where it's headed."

"I can't make his choices for him."

"Well, that's just dandy for you, isn't it? You get to enforce, bring death and destruction, but you never have to think, to choose, to risk. That's the job, right? Like every other cop who only thinks in a tunnel, you don't see anything else. It's all black and white."

"If you spend too long in those shades of gray, you forget what black and white truly is." He tightened his hand on her leg. "Don't do this, Raina. We both know the reality of the situation, no matter the outcome. Don't let it spoil the day."

"I wasn't the one who picked a fight."

"I stated the obvious. You reacted emotionally."

"You want to see an emotional reaction?" Her gaze flashed with dangerous intent. Atlas snorted, rolled his eyes. Mikhael plucked her off the horse, set her on her feet.

Since he'd expect magic, she went with the short jab that should have caught him right in his self-righteous mouth. Instead, he caught her fist, closing his fingers over her knuckles.

"Do you anticipate everything?" she asked bitterly.

"You don't want to be around the day I don't."

Raina stared up at him. A novice often made this mistake with a client. She chattered away, making it all about her, her own reactions, and forgot to pay attention to his. Mikhael's expression was set, impassive, but there was tautness around his mouth. It reminded her of the previous day, the unlikely thought that she might have bruised his feelings. Did she have the ability to actually hurt him?

Testing it, she swallowed her pride. "I apologize. You didn't deserve that, not entirely. But you being cruel to me isn't going to change my hope for him, either."

His expression altered, a subtle shift, but it eased the tension their argument had caused. It also left her floored. Her opinion *did* matter to him. Just how casual was this relationship, really? It was a dangerous thought. Thank goodness, he spoke, allowing her to push it away.

He lifted a shoulder. "I do bring death and destruction."

"You bring balance," she reminded him gently. "But you don't need to worry about me. If something happens, it's because I wasn't strong or fast enough. I don't rely on any one else for protection. That's no one's job but my own."

"Because as hard as it is to shoulder that alone, it's easier than trusting someone else?"

"Yes." Might as well give him the straight answer.

He still held her fist, but in a different kind of hold. "No one came for you, when he took you."

"After my father was killed, there was no one else who knew where to start looking." It was reality, and shouldn't cause an ache in her throat to say it, so many years later.

He moved a step closer, and was against her. When he cupped her face, she closed her eyes. Turning toward his palm, she pressed her lips there, rested her weight on his strength. "Raina," he said. "If something ever happened, I would come for you."

She put her hand over his thick wrist, evidence of his skill with so many different weapons, and squeezed. She couldn't let this much longing into her heart. She was strong enough to bear loss, but not the uncertain potential of gain. "How about we start with taking me into town?" she said lightly. "That should be enough heroics for the day. Especially if we have to deal with tourists."

~

Though it was surreal, she wasn't surprised to find Mikhael was a good companion. He patiently followed her from window to window and into the quaint shops that offered antiques, furniture, clothes, jewelry and knick-knacks to tempt tourists or self-indulging locals alike. Since Li, Gina, Matilda and a fleet of delivery vendors handled the needs of her house, she was merely delighted to have the opportunity to browse like anyone else.

Mikhael was also as good as his word. She didn't get a second glance from anyone they passed, his chameleon spellwork flawless. She almost didn't feel it, except for an occasional sense of warm air passing over her skin. When she glanced into a decorative mirror in passing, she saw an average-looking woman, attractive but not excep-tionally so. She suspected he had a similar dissembling cast over himself, since the man blended like John Cena at a reunion of the Oz Munchkins, yet no woman who passed them tripped over her own feet or walked smack into a parking meter. Pleasingly enough, though, he looked as he always looked to her. She wondered if he'd excluded her from the spell to give her that pleasure. It was both an arrogant and amusing thought. He didn't underestimate the impact of his looks, that was for certain. She liked that, because she was no different about her own. It was what it was, an asset to be enjoyed, but never to be mistaken as a substitute for true substance.

At the next antique store they visited, they were greeted by a clacking noise, followed by a piercing train whistle. The proprietor had an old model train set in operation, the cars trundling along the track cordoning several displays. While Mikhael slowed down to take a look, she went to the second level to check on a nineteenth-century Louis XV walnut armoire that had caught her eye. As she wandered through that upper level, she caught glimpses of him below, through the array of merchandise. What she saw intrigued her enough she came to the rail, leaning on it to watch him.

The set had ten cars. He'd taken hold of the controls and was putting the train through its paces, switching tracks, stopping and reversing, hooking up another car. An older man sitting on a bench nearby was discussing it with him, apparently a train enthusiast. Fasci-nated, she watched him and Mikhael enter a deep conversation, where terms like scale, track radius, gauges and steam vs diesel reached her ears.

Mikhael Roman liked toy train sets. Absorbing that astonishing fact, she bought a bag of caramel creams dipped out of an oak barrel of bulk candy, and then drifted down the stairs. Taking up a discreet position, she leaned against an old metal light post being used as a store display.

The older man was talking about how he'd built sets with his grandfather. Mikhael was courteous, attentive. He was listening, not just patronizing the man until he could get away, and even offered some feedback of his own about his experience with steam engine sets. Then he paused, glanced over his shoulder and found her there.

"Time to move on to the next store?" he asked. The other man followed his gaze, his wrinkled face creasing in a smile.

"Always a good idea to keep them moving, son," he advised. "The longer she's in a store, the more she takes a mind to buy."

Raina arched a brow but let that pass as Mikhael motioned to the store proprietor. "I'd like this set," he said, producing a wallet and handing over cash that covered the price. "No change. Please box it up and I'll have someone return for it by the end of the day."

The store owner nodded, returning with a receipt Mikhael pocketed, then he slipped a hand under Raina's elbow. "Going to get the armoire?" he asked.

She hadn't thought he was paying any attention to her whereabouts, but she should have known better. "Thinking about it. She wants four thousand. I gave her an offer of thirty-two hundred and my number if she decides to take it. With those three mirrors, it would be perfect in one of our period playrooms."

"Or your bedroom." Mikhael held the door for her, his hand at the small of her back to guide her out.

"It's not nice to read a woman's mind, Mikhael. We like to be a mystery. I had no idea you liked toy trains. You could have knocked her down on that price."

"It was fair. And it's model trains or model railways. They're not toy trains."

"True. I've never seen a movie where one was set up under a tree to delight the children on Christmas morning." She chuckled as he gave her a not-so-gentle pinch on her ass. She pushed him in retaliation, but slid closer when he gathered her under his arm, continuing their stroll down the sidewalk. "Do you want me to send Li to pick it up? They'd probably enjoy playing with it, if you aren't as covetous of your toys as Lucifer."

"Li doesn't need to fetch it. Once it's boxed up, the package will disappear and the manager will remember someone came for it. Normally, I'd send it to my cache in the Underworld, but I can reroute it to your house. There are trains scaled for outdoor garden size, you know." He glanced down at her. "You could add it to your landscape design. It'd be a good mix with the whimsical bronzes."

"I might need a consultant to help me with that. I don't know a lot about toy trains. Model railways," she amended. "As far as your new friend back there, why is it men always assume that a woman is using *his* money to shop?"

"Because a man will pay for a woman's company, in a variety of ways. Not always the direct one."

She snorted. "Well, that's honest."

"It's primal." Mikhael shrugged. "A woman has to know a man can take care of her to be worthy of her company, of her offspring. Doesn't matter how times have changed, whether she intends to have children, or how capable she is of doing for herself, she will still instinctively, chemically, gravitate toward the man she knows she can rely upon for protection if needed. Unless there's an overriding social or genetic factor in her makeup that prefers him to be the weaker one in their relationship."

"Why is it I so often have the urge to Taser you?"

"From a certain genus of female, I think that's considered a sign of affection." He eyed her bag of caramels.

"Would you like one?" she asked sweetly.

"You just want the sadistic pleasure of saying no when I ask."

"You don't know everything." Unwrapping one, she lifted it to his mouth, brushed her fingers over his lips in a way that heated his gaze. "I would have bought you a train set. Just to prove I'd take care of *you*, if I was so inclined."

"And are you?"

"You're too much of a horse's ass for me to get such an idiotic notion. But I don't mind indulging your fantasies of being a kept man."

He chuckled, gave her another pinch, this time a gentle one on the curve of her breast just under her arm. She elbowed him in his hard stomach. He kept his arm around her waist, but she slid hers around him as well, thumb hooked in the waistband of his jeans. The ripple of powerful muscle against her upper torso was a pleasant feeling.

As he guided her past a sidewalk display outside a knick-knack store, she put out her hand, making the colorful mini-flags on display flutter in passing. "So the items in your vault can be called to you when needed."

"Yes. Basic conjuring."

"It's still a pretty impressive distance," she observed. "Say you're in the forest, and there are no innocent bunnies or fawns for you to terrorize. You get bored. You call up your train set, lay it out on the ground and have at it?"

"Once, when I was in the Appalachians, pixies came out to play with it. They put pebbles and flowers into the cars. A very displeased frog."

She looked up in time to see the muscles tighten in his face in a way that was almost a smile. "They can be hyper, so I had to calm them enough they could ride on the cars without knocking them over. It was tricky to do without offending them. They're pretty sensitive."

"What happens if they get offended?"

"You get no sleep at all, because every time you drift off, they pull your hair or stick a bug up your nose."

"Good thing you don't sleep much, because you don't excel at being inoffensive."

"You just don't appreciate me the way they do."

"Hmm." She scoffed. "So how big is this depository of yours?"

"Gold digger."

"Just checking out my security options."

By early afternoon, they'd hit most of the stores along the riverfront and found a place to get a sandwich. He paid for her lunch, waving away her money. While they were eating on the restaurant's porch, he nodded to the old movie theater across the street. "Want to go see a movie? Next show starts in a few minutes."

She followed his gaze. The Aimway was a vintage nostalgia theater, a small place with a scrolled woodwork facade and movie posters framed in antique gold. Mostly they showed movies already out on DVD, but Ramona said that was part of the fun, going to see favorite movies the way they'd originally been viewed. She'd been ecstatic about watching *Gone with the Wind* on the big screen. Raina would have liked to see that one, but had made the usual excuses. Though she expected Ruby and Ramona had guessed why Raina didn't leave the house much, she preferred not to talk about it. A woman had her pride, after all.

Collecting their sandwich garbage, she tossed it away and waited, looking across the street at the theater facade while he left a tip on the table. When he joined her on the sidewalk, he laid an arm over her shoulders, fingers caressing her upper arm.

"Have you ever been in a theater?"

"Of course." Not. She'd seen movies in which people went to the movies. He gave her a look.

"Let's go see this one, then."

She blinked up at the marquee. "It's *New Moon*. One of the Twilight saga. Teenage girl angst?"

He shrugged. "Have you seen it?"

"No."

"Neither have I. We've got time, and if we don't like it, we can leave. You're interested in vampires, right?" He tapped her nails, the vampire design in red and black.

"You really need to be as unobservant as most males."

"Raina. You haven't seen a movie in a theater. Right?"

At her twitch of assent, his fingers touched her jaw, making her look at him. "Then let's go. And don't lie to me. Not now, not ever."

The squeeze he gave her this time was a firm warning, one that sent a reaction skittering through the parts of her that responded to this side of him too much.

They weren't alone in the theater, since it was a little cool for beach swimming and there were always tourists interested in the novelty of the place, but the crowd wasn't so large she felt claustrophobic. Regardless, she was glad Mikhael put them in the back row, though it was probably because he didn't like people sitting behind him. He took the aisle seat, letting her sit on the inside so he could stretch out his long legs.

Despite their light lunch, he'd bought her a small popcorn and drink, a bag of chocolate-covered raisins. He'd gotten himself a sleeve of Reese's peanut butter cups and a giant Dr Pepper. When the previews started, she leaned forward, delighted by the size of the screen, the surround sound. However, a blink or two later, she was getting annoyed. Tourists were checking e-mail and phone messages on their hand-helds, the various flashes of light distracting her as they texted. Probably sending one another inane messages like: *Hey, I'm at the movies. I got Milk Duds.*

She wrinkled her nose and tried to ignore it. They'd stop when previews were done. Maybe.

Mikhael stretched an arm behind her seat, his sprawling, lazy predator pose. As he did, a tiny spiral of energy flickered from him. Instantly, all those lights went out. She registered various levels of consternation, a few people rising to go to the lobby to see if perhaps they'd lost their signal. She leaned back into the span of his arm.

"You blocked them?" she whispered.

"I fried their batteries. Your local electronics vendor can send me a thank you."

She regarded his profile in the dim light. He was balling up a Reese's peanut butter cup wrapper in one hand, his other idly caressing her shoulder beneath the rolled neckline as he watched the previews.

"I might decide to like you, Mikhael," she murmured. "Maybe."

When he gave her a warm sidelong glance, the movie started, so she settled down in the curve of his body to watch. At the tea parties she'd held, she'd heard about the Twilight movies from women with teenage daughters. Despite her comment about the teen angst, she found herself unexpectedly swept up in it.

Elceus had kidnapped her when she was on the cusp of being a teenager, when she was learning about crushes. Since she'd had one or two before that critical turning point, she now vaguely recalled the way the heart pounded at new love, how everything was about him, nothing in the whole universe more important.

As a succubus, she was very susceptible to emotional input—when she allowed it. Even so, she knew she'd become more immersed in the male beside her than she'd believed possible. With him, she had all the elements of a crush. The heart-fluttering anxiety, the anticipation. She was hyper-aware of his arm on the seat behind her, how it slid down her upper arm, his knuckles touching the side of her breast, then slowing there, shortening the stroke, telling her that it wasn't incidental contact.

He touched her face, her neck, guiding her face toward him with firm purpose. She laid her head on his shoulder as he pressed it there, as his face dominated her vision. He covered her mouth with his, pushing her back into the seat, making the kiss deep, long and wet. Warm. His other hand cupped her breast fully, kneaded and stroked. Then he slid his palm down her stomach, letting his fingers firmly grip her hip, thumb brushing the crease between it and her thigh, intimately close to other things. They were making out in a movie theater, like teenagers, and she was loving every moment of it.

Mikhael had never imagined anyone with her experience could be so responsive. She was saturated by sexuality, nothing new to her. Yet everything in her craved and yearned and hungered, as if she couldn't get enough. Turning that mirror on himself, though, he'd been in hundreds of beds. Or rather, he'd been in hundreds of women, since often no beds were involved. But with her, it felt different. He wanted to stay in this darkened movie theater, teasing her lips, fondling her breasts, getting her more and more hot and bothered and himself the same way, all day long. He could touch her for hours. He didn't give a rat's ass about Isaac or his mission at the moment. It was just all her.

The movie had aroused her, such that when her eyes flickered toward him, calculating, measuring, desiring, there was no way he could pass up that opportunity. Not when he wanted it just as badly.

"Part your legs," he muttered against her mouth. She obeyed, making that tiny, pleading noise in the back of her throat she did when he issued a command. He slid his hand between the heat of her thighs, stroked her, knowing the panties were wet underneath thin denim. Her hand tightened on the chair, the other against his side, fingernails digging into him through his shirt.

He delved deeper into her mouth. He did want to protect her, care for her, buy her things even though she had a whole houseful of things. He suddenly understood the cultures where men brought items to the doorstep of a chosen bride, piling up skins and trinkets as proof he would do anything, give her anything, to make her his. It wasn't about the things. It was about what he wanted to give.

Raina didn't need things. She needed someone she could trust, someone who would be her equal and maybe a little bit more than that at certain times, who could provide her support when her responsibilities became too heavy, who could play with her or overpower her; whatever was needed so she didn't have to handle every damn thing alone.

While he'd been oddly touched by her amusing offer to buy him things, to take care of *him*, he'd seen that side of her with her staff. When she truly committed herself, gave her heart, she was as fierce as any male warrior. No one would harm what was hers, unless it was over her dead body. A thought he didn't particularly care to dwell upon, and then it was driven out of his head as she slid her hand over his thigh to cup his balls and erection. Her thumb stroked him, fingers tugging at the button of his jeans, not to open them, but to convey want and need. He rocked the heel of his hand over her clit, and the friction of the denim drove her even higher, so her hand convulsed. He was going to use that dissembling spell and take her right here in the movie theater.

No, he wasn't. While tempting, he wanted her to have the real experience, not one altered by magic. So he eased up, stroking her hair, tightening his fingers in it to bring them back apart. Her lips were swollen, eyes filled with that hazy desire that made him think of her twined in her sheets naked, that lush body revealed to him in its full glory.

He pressed her head back to his shoulder, squeezing her fingers before he laid her hand lower on his thigh, holding it there. She smiled against his shoulder at his self-restraint, but her fingers also closed over his thigh. An uncertain little sigh lifted her shoulders. She was smart enough to realize this was stepping outside the borders of a casual, opportunistic liaison. He knew it was something he'd never felt, which alarmed him enough to keep it to himself, for various reasons. For one thing, women tended to get all sorts of strange ideas when a man said things like that out loud.

However, based on what he knew of Raina, her reaction would probably be total horror.

CHAPTER TWELVE

"*I*'ve been marinated in teenage girl hormones."

Raina laughed, her green-gold eyes sparkling at him. As they came out of the theater, they found the day had become more overcast, but in a pleasant way. The breeze flirting along the sidewalk threatened an afternoon storm, but it was still far enough off that the pedestrian traffic could risk continued trawling.

"If you start giggling or having fits of melodrama, I'll rush you to the doctor for a high octane testosterone shot right away." She sighed, did a twirl on the sidewalk. It sent a wave of sex demon energy floating in all directions. Mikhael's spellwork had to work double time to zap it. At times the sexuality she exuded hit high peaks. As accomplished as he was, he had to stay on his toes to modulate it. Thinking about the power of the shields she put into her house to protect her staff and her clients, he didn't wonder why she stayed close to home.

"I think you got doused the same way I did. But it looks good on you."

She smiled, a mischievous gypsy temptress. She came back to his side to take his hand. "I admit, it did make me feel girlish and moony. I think that's why the movies are so popular. Women lose that side of themselves over time; not a lot of chances to indulge it. Which is sad, because it's more fun to indulge when you're an adult. When you're a teenager, the hormones can be pretty horrific and intense. So I heard."

"Never experienced them yourself?"

"I was enslaved to a demon by then," she commented dryly. "There wasn't a lot of room for them. When they happened, they manifested as homicidal rage."

He squeezed her hand. Then swung her behind him as a loud clattering disrupted the normal shopping noises. Locating the problem, he eased his hold. An outdoor display at a shop across the street had collapsed, sending inventory in all directions. Rubber balls with happy faces painted on them bounced into the street, hitting cars, rolling beneath them. One safely reached their side, coming to a stop against the foundation of the blown glass shop. Raina retrieved it, then returned to his side. "My hero, protecting me from the invasion of misfit toys. Apparently, I'm going to get to introduce you to Ramona."

Raina gestured toward the store. As he read the sign— Toys, Tea, Herbs and Magic—she grinned. "Come on. You'll enjoy this."

He guided her across the street, eying the cars who slowed while she gathered up balls. Since other pedestrians were helping as well, Raina expected the vehicles would have stopped regardless. However, whether his appearance was disguised or not, enough of his indomitable nature penetrated that no one dared even a mildly impatient expression, let alone a rudely blown horn.

She and Ruby had thought Ramona's name for the store was too straightforward, but they'd been wrong. The amalgamation drew visitors and locals alike. Her witch friend was also an agent of chaos, so something fascinating was always happening within or without, like a collapsing display. As they came up on the curb, a dozen little kaleidoscope pinwheels were still spinning on the concrete. Mikhael helped her corral those, amusing her enough that she didn't use a discreet burst of broom magic to sweep them up into a tidy pile.

"Here, let me take those. Thanks so much." Ramona had shoved a gargoyle doorstop under the display's corner to precariously balance it, but she had a placid look on her face as she moved toward them. Since such catastrophes were a daily occurrence for her, she never got flustered by them.

Today she was wearing a faded lavender T-shirt that said *Embrace the Magic* amid a spray of glitter Raina was sure would come off in the wash and cover everything she owned. She and Gina got along famously, of course. She also wore a long skirt with bell tassels that chimed pleasantly, and when she'd tapped the doorstop under the display, it had been with the toe of a zebra-striped sneaker. The ensemble was a fashion nightmare, but Ramona's enormous lavender-blue eyes, her wealth of streaming blond hair, and lithe, pixie figure pulled it off. She was an Amy Brown fairy come to life.

As she reached out to help them with her fugitive inventory, Ramona started. *"Raina."*

She'd forgotten all about the dissembling magic, but it still surprised her that Ramona hadn't recognized her until they touched. They were linked by blood, coven sisters. It indicated how effective the magic was. Guardians were too damn impressive. If supreme arrogance wasn't part of the packaging, she might be tempted to compliment him.

Ramona's eyes had widened to saucers. "You're in town."

Raina had tried to make light of what Li had told Mikhael about how little she left the property, but hearing the utter shock in Ramona's voice scuttled that. She really needed to teach her very small group of friends to have better poker faces.

"You make it sound like aliens landed," Raina said irritably.

"I would be less surprised by that." Then Ramona's gaze shifted to Mikhael. "He's not what he seems, either. Who is he?"

A warm flutter of energy, and Raina knew Mikhael had modulated the spellwork, allowing Ramona to see him as he was. Not the best idea, because her affable expression instantly turned dark as a stirred hornet's nest. "We know him. We don't like him."

Her attention went back to Raina, then to him again, reminding Raina of an owl clock. "Right?"

"Well...he's different. Here for a different purpose. It's complicated." In short, a big *not now* silent communication.

Ramona lifted a brow. "Okay, I'm confused. Normal for me, but really confused."

"Excuse me." A tall stranger had approached with an armful of stuffed bears on toy bicycles. When Mikhael's gaze sharpened on him, the stranger returned the look with a steady one of his own, his eyes the gray of twilight fields. "I believe these are yours, miss?"

Ramona turned around. "Hey, yes, thanks. Yes, those are mine." When her attention lifted, she seemed to get a little captured in his gaze.

"Miss?"

"Oh, yes. Hi."

"Hello." He gave her an odd look.

"Sorry. Something odd...about your aura. You're new in town," she said.

The stranger looked like he was reading something from Ramona as well, but more detailed, like an intricate physics text. Raina also detected something different about him, but Mikhael seemed to have a better sense of what. She shifted closer to Ramona's back.

The gray eyes never left Ramona's face. After a moment, his expression cleared, though the stranger still looked vaguely amazed. "Yes. Just passing through."

"Oh, well, then. The café around the corner has the *best* grilled cheese sandwiches. I know, I know. You're going to say, '*Grilled cheese sandwiches, really?*' But I'd take them over the fanciest food anywhere. They're like the double-decker of all cheese sandwiches. I was about to go there for lunch. Why don't we go together and you can tell me all about yourself?"

Ramona moved back into the store, taking him with her, still chattering. She tossed a glance back at Raina that said, *Gorgeous hot guy on the hook; we'll talk later about why the hell you're hanging out with Ruby's Dark Guardian, since I know you can't talk right now.*

"Should we leave her alone with him?" Raina stared after the male. He could be a librarian, tall, lean, quiet, the neatly cut hair. But then there were those fathomless eyes, the dangerous tip-off.

"Yes, he's fine. He's not here for her. And when they're not here for you, they're very gentle souls. Even when they're here for you, they can be gentle about it, depending on what kind of person you've been. He's a Grim Reaper."

"What?"

"Yeah, Grim Reaper." Mikhael squatted down in front of the lopsided display rack. Ramona had left the broken leg with its bent screw on the bottom shelf. He fixed it, then moved the gargoyle, using one hand to hold up the display as he reset the screw.

Raina re-stacked the balls and kaleidoscopes that Ramona had forgotten, but it was distracting, Mikhael doing the handyman thing. All he needed was a tool belt and no shirt. With the jeans riding nice and low in that squat. With effort, she focused on what he was saying.

"If a soul is being held back that needs to go, they call in a death angel. For the normal course of things, Grim Reapers take the lead. Most of the time they're a taxi service, but you don't want to cross one. They can pretty much kill you with a thought."

"That's reassuring."

"Your friend is in no danger. The one he's come for hasn't anything to fear as well. Elderly man, good life. Though dying is cruel, death itself can be kind. The Reaper is here to help with that transition, guide him where he needs to go."

"Oh. Why did he look at us like that? Doesn't he know the address of the person he's here to collect?"

"The moment he looks at you, he knows the how, when, why and where of your death. It makes life odd for him. They're usually very solitary."

"Oh...*oh*."

"What?" Mikhael glanced up at her. She laid her hand on his shoulder, just because it was there and her hands were empty now. It was warm and solid.

"I was wondering why he was looking at Ramona like she was a puzzle. I'll bet he couldn't figure it out."

"That's impossible." His brow creased. "The Grim Reaper knows the date of everyone's death. Even immortals like me or Derek."

"But Ramona is total chaos. If she does a spell for hair growth, it turns into a grasshopper plague. He couldn't tell. I'll lay money on it."

Mikhael straightened, pushing on the display rack to make sure it was steady now. "If you're right, that should be intriguing to him."

"She looked quite intrigued by him."

"Women." Mikhael snorted.

She let that pass, something else prodding her curiosity. "Ramona couldn't see through the spell. Can you see me, as me?"

He shook his head. "I see you as I've spelled you to look. I set it that way to detect it immediately if those sexual power surges of yours tampered with it."

"So in the movie theater, you were making out with an average-looking thirtysomething woman?"

"I still gave you large breasts." Tucking her hand into the crook of his elbow, he continued their stroll. "It doesn't matter what your outside looks like, Raina. I still see you as you are. That's how I know…" He stopped, gazing at Ramona's window display of tarot card decks and Ouija boards. Raina wasn't fooled.

"That's how you know what?"

"If I finish the sentence, you'll be angry, and I prefer you not angry. You're having a good day. I like seeing you having a good day."

He faced her with that impassive mask, as if he was prepared for her to insist. She thought about it, spoke slowly.

"It's said angels can see the nature of the soul. That they know whether someone is good or evil, or what level of corruption a soul carries. You have enough angel blood you can see that in Isaac, can't you? That's what you know."

He said nothing, and she knew he was sticking by his previous statement. He wasn't going to go there unless she insisted. She nodded once, to herself. Took his hand again. "You promised me ice cream."

"So I did." When they started walking, he pulled her close, brushed his lips against her temple. He really was very different from what she thought he was. No, not different. He *was* scary, deadly. But he was more than that, too. The shape of his soul kept shifting.

"So why did you decide on the kelpie instead of the Ferrari?"

"You made it clear the Ferrari wouldn't impress you."

"Oh, and it's about impressing me now?"

"Isn't it the male's job to impress you with virile trappings, including my choice of mount? Meaning my horse."

"I'm glad you clarified that. And my job?"

"To look disdainful and dismissive. Keep me turning on my head, trying to figure out what will work."

"I'm very good at disdainful and dismissive."

"That's exactly what I was thinking when I got your panties wet in the theater."

"That was Edward and Carlyle's doing, thank you very much."

"Together?"

"Just a personal fantasy." She sniffed, turned her head and bit the hand on her shoulder. "Besides, I can make you believe what I want you to believe, wet panties and all."

"Really." He stopped, turned her toward him.

"Don't." She laid her hand on his wrist. "It was a joke."

"Jokes like that don't make me laugh, and you know it. Which is why you throw them in, to taunt me. Want to test me here?" He lifted a brow. "I'm not averse to public displays of fucking. I can lift the spell like a stage curtain."

"Every girl's dream," she said lightly, though she knew he registered her shiver. He was the quintessential bad boy, but he was taunting a bad girl. Together they were going to be thrown in jail.

"While I'm not averse to cage play," she said, "I have a feeling they won't put us in the same cell when we're arrested."

"I'm capable of making you think I'm in that cage with you, doing things that you're powerless to stop." He was closer now, his voice husky, the eyes overpowering her. Hellfire, another moment and she was going to...

"Ice cream," she managed. "You promised me ice cream."

His look of dark promise was enough to keep her wet, but his lips quirked. He took her hand. "Come on."

He crossed the street with a casual glance. Once again, the cars slowed the minute he put his foot in the street. She told herself it was a small town, where people slowed for pedestrians, but with Mikhael, people seemed compelled to do what he wanted. She didn't know if that was magic or his charisma, or an intoxicating combination of both, but it rankled that it worked on her as well. She dragged her feet a little. "Where are you taking me?"

"There." He tugged her onto the curb, showing her the local favorite ice cream shop. "Fudge sundae, right? With nuts?"

An ice cream shop was like a bakery, alive with joyful smells that appealed to a sensory-oriented creature like herself. Once inside the door, she brought him up short to inhale. When she opened her eyes, he was considering her in that intent way that warmed her skin. "What are you doing?" she asked.

"The same thing." At her puzzled look, he ran his thumb over her knuckles. "You inhale the smells, the sounds, because it's all about pleasure and comfort. The way you immerse yourself in it makes me feel those things. Pleasure, because watching you do anything is pleasurable, and comfort, because it's a comfort to know that someone still takes time to savor something simple."

She gave a nervous laugh. She never laughed nervously. "I'll invite you to watch me floss my teeth and see how pleasurable that is."

"Raina, you could stand on your head belching the alphabet and make it sexy as hell."

Laughter bubbled out of her. The sensual roll of it turned heads. He was supposed to be helping her with that, but apparently he hadn't anticipated her laughter. His eyes glowed warmer, though, and he tugged her up to the counter. "I can do the fudge sundae," the store clerk said, "but not the nuts. Kids' peanut allergies. Owner doesn't dare risk them anymore."

Mikhael muttered something under his breath but nodded neutrally enough. "Okay, make the sundaes to go."

Raina made a face. "Crap. I like the nuts."

"No worries. You'll get them." Mikhael handed her the sundae, then took her back out onto the sidewalk. Nodding toward a drugstore a block away, he said, "That looks like a place that has nuts."

With a firm pressure on her shoulder, he eased her into one of the whimsical ice cream chairs arranged beside round tables. Though the sun was hiding behind the clouds, she was bemused to find the seat and back warm, as if heated by its beams.

"A little service I provide," he said, registering her puzzlement. "I don't want you to get cold. Wait here."

Her stomach did another little lurch at the romantic gesture, but she made an effort to hide it. "I'll wait only because I want to. Not because you told me to do it," she said.

"You keep telling yourself that. But you move off that chair, it won't only be my magic warming that beautiful ass of yours."

When he threw her one of those devastating stern looks, she retaliated by standing up, turning a circle and sitting down again, wiggling her very fine ass. She heard his chuckle as he crossed the street in those long, ground-eating strides, and it left her smiling.

If someone had told her a Dark Guardian could give her screaming orgasms, she could roll with that. But that he could make her laugh, make her feel young and silly in all the good ways...

Dipping into his sundae, she tested the strawberry topping. When she saw him at the cash register paying for the nuts, she poked two eyes and a nose indentation into his ice cream with her finger, using one of the cut strawberries as a bow mouth. Then she sucked the stickiness off her fingertips.

As he returned, his glance fell on it, as well as her sitting with her hands primly folded, a smirk on her face. "I expect a bite of yours."

"I don't share."

"Funny. Neither do I. Not certain things." Pulling the bag of salted peanuts out of the small brown sack, he used the salt shaker to crush them up before tearing open the top and sprinkling a liberal amount over the top of the sundae. "There you go."

It touched her, the expectant look he gave her, wanting to be sure she was pleased. So she closed her hand over his, still grasping the sundae to keep it steady, and caressed his fingers. "Thank you."

He sat down next to her, pulling his chair close so they were shoulder to shoulder and could people-watch as they ate. She did give him a bite of hers, and he gave her the strawberry mouth she'd made. He put it on her tongue, then dipped his finger in the fudge, painting some on her lips so she could have the two tastes together. Then some of Mikhael, because he put his lips over hers, teasing her with his tongue until she put down her spoon and touched his jaw, ran her fingers through his hair and savored the kiss to the nth degree.

When he pulled back, he didn't go far, their eyes still close. She didn't want to say anything, didn't feel like saying anything, and he didn't seem to, either, for they just considered one another for a long moment before he settled back, his arm pressed against her shoulder blades. Occasionally he took bites of his sundae one-handed as she continued to eat hers. Though they took their time, the ice cream remained cold, either a function of the shop's freezer and mix, or more of Mikhael's touching form of kitchen magic.

"So what happened, last time you were in town?" he asked. "Li said it didn't go well."

Li really needed to have a lock put on his mouth. "I couldn't hold the magic at the house and here. Too much distance between the two points."

"And the house takes a lot of energy."

"I was attracting too much attention in town, so when I pulled in more magic to camouflage myself, I had to weaken what was at the house. We had clients. The weak spot...one of them was killed. We made it look like a heart attack."

Her jaw tightened and she wouldn't look at him. "No, I'm not going to tell you which one of them did it, because it wasn't their fault, it was mine. If you want to haul anyone to Hell for it, that would be me."

"Raina." Her chair scraped as he turned her so her knee was pressed against his. Then he put pressure on that arm behind her back, slipping the other under her knees. Before she knew it, she was settled in his lap, her ice cream steadied by his brief touch over her fingers. He tilted his head. "You think I'm that kind of monster?"

"You don't deny being a monster." He was like sitting by a fire. A strong, steady flame, even warmer than the chair.

"No, I don't. I fit two of the requirements—I'm terrifying and I kill. But I'm not indiscriminate about it."

"The terrifying part or the killing part?"

"Both."

Maybe the reason she didn't fear that side of his nature was because her own kind had it, the killing part. Leaving it alone for now, she dipped her spoon in his sundae, offering him another bite of it, since she was blocking his access to it. He didn't seem to mind, his foot braced on the table leg crosspiece to hold her so she was leaning comfortably against his chest as she fed him and herself. She even gave him another bite of her own sundae.

"So what happens if you don't have your protection up around people like this?" He nodded to the passing foot traffic.

"Think sirens, sailors, sharp rocks. Only they turn on each other. Then, when I'm gone and they regain their senses, their wives are filing for divorce, the girlfriend is moving out, or they're being hauled to jail for assault, or worse. As long as it's masked, muted, they're fine. I'm just distracting, like any other beautiful woman. I can dial it up or down at Sweet Dreams to make them feel more comfortable and relaxed, help them make their choices, but I'm safest there."

"Does that ever make you feel trapped?"

"I like being able to do something like this, but really...no." She meant it. "You're right. It's my sanctuary. My place. With my staff, and the variety of guests I entertain in the parlor, I never lack for stimu-lating company. And the grounds themselves...so much ancient life there..."

"You never get lonely?"

That was an entirely different subject, one that had nothing to do with location, and everything to do with...other things. "Do you?"

He touched the side of her face, brushed his knuckles over her cheek. A variety of expressions crossed his face, things that twisted low in her stomach. "Not today," he said.

"Mikhael—"

"Funny running into you two kids."

Snapping out of her reaction to his raw honesty, Raina turned to see Derek Stormwind and Ruby, her best friend in the whole world, approaching the table. Obviously, Mikhael had seen them coming, because he showed no reaction to Derek's sardonic intrusion. It was obvious, and expected, that Derek could see through the spellwork, which meant he'd enabled Ruby to do the same, or she was proficient enough to do it herself.

"Ramona," Raina muttered. That was the last time she'd take her other best friend's casual reaction to a not-so-casual situation at face value. She'd likely contacted Ruby the second she went into the shop. Raina should have stayed and spent more time reassuring her, but Ramona never paid attention to words—she read other things, and whatever she'd read off Mikhael and Raina had unsettled her enough to call in the cavalry.

Awkward was a descriptive understatement, since Raina sat on the lap of the guy who'd fucked Ruby twelve ways to Sunday, a male who Derek considered a borderline adversary on a lot of different levels. But Raina wasn't one to get twisted up in knots over social faux pas.

"Care to join us?" She nodded at the unused chairs in front of them. When she squirmed to indicate she wanted to take her seat next to Mikhael, she discovered a certain part of him was enjoying her exactly where she was. If she moved, she'd be making that public knowledge. A wicked thought, just the kind of thing that appealed to her.

He gave her a wry look but let her slide off. Fortunately, the fit of the jeans and his seated position helped cover it, though it would be noticeable if a woman took the lingering look she would. Ruby, no matter how tempted she might be, would likely refrain in deference to her husband. Raina was happy to look at both men, the privilege of being single. Though Derek could be a pain in the ass, he was a sexy one. There was nothing fattening about a two-man visual feast.

Derek held Ruby's chair but declined to sit. "We need to talk," he said to Mikhael.

"I'm not done with my ice cream. Why don't you sit, unless that stick you carry in your ass isn't bendy enough?"

"Mikhael," Ruby said. "Please don't goad him."

The woman who traveled with Derek to aid his magical work also ran the gun shop in town, Arcane Shot, so she wore the store T-shirt, snug black and red. Ruby was beautiful, but wiry and strong, with eyes that reflected the sharp intelligence that made her capable of standing shoulder to shoulder with Derek in his dangerous line of work. A year ago, she'd been into some messed-up shit, and Mikhael had been in the center of that. That history was reflected in her obvious trepidation over the two males who'd locked gazes like bulls about to charge.

"How about both of you stop goading each other?" Raina interjected. "Yes, yes, I get it. You're both brimming with testosterone. He fucked Ruby, he fucked me, awkward, awkward, awkward, but now she's married to Derek. Monogamous fucking until death do you part, and past is past." She glanced at Ruby. "Unless you want me to fuck Derek so we can make it all neat and balanced."

Ruby narrowed her eyes. "Over my dead body."

"Good. So that's resolved. Try this, it's awesome." Raina spooned up some more fudge, nuts and ice cream and fed them into Ruby's mouth before expletives could spill out. Then watched her expression glaze.

"Oh, wow. That is awesome."

"I told you. Go get yourself one. I have enough nuts left for it." She nodded to the bag folded at her elbow.

"They don't...?"

"Pansy-assed peanut-allergy generation," Mikhael commented. "The whole lot of them, fodder for Darwin's cannon."

"His looks are only surpassed by his compassion," Raina noted. "Here, my treat."

Since Mikhael hadn't let her use any money, she pushed bills into Ruby's hand, pointed to the storefront with the meaningful glance that said, *Go get ice cream with Derek to defuse this. Guys don't fight while eating ice cream.*

However, while playing peacemaker, she was noticing other things. Like how Ruby and Mikhael were studiously avoiding eye contact. She'd expected it of Ruby, what with Derek here and all, but Mikhael's reaction surprised her. A man only looked away if the woman had meant something to him. If he had regrets. Which made her recall how he'd reacted to her poking at him about Ruby on the night he'd arrived.

She understood the dynamics between lovers quite well. Regrets didn't mean a desire to hook back up. However, there were plenty of women who'd become sloppy seconds when a male's first interest became unavailable. Being married to Derek Stormwind, Ruby was as unavailable as a pile of gold at the back of a dragon's lair—guarded by a dragon who never slept.

When Derek and Ruby went into the shop to get a sundae for Ruby and probably a twenty-four scoop banana split for Derek's enormous magic-induced appetite, she took another bite of her own treat and found it wasn't as good as it had been. She put the spoon down. "Okay, what exactly is it you want to say to her? I can get Derek to take a stroll if you need some alone time."

Mikhael snorted. "Your powers of persuasion are considerable, but if you could get him to leave her alone with me, you'd probably surpass the angels."

She nodded. He was leaning on the chair's two back legs, his boot braced on the table. Putting her foot against the chair's axis, she gave it a vicious shove.

His battle reflexes showed, because he didn't try to grab the table. He was out of the chair, letting it hit the sill of the ice cream shop window and leaving him balanced on the balls of his feet, facing her. For one weighted moment, she glared at him, then he bent, righted the chair and sat back down, this time with a foot more space between them.

"I was wondering how long you were going to pretend it didn't bother you that she was sitting close enough I could recognize her scent."

This time she went for electrical current, pulled from the air and targeted on the metal chair, dissembling spells be damned. He was back on his feet again. Even though he could take a wealth of pain, she expected it was hard to look suave when vibrating like a coke junkie. She was smart enough to be on her own feet this time, fists clenched, the chairs between them.

"As ironic as it may sound, I'm not a whore, Mikhael. Don't treat me like one."

"Then don't act like one. If it matters, say it matters. Be honest."

"Oh, yes. Because you're in the honesty business."

"When have I lied to you, Raina?"

She hoped he'd lied about a great many things, specifically the things that made her feel...wanted. Special to him. Because if he meant those things, she really didn't know what to think. And, of course, that made no sense at all.

"A diversion to avoid the truth is still a lie. Tell me how you feel about her."

"If you sit down."

She kept standing, lifted her chin. She thought he'd try to make her, but he changed tactics. Sitting down himself, he slid out her seat and waited.

She perched stiffly on the edge. She was glad the ice cream store's business had picked up, because she really didn't want Derek and Ruby to come back out in the middle of this.

"I have regrets for how I had to treat her," he said. "I couldn't have done it any differently, given the dangerous magic she was using. However, I saw the core of her. I knew the shape of her soul, as I said." He held her gaze. "If I'd been a man like Derek, I wouldn't have let him have her back so easily. But I'm not a man like Derek."

Though it hadn't been easy at all for Derek to get her back, she let that go, because that had more to do with Ruby than Mikhael.

"But for a few moments, you wanted to be a man like Derek. Because of her."

She got it, she did. Raina had no claim on Mikhael, which was why she couldn't understand why it hurt.

Oh, hell, yes, she did. The vagaries of female nature. This had been her moment, all about her and him, and now there was this other thing, this other woman that was part of it. Maybe she *was* a lot like him. She might not have a claim on him before or after, but during? She wanted 120 percent of his fucking attention, no other woman in his head, regretted or no.

"I imagined it," he admitted. "The way you imagine being an astronaut or a postman or a ditch digger. In the end, I am who I am. With no desire to be anything different. It was the regret that I had to be so cruel to her that goaded it, not a true desire to be with her, to possess her utterly, the way Derek has."

"Possession? That's what love is in your mind?"

"Yes. A possession of mind, body, heart and soul, two beings becoming one in their intent to be together through eternity. Who won't let one another go, no matter what."

"You're outdated, Mikhael. This is the generation of drive-through divorce, if your prescription mood drugs can't make you happy every minute you spend together."

"Hmm." He leaned forward. He did it slow, giving himself time to anticipate her reaction, but she didn't think anything she did would change his goal. He looked pretty set on his course. She stayed still as he rubbed a thumb on the corner of her lips, taking away the chocolate. "What you said earlier, about fucking Derek to even the score?" Those dark eyes flickered with heat, fixing on her mouth. "It's not just over Ruby's dead body that you would ever touch Derek Stormwind."

Derek and Ruby came out of the sundae shop. Raina could tell Mikhael was entirely serious, though his thumb had been gentle on her mouth. He sat back as the other couple joined them, Derek straddling a chair and Ruby sitting next to Raina, generously offering her another bite as well. Raina covered what she was feeling with her usual feline smile, but Mikhael had pulled her chair closer to his again, and now his hand settled on her thigh, his fingers casually curved to the inside of it, a touch that made it clear he had carnal knowledge of her.

He kept it there as the men spoke of more innocuous things, a lot of undercurrents happening but the exchange at least decently civilized. Derek had even brought Mikhael a beer, which was kind of like the world turning on its axis.

That wasn't the only skewed thing. She'd been okay with being swept up in this as long as she was sure, no matter her own feelings, that to him it was simply an intense fling between two unattached adults. But now, with that comment about Derek Stormwind, with this entire day, Mikhael had shifted it to a different footing.

It was hard to follow who and what he was when she was getting so many conflicting messages. She knew her thigh was warm beneath his hand, that her every nerve ending was pointed in his direction. She was so aware of him, that he was with *her* and that he was making that very clear to anyone else. She wasn't missing Ruby's pointed glance at that hand, a look slightly more discreet than Ramona's, but still a what-the-fuck look.

She must be carrying some of those hormones from their movie, because she wanted to pull Ruby off to a ladies room and say, "Did you see how he was touching me? Isn't he the hottest thing ever?" Goddess, she was losing her mind.

"There's a Grim Reaper in town," Mikhael mentioned.

"I think Ramona's adopted him for the afternoon," Raina added.

Ruby lifted a brow. "Should we be worried?"

"No. Mr. Know-It-All here says that he's not here for her. That it's all part of the natural order, blah, blah, blah."

"Sorry, this is Mr. Know-It-All." Ruby tilted her head toward Derek. "One's got to be an impostor."

"Or we're just letting them think they know everything. Female condescension and all."

"Sssh. That's ultra-secret girl code."

Raina smiled. It was good to see Ruby joking again. She gave Derek credit for that. He'd helped her friend heal from the loss of their baby and the terrible fallout from that, which had nearly taken Ruby from all of them. That won him a lot of points in her book. Not that she'd show it.

"Ice cream's done. I'd like that moment now," Derek said, looking pointedly at Mikhael.

"If you're going to do the ultra-protective, husband-of-my-best-friend thing where you threaten to kick his ass if he's mean to me, you can sit right here and do that," Raina said. "And I don't need anyone's protection."

"Actually I was going to warn him that you're a rabid pit viper and not to go to sleep in the same house with you. Unless he chains you in the basement first."

"Asshole."

"Shrew."

"Chaining her in the same room with me would be far more exciting." Mikhael wiped his mouth with a napkin and rose. "I'll walk with you, sorcerer."

He gave Raina a glance that made her visualize in great detail what being in chains and at Mikhael's mercy would be like. There went that shiver again. Ruby registered her reaction, damn it, but there was no help for it. Mikhael's specialty was dark souls, and hers just rolled out the red carpet for him. Each time he made comments like that, she knew he was drawing closer to when he'd make good on them. It didn't matter if she registered it as promise or threat—she looked forward to it.

~

"You haven't told her, have you?" Derek said, his jaw tight. They'd moved a block down the street, turned into an alley between a café and a wine shop. There was an iron gate to protect the cottage garden there, but it was open, allowing them to step out of the flow of foot traffic onto a pattern of concrete stepping stones.

"Told her what?"

"What you're feeling, what it means."

"What am I feeling?"

"We saw you across the street before we came up. The hand holding, the peanuts."

Mikhael blinked. "My God. I knew I should have concealed my nefarious peanut-crushing activities."

Derek set his teeth. "I swear, you're just like her."

"In a few days, I'll likely have to kill the wild incubus she's protecting. Possibly in front of her. How do you think she'll feel about me then?"

"You're part angel, Mikhael."

"Any other obvious statements you wish to make? Do you need to remind me that I used to spread your wife's legs and—"

Derek had him shoved up against the alley wall in a heartbeat, just as Mikhael expected. He dodged the punch to the face but caught Derek's fist in his own before it impacted the wall. Broken fingers would be hard to explain. They held that pose a charged blink in time, then Derek shoved away from him.

"The hell with you. But if you hurt her, if you hurt my wife's best friend, I will disembowel you."

"You can try."

Derek stepped to the opening of the alley, then swore, pivoted. "Is it the Darkness that makes you like this? You always had it in you, but over the years...it's become darker. I thought we were friends, once."

"You even the scales for the Light, Derek. I do it for the Dark. It may be for the same goal, but it's from different sides. I work from the shadows, you work in the light of the sun."

Mikhael's gaze shifted. Derek turned to see Ruby and Raina standing there. They knew them too well, apparently. Ruby's face was tight with concern, but it was to Raina Mikhael's attention went, knowing she'd heard his last statement. He couldn't tell much from her expression, but she was listening. Waiting.

He came back to Derek. "When a civilization becomes so prosperous it gets lazy and falls into entitlement, decadence, apathy and inertia, my job is to push them into brutality and hardship to accelerate change, bring the scales back to rights. You may save a child to ward off evil; I will cause its death for the same purpose."

He heard Ruby's indrawn breath, but he wouldn't look toward either woman, not now. "Without struggle, there is no character and strength. But some force has to provide that adversity. We work for the same goal, but on sides that can never be reconciled."

"I would have taken the thirteenth straw."

"Yes, you would have. And it would have been the wrong thing to do. I was the right person for the job."

Derek studied him a long moment. "Ruby, Raina, I need to say something to him. Privately."

Both looked ready to argue, but Mikhael looked toward Raina. "No more fighting. I promise."

"Right." She gave him a searching look. "Play nice. We'd hate to have to separate you boys." Curling her fingers around Ruby's arm, she tugged her away with her.

Derek waited until Mikhael knew he was certain the women were out of earshot, but even then he kept his voice low.

"Angels only give their hearts once, Mikhael. I know it, you know it. You have sex—insane amounts of it—but I've never seen you act like you're in a relationship. I've never seen you crush peanuts for a woman."

"I'm quarter angel." Leave it to Derek to laser in on what had crossed his mind a hundred times today, but it didn't matter.

"You've always had more of your grandsire's blood than your parents'. No matter how you amp up that bullshit Russian accent."

"You're wrong, and even if you aren't, it's my business, Derek. She won't be affected by it. She's not an angel." A diabolical ripple of humor went through him, remembering her trying to electrocute him with a metal ice cream table.

What an understatement.

He met Derek's scrutiny dead-on, Guardian to Guardian. "I won't cause her any more harm than my mission requires. Not that I feel any obligation to you, but as my...apology to Ruby, I give you my word on her behalf. I will leave her friend no worse than I found her."

Derek grunted, a noncommittal noise. "Can you live without her when you have to walk away?"

"I'm immortal, same as you, sorcerer. We live on, no matter what."

CHAPTER THIRTEEN

*H*e'd been quiet since his one-on-one with Derek. They drove back to Sweet Dreams, but when they reached the driveway entrance, she wanted to walk, so they left the car. As Raina glanced over her shoulder, she saw it shimmer and disappear. Back to the Underworld garage. Thinking about the train set, she wondered what other things Mikhael had in that cache deep in the Earth. An old toy from his youth, a picture of his mother, all indications of what he was, other than a Dark Guardian.

She knew the dangers of this kind of thinking. People were many layers, yes, but there was always one main layer to them, and she'd seen plenty of women engage in disastrous relationships by rationalizing away that one layer, giving too much weight to the less important ones. Mikhael had made it clear. He'd decided centuries ago to be a Dark Guardian, and he had no regrets or doubts in that choice. Perhaps he'd struggled with ostracism from friends like Derek, or the terrible things he'd had to do, but his one overriding layer was Dark Guardian.

Except for the unexpected bomb drop in the alley, she'd noticed he rarely talked about the specifics of what he did, as if he knew no one wanted to know. It must be odd not to talk about the thing that dominated his waking hours. And he'd said he had a lot of waking hours.

While she wasn't sure of his motives toward her, she was pretty sure he wanted to continue their...whatever their relationship was, after his business with Isaac was concluded. So if she wanted him to be a part of her life, stopping by for croissants or to share her bed, she had to be willing to understand more about that main layer.

You may save a child to ward off evil; I will cause its death. Did she want to know more?

It started to rain, but she liked rain, coupled with the solitude of walking on the road with him. Picking up on it, he didn't suggest they hasten their pace or reconjure the car. Instead, he stood while she held his shoulder to slide off her shoes and put her bare feet on the dampening ground. When they stepped off the main drive to follow a forest path to the house, where the canopies of the trees provided some cover, he delighted her by stripping off his shirt, letting his wings stretch out. One curved to shelter her head as the angle of his body did the rest. As the rainfall increased, finding its way through the treetops, the drops pattered onto his shoulders and slid down her collar bone and forearms. Turning her face up to the gray sky, she met his mouth for a rain-soaked kiss.

As it deepened, the rain grew more insistent, heavier. Thunder rolled in the distance, but it would come closer. She could sense it through the soles of her feet. Mikhael directed them beneath a large, moss-covered live oak, one of her gray-beard wizards, though deeper in the wood than those that lined her drive. Glancing up, she noted the spreading branches and remembered what he said about sleeping in them. She imagined walking through the forest and coming upon something like him, shirtless, his wings curled around him, one leg braced as he slept, those strands of hair drifting across his forehead with the night breeze.

Of course, Mikhael would never be caught asleep. But it was a nice fantasy, kissing him awake, like a reverse Sleeping Beauty.

"Want to ride out the storm up there?" he suggested.

She had clients coming in early, but they were regulars, a group of eight Army soldiers who worked the local munitions terminal. She could take some time. "If you can keep me dry."

"I can keep you warm *and* dry." He motioned to her to get onto his back. The wings disappeared, but she saw red lines like two scars curving along the inside of his shoulder blades, evidence of where they emerged. From earlier, she knew they would disappear, but she traced them now. When he bent to take her weight, she wrapped her arms around his chest. He guided her legs to clasp his hips.

"Hold on tight for this first part."

She did, and he leaped with a breathtaking flex of muscle and graceful movement of limbs, catching the first branch and then climbing up from there, taking them to a triangular cradle between two thick branches and the trunk. He helped her dismount, steadying her, and lowered her to a seated position between his thighs, bracing his back against the rise of one of the branches, their feet against the trunk and the prop of the other branch. He combed her damp hair from her face as she tilted her head back, traced the beads of water rolling down his jaw. Running her fingers through his much wetter hair, she slicked it back on his skull. When he leaned down to kiss her again, he stopped with just a space between their lips, registering her pensive expression.

"What is it?" he asked.

"I've never been romanced, Mikhael." She allowed herself a tight smile. She'd played plenty of sensual games, understood the lines and boundaries of them. "But I'm certainly not romance material, and neither are you. I want to know what you think this is."

"No male has ever romanced you?"

The truth stung a little, but she lifted her chin. "I've had a lot of sex, Mikhael. No relationships."

"Well, that makes two of us." He gave her a direct look. "No woman has ever inspired me to walk with her in the rain, or crush peanuts for her sundae. Whether or not we're romance material—your words, not mine—why shouldn't we be allowed, if only for a few days, what so many others have? Life is short, whether you live one year or a thousand."

She nodded, touched his lips. "So that's all this is?"

"It is what it is. We're attracted to one another. Not just physically. I like you, Raina. I admire you. You intrigue me." He curved a strand of damp hair around her ear. "I pursued Isaac here. You were unexpected. How that affects why I'm here or your responsibilities, I don't know." His attention moved to her mouth, that heated intensity suddenly back in his eyes, making her aware of everywhere their bodies touched in their current half-reclined position. "But I do know I want to kiss you."

"I know I want to be kissed."

The muscle in his jaw flexed. "Then why don't we leave it right there? We'll be like teenagers, like Bella, Edward and Jacob, believing that's all that matters."

Her lips curved. "Mikhael, we're adults."

"Yeah, thank Lucifer." The dark gaze held her, that heat growing. "That means no one can stop me from what I want to do to you. Except you."

She eased back a little, not ready to lose her mind to that kiss. Yet. "You never smile. You chuckle in that dry way, you have that cynical smirk, but you don't smile. What makes you smile, even if just inside?"

Okay, there it was. She was going to stick her feet into those tricky waters. Turning over to straddle him in his partly reclined position, she sat up, letting her bare feet hang down on either side of the tree. He kept her secure in his grasp, but then she adjusted, clasping his hands to hold them palm to palm between their two bodies. They twisted and turned over one another, idle caresses of fingertips as he thought over a response. Since she tilted her head back, eyes closed to catch stray raindrops on her face, his words hit her from the quiet darkness inside her head.

"A thief pulls in another man to work a job with him, a man whose character he doesn't know. When they break into the house, they're surprised by the wife. The new partner decides he's going to rape the wife, but the thief pulls him off her. The partner is a bigger man, a much better fighter, but the thief fights him anyway, makes the decision to set off one of the house alarms. Then he keeps the fight going until the police get there and arrest them both. He went to prison for ten years. But the wife is safe."

Raina opened her eyes. He'd laid his head back on the comfortable prop of the branch, was looking up through the trees, though as she watched, the raindrops made his eyes close as well. He continued speaking, encouraged by her attentive silence. "A junkie gives up on her drugs for two days to be clean enough to go to her daughter's dance recital. Even though Mom has the shakes, her daughter is happy, because she smiles at her and tells her she did good. The mother will be stoned by nightfall, won't remember anything else after that, but they'll both remember that moment.

"Another mother croons a lullaby to a baby outside their hut. She can hear artillery fire in the distance. Their small world is surrounded by tribal warfare, guns and drugs. It's very likely the child will never reach adulthood. If he does, he won't have a mother by the time he gets there. She'll be raped, mutilated, murdered. Knowing the likelihood of that, she still takes the time to sing him a lullaby by the firelight."

She swallowed, but he kept going, painting those stark pictures. "A homeless person sees a group of teens kicking a stray dog, planning to throw him in a Dumpster and set him on fire. He goes to the aid of the dog, and their cruelty turns upon him. They kick him until his kidneys rupture and he dies. But the dog has gotten away and a few weeks later is adopted by a family that finds him in the park. He becomes their cherished beloved pet for many years."

The words were simple, unembellished. But the aura of intensifying energy around him showed the significance of the images, their importance to a world that often seemed terribly lost. He opened his eyes, stared up into the trees. "These are things of nobility, a special kind of valor created against a backdrop of evil and violence. Noticed by no one except the recipients or those like me. Those moments don't make me smile, but I find a different...warmth there."

"There's a hopelessness to it," she said at length. "The idea that we only find the best in ourselves when we face the worst in others."

He said nothing, and her mind drifted toward darkness, toward memory. "Where Elceus held me, there was a small window. One night, the full moon was in the right position for a few short minutes. It filled that view, the light falling on me. A moth came to the bars. Beautiful, silky wings. Orange and blue body. It got in, couldn't get out, because that happens. It can't see the way. I was chained, so I put my hand on the cold stone, waited. Eventually it crawled on my knuckles, went still, as if it was waiting, trusting me to take it to that window. So I put it back between the bars, watched it crawl away, then fly. It tore my soul out of my chest. I wanted to be that moth, because even in its short life, it had far more freedom than I could ever remember experiencing at that point. But when I helped it, it kindled a small spark inside me. Something good. Your stories remind me of that." She pressed her lips together. "I also felt exhausted, like I'd just fought a war. Because the whole time it was crawling on the stone floor of my cell, beyond the reach of my chains, I had to fight the need to kill it before it figured out where that window was. But then it trusted me to get it there."

"Therein lies the balance," he said. "This is Purgatory. A testing ground, as I said. The choice is always ours, no matter the circumstances."

She lowered her gaze to find him looking at her as if she were one of those things that brought warmth to him. "Those who can make the right choice under duress," he said, "they're truly the extraordinary ones, Raina. You're extraordinary."

She had no desire to answer that, to do anything but look at him and give him what he wanted. He knew it as well, for now he slid his hands under her arms, straightening to lift and turn her with that casual strength so she was straddling him still, but facing away from him. He pushed her shirt up, took it over her head. As he set it aside, he kissed her shoulder, cupped her breast, tightening his grip so the curve swelled above the strapless bra. Sliding his fingers over the nipple, he made it respond through the thin lace. "Put your arms back against me, Raina."

She threaded her arms under his, her palms finding a home on the curve of hip and muscular buttocks, thumbs sliding along the crease of thigh. When he put his mouth to her rain-kissed throat, she sighed, thighs quivering in reaction.

"You can trust me, Raina."

"What..." Then she felt the conjuring, her wrists bound by his magical steel chain, connected across his lower back so she was chained to him in truth. Or chained around him. Panic leaped in her throat as the same kind of binding wound around her thighs, holding them immobile and bound to his, spread over the oak branch, feet dangling together on either side, her toes curled into his shins.

"Take it off."

"No. I'm right here, Raina. I'm only going to give you pleasure." From the tilt of his head, she could tell he was studying the pleasing visual effect of her breasts cradled in his grip.

"You have breasts a man would die for. Just the right weight. I want to tie you down and suckle you all night long."

She squirmed, which rubbed her against him. He was getting hard against her ass and lower back, and his thighs flexed against hers as she moved, an enticing coital hint.

"You're imagining me sinking my cock into you right here, making you mine."

She was afraid she was already his, for she'd allowed him to possess her in ways she'd never permitted another to do. So she didn't answer, just turned her head, seeking his mouth. He evaded her, teasing her, and she bit his neck hard, earning a growl, a pinch of her nipples that had her squirming further. His growl became a muttered oath.

She knew things about sex that would make Dr. Ruth blush, could do things that would send a man straight into a hellish, fiery paradise. But all that expertise deserted her when she was with Mikhael. Her emotions rose to the surface, and raw need drove her every action. Gripping his buttocks and upper thighs, she worked herself against him in provocative strokes, licked away the blood she'd drawn from his neck.

Catching her throat in his large hand, he pulled her head up to suck that taste from her lips, then plunged his tongue deep, sealing their mouths together by cupping his fingers around her skull, holding her to him. He bit her back, a nip at her tongue, her lips, and when her head fell back, he sank his teeth into her throat as well. He didn't have fangs, so he didn't break the skin, but he held her tight, the way male animals did, asserting dominance in a manner that had attracted females since the beginning of time.

She moaned as his fingers flicked her hardened nipples, as he kneaded the curves, pushed them together and ran his touch in that sensitive valley between them.

"Beg, Raina. Beg for what you want."

Beg, my slave. Beg for what you want.

She went cold so abruptly it was painful. She wasn't that person, the kind that let herself get mired in her past so that it could drain the current moment. But Mikhael had stripped her down these past couple days. There were consequences to giving up those shields. The words jerked her from this reality to the one she never wanted summoned.

She struggled hard, found herself fighting him. "Let me go. Take them off, now. Please."

She wondered if it was the *please* that did it, though she despised herself for the weakness. The bonds disappeared and she hunched forward, trying to get her breath, trying to protect herself, her body flushed hot and cold both. The succubus blood was close to the surface, greedy for the sexual energy swirling around them, resentful of the interruption. It made her feel primitive, out of control, no better than Isaac.

"Raina." She flinched when his palm settled on her bare back. "My energy's here. You need to feed on it."

"You just want to get laid." Though she'd tried to sound amused, flippant, it came out bitter, almost afraid. She despised the fact he could tell her hungers had risen. She'd used extra energy to make sure the house stayed safe in her absence, but vulnerability was a fuel drain. She hated that. "I need to get down."

"Turn toward me, then. I've got you."

Drawing up her legs, she turned on the point of her bottom, and he held her in his lap. Instead of lifting her to take her down, though, he slipped the button of her jeans, began to open them, his intent clear.

"No." She fought him, but he was too strong and the hunger was too powerful. He got her jeans all the way off by turning her over his lap and pulling them off her legs even as she tried her best to bite him, claw, use her magic. He took a few of the blows, absorbed the energy discharge, gave her a couple healthy, stinging smacks on the ass that shocked and aroused her enough to throw her further off balance. Then he brought her up to a straddle facing him, gripping her hair in a scalp-pulling hold. He'd opened his own jeans, so now, angling himself, he shoved her down on him, filling her to the womb, gripping her buttock with one hand to hold her snug on him.

The sensation was overwhelming. She cried out, tried to fight him some more, but he just put the other arm around her shoulders, brought her against his chest, her head against his shoulder.

"Ssshh," he murmured. "It's okay. Take the energy, Raina. It's yours. You don't have to beg for it, or even ask. It's just there, and I give it to you freely. Now and whenever you want it."

She was too much of a mess, didn't know where to begin, but he'd figured that out. He tipped her face up again, and she shut her eyes, not wanting to see. Brushing her mouth with his own, easy touches, he swept his hand down her spine and back up again, awaking all those pleasurable nerve centers. Then he began to move, using the hand he had on her ass to help him, gripping her smarting cheek to lift and lower her, a slow thrust and retreat that immediately centered her succubus blood on the focal point of that energy, the dense buildup. Saliva gathered in her mouth.

*You don't have to beg, or even ask. I give it to you freely. Now and…*for all eternity. Did she just imagine those last three words had hung unspoken in the air? She stared into his opaque eyes, the taut mouth. He'd just proven he wasn't a kind or merciful lover, but she didn't respond to those qualities when immersed in these dark shadows. His determined, ruthless nature pulled her out of them. He understood *her* nature.

Whatever shields she thought she had against him just disappeared. She began to move with him in that rise and fall, his knowledge of her body's response irresistible.

"He has no hold on you anymore."

"I know. I made sure of it."

He gave a fierce, satisfied nod. "If he was still alive, I would make him suffer three times over for everything he made you suffer."

She trembled harder. "Mikhael, don't."

He thrust deeper, earning a cry. "When I demand you beg, Raina, I demand it for your pleasure and my own. Not to harm you. Never to harm you."

"I know. I know." God, her throat was aching, a place so raw and jagged inside.

"Let the tears go. Let it all go."

Something like a sob tore from her throat. "I can't cry. Tearless… witch."

When she'd been with Elceus, that had been a mercy. She'd never shown him a single tear, never begged, no matter how much he tried to make her beg for nourishment, for release from pain, from darkness, from punishment. She'd always been smarter than him, knew he needed her more than she needed her own life. Her sanity.

"It hurts too much, Mikhael. I can't climax. Please…you release. Let me feed on you."

The muscle in his jaw flexed, his eyes sparking, but he gave her a short nod, understanding. Curving her arms around his shoulders, she pressed her face into his throat as he increased the speed and power of his strokes. Her emotions might be too raw to allow a climax, but it was a pleasure to feel his cock inside her, to feel all that male strength.

She held on to that, savored it as his muscles became tensile steel beneath her greedy hands, stroking, touching, enjoying his body, the appetizer to the main course.

When he released, the heat of his seed sent sensation spiraling up through her belly and rushing through all her nerves. She caught the energy, drew it in like sunlight. She could draw all the life out of the sun, but Mikhael could handle it. He was hotter than the sun, would be burning long after it winked out and left the galaxy in darkness.

Clenching her muscles around him, she milked him, earning a guttural, animal noise from deep in his chest, a harder clutch of his fingers on her ass, another spurt of seed. God, he felt so good. Her sex spasmed around him, wanting the orgasm despite the emotional train wreck that had delayed its release. Bless his black heart, he picked up on it. Pushing her back so he could reach her breast, he closed his mouth over her nipple and began that deep suckling that she felt all the way to her womb. He kept thrusting, even as he completed.

It was like the decadence of dessert after a perfect meal. She screamed when the hard-won climax hit her, and he bit down, adding pain to the pleasure of it. The energy swirled over her skin, penetrating every pore. She inhaled him, drank him, soaked in his energy and found strength again, found balance.

Because, as she'd said, balance was what a Dark Guardian did.

CHAPTER FOURTEEN

*J*t was in the aftermath that she felt it. Cathair passed over them a moment later, his screech ensuring she received his message, loud and clear. Gooseflesh rose along her arms. *Shit.* "Trouble. We need to get back to the house, now."

She was already trying to move back, though Mikhael caught her. "Hold on a second. You don't want to break a leg. Or snap something off you may need later."

She made a face at him and lifted straight up, standing on the branch with easy balance. The energy had restored her, such that the woman Mikhael saw now was his usual self-possessed, half-breed witch. Before he could react, she'd taken a step out into space, using the air currents to carry her down with a sparking of the elemental energy.

"If you'd told me you could do that, I wouldn't have carried you up here." He dropped her jeans down to her, sending her shirt fluttering behind, though he held on to the panties and bra. No sense slowing her down.

"Exactly. Don't whine. You got the chance to impress me with your manly strength. Meet me there." She'd yanked on the jeans and shirt and was gone, moving fast, reminding him of how Isaac had moved. There was a fluid grace to her movements the incubus lacked, though, probably because she wasn't frothing at the mouth in terror.

He tucked everything back in, grabbed his shirt, stood up and took flight. It wasn't anything related to Isaac. He would have felt that, so it must be something involving her sex demons and their clients, something she would feel. He got there when she did, except she was already heading through the front door. He sensed it clearer then, confirming it was local trouble.

Regardless, when she reached the second floor, he was a step ahead, insisting on it, despite the fact she nearly elbowed him aside. He gave her props for determination, since he was twice her weight. She came to a stop.

"You need to let me handle this. It needs my touch, not yours. Trust me."

He assessed the array of dangerous vibes coming out of the second-floor parlor. "I stay at your side."

"How about at my back? *That's* where I need you." When she held his gaze, Mikhael weighed options, nodded.

"You've got it."

"Okay." Taking a deep breath, she moved forward in her usual sauntering glide, into direct view of the parlor occupants. The room was much like the one below, but up here, group play was permitted. A couple staff were in role-playing costumes, some of the bondage devices looked to have been in recent use, and there was a lot of naked flesh. At the moment, all that flesh was crowded to one side, and the agitation coming from them bent the dense space of the room outward.

As she crossed into that space, temper sparked in Raina's eyes. Even before he stepped in behind her, he detected why, because at that moment Isaac pinged on Mikhael's internal radar. Focusing, he found the incubus had hit the perimeter of the property, and suffered the consequences of it. The magical barrier had knocked the incubus completely out, a satisfying result which allowed Mikhael to keep his full attention on what was happening in this room. He'd deal with Isaac shortly—if Raina didn't tear the young sex demon to shreds first.

It was obvious an incubus's wild magic was at the hub of this situation, buried amid the chaos of fear and anger. An incubus not integrated into Raina's spellwork for her staff. The residual of it swirled through the room still, punctuated by the hostility vibrating from the clientele. Compounding the problem was the fact they weren't innocuous businessmen, but a group of trained servicemen. Isaac's uncontrolled energy had also made it more difficult for the succubi to tone down their own charms. It was lucky Raina's protections were as strong as they were, because otherwise Mikhael knew they would have been looking at a roomful of bodies.

He wanted to curse out loud. She'd been having a good day, had believed it would be safe. He'd told her it would be. Now she was angry with herself, which pissed him off. She was also mad at Isaac, which didn't bug him as much. Maybe now she wouldn't mind him killing the little bastard.

Stepping into the room behind her, he swept his glance over the soldiers. Their tension was targeted at the center of the room, where one of their buddies had a sidearm and was apparently caught up in a full-blown PTSD episode. A mixed blessing, because it had brought them back to their senses, somewhat, but they were still too messed up by Isaac's disorienting vibes to be much help. Except they had shifted in front of the staff, automatically protecting civilians.

Mikhael focused on the man who had Li pushed to his knees, a lock on his neck, the gun pressed right against the incubus's skull. A kill shot, even for a sex demon.

"Lawrence," Raina said in a firm voice. "What are you doing?"

He turned pupils the size of pencil tips toward her. "He's a fucking informant. He's going to tell us what I want to know, or I'm going to shoot all his buddies there." He nodded toward the others.

"Those are *your* buddies, and my staff, Lawrence. I need—"

"It's not safe here. Come get behind me."

She moved toward him while Mikhael bit down the urge to hiss. "You're in Sweet Dreams, Lawrence. My house. You came to spend time with Gina and Marisa. Did you enjoy them?"

His brow furrowed. He was sweating and his finger trembled on the trigger of the gun. The gun was too close to Li for either Mikhael or Raina to make a move. Spellwork could be used, but they had a human audience, and the man was too worked up. By the time the spell was launched, that trigger finger could squeeze.

"They aren't here," Lawrence said. "Gina and Marisa aren't..."

"Of course they are. They're right there." Raina gestured. Gina and Marisa emerged from the knot of sex demons. Gina wore a lavender corset and stockings that made her look like a sensual fairy. Marisa wore only a pair of thong panties. A lot of fragile pale skin, but at least they looked nothing like enemy combatants. Gina was bleeding from her temple, a clip from that gun. Mikhael gave both women credit for guts, if not brains, as they moved forward at Raina's gesture. A couple of the soldiers moved as if they'd stop the girls, but Mikhael caught their attention with a sharp note in his throat, shook his head. He supported their intent, but Raina was right. This was her turf. They had to trust she knew what she was doing.

Li had his gaze fastened on her. The moment his mistress had entered the room, he'd looked less scared. They trusted her. Believed in her. Believed she could get them out of anything. People only believed that if she had actually proven it--repeatedly.

"You're not in the field, soldier. You're not in Afghanistan." This came from one of his comrades. "You're home. You're pointing a gun at a civilian, threatening women."

"Shut up." Lawrence snarled. "Don't try to confuse me."

"He has no reason to lie to you, Lawrence," Raina continued in that reasonable tone. "You know I have a strict rule about firearms above the first floor. The only weapon you bring up here"—her lips curled in a seductive smile—"is the one between your legs. Isn't that right, Steve?"

She shot the soldier a meaningful look, and thank the gods, Steve picked up her direction. "Hell, yeah. But that's probably why he had to bring the gun, Miss Raina. He's not got much firepower down there."

"Give him another beer," came from another of the group. "Maybe it will pump it up."

Lawrence's gaze shifted. Their laughter, though a bit forced, held the camaraderie he knew. The men were getting their feet beneath them, trained to respond even when they weren't at full capacity. They'd just needed the direction.

"No," Lawrence said, but he looked uncertain. "No, it's not safe. He said so. That skinny, pale guy said it wasn't safe here, that the enemy is here, hiding, and no one's safe."

"Where is the skinny guy? Show him to me." Raina gestured.

Lawrence's gaze crawled over the room, desperate, showing his doubt of his present reality. "Not here. He's not here now. He must have run." His hand trembled.

"Please, don't. Lawrence, you're about to hurt someone I love.

Please don't." Raina took several steps forward, and now there was just a pace between them. Mikhael gauged his distance. Hell with it. He'd use magic and worry about explanations to the humans later. But he'd feel a lot better about the chances for Li if Lawrence would shift the gun. Unfortunately, that could leave it pointed at Raina.

Magic was unleashed, but not his. Raina's sexual energy unfurled, controlled, targeted. Lawrence's attention fastened on her as she closed her fingers on his gun hand, stroked. Pushed it toward the ground. Li slid free as the human stared at Raina. Tentative, the soldier reached out, slid a hand along her face, cupped her neck, tightened, lust translating through the urgency of the grip. She held that inviting smile as, with the other hand, she gestured. Gina moved in to help the incubus, since Li was bleeding, limping.

"It's all right," she told Lawrence in that sultry purr. "You're among friends."

The ceiling fan, on an automatic timer, switched on, started to rotate. The male didn't even blink, so spun up in Raina's web, but the wind currents stirred up those lingering incubus vibes Isaac had disseminated. They infiltrated those more pleasant feelings Raina was using to fog Lawrence's mind, confusing them. And a confused soldier, thinking he was in a combat situation, was a dangerous weapon.

Mikhael registered the second things changed for Lawrence, when the beautiful woman before him was no longer what Lawrence saw. The enemy had moved into his space. He shoved her back and the gun hand shot up, his finger squeezing the trigger, point-blank at her chest.

Raina lunged inside his guard, knocked his arm off center so the shot sizzled over the delicate juncture between throat and shoulder. In the next blink, Mikhael had control of his arm, forcing the gun up so the next projectile went into the ceiling. There were shouts and a short scream, and then Mikhael had him down on his stomach, Raina sitting on his other arm.

"Don't hurt him," she said.

The directive hadn't been necessary. He had the male down, restrained, but wasn't causing him any further distress. As he'd told her, he wasn't that kind of monster. Though from what was roiling in his blood, he realized he might have become one if that bullet had found its target.

"It's okay," she murmured. "It's all right." When she put her hand on the man's head, he realized, wryly, she wasn't talking to him. "Easy, Lawrence. It's all right."

Under her touch, the man stopped struggling. Then he began to cry. From her stricken expression, Mikhael saw Raina would have shed tears, if she could. She sat on a man who'd witnessed brutality, who'd exercised it himself for a seemingly just cause, but right or wrong, it had happened because of the senseless cruelty and madness of the human world. Once a man was mired in that often enough, he knew it would never make sense, that the soul held so much darkness it was a wonder the world continued turning day after day and hope lived at all.

Raina knew that truth. Maybe it was why she understood Mikhael enough that it didn't stop her from hanging out with him. An odd thought, one he wasn't ready to examine at close range, feeling a little too much kinship with Lawrence under her stroking hand.

"I've got him, Miss Raina." Steve knelt beside them. "I'm so sorry about this. He's only been working the terminal with us a couple months, so he's still figuring things out. We'll pay for the ceiling. Let us take care of him."

"I know. It's not his fault, or yours. Take him downstairs, do what you need to do for him." She squeezed his shoulder. "Get him the help he needs."

Tucking the gun in the back of his jeans, Mikhael helped Steve and his buddies get Lawrence up. Raina turned her attention to Li and Gina. By the time he'd returned from the downstairs, she'd verified their wounds weren't serious, not for their kind, and sent them for medical attention in the kitchen. She was opening the windows to air the room out. He'd learned from Marisa that the next patrons weren't due for an hour. There was blood on Raina's shirt, but with the off-the-shoulder style, he saw the bullet's track had been a graze, leaving no more than a burn mark. The blood was Gina's, from her head wound. Raina must have hugged the girl. Even knowing that, he had to force himself to give Raina room, not to crowd her into a corner to touch the superficial wound, check it, touch all of her. That gun going off, targeted at her chest, kept replaying in his mind.

She wasn't in the mood to be coddled. A storm was building around her, because nothing pissed her off like an attack on her home.

She channeled it, though, held on to a cold rationality, running down the to-dos. She obviously knew how to handle a situation like this, had likely done it before. He wasn't surprised. She seemed able to handle everything thrown at her except how he unlocked the ghosts of her past. Even so, she kept letting him in. It made him feel a way he'd rarely ever felt. Bonded to another.

He followed her downstairs to her office. When she went to her desk, he caught her there at last, closing his hand around her elbow. She turned, a frown on her face, but as he examined the abrasion left by the bullet with his fingers, she didn't flinch.

Extricating herself from his grip, she pulled a pearl-handled switchblade out of her desk. He got a glimpse of a wicked six-inch blade, then she'd retracted it, tucking it into her jeans pocket. She faced him, hands on hips, and that hardness to her eyes wasn't much different from what he felt about the matter.

"So. Shall we go find our *skinny guy* who started all this?"

"He's unconscious on the south lawn," Mikhael said. "That's where he hit my perimeter boundary. Probably zapped him with about ten thousand volts. If he wants kids, they'll be born with four heads."

"Reproducing is not going to be an issue. I'll handle him."

He considered the set of her chin, the fire in her eyes, nodded. "You wanted him alive. Though I'm not sure why, I figure it's my place to remind you of that, since you're acting like you're going to filet him."

She looked daggers at him, and he had to suppress a smile. He hadn't had that urge in a very long time.

"We need to hurry. I have a client at eight."

"Excuse me?" He stopped her with a hand. A firm hand.

"I have a client tonight. I do take a few of them, Mikhael."

"Then I suggest you cancel. I told you: while I'm fucking you, no one else is." Actually he was feeling like that needed to be the case from here until the indefinite future, and he cursed Derek for putting that bug in his brain. Damn angel blood. He could manage it. He would. But she wasn't screwing some guy right under the same roof with him.

"Well, it sounds like you aren't, then." Her eyes glowed with green fire, telling him she wasn't tolerating any exercise of testosterone at the moment—except her own. "Because this is a very important, very valued client. You can watch, if you want. Maybe you'll learn some-thing about handling women."

"Raina." His tolerance had limits. He reminded her of it in those two syllables.

She closed her eyes, made a visible effort to step back from the events of the past hour. When she reopened them, her expression was calmer, but more detached as well. "It was a very nice day. Thank you for it. But this is what I do and who I am. After I resolve this, you can take Isaac and go. He's violated the most important rule of being in my home, so I relinquish him to you. I trust you enough to do the right thing with him, but more than that, I won't risk my family. You can both leave."

Just like that, she'd turned away, all her shields in place as if he'd never even darkened her door. Or allowed her body to yield to his. He caught her elbow again, drew her back to him. "As warm and fuzzy a farewell as that is, it doesn't change the fact that whoever took the item is going to track him here."

"I'll tell them he left with you, and that will be the end of it. They have no business with me, and they won't make it past the protections on my property."

He wasn't leaving her undefended, no matter how capable she was, because they still didn't have enough knowledge of what was coming, except that it scared the shit out of Isaac. While she was pretty damn formidable, he didn't want to take the chance. Plus, he wasn't done with her yet. That was the long and short of it.

"Not going, Raina. Not yet. No matter how much you pretend you want that."

Her look would have shriveled the vital parts of most males, but he held his ground until she turned and left the room. Gods, even when she was angry, she still had that distracting pendulum walk. Right now, it didn't make him think of sex as much as it made him glad she was still breathing. He still had a perverse urge to choke her, though.

She had a client. Yeah, if she thought that was going to happen, there might actually *be* a dead body here tonight.

"Isaac. Wake up. *Wake up.*"

Raina jabbed Isaac between his bare toes with the blade, bringing him jolting out of unconsciousness. She moved back as he twisted to his side and retched into the grass. She stared down at him until he sat up, looked sullenly at her. One look at her face, however, and his became far less belligerent.

"You just couldn't believe me when I told you that you were safe here, could you?" She squatted, met him eye to eye, aware of his shifted attention to Mikhael, standing like a dark cloud behind her. She didn't know if the menace was because of their argument or because he was turning up the scary volume to help her with Isaac, but she didn't care, not if it got the job done.

"I gave you sanctuary. And you nearly got my people and clients killed trying to create enough of a distraction to cover your escape. Well, congratulations. Door's open. Go." She pointed to the woods. "The second you step off this property, you're all his, to extract information, to do whatever he wishes to you. If the female demon doesn't get you first. When you hurt my family, you don't get a second chance to do it."

She rose, pivoted. She made it a good six steps past Mikhael before Isaac rallied.

"Wait. Miss Raina. Wait."

She kept going another ten paces until he repeated it, and she heard him trying to scramble after her. She turned.

"Wait." He swayed, fell back down. She didn't move as he struggled to his knees and stayed there, fingers templed on the ground to hold him steady. "Fuck, what was in that barrier?"

"Something that would have killed you if you had prolonged contact with it." Mikhael shifted to one hip, crossed his arms across his chest. Scratched his jaw with a jagged hunting blade twice the size of Raina's switchblade. Isaac turned three shades paler.

"Please." The gaze he turned toward her was full of misery. "Please."

"No excuse, no babbling attempt to persuade me?"

Isaac shook his head. "I like Gina and everyone, but no one protects our kind. Not even our kind. It was just a matter of time before you sold me out. You're fucking *him*."

Mikhael kicked him in the side, flipped him over. Isaac yelped, then cringed as the Dark Guardian planted his boot on his chest. "You talk to her like that again, you won't have a tongue left to save your worthless hide."

Raina glanced at Mikhael's dark and forbidding expression. An impartiality settled over him when he faced something like this. A variety of contingencies were likely going through his mind right now, calculations and considerations. He was apathetic to the terror of the creature utterly helpless to him. It was chilling.

"No one protects our kind," Isaac repeated in a broken whimper.

"I can't imagine why, since we're obviously so trustworthy and loyal." She studied him. The incubus looked perilously close to tears, which could be an act. It could all be an act. It didn't change the truth of his circumstances, or that she understood what he felt. Damn it.

On certain things, she didn't second-guess herself, or agonize over decisions. She was likely to regret this one, but she knew she was going to do it. No use beating it to death in her head. "You will apologize to all of them, especially Gina and Li. After that you'll be confined to one of my guest houses, reinforced by my protection and the Dark Guardian's. You won't leave that house until this is resolved. Then we will decide what shall be done with you."

He nodded. "All right. Yes, ma'am."

"Oh, please. That's pouring it on a little thick." She was still angry. Now that she knew her people were safe, what bugged her the most was how her nice day had been ruined. She'd taken a risk, and it had resulted in this. And she resented the hell out of it, it didn't matter how petulant that was. She'd wanted one goddamn day.

It was just one day, she reminded herself. She'd had plenty of good ones, so she needed to suck it up. But this had been a damn near perfect day.

"Go to the guest house there." She pointed to it. "Mikhael or I will be there shortly, and we better find you sitting in a chair like an altar boy. Touch nothing."

As Isaac scrambled off, still staggering like a drunk, Mikhael approached her, but Raina moved away, out of reach. "Tell Matilda you want something for dinner. Doesn't do any good to tell her what. She'll prepare what she thinks you should eat. Or you can go out, so you don't have to be here tonight, if that's what you prefer. There's a good steak house right off of Main."

Marisa was coming toward them. She'd have a report on Li, and a hundred other details Raina needed to handle. Then she had the eight o'clock, followed by hostess duties from ten o'clock to closing. She was already running it down in her head, using the routine to settle her temper and her nerves, when Mikhael touched the small of her back. If she could have shrugged him off with grace and no evident agitation, she would have. Instead she set her teeth, looked up at him.

"Are you brushing me off?" he asked.

"I have things to do. I run a business here. That's the truth of it, Mikhael." She touched his forearm then, a contact she didn't let herself feel. She couldn't afford it right now. "Getting my staff calmed down enough to perform at the right level tonight will take me a while, not counting all the other things I need to do. We'll talk later."

He studied her. The truth was the easiest lie, so she let the harried expression show, a woman up to her elbows in alligators. Two more of her people were coming out looking for her, reinforcing it. Brush-off or not, she did have things to do, and if he couldn't help with that, he was just in the way. Plus, having him in her field of vision made too many things rise to the surface. She was trying to lock down a montage of images. Nearly being shot, riding a kelpie, eating a sundae, staring into his eyes in that tree as she wondered what was truly growing between them.

He hadn't given her a straight answer, but she knew the answer. It was nothing. A pleasant interlude. This, in front of her, that was her life. It was a pretty damn good life.

"Do what you need to do. I'll get your staff calmed down."

He meant it, which was shocking enough, but the fact he'd decided to help her was even more unsettling. He touched her arm, a firm grip. "I'm here, Raina. You're not in this alone. Let me help."

She gave him a stiff nod. "If for no other reason than I'll be fascinated to see what you do to calm them down."

"I'm sure you have a game of Twister somewhere in the house. Twister calms everyone down."

She looked down, pressing her lips against an aching smile, and he touched her chin. When she lifted her gaze, he bent. He didn't kiss her mouth; he did something far more devastating. He pressed his lips to that graze on her shoulder, keeping his kiss there long enough that a tremor went through her lower belly. Her hand found its way to his head, fingers burrowing in his hair. She laid her forehead against his temple.

"I've been through far worse, Mikhael," she said. "It's okay."

His arms went around her, held her close, and she relented, curling her arms around him under the strong grip of his. "Don't do that again," he said against her neck.

"We have very few gunfights. Except on Ride a Cowboy night."

Lifting his head, he did that gentle stroke over her hair. She was aware of Marisa's fascinated regard, but then he let her go, pivoted and strode toward the house. She didn't know what he said to Ana and Luke, the other two who'd come out, but they turned and followed him.

"Li's doing fine," Marisa said. "Gina says she's all right, but I think she'd be better off out of it for tonight. Li says he's ready to go. What do you need me to do?"

CHAPTER FIFTEEN

*R*aina worked with the cleaning staff to make sure the upstairs parlor was restored to its normal appearance, atmospherically and physically. She handled the former and the maids handled the latter. But when she was done, her curiosity got the better of her. Laughter and occasional raised voices, like kids clamoring to be next for a treat, kept drifting up from the first floor. Following the sound to the lower parlor, she discovered Mikhael had indeed found a way to settle her staff, get them in the right mindset.

With tarot cards.

Somehow he'd found out that Min did readings. In the past, they'd occasionally whiled away a rainy afternoon with the activity, so once he had them pointed in the right direction, it seemed several of them had volunteered to have their fortunes read. Min's interpretations were being subjected to the peanut gallery formed by the rest of them, the source of laughter and raised voices.

It wasn't just the choice of activity that amazed her. As she stood in the parlor doorway, she realized he'd taken to heart what she'd said about them being children in many ways. He'd apparently moderated his behavior accordingly, because instead of maintaining a cautious distance from him, they were clustered around him like kids around a mall Santa Claus. Okay, maybe not that bad, but still...

Min had talked him into having a tarot reading, so he was the one in the hot seat across from her now. They'd already taken him through several questions. About half of Raina's staff crowded around the wingback chair he was occupying, the rest around Min.

Sophia was kneeling next to Mikhael's leg, her bosom pressed into his knee as she leaned over it and offered alternate scenarios, since she and Min both did tarot and regularly argued over interpretations. Catalina sat on the other chair arm, and Mikhael had his hand casually laid along her hip and thigh to steady her as she twisted around to exchange quips with Saul, standing by Mikhael's one shoulder, Luke hanging over the other. It couldn't be comfortable to a warrior like Mikhael to have them at his back like that, but he showed no sign of it, exercising his dry wit to win nervous laughter and draw them out.

It was like leaving a room before an execution and coming back to find the hangman and sentenced sharing a Coke and a smile. Cue the swelling overture that assured the viewer that anyone could get along, as long as a soft drink was involved.

She noted Mikhael did appear to have a Coke, which almost made her smile. It broke free when Ana stole a sip from it, thinking he wasn't paying attention. *Good luck with that, sweetie. The man misses nothing.* Sure enough, he pinched her, telling her to behave, and though she jumped, he won a cautious, playful smile.

"You have to phrase your questions in a more open-ended way," Sophia told Mikhael. "Tarot's not really good for yes/ no answers. It's not an eight-ball reading."

"You're not old enough to know what a magic eight ball is," Mikhael scoffed.

"All that stuff is retro now." Aiden smirked. "You probably remember it as going to the Oracle at Delphi for guidance."

"Actually, the village wisewoman just read the bones." Mikhael gave him a quelling look. "Stripped out of mouthy youngsters."

"She is right," Min said shyly, looking down at the cards. "It's better to be open-ended. And you really have to choose the questions. I mean, it's worked okay with me choosing some standard ones, but you should at least choose one or two. Something that's important to you, not like your last question." She dared a reproving look at him. "The Universe doesn't like to be mocked."

"PB and J or bologna and cheese for lunch is a very important question to me. And the Universe has no problem mocking *us*. Turnabout is fair play."

"Choose a question about love," Ana prompted.

He slanted her an amused glance as Luke and Saul groaned. "Girls always want it to be about love," Luke said. "Min said it had to be important to *him*."

"Love is important to men," Ana protested. "He can ask about it in a way that means something to him. It doesn't have to be girly and romantic."

"Yeah, like: *Is forever love possible with a large-breasted porn star who can suck chrome off a trailer hitch?*"

"I'm in love just hearing about her," Mikhael agreed with Saul.

When Min shot them all a searing glare, Mikhael lifted a hand of truce. "All right, then. Let me think."

Raina couldn't deny how the scenario looked. The way the males were looking at him and the females were drawing closer; how they were all being respectful, but also trying to tease, to engage his attention. That authoritative demeanor of his, patient and yet projecting the boundaries of his tolerance. It could be wishful thinking, but it was what a strong male role model should provide. Very few of her staff had experienced such a thing in their lives, but it didn't mean they wouldn't latch onto it.

Mikhael might be horrified by her thoughts, or he might know exactly what he was doing. Now that she'd stepped in the room, she discovered it wasn't all clever intuition and his nonexistent charm that had achieved the impossible. He was putting off a hum of low-level energy that dampened their fears, helped them put away what had happened earlier. But he was also giving them what she herself had enjoyed—the cynical yet somehow appealing edge of his humor and patience.

Then he asked his question. "What should be the highest priority in my life...love or duty?"

She stilled. While he hadn't acknowledged her, she was sure he knew she was there. Min drew out the cards. She was using the Gaian Tarot, another exceptionally appropriate choice. Between her and Sophia, they had over two dozen decks, but the Gaian deck was the one that was about healing, about soothing the agitated heart while offering guidance to bring the viewer back in rhythm and harmony with natural forces. Typically, both females allowed the one being read to choose the deck, and she saw the basket of their inventory behind them. The fact Mikhael had picked the one that reflected his goal with them was just...fascinating.

He's centuries old, Raina. He knows shit.

She gave herself a mental chuckle. Yeah, he did. Maybe that, even more than the low-level energy around him, was why Sophia was at his knee, and the boys felt brave enough to make male-bonding jokes. Raina herself had experienced both sides of this particular Dark Guardian, hadn't she?

She tuned back in to his question. Love or duty. What had prompted that one?

"Six of Air," Min said, showing him the card. Her brow furrowed. "In some of our decks, that's about victory, but in this deck, it's about celebrating the day with people who mean something to you. It suggests that you don't really celebrate your successes with anyone. You do your duty without acknowledgment."

"Acknowledgment isn't necessary. Just commitment to the task at hand."

Min nodded, but when he met her gaze, she quickly shifted hers to Sophia. The young woman was considering the card as well, but she had the temerity to voice what Min wasn't. "I think this card is saying you need to let love take a higher place on your list of tasks." She nodded to another card. "Remember when Min asked how you see the people around you? The Nine of Fire came up. You maintain an even balance by avoiding people, but you can't. You're going to transcend, but your path to enlightenment may be different than you expect."

"That's pretty vague." Mikhael grunted. "Good for roadside fortune telling."

"Like when you drew for *where does he get his strength*." Luke pointed to the table and scoffed. "You pulled that Ten of Water, Min, which you said meant he gets strength from other people's happiness."

Mikhael gave him that direct look that could wilt courage at a hundred paces. "Is there something about me that suggests that's not true, Luke?"

Luke paled, stammering. "W-Well, I meant that—it's just that you're—"

"It's true. He loves puppies, and nothing makes him happier than kissing babies and helping little old ladies across the street."

Heads swung toward Raina, a wave of chuckles running through the group. "Actually, it is true," she said quietly. "The card wasn't wrong, Min. He sees happiness in unexpected places. Places the rest of us don't see it."

Min looked between the two of them, since Mikhael had turned his gaze to Raina. Seeing him among her family like this, Raina couldn't hold on to her anger or detachment from earlier. He heard a mother's lullaby in the middle of a war-torn jungle, after all, when others only heard gunfire, screams. When everyone else felt hopelessness, he saw faith. Yet he was a Dark Guardian, knowing the dark side of the soul better than anyone. He'd known her soul in barely a blink.

A little overwhelmed with the revelation, Raina leaned against a chair, nodding to Li with forced casualness. Her senior staff member was pale but determined to be here. He gave her a quick appraisal of his own, telling her he was making sure she was all right as well. Her heart filling with love for all of them, she came to him, put a hand on his shoulder.

"The Six of Air also comes with a warning," Min said, drawing their attention back. "It says you shouldn't deny yourself love, or rather, that you should make sure you don't die without love...or having loved fully."

As Mikhael regarded the card in silence, Min shifted. "Two more. You get two more questions for the reading to be complete. Unless you're tired of it."

"See if your mistress has one she'd like to ask for me, one she thinks is on my mind. Or hers."

"I'm not sure it works that way, but sure." Min shrugged, looked toward Raina.

"He's just being lazy, getting others to do the work for him." Raina snorted. "But all right. What were his other cards?"

"Two of Earth for his most important goal. He has to balance his emotional against his non-emotional self, face a gut battle against what he thinks is good and what he thinks is evil."

Raina pursed her lips. "Pretty accurate on that one."

"Not necessarily." Mikhael shifted in the chair, stretching one long leg past Min's dainty feet. "My most important goal is finding a Hooters where the faces of the female staff are as excellent as their bodies."

"Don't let me stop you. Door's right there." While the others

JOEY W. HILL

grinned at her sugar-sweet tone, she cocked her head. "Okay. I have one. How do others see you?"

Min laid out the card. Sophia lifted her gaze, the two girls exchanging a concerned glance. "Well..." Min cleared her throat.

"Min."

Raina knew that tone Mikhael used. No-nonsense, requiring a truthful and direct answer, but Mikhael added something to it. A gentle note. He was still aware of his goal here. Always focused, she reminded herself.

"Just tell me," he said. "I'm not going to be offended."

"You can't know that until you hear what I say." Min was young but no fool. Raina was amused and proud at once.

"If I'm offended, I promise not to grow three heads and eat everyone in the room."

She tittered, covering her mouth with a slim hand. She wore several rings with garnet stones on them. "All right, then. But remember, you promised."

"If I break the promise, you'll be chewed up and swallowed so fast, you won't feel a thing."

She giggled again but looked down at the card. "Eight of Fire. Most see you as a means to an end, taking them where they want to go. You arrive in the nick of time so often, it's kind of mysterious how you do that, like you're an EMT or firefighter. You're seen as a... rescuer."

Raina saw myriad reactions to that, ranging from *boy, was that one way off* in Saul and Luke's exchanged look, to Min and Ana's more pensive consideration. The girls were evaluating the way he'd acted this past hour, how Raina herself acted toward him. What he'd done upstairs with the gunman. They were probably realizing, as she had, there was far more to him than it seemed.

He nodded, glanced at the clock. "All right. Your next clients come in soon, and I don't want to get you in trouble with your boss."

Min smiled at that, but she shook her head. "You need one more question for the reading to be complete."

"All right, you choose then. Quickly."

"Okay. This is one...I think this would be a good one to ask. Why do you want to be remembered?"

Mikhael grimaced. Raina already knew being remembered wasn't a priority to him, but he shrugged, humoring Min. "Go ahead. See what comes up."

Raina moved closer. She stood at the back of Min's chair, close to Luke, who'd shifted over there. Mikhael's gaze rose, touched her, as Min turned the card.

"Wow. Explorer of Fire."

Raina looked down at a masked man walking through a winding ribbon of fire. Like a man walking through the Underworld.

"This suggests you want to be remembered as the Knight of Fire. You don't hesitate to move into danger, but you don't endanger others. Your work is very important to you." Min cleared her throat, glanced up. "You strive for perfection in ways that may not be sane, but this isn't the card of someone who cares about sanity. You reach into fire to pluck out the steel. You want to be remembered as one who created your passion and guarded your loved ones."

Knight of Fire. Raina knew he never took himself that seriously, because he didn't really think about things that way. He was a Dark Guardian. That was what he did.

Thinking about what she'd learned about him in the past few short days, she realized the tarot did bring it all together. Knight of Fire... Valuing happiness in unexpected places. A man who needed to make love a greater priority, so he didn't die without giving himself that experience. A man who might be facing that choice even now.

She didn't dare let herself think beyond that. It was past time to go to work.

She returned to her downstairs office, focused on the practical. She shuffled appointments for Li and Gina, because she was giving Li the night off, no matter what he said. He would work with Aiden on one client, a female who wanted to be taken by two males, and he could get his energy from that session. Aiden would rein back his appetite for Li, give him the lion's share, because Li would need it due to the trauma.

That accomplished, she sat back. Thinking about the reading, her thoughts went to Isaac. Rising, she took the garden exit, moving toward the guest house. To her enhanced senses, the newly erected perimeter barrier hummed like a high-voltage electrical fence. She was sure Isaac could hear it, feel the reminder, but she passed through it safely. He was sitting on the porch, staring off into the woods morosely, probably waiting for Death to step out. He knew he was out of options.

Taking a seat on the top step, she pulled an apple out of the sack she'd brought and polished it on her skirt before beginning to work on the skin with her paring knife. She didn't speak for a while, but he watched what she was doing. "I was listening to Min do a tarot reading," she said at last. "She thinks the purpose of the cards isn't to deliver answers, but to give you guidance to determine your own destiny, make the best choices. Maybe I should send her out here and let her read for you. Would you like her company? I'll send Saul with her, but I expect you aren't going to hurt her, are you?"

He shook his head. "I don't hurt...others like us. I didn't mean to do that."

"You did mean to do it. But you didn't want to. I get the difference." She finished the skin, offered it to him. He took it, playing with it, wrapping the winding around his wrist and then tearing off a piece to eat. "You've been taught that kindness and compassion are weakness, Isaac. You take advantage of people who offer them, because they're not to be trusted. If that kindness is tested, they'll cut and run, sell you out, won't they?"

He didn't answer. "It doesn't matter how long we live," she continued, "there's always room to learn something unexpected. You've had a rough go of it. In order to change that, you have to have a certain nobility of character. I don't know if you have that. I can't see it in you, but that doesn't mean it's not there, buried under all the shit you've been covered in for far too long."

He looked away, blinked. "Don't waste fake emotions on me, Isaac," she said gently. "Tears, false remorse...what matters now is what you truly are, not how well you pretend."

He nodded, averted his face farther. She could feel the misery coming off him, the resignation and hopelessness. Stuck between a rock and a hard place.

"Come here," she ordered. "Come sit with me."

He rose from the couch, knuckling at his eyes in that embarrassed male way that said the tears had been real, uninvited. She lifted her arms, let him lie down on the porch boards and put his head against her breast, his arms loosely around her waist. She rocked him like a large child, smoothing her hand over his brow, down his upper arm.

"I don't think I can change. But I wish I could."

"Well, wishing is always a start. A nap is a good start as well. I'm going to wrap you up in a sleep spell now."

He stiffened, sat up. "No."

"When was the last time you slept? Really slept?"

"It doesn't matter. I can't."

"Inside the boundaries of my property, you're safe, Isaac. I could put you to sleep without your consent, but I want you to give it. You're exhausted, and it only increases your fear and desperation. Sleep will help you feel more in control of your destiny." She feathered her hand over his brow. "It will be a true, deep sleep, no nightmares or fears. Wouldn't you like to be unafraid for a little while, see what that's like?"

"She was like this at first," he said abruptly. "Motherly, kind. Then, when I told her I didn't want to do what she wanted, she hurt me. Hurt me until all I knew was fear, until I flinched when she blinked, and that made her laugh. She had a terrible laugh. She killed Tara, like she was nothing. She *was* nothing to her."

That woke some dark memories, for certain. Raina kept her fingers loose and open, though something furled up in her chest like a dying flower. "The way we feed on sexual energy?" she said carefully. "That's the way some creatures feed on fear. She used you for a purpose, but her ultimate purpose was pain and suffering. I can't prove to you I'm not like that. You have to use your own judgment, trust where you've never been able to trust before."

It turned her mind to Mikhael. On a certain level, she was asking Isaac to do what she refused to do. She hadn't given him that full surrender he sought. He could coerce it from her, tapping into her deepest cravings, but he'd held back, waiting. True victory for them both was when she trusted enough to give him everything willingly. It was too soon for that, maybe. But then again, in an incredibly short time he'd opened up things she'd never given a male. She was sitting here, contemplating giving him the rest sooner than later, right? Case in point.

She trusted her intuition in so many ways. Though everyone else might tell her she was crazy, it was possible Mikhael was one of those rare people she could trust.

Isaac withdrew to the porch swing. "I can't," he said. "I'm sorry." He combed back his blond hair, a casually sexy gesture, innate to being an incubus, not calculated. She could see the tension, feel his rabbit instincts readying him for flight.

"All right." She nodded. "You can't consent, then. But I am going to make you sleep, Isaac. It's what you need. Though you won't believe it, you'll be safe while dreaming. You'll wake up safe, and here."

"No." He scrambled off the swing, but, of course, there was nowhere to run. "Please don't."

She lifted one hand, gently twirling it in the air, a modified royal wave. Like shades rolling down, his lids drooped, then closed. She was swift enough she caught him before he hit the porch boards. He was heavier than she'd expected, but incubi were lean muscle, after all. Lowering him to a supine position, she considered the best way to get him to the bed. The guests hadn't yet arrived, and even if they had, if they were gazing out the window rather than absorbed in their chosen companion, she needed to do some retraining. She would levitate him, get him inside that way.

Or she could rely on manual labor. Lifting her gaze, she discovered Mikhael standing in the front yard. As the tarot reading came back to her, as well as the thoughts she'd just been having, her stomach made a funny hop. Anticipation, anxiety, inevitability.

"Need some help?" he asked.

When she nodded, he came up the steps. She propelled herself into motion with a jerk, a convulsive twitch. She was going to get Isaac's legs, but Mikhael waved her off. Squatting, he slid his arms under the young male and lifted him. "Where?"

The guest house had an open layout that included a bedroom, sitting room and kitchen. As Mikhael laid Isaac on the wide couch, she took the crocheted afghan along the top and draped it over him, smoothing the hair on his brow. For the first time, the feral look was gone, leaving a young man who would be likeable if he smiled, if he didn't carry a scavenger's scuttling fear in his eyes.

She left him there without a word, moved back onto the porch and down into the yard. When she reached the gate, she turned to Mikhael. Even hearing his footsteps following close behind her, it was still unsettling to find him right in front of her. "Tarot readings?"

"Parlor tricks. It seemed to help them."

Tarot was far from parlor tricks, but he knew that. It was just the way he was, never taking anything seriously in an obvious way, even while he looked at the whole world without smiling.

Her world was about to fall out from under her, but she made herself take a step toward him. A small one. His brow furrowed at her look. "You've gotten pale, Raina."

"I never break my word."

"That doesn't surprise me to hear." Then his expression sharpened, catching up. "What are you promising me, Raina?"

"Me." She swallowed. "Tonight, after my client. However you want me. I'll come to your room and you can do...the things you've talked about doing. The things we both want." The last words were a whisper.

I flinched when she blinked. Goddess, she knew what that kind of terror felt like. But it didn't have to touch this. Not if he was worthy of her trust. She was banking everything on the idea that he was.

Mikhael saw it all, felt it all, she was sure. "All right," he said quietly. No *Are you sure?* No comfort, because he wouldn't offer that, not right now. It gave her the ability to stay strong, to not back away from it. He compounded it, showing his ruthless streak.

"So promise me. Give me your word."

"I give you my word. For tonight...I give you myself. Everything."

That was it. Her courage deserted her. Pivoting, she moved toward the house, ignoring the way her knees wobbled, hoping it didn't show too badly. She had a client. That's where her mind had to be now. The rest would be for later.

He thought he'd be rational about it. This was a bordello, and Raina ran the place. She had clients she handled personally, just as she said. She'd told him if he didn't like it, he could find the door. She'd also told him after she finished tonight, she would be coming to him, giving him something she'd never given another.

The second wave of clients arrived, were escorted to the parlor. He could make out the sounds of foreplay, flirting, pleasure being given, pleasure received. Raina's throaty laugh as she greeted guests, coordinated their desires. He watched the clock tick toward that eight o'clock hour.

Eventually some were taken to private rooms. Gina and Marisa were entertaining in the bedroom above him; Catalina and Min played a game with someone in the lower level library that involved a lot of suggestive laughter and the occasional sound of a riding crop slapping bare flesh. Luke passed outside his door with his arm around the one named Mark, telling him that he had something very special for him... if he was a good boy.

The parlors got quiet. He tuned in to Isaac periodically, verifying he was still in that deep sleep. Otherwise, Mikhael lay stretched across his mattress, every muscle tight, every sense stretched out for one taste of her. Sexual energy was released through the house, coming through the vents and wafting across his ceiling in colors of blue, purple, gold, shimmering silver...

There. Her specific scent, her arousal. That gold and green like her eyes, tinged with blue and rose, an emotional response as well as a physical one.

Fuck rationality.

There was too much swirling through the air for him to pinpoint her location exactly, unless he focused, and he wasn't really in the mood for focus. It wasn't that big of a house. He could go room to room if needed. He started with her room, though even before he turned the latch at the bottom of her stairway he knew she wasn't there. No matter her feelings for a client, she'd never entertain inside her personal space. He'd been the only one to take her there, to make love to her in that far-too-small bed.

He was well aware the house had a mind of its own. A vibration of power, and the latch refused to turn. "Not the moment to fuck with me," he said. "I'm a fire element, and you're all dry timber. Really want to go toe-to-toe?"

There was an insolent creaking of boards, then the door opened with a petulant bang against the stairwell wall. She'd probably blame that hole in the sheet rock on him.

As he reached the top of the steps, Cathair was on her balcony, eying him balefully. She must have been running late, for she'd left a pile of clothes on the spread. He picked up a long piece of filmy cloth apparently meant to wrap loosely around the body and shadow what was beneath, not conceal it. He could just imagine her standing on the balcony with the wind fluttering the ends away from her, her dark hair wildly whipping, an invitation to sex and sin under the moonlight.

"Going to Heeelll," Cathair promised.

"Not before I have raven stew...with carrots." Mikhael bared his teeth at the bird. The raven cocked his head, unfazed, and defecated over the rail.

He thought about a carefully aimed smack that would spin the bird off his perch and dislodge a few tail feathers, but decided against it. Messing with a witch was one thing, but messing with her familiar? Vicious as mother bears about them. Besides that, if he was going to deliver a smack or pluck any tail feathers, he'd much rather do that to the witch in question.

The library was empty. Min and Catalina had apparently taken whomever they were entertaining elsewhere. Ellen was in the empty parlor, setting out decanters and plumping pillows. She turned in surprise as he came in, probably because the room temperature went up several degrees.

"Where?" Mikhael said ominously.

"She's with a client," she said. Apparently something altered in his expression, because she added, with a perilous crack in her voice, "We never disrupt a client's privacy unless it's a matter of personal safety."

He took a step forward, the couch pressing against his knees. "I'm about to break that rule for every fucking client in this house. I will kick in doors until I find her. Plus, she invited me."

You might learn how to treat a woman. Okay, maybe she'd been being a smart ass, but he'd take it at face value.

Ellen had shifted nimbly behind the couch so he wasn't standing too close. "Let me buzz her, make sure it's okay. But if she doesn't answer..."

"Ellen." Placing his hand on the couch, he sent it sliding away from the wall with enough force it turned the Persian rug into an accordion before it. He had her cornered. "Where? *Now.*"

"Third-floor ballroom," she squeaked.

He was being a bastard of the first order. Though his reputation might be fearsome, he rarely felt anger or showed it as such, but right now his blood was boiling. Somewhere in this house, another man's hands were touching her, his mouth...

With a curt nod, he pivoted and started out the door. Then he stopped, sighed, turned back around. While Ellen watched him with astonished eyes, he moved the sofa back in place, kicked the rug flat once more, then strode from the room.

When he reached the top of the carpeted stairs, he heard music. A smoldering Latin beat. Going down the hall, he passed open doors that showed other sitting areas, private play rooms, some occupied by those who liked the chance of an audience. He didn't look into them, which was probably good. Even so, when he passed, he heard those doors closing, the violence vibrating off him enough to put a damper on the exhibitionism urge.

The square footage of the house had to be magically enhanced, since there seemed to be no end to the damned winding hallways, spacious areas and bedrooms, little cozy nooks for rendezvous. At last stopping before the double doors that obviously held the ballroom, not just because of the grand cut of the doors, but because he could sense her energy signature here, he heard Raina's sultry laughter. A male's rumbling voice responded, and murder painted everything red. The surge of bloodlust startled him enough to make him stop, close his hands into fists, take a deep breath. What the hell was the matter with him? Did he really expect her to take off from work the entire time he was here?

If work meant fucking some other guy, hell, yes, but he knew how unreasonable that was. Unless his unreasonable reaction was exactly because of what Derek had said. If it was, he *really* needed to turn away, do what he'd told Derek he'd do. Back away, leave it alone. It didn't matter what was true in this case; it mattered what was possible.

Yes, she was willing to give herself to him tonight. Yes, she responded to him on an emotional as well as sexual level, and he was intrigued by her. Captivated by her. But he'd been fucking everything that moved for hundreds of years and moving on. He hunted her kind. There was a whole laundry list of reasons why it wouldn't work out.

One of them being she was behind that door, offering her body to someone else.

He was going in circles here, his logic off somehow, but he couldn't work it out. He needed to go back downstairs, offer a stiff apology to Ellen and get a drink. Go for a walk. Maybe go poke Isaac in his sleep with a sharp stick, just to make himself feel better.

He stared at the doors. He could kick them open, but Raina would fly into a glorious rage if he damaged the mated swans carved in the panels. Instead, he turned the latch and stepped into the room, prepared to shed blood.

CHAPTER SIXTEEN

*T*he ballroom had a polished floor, a chandelier, elaborate moldings and a ceiling painted with cherubs and clouds. It recalled a nostalgic, graceful time when such details mattered. Raina was in the arms of the male Mikhael had imagined breaking into several pieces, but the scenario wasn't exactly what he expected.

"How often did you and your wife get all the way through the *bachata*, Jorge?" Raina asked, laughter in her voice. "Before other urges took over?"

Her dance partner chuckled. "Some things are private between a man and his wife, even with a lovely confidante such as yourself. But I will say...not often."

Jorge was in his seventies, a very fit seventy, given that he was in the middle of a demanding Latin dance that had him and Raina pressed close to each other, hips moving in tandem together, his thigh between hers. As they moved with seamless synchronicity, he lifted her hand over her head, turning her, and then released his grip so she could comb her fingers through her hair in sensual display.

His hands slid to her bare back, her hips. She wore a short skirt of stretchy fabric that barely hugged her ass, and a halter that was a gauze sash crisscrossed over her breasts and knotted between them. Underneath she wore nothing, revealing the dark smudge of her nipples. Her hair was down and flowing, her eyes made up so they looked dark green and mysterious, lips red and wet like a Latin gypsy girl.

Mikhael moved silently to the shadowed corner, for the room was lit only by candles. He knew Raina was aware of his presence, but the man seemed oblivious. He didn't blame him.

"I liked this dance," Jorge said, "because we rarely had to let one another go. I was able to keep her close throughout the steps. Away from other men."

"But I thought you like the teasing dances as well. Like the tango?"

He smiled against her hair as he pulled her back to him. Raina rotated her hips against his body as his fingers spanned her bare midriff. "Ah, she liked to tease like you do. Drove a man mad."

"That's what women do. Make you crazy, make your blood boil." She turned again in his arms with a little sigh. "But then you have your revenge. Your lust makes us breathless."

And she was. It wasn't faked. She wasn't seeing an old man, treating him with patronizing indulgence. She was seeing a man who danced this dance with true masculine style, who'd overwhelmed his wife with it, with the sexual beat that it was meant to have. When Jorge's hand moved to her lower back, or so close beneath her breast he had to be feeling the heavy weight on his knuckles, she responded to it, responded to his skill as a lover. Mikhael pushed down an absurd attack of jealousy toward the septuagenarian. Yes, he was vastly older than Jorge, but that was different.

On the elaborate turns, the kicks and footwork, they were well matched. Jorge was more skilled, suggesting he'd taught Raina the dance over multiple sessions, her natural sensuality making her a good student. Mikhael let himself be absorbed in her every movement, the undulation of her made-for-sex body, the beauty of it. She could have been Jezebel, Bathsheba, Helen of Troy, but she was Raina. A fascinating, complex creature that could fog a man's senses to the point he'd miss the real treasure.

She gave herself to this, to this moment and this client, embracing what she was to savor it, to give him an unforgettable experience as well. That tapestry of her unique magic was in the air, swirling around them like a multicolored fog, the silken tendrils splitting and curling with the air currents raised from the dance.

Though Jorge was as stimulated as himself by the vision she made,

Mikhael didn't sense this was going to end in sex, and not just because he wasn't going to permit it. This was about something else.

As the music changed, became a deeper, more emotional beat, the pace slowed. She leaned up against Jorge, stroking his hair as he buried his face in her neck. "Sshh...it's all right. Dance with me, Jorge. Just dance."

They maintained that position for the duration of the song, the man holding on to her, lost in the memory of the woman he wished he were embracing. But when the beat changed up again, Jorge straightened, gave her a strained smile, tears in his eyes. Then he launched them into a fast samba.

By the time that dance was done, they were both sweating, and she was smiling as well. She'd missed a few steps during the dance, and he'd helped her correct them. When they eventually came to a halt, she squeezed his hands, then moved across the room, hips swinging. Reaching the corner beside the music player, she bent to get him a towel, revealing she was wearing a black thong beneath that small skirt. While Jorge fully appreciated the view, Mikhael swallowed back an animal growl.

When she came back, her gaze flickered over Mikhael, but then returned to her client. "That was marvelous. I can eat a bigger breakfast in the morning and suffer not a moment of guilt."

"Chica, you never experience guilt. You know your beautiful breasts and that gorgeous bottom of yours are exactly the size a man wants. I forbid you to lose a pound from them." Sliding his fingers along her face, Jorge then dropped that touch to stroke a curve, considering. Raina tilted her head toward it, then looked up at him.

"Tonight?"

He didn't say anything for quite a while, just stroked her breast, her bare side, his eyes seeing something else. Someone else. At long last, he looked up, shook his head. "No. Thank you, *querida*, for offering. As always."

"I offer for very few, Jorge. The invitation is always there for you."

"Perhaps not. I have heat burns between my shoulder blades." The man turned then, giving Mikhael a direct look. "This one is asserting a claim on your affections."

So he'd known he was there the whole time, and hadn't missed a step. He'd probably added a few of those more blatantly sexual moves to prove the point. Pretty ballsy old bastard.

"He only has my attention for the moment," Raina said. "You have my heart forever."

Jorge kissed her hand and held it to his chest. "If my Juliana hadn't taken mine with her, I might have offered it to you. But any man would."

"No. Men offer women their souls, but rarely their hearts." Raina touched his face. "Thank you, as always, for teaching me to love your dancing."

"Thank you." Jorge kissed her hand again, then turned to Mikhael. "I relinquish her to you, but only because your jealousy has propped up an old man's ego."

Mikhael nodded, but he couldn't inject a great deal of warmth in the gesture. *He only has my attention for a moment.* Knowing it was gentle charm, it still didn't sit well, hearing it aloud.

Raina escorted Jorge to the door, her hand on his arm. "Be sure to have Gina schedule your next appointment. Maybe one day you'll cave and let me ravish you...old man."

Jorge's chuckle filtered back through the doors as Raina closed them. Turning, she leaned against the panels, considering Mikhael.

"Were you planning to pull some slobbering naked fool off of me?" she asked lightly.

"Actually, I'd planned something more violent. Bludgeoning him into bones and pulp, then spreading your legs and fucking you next to his bleeding body until you screamed my name."

Her eyes darkened further, the makeup making them even more tantalizing. She moistened her lips. As she came toward him, her posture tilted her breasts up, drew his eyes to the way they strained against the gauze sash.

"Do you worry that he's not moving on with his life, coming here to dance with the ghost of his dark-haired wife?"

She shook her head. "No. He has children, grandchildren. He runs a business in town, is well tied into the community. This is his secret gift to himself. Some people only have that one person in their life, and they'll never find another, because that was enough. Perfection. He's one of those."

Stopping a few feet away, she twisted her hair up, holding it to let the cool air touch her nape. The position cocked her hips provoca-tively in the heels she was wearing. "Can you dance?"

"I can manage a step or two when pushed to it."

"I expect you excel at this kind of dancing. At all sorts of dancing."

"What I want is for you to dance for me, Raina. Make me hard the way you made him hard."

She pursed her lips, her lashes lowering. "You're already hard." But she rolled her hips in that figure eight movement that could scramble a man's brain, pivoting on her toe as she did it, so he saw it from every angle. She gave him a smoldering look over her shoulder.

Rising, he held out his hand. She backed away, continuing her dance, untying the sash that formed her revealing halter top as part of her choreography, her hips shimmying in the brief skirt. She worked her way around him, her fingers trailing along his back, his waist, his hip, and then she pivoted away again, the sash fluttering out.

He caught it, yanked, and sent her spinning back against him. Putting his hand low on her back, he dipped his fingers under the short skirt to tease the indentation between her buttocks. When her lips curved, he knew she'd taunted him deliberately to see if he'd take over. She had no idea how deep and dark a place that was for him when it came to her. But he was about to show her.

"You're done with your client. Time to deliver on your promise."

She gave him a look, moved to the wall, and was brought up short by the sash still loosely looped over her shoulder and around her rib cage. She slipped it off her shoulder, her gaze holding his, and he released one end. As he'd hoped, she did a slow, graceful turn to fully free herself, and her end of the sash fluttered to the ground, leaving her upper body bare and him grasping the other end of the sash. Giving him a satisfyingly smoldering look, she went to the intercom system. As his gaze coursed over the line of her back, Mikhael heard Ellen pick up. "Yes, Raina?"

"Has Marisa finished with her appointment?"

"Yes."

"Have her rotate hostess duties with Ana and Li. They can let me know if they have any problems."

"All right. Have fun." The mischief and amusement in Ellen's voice didn't translate to the intensity of what was happening in this room, but then Raina clicked off and it was just the two of them. He came to her where she stood by the doors, slid his arms around her, lifted and brought her back to the middle of the floor. Her heart was pounding, her lips parted. He inhaled her scent, a drug he would always crave.

Lowering her to her back onto the smooth wood, he let her legs slide between his like a dance maneuver in truth, but when he knelt, he placed his knee between hers, laid his hands on her thighs and parted them, pushing them out and up, bending her knees. He felt the quiver, that female acknowledgment of him looming over her, a potential threat or temptation.

"Put your arms over your head."

That trembling increased, but she did it, with a lift of her chin and a fire in her eyes that said she was doing it because she wanted to do it, not because he'd commanded it. The two went hand in hand with her, and she knew it as well as he did, no matter what games she wanted to play.

"Dance for me now, Raina." He cupped her buttocks, put his weight on his heels and lifted her up to his mouth, pushing back that skirt with the pressure of his mouth coming to her sex. He teased the labia and clit through the satin of the thong as her hips bucked, rolled, the most carnal dance of all, and a gasp broke from her lips. She was wet, whether from her dance with Jorge or from Mikhael watching, he didn't know, but it didn't matter. He was the only male getting to taste that sweet honey.

He flicked her clit with his tongue, swirled over her labia until the insistent grind of her hips said she wanted him penetrating, his tongue fucking her, or his cock. He'd make her wait, his gaze devouring the quiver and movement of her generous breasts. But he took her close to the climax, pushing against the clit, that satin friction helping him until she was panting, her face flushed. Then he backed off, because he knew how he wanted her this time, and for that he had to have her hot and wanting, no room for fears in the heat.

Turning her over on her stomach, he caught her hands, tied the sash around her wrists and then wound it all the way up to the elbows, cinching them close so she felt the strain in her shoulders, but not enough for true pain. Just the arousing discomfort of bondage, of knowing he was making her helpless. When he turned her back over, her bare breasts thrust out, tempting him.

"Mikhael."

"Sshh. No talking unless I give you permission. Just feel it, Raina." He folded her over his shoulder, rising to his feet. He had one hand steadying her by the waist and hip, but before her tension could take over, he put the other back between her legs, finding that wetness and stroking it, keeping up the manipulation that had her making little frenetic jerks against his shoulder, as well as pleading noises that drove him crazy.

Leaving the ballroom, he went down to the private playroom he'd seen on the way. It was empty, so he didn't have to bark at anyone and send them scuttling. Shutting the door with his foot, he brought her back to her feet in front of him. Tied deliciously, her breasts thrust out, shoulders back, unsteady on her heels so she had to depend on him to keep her balanced. Her hair was disheveled, and he pushed it back from her face, tightening his fingers on it. Her eyes were wide, lips parted, and he saw the uncertainty trying to break through, the fear and memory. She was on the brink of terror, and her gaze went to him, panicked.

"Easy," he said quietly. Pushing her down with that hold in her ebony locks, he supported her until she made a safe descent to her knees, then kept holding her hair so she had to look at his face, the way he was devouring her with his eyes. It was the picture in her lower parlor, and he saw that memory kick in, calm her somewhat.

"What music do you play to relax?"

"Enya," she managed. "Watermark album."

"Pick another. Enya sucks the testosterone right out of a man's balls."

Her lush lips curved. "I have a couple clients who'll disagree with that."

"They don't count, because something's obviously wrong with their wiring." He cocked his head. "Did you just talk about other men you've had? Didn't we discuss that?"

She tossed her head, trying to free her hair from his grip, but that just made it constrict. "I don't recall."

"Let me see if I can help you remember."

There was a padded spanking bench in the room, beautiful crafts-manship, like everything she bought for Sweet Dreams. Bringing her to her feet, he guided her over to it, made her stand there watching him as he ran his hand over the cushion and woodwork, appreciating it. Then he pushed her down to her knees on the one step and folded her over it. She was quivering again, and he made an incoherent murmur as he secured her to it with straps, enjoying the look of her breasts propped over the opposite side. He combed her hair forward as he put a slim functional collar on her, snapped a tether to it and hooked that tether to the base of the bench. Then he bound her knees to the step, spread apart so he could see what was between them from any angle he wished.

She was silent, but her body was a tuning fork, vibrating with so many responses he couldn't stop watching her, registering every minute change. He'd worked her up in the other room, and now she was well on her way to mindless arousal. Her hands were opening and closing helplessly in the straps, making him even hotter.

Helpless and his. He stroked down her back, then pulled his blade and cut the skirt off her with a sharp touch of steel, doing the same to the thong. He yanked it all free, leaving her naked except for her restraints and the glorious hair.

"Mikhael."

"I'm here."

She swallowed. "Mikhael." It was a bare whisper, and something he couldn't resist. Kneeling before her, he lifted her face and kissed her mouth, tugging on the collar. She put a lot of raw need in that kiss, nothing practiced about it, inciting pure male satisfaction. It was desperate, greedy, and it lit a fire inside of him that would be assuaged only when he was balls deep inside of her. But it also called forth something else.

He traced her lips. "I'm right here. You can trust me."

The room was all rich velvet, hushed anticipation. He picked up a blindfold. Her expression changed, skin paling, but he shook his head, slid it over her eyes. "You're with me, Raina. You're safe. You're mine. Just feel."

Trembling had become shaking, but she wasn't saying no. She was getting lost in it, lost in a miasma that could go straight to a heavenly space or right into hell, if he did this wrong. But he wasn't going to do it wrong.

Her sexual energy had turned almost completely flame orange, with some bare slivers of green that indicated she wasn't entirely immersed, that some parts of her were still working through the past. He was going to help her burn that house down.

⁓

It was a different side of him. Tender wasn't the right word. Maybe tender implacability fit, because he wasn't going to release her even if she begged, and that refusal was part of what she craved. She knew she was safe and he wouldn't harm her, no matter what. It was the first time she'd felt that at the hands of a male. She'd promised him everything. Now she called on the courage that had served her in all other parts of her life and gave it to him.

"C-Can't s-stop-p shaking," she admitted, and was rewarded by a fierce satisfaction in his voice.

"That's the way it works at first. When it's done right."

"I-I know. Just n-never felt...felt it...m-myself."

He rose, trailing his fingers down her back again so she could feel he was still there. "I've wanted to do this since the first day I met you."

The clap of his palm against her bare buttock was loud in the velvet room. She jumped but felt a flash of desperate humor, knowing that there were several levels to his declaration, but then she had no space for humor, for any emotional retreat at all. He gave her a good spanking, until she felt the heat from both buttocks and flinched at the sting, but she didn't want him to stop. When he slapped her between the legs, she moaned. As he came back around, she was squirming and panting, as close to begging as she'd ever been. He knew it.

"Want to say something to me, Raina?" He wouldn't use the word that had plunged her into that bad place before, but eventually, she thought maybe he could. He'd wipe all that away with every kiss, every touch.

"Please..." It came out so soft. "Please...I need you inside me."

"No place I'd rather be."

As she heard the sounds of him stripping in front of her, she imagined seeing the weight and beauty of his cock. Her tissues contracted, weeping for him. She was so hot, so close.

"You don't go over until I say so. Tell me." He caught her chin.

"I understand."

His lips twisted. "Understanding and obeying are two different things. I want to hear you say, *I'll obey.*"

There were a lot of different things behind that word as well, such that she had a harder time with it, but he waited with the patience of a damn rock while her body shuddered with desire.

"I'll obey." After all, if she changed her mind and didn't obey, there were darker, more delicious punishments he could dish out in this room. She wanted to find out what those were, let him take her to more firsts than she'd ever thought possible.

She heard him snort as if he divined her thoughts. Yet when he moved behind her again and guided his cock into that heated gate, she felt him fighting his own reaction.

"Fuck, you're wet. And sucking on me like a vise."

Her muscles clenched around him as he pushed in to the hilt. She groaned, head jerking up against the tether, reminding her of his bindings.

"That's it. Fight me if you want, but you won't get away from this, from where I'm going to take you. You're mine, Raina. No male can own your soul the way I can."

Her response was lost as he began to thrust, driving her hips against the bench, slapping his pelvis against her reddened buttocks. She cried out on every stroke, those lovely female animal noises that said she was being pleasured beyond rational thought. His cock was impossibly thick, and she imagined his balls boiling with the seed he wanted to jet deep inside of her, mark her so there was no doubt.

"Mikhael...I can't...I'm coming."

"Come for me, then. Come now."

She exploded, no other word for it. The scream that tore from her throat was the most intense she'd ever experienced, her slickness clenching over his cock in that tight fist that dragged him right over the edge with her. He was braced over her, hands on the bench, chest pressed to her back, mouth on her shoulder, their bodies moving in tandem much like hers and Jorge's had, except Mikhael was hilt deep inside her.

"Jorge's not going to get this close. No male is," he muttered in her ear.

No male ever had. She didn't say that, but right now she believed him, belonged to him utterly, because she wanted to do so.

~

It didn't end there. She'd promised him everything and he took it. A couple times she blacked out, and when she roused, she was always in his arms, with him cosseting her. He never took off the blindfold, made her dependent on him throughout, her senses straining to respond to his every command and touch.

He tested out all the equipment in the room, brought her to climax three times before she started to lose track. Every time she fed on his energy, she just came back stronger. She couldn't have held back her need to drink if she tried, so she became sated with it and savage, reduced to a primal creature who only wanted more.

Which made her eventual exhaustion all the more remarkable. She'd never given out before a lover. When she was limp and sated, Mikhael carried her out of the room and to the second level, to his bed. They'd given him the royal master suite and it suited him, looking like a king's chambers. Putting her on her back, himself between her legs, he took her one last time. She made a feminine note of distress as he parted abraded tissues, adding just enough force to remind her she was his, but not enough to be unbearable, holding her on that knife edge of pleasure, pain and service.

Before he released inside of her, he made her come one more time with his skill and her overwhelming desire to please him.

She might have called him *Master* a couple times. It was a hazy, disturbing memory, mainly because she'd meant it with every ounce of passion she gave him.

At last, she lay in the curve of his body, limp and unresisting as he stroked her breast. His other hand traced small circles over her clit, because he'd told her to keep her legs parted for him. Occasionally he leaned over her, suckled her nipple gently, his toy to play with as he wished. It caused a slow liquid river of arousal through her body.

When the night deepened, he folded his arms around her, holding her close to his chest, and they fell into a postcoital coma together.

~

It was past three a.m. No disturbances in the house, some sessions still happening, but it was winding down. Her brain cells were still sluggish, but with her cheek pressed to his chest, listening to his breathing, she knew he was awake. He probably knew she was awake, but he said nothing, so she started thinking.

When he made love, had sex or fucked her, it was always in line with her feelings of the moment. An exceptional sexual Dominant figured that out. He anticipated the need of whoever he was with. Some small part of her was bothered by that, because maybe he exercised that trait on anyone. He'd done it to Ruby, after all.

She thought back to their trip into town, the way he'd protected her there, even when she didn't need it. Dark Guardian. Light Guardian. It didn't matter. Maybe because she was a creature of darkness herself, she was beginning to believe Mikhael, that the cause they served might just be the same.

He arrives in the nick of time...he gets strength from the happiness of others...love versus duty...

He acted as though he were uniquely charged with her protection. Unless Lucifer had mandated that, it was something Mikhael had mandated himself, for his own reasons and desires. She didn't question the sanity of the thought the way she might have a few days before. Instead, she moved closer to him. His arm tightened, all that hard muscle against her back.

She'd spent six years of her life in hell. She'd learned her Craft, continued to learn, such that no one was taking her down without a fight. But being able to take care of herself didn't mean she felt safe. Once being that kind of victim, a person never felt safe, no matter how they tried.

With him, she did. Life was a funny thing.

Succubus or incubus, there was a killer instinct to her kind, in the blood she carried. It made the sadistic side of Mikhael's personality a soothing balm, a tonic on that homicidal urge. It was something she likely couldn't explain to Ruby or Ramona, but he got it. He couldn't be harmed by it, either. He could take it, and that meant something.

Running a hand over her buttock, he pinched her gently, but enough that she felt the soreness from his spankings. It gave her a shiver. "What?" he asked.

"With Ruby, you were brutal, merciless, unkind even."

"She told you that?"

"I could tell. But that was what she needed, wasn't it?"

"With what she was playing with at that time, yes."

"So you did it to help her."

"Don't set me up for sainthood on that one."

"I didn't say you didn't enjoy it." Raina scraped his chest with her fangs, pricked him. "But it was tempered by your heart, by what she needed from you. Which makes me wonder what you need."

"I don't think about that."

"Everyone thinks about what they need and want."

"I'm bound in service to the Underworld for all eternity. That's what I do."

"You're here with me, in this bed. Lucifer didn't dictate that. So I'm something you want, at least at the moment."

"You are definitely that. In fact, I want you right now."

"You couldn't possibly."

In answer, he pressed her to her back. She couldn't help a shiver of trepidation, because she really was sore, a unique experience for her, but he held her gaze and her legs parted for him. When he slid into the slickness left from their climaxes, he went slow, easy. He would never ask, never allow her to refuse, and that just made her more willing. She lifted a hand, stroked his cheek.

"You're not a kind man, but I do think you're a good man. A man with integrity."

"I can accept that. If it gets me laid."

Seeing the gleam in his eye, she punched him in the side, none too gently. "Ass."

He thrust deeper, and she let out a gasp at the sensation. When he gripped her wrists, she tensed, but he nuzzled her throat until her hands opened up, and she gave herself to the way he felt pressed up between her legs, her heels resting high on his thighs.

"I can feel your magic like the blood coursing through your veins," he murmured against her throat. "I can feel you wrapped around me. I like it. I like being here with you."

Gentle intimacy. Unexpected from him. She'd always been guarded about her feelings, not in a bad way, but because she weighed everything for the proper response for clients, for her incubi and succubi. Sometimes she shared her thoughts with Cathair, sometimes Ruby and Ramona, but with them it was mostly maudlin moments that didn't really mean much.

"Just say what you feel, Raina. It's all right."

"You're heavy."

He chuckled, nipping her throat. "I won't move until you tell me what you feel."

"I like having you here, too. For now. Until you irritate me."

He continued that nibbling on her neck, easing his way down to the rise of her breast, making her heart squeeze in on itself as he stayed so tender, treating her with reverence. But not an arms' length Goddess reverence. The type of reverence that came with the seeds of love.

Okay, that thought stiffened her like a board. "I need to get some sleep. I need to go to my own bed."

"When I'm here, this is your bed, Raina. It's a much better fit for my size." He caught her chin. "What's wrong?"

She shook her head. "Old demons. Leave it, please?"

Mikhael studied her a long moment. "Can you sleep in my arms, Raina? Just sleep and not worry about anything for a little while?"

She wanted to sleep in his arms more than anything she'd ever wanted. That was what was worrying her the most.

"It'll be all right," he said. He slid out of her, apparently content with simple penetration. Settling her on her hip, he guided her legs so her knee was nestled between his thighs, up against cock and testicles, their warmth and reminder of male presence. "Sleep. There's nothing to fear."

Except him, and the way he made her feel. Curling her fingers in his chest hair, liking far too much his arms being wrapped around her, Raina closed her eyes. She willed herself to the escape of dreams, even knowing dreams might very well be the problem—old dreams, wishes that she'd lost long ago.

CHAPTER SEVENTEEN

When they woke just past lunchtime, Ana and Min brought them a light repast, a kind surprise. The girls, getting an eyeful of Mikhael's body, the sheet low on his hips, wanted to pile in and share the croissants and strawberries with them. Raina sent them scampering with threats of hair-loss spells and rashes. Mikhael had looked amused at her desire to keep him to herself. She'd been a little unsettled by it, as well as the fact that, though the girls wore lingerie that hid very little, his total attention was on her.

Even as they set the tray on the side table, he'd started placing hot kisses on her throat, tugging at the sheet to get access to her body, barely waiting until they were gone to take her again, all before eating. Then he fed her from his hand, refusing to allow her to feed herself, underscoring his claim of the previous evening. She didn't tell him the fantasy was over, that her submission had been for that one night, because quite frankly, she wasn't sure if she ever wanted it to end.

But the world eventually intruded. Li came in with a scheduling issue and a reminder that tonight's bachelor party, a group of thirty, had several issues that would need her attention. She told him she'd be there shortly. As she left the bed, she noticed Mikhael went still, his focus internal. An arc of power flickered off him, an arc not his own, which made her go on alert.

"Mikhael?"

He held up a finger, keeping that internal focus, and she realized then he was listening to someone. Someone speaking in his head, and the message wasn't entirely welcome. When his expression cleared, he looked up at her. "Lucifer wants me back in the Underworld for a short meet."

"Of course. I have a conference call with God later today." She plucked his custom-tailored dress shirt out of the closet, considering it her due since he'd carried her down here naked last night, uncaring of who they met in the halls. Now she put it on, ran her fingers through her hair. Time for a reality check, and what better sign than a hail from the Lord of the Underworld himself?

"I shouldn't be gone long."

"You don't report to me, Mikhael. We had sex, not a marriage ceremony."

She knew if she stood in front of a mirror, she'd have bruises, marks from his mouth, his hand. And she'd be glowing from all of it. But this was a fantasy and, like all fantasies played out in this house, it had a beginning and an end. "While I'm there," he said, his eyes on her, "I'll follow up on some leads about who might be chasing Isaac. I should be back late tonight, but with that tracer on him, and the protections I've put with yours to reinforce your perimeter, I'll be aware if anything happens. You won't have to be concerned about you or your staff."

"I can take care of myself." She tossed her head, gave him her sexy smile. "I'm not worried about that. Go do your thing. I have a life, you know. Can't be lazing around bed all day."

He rose, unconcerned about his nakedness. Goddess, the man was beautiful. When he came to her, she saw he had some bite marks and scratches as well, which absurdly pleased her, though it didn't dispel the apprehension in her stomach. Like some melodramatic teenager, she felt like he was never coming back.

"Raina." He lifted her up to sit on the dresser, putting himself between her knees. "There's nothing to worry about."

Her temper sparked, more with herself than him, but she preferred to lash at him. "I *know* that," she said impatiently. "I have a busy schedule today."

"This is different for me, too."

That stilled her, her attention snapping to his face. "I'm coming back," he continued, "not just because Isaac is here, but because I want to figure out what this is. I look at you, and I want to keep you. Protect you. Never let you go."

There was another word hovering there, for both of them. Mikhael knew she was no more prepared to hear it than he was to say it. It had been three fucking days and, while he knew what he knew about his own kind, she was another species. Succubi rarely mated, and the ones that did were practically an urban legend, probably because of their insatiable and deadly sexual appetites. She wasn't full succubi, but she surely had an insatiable appetite. So did he.

In fact, his appetites, even for one of his kind, were considered somewhat excessive. He wondered if there'd been a reason for that, and that reason was in front of him. He kept that to himself, though. Even with a succubus's sensibilities, Raina wouldn't appreciate the theory that his need to fuck hundreds of women had been preparation for her. She could put a spell on his dick that tied it into a half hitch. He might be able to counter it, but he'd rather not take the risk.

But he *could* fulfill all her needs on that score, and would be damn sure he did—often.

"All right," she said, giving him her faint smile, the one that came from the uncertain, vulnerable place inside of her. "Go do your thing, and get your ass back here. Succubi aren't known for our patience."

"I saw a few toys in that drawer that might help you pass the time." He caught her chin, his fingers stroking before he pressed a kiss against her throat. "But record it; else I'll make you do it all over again in front of me."

"Sounds terrible."

"It will be if I tie you up and keep using the toys on you, but never let you come."

"Sadist."

"You love it. Masochist."

She pushed at him. When he kissed her fingers, her eyes stilled on his face. "You smiled. Mikhael, you smiled."

"I'm sure it was a mistake." But he squeezed her hand hard, glad to give her something that pleased her. Then he kissed her until she was breathless. "To think about me when I'm gone."

"You better get back fast. That kiss will only last me an hour. Then you'll be a distant memory."

~

That taunt had been a *big* mistake. The good kind. A succubus was never sore from sex, because only another sex demon could have that much sex. Or, apparently, a Dark Guardian. She was quite aware of the speculative glances, the hidden smiles as she moved with slow dignity through the house that day, refusing to limp, hobble or groan. If she had to sit, she chose the edge of a chair. So she did a lot of standing.

When Gina came to her late afternoon, they had the schedule under control, the night's preparations down to a few to-dos. Raina was taking a fifteen-minute catnap, stretched out in the side garden, basking in the sunlight while Cathair made a mess in the birdbath, flapping his wings and spraying drops of water on her. Feeling Gina's approach, Raina cracked her eyelids.

"If Catalina has changed her mind one more time about the outfit she's wearing, tell her I'm going to turn her out naked in front of those thirty horny men and tell them she's a no-holds-barred, all-you-can-eat buffet."

Gina chuckled. "No. I'm here for you."

Curling her fingers around Raina's wrist, the young woman tugged her to a sitting position. Curious, Raina rose to follow her. Gina led her through the gardens, around to the back of the estate, to the spa house attached to it by a covered walkway. She'd had it added a few years back, another attraction for female clients. Now her staff had run a fragrant bubble bath in the tub that could hold twelve. Marisa was there, and Li, and Ana. As she stood, unresisting and moved, they undressed her, helped her into the tub.

"Just soak for a while," Marisa said. "Then we'll give you a massage."

Ana stripped to come into the tub with her. She'd brought the herbal remedies that were often used on clients after a vigorous session, but it was the first time Raina had experienced them. Ana attached the mix to the gentle sprayer and applied the diluted rinses where needed, inside and out, shifting Raina as needed. Mikhael hadn't left an orifice unclaimed, and as Ana's touch whispered over her, Raina's mind drifted over those provocative memories. Goddess, he'd been deliciously insatiable, unstoppable.

When they helped her out of the tub after the perfect amount of soaking time and laid her down to apply oil-based salves to those same areas, as well as the scrapes and bites, she let out a simple moan of pleasure.

"He's a great big animal, isn't he?" Li murmured, amused. He'd begun her massage, starting at her feet and calves, while the girls worked higher up.

"The best kind," Raina mumbled. She decided then and there each of the staff would have a turn at this monthly, because it was pure heaven. She wasn't certain that Li helping with the massage would meet her Dark Guardian's approval, but such casual intimacy was a sex demon thing. Ana and Min would have joined them in bed this morning without hesitation, following her direction to give both her and Mikhael pleasure, if that had been Raina's wish. Afterwards, if she told them Matilda was making chocolate chip pancakes for breakfast, they would have rushed downstairs, squealing like Christmas morning.

Mikhael might discover there were a lot of upsides to calling a bordello home.

She stilled at that thought. She knew the word unspoken between them this morning, both of them too jaded to speak it. While the potential of it was hard to deny, all she'd known of him three days ago had been the rumored reputation of Dark Guardians and Ruby's account. There were still far too many things to learn.

But was she willing to try, if he was?

Shutting her eyes, she turned herself over to her sex demons' care. Tried not to worry that her boyfriend being away from her would give him the chance to decide he liked someone better. Or worse, prove he'd only been killing time with her. Goddess, it was crazy. Did never having been in a relationship, a real one, mean she had to start from the very beginning, go through all the adolescent feelings she'd never had a chance to experience? If that was the case, she'd just cut her own throat now and save herself the humiliation.

Her staff was being too damn quiet. "*What?* Why aren't you all talking?"

"Actually, we've said a couple things to you," Li said. "You've been lost in your head."

More than that, the rest of her dozen staff had arrived. Some were ringed around the pool, dipping their feet into the water's flow. Saul was lounging on one of the tanning chairs.

"I'm sorry." Raina sighed, reaching up to stroke Li's face. "Are all of you all right? I know it's been a bit unsettling, having a Dark Guardian among us."

"We're fine. He's not so bad. We've all dealt with scary evil before. He's scary...predictable. He tells you his rules, and he doesn't change them."

"So you don't think he's evil?"

"No." Gina looked puzzled that she'd even asked. "You wouldn't have anything to do with him if he was. Unless you had to pretend to protect us. You don't act like you're pretending."

Just that simple. And it was true.

"Though the point of good faking is no one knows," Li teased. "And Raina can convince anyone of anything."

Amused, Raina relaxed a little more. Sometimes she forgot how much she enjoyed her staff. "So what do you think, Li? Am I pretending?"

"No. The only time I've seen you pretending is when you were acting like you *didn't* want him."

"Wanting and liking are different things." Raina pressed her lips together. "I do like him, sometimes, but I keep looking for his agenda. Anything he wanted to take, though, he could have already done it and been gone."

"Except what he wants is you."

She lifted her gaze to Saul. He'd brought the softening oil they all used to make their skin pleasing to their clients. Li shifted out of the way so he could apply it. They knew she liked Saul's massages the best, because of his strong but gentle hands. She wondered what kind of massages Mikhael gave. Or if he'd like a massage. He wouldn't want one from Saul, no matter how good his hands were. Her lips curved at the thought. One thing she didn't get from Mikhael was a bi vibe. Her tall, dark and brooding male was pure hetero.

"He's chosen you," Gina agreed. "You can tell." She sat on the edge of the pool, her feet in the water. "He wants you."

"It's an intense affair, that's all. He'll move on eventually. I'll enjoy him until then."

"You don't say anything about you moving on. Which means you're just protecting yourself. You want him, too. You miss him. You're worried." Saul rubbed her foot, massaging the arch in a way that had her eyes crossing. "Your aura has gone into full blood-mating mode."

Oh, hell. "It's a misfire." But as soon as he'd left, a heavy ache had developed in her chest, a sense of loss strong enough to be painful. She'd rationalized it, tried to push it off, but it didn't change the throbbing agony behind her breast bone. It was even projecting off her skin where an incubus could see, because the males could detect when the females had chosen a mate. Succubi didn't usually do that, or if they did, it was temporary. For a witch who happened to be half succubus, it might be different.

"It doesn't mean anything."

Helping her up without comment, Saul guided her to the salt spring. She closed her eyes, laid her head back on the edge so Min could rub her temples with eucalyptus and lavender. "He's a Dark Guardian. Would you all really want him hanging around?"

"He says he doesn't pursue demons like us, because we're not causing harm. I believe him." This from Ana. "He *is* scary, but he doesn't lie."

"Yeah," Saul said dryly. "Right after that, he said— pleasant as you please, and with a heavy Russian accent—*Those who cause harm, I hunt down and tear apart, like paper dolls.*"

Mikhael, you ass. But they were right. He was savage, dangerous... and brutally honest. *This is different for me, too.* He'd said that, and meant it. So maybe he didn't know what to make of it any more than she did.

"Tonight's the full moon," Marisa said. "Are you going to do your midnight thing?"

"We'll see how the bachelor party goes."

"We can handle it." Saul nodded to Li, Luke and Aiden. "You've taught us how to simmer things down if needed, to monitor the energy patterns. We'll watch over the girls."

"Are you all becoming all grown-up and responsible on me?"

"We wouldn't risk shocking your system like that. You might short-circuit." Luke had gotten into the salt spa across from her and now let his foot slide along her knee, trying to worm his toe between her thighs. He pulled back with a laugh when she splashed him. Then he sobered. "We can handle it, Raina. Go do your thing."

"It recharges you," Marisa said. "We know how much energy this takes. In fact..." She glanced at the other girls. "We've been talking. We know we're not witches, but we know lots of people who aren't born with that talent do energy work. With us being sex demons, it should make us more capable at it than them, right? We think you should start teaching some of us how to more actively help you, to protect the house, protect the clients. Let us share the load."

Raina straightened, studying their uncharacteristically somber faces. "Where is this coming from?"

"When you went to town, you looked happy, excited," Li said. "You don't look like that. Ever. It made us all think about it. I've been with you for six years, and you've never had a boyfriend, or a date. Don't get me wrong." He looked around him. "Your life doesn't suck. You have an awesome place, and you enjoy life. But you should be able to go into town to see a freaking movie without it being a major deal. You should be able to go out on a date. You should be able to fall in love, if that's what you want to do."

Gina slid into the water to cuddle under her arm, while Ana did the same on the other side. When Luke met her gaze, her usual prankster was serious, a trace of sadness in his eyes. "Every one of us owes our lives to you, mistress," he said quietly. "You've given us your love and protection, as well as kicked our asses when we needed it. It's time for us to do the same for you. We haven't done much for you except make you a boatload of money. We can do more than that."

Raina chuckled. "Don't underestimate how tolerable that boatload of money makes you all. I saw an armoire in town I really want." She shoved at Luke's shin with her foot, but then looked around at all of them. "You've done more than that. You're my family and, as someone reminded me not too long ago, our kind needs family. Thank you. All right, I'll think about sharing the load. And I will go out into the forest tonight. But I won't be far if you need me."

"You never are," Li said. He was kneeling behind her on the lip of the spa. Now he bent, sliding his arm across her front to embrace her.

The others took his cue, enveloping her in a very reassuring group hug, one that helped ease that ache...somewhat.

~

Most of her experiments with spellwork and potions, or manipulations of power to increase her skills in the Craft, were done in the cellar or her room. However, on full-moon nights, when she could, she went to the forest. Her staff was right. She needed a place to stretch out her mind and senses, and there was no better time for clarity. As she moved into the clearing she used most often, deep in the forest around her property, she reassured herself once more that she was close enough to feel if they needed her, but far enough away that she could get the space to figure things out.

Every witch was affected by the full moon. Before Ruby was traveling so much with Derek, sometimes she and Ramona met on Raina's property to do the monthly rituals, but often Raina did them by herself. There was a practical purpose. The primary order of business was channeling the Goddess's light to reinforce the house protections. But the opening of the ritual was always about celebration, uncloaking beneath the light of the moon, feeling the Goddess's supremacy fill the blood, that ancient connection that witches, particularly female ones, had shared with Her since the beginning of time.

Medieval superstition said Satan came to dance with the witches, fornicate with them all. A smile touched her lips. More likely, someone witnessed a male witch wearing a horned headdress, channeling the Lord, the Lady's Consort, and coupling with the head priestess to draw down energy. The Great Rite. Of course, witches celebrated the sensual, so it wasn't beyond the realm of possibility that they all joined in on that pleasure after the main magical work was done. In simpler times, a lot of birthdays likely could be traced back to such uninhibited celebrations.

She drew deep breaths, centering. She'd cast her circle, called Quarters, let that power fill her, thanked it for its presence. Now she pushed the cowl from her face, untied the silken cord and let the velvet robe drop from her naked body. On a nearby tree, she saw the gleam of moonlight on Cathair's feathers, the flash of his eye as it became crimson, affected by the magic swirling around the protected circle. Here she could let it free, the succubus and the witch, the flow of the power bathing her in heat, making her movements languid. It was here things became still, the world stopping at this one point so she could open herself to whatever wisdom was offered. The Lord and Lady knew her past, her present, her future.

She blamed them for nothing she'd endured. The Wheel was the Wheel. It turned the way it was meant to turn, and everything she was in this moment was because of the path it had taken her. She was strong, Their child in all ways. As she stilled her mind beneath that light, she let it fill her, became utterly still, waiting to see where it led her, what it had to show her.

Isaac's face swam up into her mind. She was missing something with him. She saw darkness around the young incubus, uncertainty. Balanced on the knife edge of survival, he based his decisions on that, not on good or evil, and that was dangerous. It meant he was going to hedge his bets. He was going to play both sides. Right now he was locked down on the compound, but if the female demon reached him, he would do what needed to be done to survive. It could get them all killed, including him.

She suppressed a sigh. Could he be saved? There was no clear answer to that. There might not be enough time for him to build trust, confidence. She could only shield him as much as possible and hope when the female demon was handled, there would be that opportunity for him. She sent a bolstering shot of white light to the young incubus.

The power swirled, making her body sway in a clockwise motion. Closing her eyes, she let its weight settle, steady her, point her to the path. Right to Mikhael.

What did he really want? What were they to one another? She had zero experience in this kind of relationship. She'd never considered having a permanent lover, but he might be offering. Dear Goddess.

Opening her eyes, she stared up at that pale sphere. She wanted him, a feeling that had no end. While she had a blood craving for him, to take his limitless energy, she also wanted to give it back, twine it together until they were one being. It didn't matter that they'd known each other for three days. She'd been waiting, and so had he. They were the intersect point in the universe for one another, the turning, key moment.

I've had a lot of sex, Mikhael. No relationships.
Well, that makes two of us.

A moment was just a moment. It was the only sure thing, and she knew better than to count on more, particularly with who and what she was. But right now, with the moonlight upon her, her woman's heart and soul wide open to the Goddess, who understood the female heart like no other...she hoped.

Mikhael had every intention of materializing outside the house, out of sight of guests, but close enough to be inside with her in a matter of a few strides. But when he changed his mind and appeared farther down the winding drive, he realized some internal radar had known she was out here in the forest. It recalled their pleasant time in the tree from the previous day.

Shrugging out of his shirt, he made it disappear, then winged over the trees. Lucifer's meet had been the expected status report, but something a little more than that as well. The Angel of Darkness knew about everything. When he dismissed Mikhael, he had only one thing to say: "Love *is* the duty, Guardian."

He wasn't sure if it had been a warning or affirmation, but Lucifer wasn't the chatty type. Mikhael's mind left that puzzle as he located the power center that marked her location. Silent as an owl, he landed on its outskirts.

The moon basked the clearing with light, and he couldn't fault the Goddess's desire for illumination. The robe pooled around Raina's ankles was a velvet garnish to the pale beauty of the body rising from the crumpled fabric. He could feel the power coursing through the ground, coming at her call.

She was seeking guidance and, if he knew her, it was what to do about Isaac, about him, about those she protected. During this ritual, her shields didn't exist, all of her given up to the Goddess. She sought answers beyond what pride, ego or her territorial instincts demanded.

She was fully in its grip, the way her head tilted back, eyes closed. Her arms stretched upward, fingers reaching for the sky as she accepted the Goddess's energy and arched into its current, a naked, feminine hourglass connected to the Earth and all the elements.

Shadows and moonlight swirled around her, a channeling of Dark and Light together. Watching those two forces come together, he found an answer to the question he hadn't known he'd been asking himself.

When he stepped through the circle, it allowed him passage. He was welcome here. It was a telling thing, because it meant her unconscious welcomed him. She was connected to things beyond the Veil, her body swaying in a slow, clockwise rhythm in the center of the circle, her fingers fluttering. Then she felt him. She tilted her head down, delicate chin tucked to the left, and he realized it was the same pose as the pencil sketch of the collared beauty on her wall, only her neck was devoid of such a sign of ownership, of possession by a Dominant lover.

Being taller than her, it was easy enough to step up behind her, align their arms, put his fingers in the spaces between her outstretched ones. She hesitated a moment, then she let her fingers curve and clasp his. He felt it then, the melding of Lord and Lady, as if They'd been waiting for the two of them to come together like this. He was aroused, he was moved, he was completely bonded to this witch. Everything made sense, and it had been a long time since everything had made sense.

"This isn't a Great Rite ceremony," she said in a throaty voice.

"But it can still be sacred."

His own voice was unsteady. It created a flash of surprise in those beautiful eyes she turned his way.

The world was a reflection of the souls that inhabited it; a seesaw between Dark and Light, rarely in balance. It kept Guardians like himself and Derek busy. But this one vessel, this woman, represented the best of the Dark and the Light. That was the answer he'd seen in the spiral of moonlight and shadows. She embraced her succubus nature, obeyed and accepted the dark power that was part of it, and tempered it with justice, compassion and laughter.

She was a bad girl with a heart of pure Light.

He was a Dark Guardian who served the Light from the Dark side.

Most of his service required immersion in Dark energy. The core of pure Light, the gift from his angel grandfather, was what twined with his dark inclinations, made him one of Lucifer's top Dark

Guardians, unable to be swayed or corrupted by the influences of the grim world he inhabited, even while using its more violent methods to perform his role.

He knew there was good in the world, though he was steeped in the darker sides. As he'd told Raina, he was more apt to notice and cherish a glimmer of light amid darkness than the blast of the sun at the height of the day. Puppies and innocent babies didn't interest him. He wasn't cynical; he just stood apart from it.

Raina connected him. Her darkness, when he clasped it to him, connected him to the fierceness of that light, because she contained both. In this circle, he felt its touch, let it wash through him, purging any debris. Leaving him balanced.

She leaned back against his body, drawing strength from him as the Lord and Lady did from each other. The shared axis of the world on their shoulders, their universe. In this sacred circle, there was no reason to argue it, analyze it, refuse it. It was perfection. It was love.

The word came to his lips as it had this morning, but he couldn't say it. He wasn't sure if it was because it was too soon for her to hear it or if all his centuries of life hadn't prepared him to risk the agony of possible rejection. He knew a lot of things about time, though. It passed too fast, but it was also infinite, so there was a choice to be made between the moments seized and the moments savored...and the proper timing for both.

"I need to close the circle," she murmured.

He released her so she could do that, bid farewell to the elementals who had gathered. He could feel their presence, see their auras, see their slow melting back into the sky, the earth, the forest. The flutter in his peripheral vision had likely been Fae spirits.

There were whole alternate realities in the peripheral vision. A human might see a dragon there, but when he turned in that direction, he would see only a bush shaped a certain way. The dragon was there, however. Right beyond the grasp of the known senses.

He wasn't surprised the Fae had come to her circle. Raina had the appeal to call up every fantastical creature he knew. Except the unicorns, who stubbornly refused to respond to anything but flaxen-haired virgins.

Their loss.

When Raina completed the circle closing and turned to him, he had her robe in his hands. He slid it over her shoulders, made a quiet noise for her to keep her hands at her sides, and then freed her hair from the collar himself, letting it spill loose and wild over his fingers. Looking at him for a long moment, she retreated to a flat-topped rock he assumed had served as her altar in times past for more concentrated spellwork. She used it now as a seat to steady herself as she began to braid her hair. When a moth fluttered across her nose, she wiggled it to dispel the itch, the passing sense of silken dust. It made him smile. Dropping to a squat near her, he tented his fingers on the ground. "Pretty thing," he observed.

"The moth?"

"You. Braiding your hair."

She paused, then kept on with the braiding, but he noticed her rhythm was less smooth. He'd made her self-conscious, a surprise. "No one's ever called you pretty?"

She shook her head. "I'm beautiful, sexy, mesmerizing. Pretty is... comfortable. Emotional."

Intimate, familiar. She didn't say that, but he knew that was what she meant. Ironically, neither of them hesitated when it came to physical danger, but they were both overly cautious creatures when it came to emotions.

"Pretty is a word a lover uses when he sees more than your outside," he said. He curled his hand around her bare foot, rubbing his thumb on the arch, then bent and kissed her toes. When he looked up, he could tell he was discomfiting her. Good. He intended to do more of that.

"You *are* beautiful, sexy, mesmerizing. But right now, you're pretty. When you sleep, you're pretty. Soft. The other morning, when you were about to go downstairs, Cathair was nattering at you for a treat. You sucked in a breath, rolled your eyes, but you went back and gave him a plum from your fingers while you talked to me. It made your hand sticky, but you waited until he finished. When you bend over to look at something on your desk, you pull your hair to the side. When you pass the hall tree mirror, sometimes you make a face at yourself."

"You've been watching me." She'd stopped braiding. Reaching up, he unraveled the braid, combed it back out the way he liked it, pressing against her knees as he did so.

"Since the very first moment. There's a girl there, along with the woman. I like it."

She didn't smile. "I see the boy in you as well," she said. "The one who crushed nuts for my sundae."

She touched his face, but it was more query than caress. "Men will do romantic things when they're infatuated, in lust, but they don't go out of their way on the small things. They go for the grander gestures to seal the deal faster. It's a very primal game. But you bought peanuts because it was nice, and you thought I'd like it. You have a soft side, Mikhael, a side that likes to please a woman emotionally as well as physically."

"I'll deny that to maintain my reputation."

"Doesn't change the truth of it."

"Also doesn't change what I am."

"No. It doesn't." Drawing a breath, she slid from the rock.

Sensing the mood shift, Mikhael rose, facing her.

"Give me the truth, once and for all," she said, a steadiness to her gaze that belied the tension he sensed in her. "What is this, Mikhael? You came here to do a job, and, after it's done, you're leaving. Yet you're courting me. You're stirring up emotions. You say I'm not a project, the way Ruby was, but what other purpose can you have for drawing me out this way? You say it's different for you, but how am I supposed to believe that, knowing who and what you are?"

"If you're looking for a guarantee, Raina, I can't give you one. But I'm not playing a game."

"I know there are no guarantees. You made it clear that your duty, your obligation, the oath you've taken, it comes first. So how do I fit into that plan? Or do you want me to believe you've become moony over a succubus, the madam of a bordello? Something so tainted that neither Hell nor Heaven claim it?"

"That's not true." His temper sparked, unexpectedly. "You don't believe that about yourself."

"I don't believe it, but a lot of others do."

"What I feel is what I feel. I want you."

"Today, for a year? Forever? Or do you have a specific contractual term in mind? How long do I pencil you in for?"

Forever, if you know what's good for you. He considered her, his brows drawing down. "You're picking a fight for no good reason, so what's really bugging you, Raina? This isn't a fucking session with a client, where you orchestrate it based on their needs and hourly rate."

She flushed, the green-gold eyes firing. "I didn't say it was."

"No, but you're not defining it any more than I am. You've never had a male you couldn't completely control. The bitch of it is, you've been looking for someone to take the reins your whole life."

He stepped forward, she backed up, into the unyielding trunk of a live oak. When he slid a finger down her cheek, he pressed against the soft skin, made her feel that firm touch under her chin, down her throat so she raised it, swallowed, though her jaw was tight, the eyes still angry, uncertain. "That's the real problem, isn't it, Raina? You want someone to take control, but nothing scares you more, because you've been in a situation where they did all the wrong things. You can't control how you feel about me, or how I feel about you. We're not always going to be able to predict where that will take us. If you've never had that experience before, why is it so difficult to believe it might be the same for me?"

Because you're a Dark Guardian. Because you're not saying it outright. Because I need to hear it and believe it. But Raina was too damn cowardly to ask him to say it. If he refused, she would feel like a cat who'd stepped out in front of a semi. If he did say it, and she heard the lie in his voice, she would feel like a whore in truth. She'd have to act like one to laugh it off, to take this back to safe footing, and that wasn't where she wanted to be with Mikhael. She wanted to be real with him, now and always.

He was right. She was picking a fight over nothing, though it was motivated by something a lot larger. She was in a situation she didn't know how to handle. While it had given her clarity, tranquility for one moment, the ritual had also made her vulnerable, and reality was intruding, the ghosts of the past. It was all bubbling too close to the surface. She was going to say things, things that would give him the ability to destroy her. She was falling in love with him. She wouldn't compound that absurdity by believing the same had happened to him.

"I need some space. I'm going back to the house." She said it without anger, but he held her there, his voice low.

"Don't let him keep you chained in that cage, Raina. Tell me what you want."

Her throat ached, but she managed the words in a steady voice. "If neither of us is willing to put our feelings out there, then we're not ready to trust one another. It's too soon. Let's leave it there for now. But I need...I just need to go. Let me go."

She pulled free and did what she swore no man would ever make her do. She ran from him.

CHAPTER EIGHTEEN

*I*t didn't matter what Mikhael made her feel, how he unleashed those deep cravings in her to trust, to surrender, to submit. She depended on herself, remained in control, and that was how it was going to stay.

Despite the manic pep talk, she was shaking when she came in the house. Li was doing his yoga, his chest flat on the floor in a way that made her hip joints ache just looking at him. Straightening to his elbows, he sent her a thumbs-up. "Good timing. Bachelor party just pulled out." Then he frowned, looking at her face. "You okay?"

She wanted to say yes, because she was the one who could handle anything. They never needed to worry she was going to fall apart or let them down. Damn it, it was just an infatuation. One that had gone beyond skin deep into the bones, such that they were rattling like a skeleton in its grave on a desolate, windy night.

A chill swept through her. Li snapped upright, his eyes narrowing, alarm spreading over his features. Raina turned toward the closed door, felt the vibration.

"Get down!" She spun, launched herself at Li and took them both back to the floor. The front windows exploded inward as she leaped, a million projectiles she warded with a fast shield that caught most of them. The rest buried into her flesh like tiny arrowheads, tearing holes in her robe, damn it. Her favorite ritual garment, blessed by over a thousand full-moon ceremonies.

She sprang to her feet, yanking the athame out of one of the deep pockets. "Stay here," she ordered Li. "Keep the rest of them inside."

The ground was still quivering as she ran to the door. The stained glass transom, an original piece over a century old, was in pieces on the floor. She was going to have someone's hide. Then she caught a glimpse of what was happening on the lawn, and none of that mattered.

"Raina, wait!" She heard someone at the top of the second-level steps, perhaps Marisa, call her name. Yanking open the door, she flew down the stairs and went to Mikhael, lying motionless by the destroyed fountain. Nearly half a ton of exploding concrete had hit him. His skull was a bloody mess, likely caved in, and he was covered by enough of the debris she knew his spine had to be snapped, bones broken. He was sprawled on his stomach, all that strength and beauty limp and lifeless. She wanted to roll him over, wanted to see what she could do, but there was too much to move and no time to do it.

He was a Dark Guardian, damn it. Nothing could kill him, right? He was just knocked out. She had to buy him space and vital time for his supersonic healing powers to kick in, that was all. Taking a stance over him, she gripped the athame and channeled all the power she had into it, preparing herself for what was coming up her driveway now.

How the hell had *that* gotten through the protections around her place, her own and Mikhael's?

It looked like a human female, followed by four mutated creatures unmistakably part of the demon ranks. Thugs, muscle to do the things the female didn't have the patience or time to do for herself. Of course, from the power Raina felt emanating from her, she could do pretty much any damn thing she wanted to do. She was looking at the harrowing evidence of it at her feet.

Reversing the channel of power in the athame, Raina brought it down around herself and Mikhael, beefed it up to the highest power setting possible. Just in time.

The female disappeared. A blink later, she phased in front of Raina, no more than an inch outside that protection. The phasing looked like the snow of a television coming back into focus, all the atoms reassembling themselves, and pushed against Raina's shields like a fucking ton of bricks. *Holy shit.* A phase demon. They were extinct, ancient beings long gone from the world, like the Titans.

Apparently not. Some twisted god must have unearthed one, just like Zeus unleashing the kraken. Or worse, this demon had unleashed herself, gone completely off the reservation.

The she-demon touched the edge of the protection, watched it sizzle along her fingertip. Raina cinched it in closer to both her and Mikhael, because though a phase demon could phase through any protection field, hence their name, they couldn't occupy the same space as the one they were attacking. Unfortunately, that limited Raina's options. She was all too aware her succubi and incubi were now entirely vulnerable because the net of their protection was a perimeter, not a cloak, and there was no time or energy to spare to change that.

As the finger phased out of existence, then came back into focus, the female cocked her head. She had the large gold eyes of a rabid tiger and fangs just like one, which elongated now until they curved under her chin. Her nails likewise lengthened.

"You need a manicure," Raina said evenly. "If you're trying to scare me, I've had clients with scarier appendages than that."

The female smiled, and it was the stuff of nightmares, like a clown doll in a child's room. The toy with a harmless grin that looked entirely different when the child woke in the middle of the night and stared at it through the dark.

"Isaac said you were a badass, afraid of nothing." The demon sounded so much like Bette Davis, Raina was certain she'd stolen the diva's voice from some graveyard archive. "But I'd expect no less of the sex demon who took down Elceus. Drained him like a husk, broke your own chains and swore you'd never be chained again, didn't you?"

Raina arched a brow. "You've been reading my social media profile. Sorry, I didn't catch yours. Name?"

"Erica." The demoness blinked. Her lashes were long and thick, drawing more attention to the mesmerizing eyes. Raina made sure she didn't linger there long. Erica might look like she was slouching in a dangerously casual way, but she was pushing hard against those protections, testing them. Raina's limbs quivered as she did her best to hold without appearing to commit any effort to it. At this stage of the game, it was all about the posturing.

"Erica? Soap opera fan?"

"You're showing your age, dear."

"I get the Soap channel. Full cable service out here, thanks to the barn-sized satellite. Are you here for the spank-me package we offer, or do you have another agenda?"

"I'm here for two things. Isaac. And you."

She felt a touch in her mind. Cathair, in the shadows of the tower balcony.

Get Derek. Go get him. Go now. It was dark, he had the cover, and it was the best plan. She needed help.

When he took flight, he was as silent as a whispering wind. It didn't matter. Erica's gaze snapped up.

She sees you.

Cathair shot high into the night sky. When Raina dared to pull her attention from Erica for a blink, she saw a shadow form behind him. Reacting fast, she sent a ball of white flame at that shadow and repelled Erica with a propulsion blast at the same moment, hoping to knock both back a few paces.

There was a shriek in the sky, and an eagle shot out of the flame. Beating his wings and somersaulting until he put out the fire, he closed in on the raven. As they plunged into the forest together, Raina heard the cacophony of the birds engaging, then Cathair's mortal cry. Pain exploded in her chest.

No. No. Raina snarled as Erica took advantage of her distraction to land a blow under her guard, a jolt nasty enough to unbalance her. She threw up her shielding again but had to go to one knee to brace it, holding herself over Mikhael's prone body. *Oh, Cathair. Sweet old bird. Damn it.*

As she crouched, panting, she used the point of her wrist to swipe the blood from the glass off her forehead. Her mind was spinning over the options; oh so helpfully, her adversary was already cataloging them for her.

"You won't last very long this way," Erica said, strolling around the fountain remains. "Your every movement underscores the weakness of your position."

She disappeared when the ground erupted beneath her and tree roots from the nearby live oaks clawed up out of the earth, their jagged edges ready to rend demon flesh.

"Underscore that, bitch," Raina muttered. When Erica's voice came from safely within the tree cover a few hundred feet away, she felt some small satisfaction, but not enough. It had probably been stupid, dropping her protection for even that bare moment, because putting it back up was like starting a car. It used more fuel. Erica's thugs were circling, the pack waiting until the alpha bitch wore the prey down so they could move in for the kill. They were close enough for her to see they were horribly maimed. Nothing to affect their strength, but grotesque alterations. Extra fingers, slits around their eyes and noses, chains of tumors around neck and wrists like macabre jewelry.

"Some people will put a litter of unwanted puppies in a burlap sack with a few bricks," Erica said in that starlet voice. "Though the puppies are whining and crying, the human ignores them, doesn't care. He drops that sack into a lake. Walks away, knowing the puppies are in there, fighting for their lives, fighting to breathe."

Erica phased just outside Raina's protective cloak once more. This time she stayed partially phased, so Raina couldn't get the jump on her. Though her unworldly gaze sparked with heat, it chilled Raina with its pleasurable malice. Evil was her fetish; malevolence got Erica off. "What you protect in that house are a bunch of unwanted puppies."

Raina's eyes narrowed. "They've done nothing to you."

"You know that saying, *kill them all, let God sort them out*? I really don't give a shit. I assume you do. You and I both know your protection isn't doing a damn thing for them right now." The she-demon glanced down at Mikhael. "I'm not of a mind to kill a Dark Guardian. For one thing, they're incredibly difficult to kill, like one of those campy slasher films. Everything you do to them, they just pop right back up, eventually. Unless you hack them into pieces, take the body parts at least a thousand miles apart, and burn them with oil. So much work."

As she turned a speculative gaze to her crew, Raina could see her considering it. Anything Raina said would turn her toward it, because Erica would know she was trying to protect him. So she'd have to fight her off, because no way in hell this Underworld skank was touching Mikhael.

"No time for that," Erica decided. "I've stayed off the radar a long time. Having him alive and giving him a decoy to blame for all this will work better for me than having Lucifer digging into who killed one of his precious Dark Guardians. They're his elite hit squad, you know. Treasures them like sons." Glancing down, her face split with that horrible smile again. "Especially one with angel blood. Nope. Don't want that kind of attention. A girl knows when it's wise to be coy."

As the demon fixed that intent gaze on her, Raina tensed. "Come with me without a struggle and I won't kill everyone inside the house. You can sense their well-being, so you'll know if I'm lying or not. I'll leave him where he lies."

Raina snorted. "You'll just come back later and kill them, after you have me where you want me."

"Possible. But it does give you time to come up with a plan to thwart me, doesn't it? The alternative is I send my pets in there and they eat them alive. Sex demon is their favorite aphrodisiac. Better than oysters, because they can fuck them, then kill them. You have some delicate morsels."

If only she'd considered it long before Marisa suggested it, teaching them how to handle the shielding magic and their own protections. She'd focused so much on keeping them safe, she'd forgotten the best thing to do for those she loved was to teach them how to fend for themselves, stand on their own two feet. But now wasn't the time for regrets. Raina had powerful friends. Plus, no matter what she meant to the male on the ground, when he woke up —and he *was* going to wake up, damn it—he was going to be majorly pissed off. He'd hunt this bitch to the ends of the earth. Unless Raina figured out a way to disembowel her first, her new mission in life.

She tried not to look at the paleness of his face or wonder again how badly he was hurt. *You let a girl get the jump on you, Mikhael. When this is over, I'm so not going to let you live that down.*

"Fine. But first I do this." Using the athame, she nicked Mikhael's wrist, brought it to her lips and swallowed the blood. Now she could sense his existence the same way she could her sex demons. Another way succubi were like vampires, in their ability to track through the blood. One big happy blood-sucking genus.

As she remembered Mikhael's dry humor, she pushed away the thought of what it would feel like if his life impression disappeared off her radar. Of course he'd tease her about that, say something like *I knew you cared.*

"Bring out the youngest female. We'll start with her."

"No," Raina said sharply. "I'm going with you."

"Too late. An example is in order. I didn't give you permission to take the Dark Guardian's blood."

Raina curled back her lip. "I don't answer to you. If your filth takes one step onto that porch, I will fight you. Those in the house will fight you. We might all die, but what you do to one of us is a strike against all of us. You take me now, all your minions with you, I go quietly. For now."

Erica eyed her, but Raina knew she was going to win this one, because she meant it. It was like she'd told Mikhael the night he'd come: *I won't be your doormat.*

"Fine." Erica shrugged. "Drop your protection."

"I'll come out to you." The protection would hold. She'd dedicate every ounce of energy to it as long as she could, no matter how it depleted her. Li and the others would know what to do once they were gone. The question was would it be too late?

She did know what it was to be out of control of the situation. She didn't want her argument with Mikhael to haunt her now, but if she'd needed a slap in the face about the difference between his idea of control and Erica's, she was getting that life lesson now.

Awesome, I get it. You can let me wake up now.

Li would do what she'd sent her beloved Cathair to do. Call Ruby, call Ramona. Get Derek. Goddess, the Light Guardian would never let her live it down if he found out that calling him had been her first thought when Mikhael went down. Given the adversarial relationship between the two males, Mikhael himself might have preferred the dismemberment and burning-oil option.

He'd get over it. Please, Goddess, let them all live to get past this moment.

The Lord helps those who help themselves. Raina was a strong believer in that mantra, whether divine power showed itself as God or Goddess, or an amalgamation of both, so her prayer fit accordingly.

Give me the strength and opportunity to take this bitch apart. And make her suffer for Cathair. Please also let Mikhael be okay. But don't tell him I asked for that.

CHAPTER NINETEEN

I've never lost a battle yet.
How do I know that's not an exaggeration, a boast? A lie?
Because I'm alive.
Do you anticipate everything?
You don't want to be around the day I don't.

"You should thank me for telling you how to kill Mikhael. It's always good for a woman to know how to get rid of a man, because they all become irritating."

Speaking of irritating. Coming back into painful consciousness, Raina tried to cling to the memory of Mikhael's voice, but it was no use. Erica never got tired of hearing herself talk. In all fairness to the psychotic demon, she didn't get much stimulating company, since her base of operations was a hole in the middle of nowhere, a rabbit warren of sorts. Plus she was surrounded by thugs who couldn't speak, just grunt and drool.

Raina had no idea where they were, because she'd been put in a sack. To thwart any of Raina's attempts to use magic to track her whereabouts or leave a trail, Erica had taken other measures as well.

Raina had bitten down on the instinctive panic as the fabric tightened around all of her, immobilizing her arms and legs. The suffocating feeling was alleviated only by the small hole Erica cut into the mouth area, managing to slice Raina's lip at the same time. "Are you familiar with the principle of the iron maiden?"

Raina had cried out as it felt like her body was speared in a hundred different places by sharp, short spikes. "A very real illusion, one of my favorites. No bleeding out, but oh so deliciously painful. It keeps your mind on things other than causing me problems. Here we go. I'd say hold on, because it's a bumpy ride, but you can't hold on to anything, can you? Entirely at my mercy."

One of the thug demons had thrown her onto his shoulder, his ham hands handling her like a bull juggling china. That was when she lost consciousness, because whatever vortex they'd gone through to get to Erica's hiding place had caused her head to hit something hard and unyielding. Rock, she thought, now that she was getting her bearings. She was no longer in the sack. She was in a cramped cage, naked. There was a steel collar on her throat and cuffs on her wrists, both spelled the way Elceus had done it to keep her succubus powers from working.

It was like waking up back in time, a time that still caused her nightmares, as Mikhael well knew. Erica had intended it that way, so Raina fought the fear, fought it with everything she had. She wasn't a victim. She was never going to be a victim again.

Mikhael was right; she did love movies, and now she remembered *The Man in the Iron Mask*, Leonardo DiCaprio declaring: *"I wear the mask. It does not wear me."*

She had a problem Leonardo didn't have, however. She was weak from blood loss and getting hungry. In short order, she'd be headed into ravenous, and it wasn't the human side of her that wanted to feed.

Erica gave Raina an appraising look. "Salivating a bit, aren't you? The pain helps accelerate that. But you're not quite hungry enough. I want you so hungry you'd drain a baby if I gave it to you."

Raina's gaze narrowed to slits and Erica laughed. "Before you can give one of those tiresome speeches about how you'd never do such a thing, don't worry. I'm not going to do that. I need your help with an experiment. I'm a student of your Craft myself, and I think, with your gifts, you can kill an incubus the way you can kill a human male. Your unique blend of witch and succubus magic will not only suck him dry, but make his power yours. You could become far more powerful than you are now, perhaps able to drink life energy with merely a look. You'd serve me far better that way."

Fucking hell. Yes, in her studies, Raina had suspected the ability to do what Erica described lay within her grasp. For obvious reasons, she'd never pursued or honed it. However, both the Underworld and heavens were aware of the potential, which was one of the many reasons Raina knew they both kept a close eye on her relationship with her sex demons. When Isaac ran to her sanctuary, Erica had done her research, probably torturing an Underworld archivist. She'd discovered there was more of value at Sweet Dreams than Isaac. Raina and Mikhael had both focused on Isaac at her target. Now Raina and Isaac were both in the demoness's hands, and she was wanting to play mad scientist with abilities no one should ever use.

When the she-demon looked pointedly at the far wall, Raina saw Isaac there, tethered by chain and collar, the chain bolted to the floor. The young incubus had been badly beaten. Not enough to be unconscious now, but possibly earlier. He was staring at Erica, his body rigid with terror. At Raina's searing look, Erica shrugged.

"He was cooperative enough, telling us when you were both away from the house so I could set up my ambush. But when I was going to let my demons have their way with you while you were out, he got very difficult. Fortunately for you, they expended their sadistic cruelty on him while you had your nap. Kept them occupied and out from underfoot."

Raina met Isaac's gaze, though it was a little difficult, since his eyes were nearly swollen shut, his nose broken and mouth torn. "I'm sorry," he said, his voice a rasp. Even that sent him to coughing blood.

"Oh, enough about you." Erica gave him a kick as she went by him. Isaac didn't make a noise; he just became paler and shuddered.

Raina made herself look away, take note of her surroundings. It was a large cavern, uncomfortably warm, thanks to a gaping pit in the center that emanated heat.

"Do you like my fire pit?" Erica caught her scrutiny. "A direct drop through the Underworld to the Earth's core. It goes on for miles. I've thrown creatures down there, just to see how long I can hear their screaming. It takes a couple moments for that short, lovely shriek of death to reach my ears, long after they're already burning."

Raina didn't respond. She saw other tunnels leading off from this one. Escape routes, or rooms for more supplies? Erica's demons would be coming and going eventually, giving her intel on what lay beyond this chamber.

"In your pathetic attempt to determine your escape options, you haven't noticed my newest acquisition. Other than you, of course." Erica nodded to the far wall, where what looked like a silver flute with elaborate markings and scrollwork was laid in brackets. "With that, I can take a soul, hold on to it, make the body do as I desire. Forever. The power that thing holds will enhance my own considerably. I can use it as a battery charger. Even better than a vibrator, something I'm sure you know a great deal about, with your tedious attempt to suppress your succubus power. You won't be doing that anymore."

She would happily shove that thing where a vibrator would go, just to see Erica yelp. But Erica was on to another topic.

"I'm sure you're worrying about the Dark Guardian. Don't waste your concern. That particular male is very affirmative action. He likes his pussy as diverse as I like my weapons. You were just his latest notch. But don't get down in the mouth about it. No one wants to be an angel's chosen. There's no divorce for them. They only choose one love, ever. He never has, though. Almost thirteen hundred years, if you can believe it. Too much human to him, too much darkness."

"You can save your breath," Raina said. "Succubi don't look for love. He was a great piece of ass."

"Your tongue is sharp enough to be entertaining. That's good. The day it's not, I'll have it cut out. Or split. You'd look good with a forked tongue. I like altering my acquisitions, sculpting them to please my eye." Erica glanced at her four minions.

Her words explained their grotesque appearance. They seemed bloodlust sated, logy and almost comatose. Probably a trance spell to store their energy until she needed them. "Of course, since you'll be serving me as a succubus, I'll keep you intact. Best to let your looks do the work, rather than wasting that tasty energy, compelling my intended targets."

Raina shifted to a squat with effort, since the cage was so cramped. Her flesh was pressed up against the four sides, so she couldn't get away from anyone poking at her from the outside. When she tentatively reached out with magical senses, an unpleasant frisson of electricity sizzled through her finger joints. *Shit.* Erica had also put up a ward against her non-succubus magic.

The cold in the pit of her stomach was fighting to become fear, outright panic, and she viciously clamped down on it. She would never be afraid again, no matter what she faced. It was her Scarlet O'Hara oath to herself, the underlying symbolism of *"I'll never be hungry again." I'll never let anyone determine my destiny again. You have me now, but no one stays on guard forever.* As Elceus had proven.

She wanted to believe Derek could find her. He had a long reach. He also had Ruby and Ramona for backup. Then there was Mikhael. Her heart clenched as she envisioned him on the ground again, and then before that, their...disagreement.

She knew Mikhael was right about that as well. Damn know-it-all. Her fear had been about the war between wanting him to take over, to surrender to him, and how it connected to her past. Not a fear of him mastering her. All the dark chambers of her heart, mind and soul had known it, hungered to call him Master. The resistance, the fighting it...that was the way it was between them. If they pursued any kind of relationship together, it would be as much about those fights as it was the sex. They liked that about each other.

If she wasn't so cold, so dirty, stiff and in pain, and basically at the mercy of a demon psychopath, she might have smiled over it. As it was, her eyes got that achy feeling they did when she wanted to cry but couldn't, thank goodness.

Oh, Mikhael. She wanted to touch his face, hold him, feel his strength. She remembered what he'd said, the night she'd woken from her bad dream.

No more nightmares getting past me.

Well, you fell down on the job, Dark Guardian, so I expect you to treat me to ice cream sundaes for the rest of my life. With nuts. Hope you have deep pockets.

She felt his life spark from the blood she'd taken, but she didn't know what that meant, if he was even conscious. She didn't know how long a recuperation he would need from an injury that severe. Though she could feel him, it was very faint. She told herself that was geography, not a reflection of his condition. They were deep underground.

Whether Mikhael would try to come after her or not, Erica was too smart to leave any kind of trail. So Raina needed to focus on her own wits. This type of situation required being hyperalert, 100 percent attention at all times, so no opportunity would be missed. It was a macabre form of Zen. There was no past or present, only the very horrific now.

"How is it you're even alive?" Raina asked. "I thought the Dark Guardians had kicked your asses centuries ago."

"Lucifer felt we'd overstepped our bounds as a race. It was genocide." Erica turned away from a cauldron, where it appeared she was cooking up something especially nasty. Her lip curled back in a sneer, her eyes fierce. "I escaped the slaughter."

She shrugged. "In truth, I don't miss the rest of my kind. We never cared much for one another anyhow. More power for me now, right? Lucifer sent the Dark Guardians to wipe us out back in..." She paused, appearing to count it out on her taloned fingers. "Oh, heavens, back in 800 AD sometime. Time does fly. Mikhael wasn't even a Dark Guardian then. Barely a hundred. Bet he was a cute, delicious little baby. Like chicken fried on a stick. Anyhow, I saw the writing on the wall. Put myself down here in a dormant state. Erased my life existence from the cosmic map. There's a price for that kind of magic, of course. Always is. Had to be cognizant of everything, even though I was completely frozen, inert, a part of these walls. Broke free about fifty years ago and I've been learning, staying low. Accumulating assets. World has changed a lot, physically at least."

Erica cocked a brow at Raina. "You think if you keep me talking, you'll gain an advantage. Not that I want to crush that hope right away; it's so much more fun to destroy it in various little ways over time, but I don't want to deal with a tiresome resistance."

The demoness pulled a hot iron from the fire, twirling it like a baton. Raina steeled herself, refusing to cringe, forcing herself to mark what Erica was saying and not lose herself in that dull orange glow or the image of her flesh being burned by it.

"Mikhael never saw me coming," the she-demon said. "I knocked him out with that fountain. With you gone, he won't know I'm a phase demon. He'll pin it on some rogue demon element, one I'll throw in his way with your scent, your blood, and the pursuit will stop there. I feel sorry for that scapegoat. You're a very choice piece of pussy. Mikhael will make the poor thing suffer.

"In the meantime, I'll continue to be a shadow in the night, able to do as I wish. Especially with a soulkeeper in my possession, thanks to Isaac's help." Erica paused at the wall, reached out to touch the silver flute. It looked like what the Pied Piper of Hamelin would use to call children away with him. "Tally that up with an accomplished witch who also has the power of a succubus, and I scored big this week. "Oh, and in case you're thinking the puppies will figure it out for him, they couldn't see me, any of us." She glanced at her minions. "All they saw was you out there, talking to yourself and standing over his body. You should be glad of that, because otherwise I would have turned your place into a slaughterhouse. Perhaps in time we'll go back for them, add them to my little cache. A girl can never have too many weapons, and a small army of sex demons...priceless."

Raina closed her fingers on the bars. Erica's eyes followed their emergence from the cage like a snake about to strike. "Why is it the villain always wants to ramble on about her plans and how clever she is?" Raina asked pleasantly. "Is it to torture her victims further? Or to prop herself up with a sense that she's more than an evil, crazy psycho that no one really wants around?"

Erica jammed the iron through the bars, against Raina's right breast. She screamed, no help for that, but it was a scream of rage. Those bars were her anchor point, her grip on them like the edge of a cliff. She wouldn't fall, no matter what. The gaze she kept locked on Erica was filled with hatred and the promise of retribution, not fear. No room for fear.

She was prepared for cruel and evil; she'd been through that. The fear she'd had then, that had consumed her for so long, was eventually replaced by fury, and that had helped her break out. Rage and power had joined with her succubus blood, and she'd been willing to dive as deeply into darkness as Elceus himself to take him down.

That experience had given her the ability to understand what Mikhael meant, about the darkness in his heart being something that could be used for good. But it didn't stop it from being darkness.

Raina convulsed against the bars as Erica kept the iron pressed against her. Her lips curled back, fangs showing, and she snarled at the she-demon. The pain was excruciating, eating away at everything that was keeping that fear at bay, so she fought it harder. Shoving herself against the brand, she reached through the bars and closed her hand over the iron, holding it even when Erica tried to jerk it back.

"You...can't make me...do anything," Raina said. "You might as well...kill me now."

Erica finally yanked the iron away and it clattered to the floor. She stared at Raina, who was panting, her burned breast pressed against the cage.

"Elceus taught me everything about enduring pain." Raina spat through the bars, and the demoness, not expecting it, got hit with the spittle. Score one for her, though she was aware of Isaac shaking his head, trying frantically to dissuade her from poking the tiger with a stick. It didn't matter, not when the tiger already had you in her sights. At that point, it was all about who backed down first.

"I may not be able to teach you about pain, succubus." Erica picked up the iron and considered it, her eyes running down Raina's body with malevolent promise. "But I know, no matter how you resist the pain, you can't resist hunger. Eventually, you will drain Isaac."

"Not happening. The hunger doesn't override my will. Not ever."

"You're lying. Even if you aren't, he'll beg you to do it." Erica slapped the iron back into the brazier and met Raina's gaze. "Because until you feed on him, I'm going to have more fun with you, and my demons are going to have more fun with him. I absolutely love having more than one toy to play with."

～

Mikhael drifted into consciousness, a hazy sort of fur over his memory, such that he came awake without opening his eyes, getting his bearings. He was in Raina's front yard, surrounded by what smelled like torn-up grass and broken concrete. Derek was there, kneeling beside him.

Some others were there...the incubi and succubi, probably up on the porch, along with Ruby and Ramona. No Raina. Her scent lingered...her blood.

His gaze snapped open and he surged up. He didn't contain his instinctive reaction, but fortunately Derek did, grounding the electrical energy that shot off him and struck the ground in four places, lightning smoking off the grass. One of Raina's rosebushes disintegrated into a pile of ash. *Shit.* She was going to nail him for that one.

"Where is she?"

"I'm going to lift the veil on your memory now. I didn't want you coming up thinking you were still in the midst of a fight. Mikhael, look at me. Tell me you understand."

He shook the clouds out of his head, and they stubbornly stayed fixed there. He focused on Derek, whose mouth was tight and eyes dead serious. Something bad had happened. Very bad. And Raina wasn't here.

"Get your shit out of my head before I rip off your arms."

"Good enough." Derek nodded. It was like a breeze going through his mind, an easy removal. Any other time Mikhael would have been impressed with the Light Guardian's command of mind magic, since exercising it on a Dark Guardian, even an unconscious one, wasn't the easiest task. But what filled his mind was enough to eradicate any desire but one.

He'd been on his way to her porch. He'd intended to walk up those stairs, kick in the door, sling her over his shoulder and take her somewhere they could talk this out, once and for all. He was going to lay it all out for her, whether or not it scared the shit out of her. And him. He had time, he could wait her out until she believed him. Until he got steadier with it himself.

A power surge, coming from behind him. He tried to turn, but the percussion had already hit, the fountain exploding, and then...nothing.

Nothing. A scent he remembered vaguely, putrid, decaying...

"What did you see?" His gaze speared the sex demons on the porch. Li was paler than usual, probably because Mikhael sounded like he was going to eviscerate anyone who didn't give him the right answer. Which was probably why Derek answered, and Ruby stepped in front of Raina's charges, though her expression held a disturbing compassion. As well as a great deal of worry for her friend.

"Raina was standing over you, protecting you from something," Derek said. "Something Li couldn't see, but she was talking to it. It didn't stay long, and he only had one side of the conversation."

Derek shared the details of it with him, a comment about a soap opera, nothing useful. Raina obviously hadn't known they couldn't hear or see her opponent, else she would have given them more. "Then she vanished."

"How did you get here?"

"Cathair." Derek's jaw tightened. "She always said she'd never call on me for anything, so when he came looking for me, instead of Ruby,

I knew it wasn't good. He kicked the ass of an eagle to get to us, and he's hurt bad. Very bad, I'm sorry to say. Ramona is tending him, since she's better at that than this kind of thing. Cathair couldn't see who Raina was facing, either, but he picked up from her mind that it was the female demon you expected. Isaac's gone, too."

"Nothing should have gotten through that perimeter undetected."

"I walked it while you were healing, and I got nothing, except the tracks of four low-level demons, thugs she probably compelled to help her. Once she got in, neutralized you, she had them cross those warding lines. They all disappeared in the same spot. No trail. What did that demon take that would make her want Raina as well?"

"She took a soulkeeper."

Derek considered that. "To use that, the user would need to be able to detect the moment a soul is about to be released."

"A sex demon can detect that. She took Isaac."

"But with Raina, she gets that, plus a powerful magic user." Ruby spoke from the porch. She'd put her arm around a white-faced Gina to reassure her, but her next words were less than reassuring. "More powerful than she seems, which is already formidable."

"What do you mean?" He'd made it to his feet and took a step toward the porch, gaze narrowing, aware that Derek shifted with him, keeping an eye on him. Fuck him.

Ruby pressed her lips together, expression strained and worried. "Raina doesn't tap into half of the power potential she has, Mikhael. She doesn't want to attract unwelcome attention from the Dark or Light Guardians, because she knows what she does here already has her flagged."

Mikhael bit back a vile oath. "Damn it, Isaac running here brought Raina onto the demon's radar. She knew she was getting double bonus points if she got them both."

"You had a tracker on the incubus, right?"

"They're too far gone. I've got nothing on him now."

Goddamn it.

Derek's steady blue eyes held his. "We have nowhere to start to find her. I can go to my sources, you go to yours, see what we can pick up. Then—"

"I know where to start. Give me a minute. You may need to do that wake-up shit with me again."

Derek didn't question, just leaned on his white ash staff and nodded.

Mikhael moved to the broken fountain. Water was still trickling from the spout, spilling into the broken basin and running into the ground. Rebar was sticking out of one of the broken pieces, so he struck the concrete repeatedly with his fist to make it crumble, free the iron bar. It was helpful, cathartic, and he ignored the reaction from the porch as he decimated it in two blows. Then he positioned the rebar over his heart, closed his eyes.

I'm here, baby. Reach out to me.

He shoved it in, aware of several cries, even a somewhat gratifying gasp from Ruby he was sure would chap Derek's ass. Then he was on one knee. He held on to consciousness with everything he had, casting that lure, casting it wide, in all dimensions. *Come on...come on...*

He fueled himself with vicious, lethal rage. Someone had taken her, would hurt her. She'd been there before, which meant she would see what was coming at her. She'd fight like a bitch straight from the bowels of Hell, because she didn't know when to shut up, back down, and they would hurt her even worse. He was going to make them suffer three times over for anything they did to her.

Just before consciousness left him again, he felt it. A single ping in a universe of darkness. His lips stretched in a grim, deadly smile, and then he fell to the ground and was out again.

He opened his eyes to see Derek kneeling over him, gripping his shoulder, bracing himself with his staff. The metal inlay against the carved wood flashed in the early-morning sunlight. The Light Guardian removed his touch when he saw he was awake. "You got her?"

"Got her."

"Then let's go get her back." Derek offered his hand and Mikhael clasped it, getting back to his feet. Gods above. Running his hand over the back of his head, he found his hair caked with blood and unmentionables.

"I believe it was your brain matter. Ruby and I knocked the concrete off you. Pretty much ground your spine and a lot of other bones to dust, crushed internal organs. Good thing your dick was under you, even though I assume the puny thing's probably still intact."

"Feels like it." Mikhael cracked his neck, his knuckles, shrugged his shoulders. He'd donned his shirt when he'd chased after Raina, so now he tore off the tattered fabric and let the wings spring forth, stretching them out with an assortment of bone pops that had Derek wincing.

"Done with your Hulk impersonation?"

Mikhael gave him a searing glance. "Underworld. The old chambers. Deep. Close to the Well."

Derek sobered. "What the hell would be holing up there?"

"I can't feel it. I can only feel her."

"You staked yourself to pick up her reaction to a typically mortal injury. So she is your chosen."

"I never denied it. Just what it should mean to her."

Considering that, Derek nodded. "Not real stable area through there."

"No. She should not come." Mikhael nodded toward Ruby.

"*She* is coming." Ruby, proving her hearing was as sharp as ever, came down the steps with a fierce look on her face. "She's my best friend."

"No." Derek stepped forward, his face resolute. "Ruby, you can't go there. For one thing, we're going to move fast. Mikhael and I both know the terrain."

"You're familiar with it," Mikhael corrected. "*I* know it."

"You really want to compare dicks now?" Derek scoffed.

"No. We need to go. Now."

Mikhael had felt her, just long enough to sense her whereabouts, but he'd also sensed intense pain. She was fighting a losing battle against terror, and Raina didn't allow herself to feel fear. Someone was taking her back to those dark places in her memory, the places he had touched, soothed. The rage boiled in him, made the ground beneath his feet quiver. Those on the porch felt it, shrank back.

"You've transported me before," Ruby was insisting. "I just hang on, and we get there."

Derek's mouth tightened. "Ruby—"

"There is no time to argue with her. *No*," Mikhael snapped. "You are a powerful witch, but you are carrying a child. You will not put it at risk."

Ruby's mouth closed like a trap. Though she sent him a scalding look, he could tell he'd ended the argument. It didn't matter anyway. She couldn't override his will and Derek's together, and though her husband had been willing to handle her more diplomatically, there was no time.

"We need to go."

Mikhael pivoted, strode away to give them a moment and to prepare for the swift transport. It was best that he and Derek not do the transporting close together, because the energy streams could bump into one another and cause an even rockier trip than it would be otherwise. Going near the Well was like going near Scylla and Charybdis. In fact, the Well was probably the origin of the mythology.

Derek caught Ruby's waist, brought her to him when she would have shoved him away. "How did he know?" Her angry whisper reached Mikhael's ears, but he didn't turn.

"He's a Dark Guardian. He can sense life and death the same as I can. Be safe, stay here and take care of her people. We'll bring her back. I promise."

A fierce kiss, a murmured exchange of words, and then Derek was striding toward Mikhael while Ruby stayed where she was, eyes worried, face pale.

Derek planted his staff. "She's pissed, but she knew you were right."

"Anytime you need help handling your woman, telling her what her place is, just let me know."

"Uh-huh. Step out of the way when you land, because I'm following close. Don't want to end up with my head shoved up your ass."

"I wouldn't want to make your fondest dreams come true."

Mikhael closed his eyes, found his bearing, and summoned the energy to get there as fast as possible with his body intact. He was going to need everything in working order to tear a demon apart. He wouldn't let the ache in his heart get in his way, the bone-deep terror that they might be too late.

He never felt fear. He wouldn't tolerate it now.

CHAPTER TWENTY

*T*he Well was a river. A boiling river of lava that surrounded the earth's core like one of Saturn's rings. There were creatures who dwelled within and on the banks of the Well. Impervious to heat or cold, they were blind, mole-like beings who saw without eyes. They felt heat, anything with life energy in it, and hungered to suck that energy out of the soul like the center out of a Tootsie Pop. They were oracles, messengers, as well as repositories of all the knowledge they'd ingested. If anything happened in this part of the Underworld, they knew about it, but getting their wisdom and surviving it was a rare occurrence. While they wouldn't necessarily mess with a Dark Guardian, it was different when he planned to stride through their ranks like a wheat field.

But Derek had never seen Mikhael so focused, so deadly. He wasn't waiting for anyone, didn't care for negotiation or hesitation. When he yanked one of those dark slimy creatures off the river bank, it came up in his hands with the sound of a suction cup. The Well dwellers could be various forms, but this one looked like a large vole, with a short, thick body, stubby hands and feet, and sharp yellowed teeth beneath its eyeless face.

As Mikhael seized it, forked red light illuminated its skeleton, a power surge to repel the Dark Guardian. Mikhael countered it, so the magic slammed into a wall he turned into a net over the Well dweller's form, such that the creature's magic activated inside of it. It shrieked, but it couldn't get free of it, or Mikhael's grasp, like a baby with its finger in a socket. Derek brought up his staff, and the blue light that shot from it was like a lighthouse beam, a heated glow that swept around Mikhael and himself. It turned the ground to acid, driving off any who were unwisely thinking they might take advantage of Mikhael's focus on the single Well dweller.

"Where? Female demon, with a captive. And an incubus."

A chittering, the language they spoke. The thing's four nostrils all flared indignantly. Its teeth looked like boar tusks. Mikhael didn't seem the least concerned about that. Tossing the creature aside, so that it rolled down the bank and into the eager grasp of the lava, he nodded to Derek. "She's holed up in the catacombs. She's taken over a section of them, guarded by about a dozen demons. Muscle, but some magic users."

"She's probably blood-connected to them. She'll know we're coming."

"Then we don't need to kill them quiet. I take the lead. Follow close."

He didn't give Derek time to argue, already moving away. As they left the Well behind, they moved into rougher, less predictable terrain. Lava spouts, unstable earth and dark abscesses, dangerous boiling mud pits that were concealed in the shadows of rock projections that looked disturbingly like teeth. Teeth that protruded in macabre shapes and random directions.

It was like being in the mouth of a dragon in need of dental work.

Mikhael's wings took him over some of the rougher spots, and Derek used short bursts of levitation, but the Well had a mind of its own. When the ground gave way on one of his landings, Derek let out a curse, falling chest deep before he could catch himself. The heat of the lava flow that ran a few feet beneath the crust was a burning lick along his boots, but before it could do more than singe, Mikhael's strong hand closed on his forearm, his wings beating hard to pull Derek from the greedy opening. The Dark Guardian dropped him back on the ledge, a safer distance from the hole.

"Hell, it burned my boots." Derek knocked the flame off the dragonskin with his staff, expelling it. He dropped in closer behind

Mikhael then. When it came to this kind of work, neither one of them was going to get into the whose-dick-was-bigger bullshit. Mikhael was right; familiar alone didn't cut it down here. If Derek got knocked out of the game by the damn trip to get there, Mikhael would be facing what was ahead on his own.

The rock formations became more frequent, the teeth consolidating into cliffs that curved over them on both sides, eventually transforming into a closed archway. The ground opened up beneath it, forcing them to walk a narrow ledge of rock against the cliff side. Five hundred feet below, a wide lava flow was visible, the heat felt even at this distance.

A rumble through his soles, through the wall next to him, and Derek anticipated, thrusting up with the staff as Mikhael grasped his forearm. The contact allowed Derek's domed shield to protect both of them, the rock that fell from the cliffs above bouncing off it and around them like giant hailstones. He'd protected the ledge integrity as well, and now Mikhael's shielding joined his, the two locking together to stabilize it.

Once the avalanche was done, Derek swept the area above with expanded senses. "Just random. More of the Well's carnival routine."

"I agree. Our enemy still lies ahead." Mikhael jerked his head and they were moving on. Within moments, the catacombs rose up like a malevolent beehive before them. The Dark Guardian didn't take the upper passages, heading without hesitation into the mouth of a tunnel that would take them farther down.

Though they both knew the female demon would detect their coming as soon as they engaged her perimeter guards, stealth was the order for now. They moved soundlessly, Mikhael's wings tucking in close to his back and then dissipating so as not to scrape the walls, since the initial passage was narrow. When the tunnels widened out, they became a chain of larger chambers connected by dark hallways. Derek and Mikhael both came to a halt, Mikhael turning to meet Derek's gaze. The arcane school had been centuries ago, but now, without thought, they fell into the hand, eye and body language signals they'd developed then.

Feel it? Ancient. This demon is old.

Mikhael nodded. They resumed their course, but now there was no banter, two warriors moving toward a battle they knew was going to be tougher than expected. Derek kept an eye on their six while Mikhael scouted forward, a sweeping sphere of surveillance.

When the tunnel narrowed again, Mikhael brought him up short. Derek felt it at the same moment. A low-level warding just ahead, so close Mikhael could reach out an arm and touch it. A trip wire.

Mikhael directed them both to hug the wall, nodded to Derek. This was precision work, and of the two of them, Derek was better at that. No room for ego here. Somewhere ahead, the woman his wife loved was being harmed, held against her will. They were getting her back. It was obvious there was nothing else as far as Mikhael was concerned. Hell, Derek loved the prickly bitch himself.

Derek focused on the warding, felt the shape of it, the make. Dropping to one knee, he summoned the magic, rolled it into a ball in his hands, and then gently tossed it over the warding mark. It spread out along the surface, a bluish tint. "Go now," he mouthed, and he and Mikhael stepped through it, like ghosts passing through a wall. A moment later, the magic dissipated, and the trip wire was intact again.

Mikhael made the short gesture that said their opponents were around the curve of the wall, about a hundred yards of ground to cross.

Derek closed his arm on Mikhael's. *Chameleons.*

Mikhael's eyes narrowed, then he felt what Derek had. His lips curved in that grim, dangerous way, and he nodded. They would have turned the corner and run right into a wall of chameleon demons, able to blend into the colors and energy of their surroundings until the last moment when their opponents—or victims—charged right into their grasp.

Paint ball? Derek lifted a brow.

Mikhael nodded again, that glint in his gaze. *I go first. Let their leader reach me.*

They counted it down to five. Then they were in motion, stealth replaced by savage speed, an infantry charge.

Mikhael moved swift as a panther through the narrow passage, bursting out into a wider area. Stone pillars had the look of cypress trees, trapped in the sludge of a foul-smelling swamp, the air rife with sulfur and toxic fumes. Derek realized immediately they were dealing with twice as many as the Well dweller had warned them about. The lying sack of shit. With a snarl, he cast the paint ball spell, as they'd dubbed it years ago. The orange miasma spun out from his staff, swirled through the air and settled on everything living, everything in motion. Ugly muscle. That part had been true, even more than expected. The demons bearing down on them had been mutilated, their faces a horror of cuts and alterations. They were also slathered in protection like kids in sunscreen, the intent of that magic to keep Derek and Mikhael from impeding their main talent—brutal killing strength.

His staff became a lethal blade, and he threw out a slowing spell to protect Mikhael, no matter what the bastard had said. But the leader was already in full charge toward the Dark Guardian. Or maybe Mikhael had made a beeline for him, the biggest thug of the group, a giant ogre-type creature, with hands designed to crush elephant skulls.

Mikhael leaped right at him, his wings out once again to give him propulsion. Fists clenched, arms locked, he plowed right into the creature. Or rather, right through, because he plunged his hands into the creature's chest up to the elbows, his feet braced on the demon's massive torso.

The Dark Guardian's face was a mask of murderous bloodlust that curdled even Derek's bones. Mikhael snarled like an ancient demon from the deepest level of the Well. The ogre screamed, tried to dislodge him with powerful fists and rippling arms, but the shift of power in the chamber was a sudden tide of heat. Even those bearing down on Derek came up short, confused, turning toward the struggle between Mikhael and their leader.

Mikhael ripped the heart out of the creature, flipped back off him and landed on his feet in a crouch, holding the oozing, dripping thing in one hand. But he wasn't done. The dark aura of his magic, now inside the demon's protection, spread over the creature. The she-demon had allowed for things that would try to sap their strength, but she hadn't anticipated this. Hell, Derek hadn't, either. With fascinated horror, he watched the demon's skull peel back like a grape and then, with an explosion of blood, sputum, and one final agonized shriek, it turned inside out like a purse, falling into a heap of still quivering, jerking matter.

A moment of silence reigned in the large chamber, the only sound the rasping, snorting breath of creatures with long fangs and wide nostrils. Then two dozen denizens of the Underworld were scattering, scrambling back toward the dubious protection of those cypress pillars as Mikhael straightened and moved forward. He strode knee deep through the gore of the thing he'd just demolished, looking neither left nor right.

Apparently it was a big mistake to attack a Dark Guardian and let him live. *And* take his girl.

As Derek filed away that important tidbit of information, he fell in behind Mikhael. He knew what a Dark Guardian did, what their capabilities were. But it was the first time he'd seen it exercised in quite that way. Then he thought about what he might do if someone took Ruby, and he was right on Mikhael's heels, moving almost shoulder to shoulder with him.

They went through another narrow passage, then wider areas, but the message had been passed. As they descended farther, the heat intensifying, nothing else bothered them. For now. She'd have something more powerful waiting for them. They couldn't lead merely with the dangerous vengeance he felt pulsing off Mikhael right now. When a male was in a rage like this, he needed someone to cover his back. Not just physically.

So when they slowed, taking account of the terrain, both of them sensing their prey waiting in the nest of chambers just ahead, Derek touched Mikhael's shoulder.

Mikhael shrugged him off. *I can feel her. Raina. She's close. They're all close.*

Derek risked the whisper. "Is she worth it?"

Mikhael, his mind in a blood haze from the latest kill and focused on the next, most important one, stumbled over the unlikely question, the strange familiarity of it. He turned his gaze to Derek.

The Light Guardian had a grim curl to the corner of his mouth, something expectant in his eyes. When Mikhael figured it out, he stared at him. Derek couldn't be yanking his chain at a time like this. He'd lost his fucking mind.

"You're quoting *Prince of Thieves* to me?" he said, disbelieving. "Kevin Costner?"

"Raina got us hooked on movies." Derek kept the whisper, as well as that same, steady expression.

Mikhael rubbed a hand over his face, rolled his shoulders. Derek always kept his wits about him. He remembered that, along with a lot of other things about him. He got it, then. He understood. And though his blood was pumping hot, his darkness up close and personal on the surface of his skin, Mikhael gave Derek the answer he was seeking.

"You remember the stillness lesson? Each time we moved, even from merely breathing, we were electrocuted?"

Derek nodded, his blue eyes darkening.

"You said I was focusing too much on what would happen if I moved, and not so much on being still. You were electrocuted fourteen times communicating that through body signals. I did not forget that. Or the lesson. My rage won't cloud me from my goal."

His gaze locked with Derek's. "And to answer your question, she's not only worth dying for; she's worth living a thousand lifetimes."

"All right, then." Derek bared his teeth in a grin, shifted the staff to his left hand. He charged it so that the ripples of power brushed Mikhael's skin. "Just so I'm not risking my life for your latest piece of ass."

"I'll be sure my *last* piece of ass knows you made that comment. She liked my wings, sorcerer. Couldn't take her eyes off of them."

"Dream on, Dark Guardian."

Raina couldn't think past her hunger. Erica hadn't used the iron again, but she'd used that spike spell, fire spells, things that didn't mark her but hurt as if they were puncturing, scorching, breaking. After each session, she was hungrier. Under this kind of body trauma, the stronger succubus blood kicked in to help the human side endure, to survive. The phase demon knew it.

Erica's latest trick was to break her fingers. It even looked like the fingers were bending and cracking, and though Raina knew it was an illusion spell, it didn't matter. The pain was real. The only good thing was it made her human blood useful, driving her to a faint.

As terrible as all this had been, nothing had been as bad as feeling that spark that was Mikhael wink out in her consciousness. It had been brief, a stutter only, and then he'd been back, but for one short moment he'd actually felt...gone. She hadn't expected her reaction to that, an overwhelming desire to scream out his name, throw herself against the bars and go after Erica, no matter the consequences.

Now, swimming in the blackness, she tried to stay there, to stay away from all the fear and pain, fighting the pull back to consciousness. But it was useless.

She'd been moved. She was in another cage, with Isaac, and it was only big enough for there to be a couple feet between them. He smelled...delicious. She was stronger, far stronger than Isaac. He was her kind, but he had the sexual energy she craved.

"There you are," Erica crooned. "He's a tasty morsel, isn't he? All he needs is ketchup."

Isaac stared at her with resigned eyes. He knew. He knew this was it. *No.* This bitch wasn't going to dictate to her. Raina groped at the steel collar around her throat. When she'd first woken and discovered it on her, she'd struggled with it, panicked. It had burned her hands, burned her throat if she fought against it too hard. Now she locked her hands on it, shoved it hard against her windpipe.

"What are you doing? Stop!"

She would burn through her neck, kill herself before Erica made her commit such an unforgivable crime. Always on her own terms. Always.

"No, no, no!" Erica couldn't phase in the cage with them. To stop Raina, she had to become corporeal, within reach, and then Raina would tear her skinny ass up.

Come on, make my day. Fuck, this hurts. Oh, God, it hurts. Mikhael...

She might have wailed his name even as she gritted her teeth and kept the steel in place. Until strong hands were on hers, pulling her fingers off it. Not Erica's hands. Isaac's.

"No." He was crying. *"Stop."*

She fell back, panting, and as she did, he brought his wrist to his mouth, tore open the vein.

Sexual energy was what drew a succubus, but sexual energy coursed through the blood, so a bloodletting increased its potency tenfold, turning a ravenous creature into an absolutely out-of-control one. She was on him in a heartbeat. No time for a howl of protest from her conscience, no time for anything but sating that hunger.

He was already naked, so closing her hand over his sex, pouring her energy into him to arouse him, to bring him to a climax, was as easy as breathing. She wasn't taking no for an answer, in the full glory of her power as a succubus, but beyond that, he was helping her, holding on to her waist, his face buried into her midriff as he shuddered and bucked. She brought his wrist to her mouth, drank deep of the blood as she did the same with his sexual energy. His cock spurted, his fangs scraping her in reflex as she fed on that power that could sap a mortal female, take her life. He had done it, over and over again. Now she fed herself on that, grew glutted and strong...and horrified.

She shoved away, backed into the corner of the small cell, breathing hard. But Isaac followed, dragging himself to her. His fingers curled around her thigh, holding on. Raina looked down into his face as he rolled his head to look at her, so sad and tired.

"It's okay," he said. "I owe you."

"No." She shook her head, tried to figure out how to fix it. "Feed from me the same way. Take some of it back."

"Don't think it works that way. She was...right. You can do it. You can drain our kind, as well as humans. Makes you more powerful." His voice dropped to a whisper, his gaze suddenly fierce. "More powerful than her, in time. You'll take her, then."

She gathered him to her, held his head in her lap. He nuzzled her like a cub, then let out a little sigh. He died, just like that. It was always quick, that kind of death. No time for long speeches or tears. But she didn't have tears to shed over him.

She'd killed him. She'd done what Erica wanted.

All of it came back, every act of cruelty done to her, to her kind. She knew how Isaac felt, but of course she'd always known how he felt. In this moment, however, the bitter resentment stirred, took over, became a hatred that could make her despise everyone who wasn't succubus or incubus, even Derek, Ruby and Ramona. She was tired of being used, tired of monsters like Erica trying to take advantage of abilities that weren't theirs. She was...enraged.

Erica wanted her off balance, wanted the horror of what she'd done to overcome her. The truth didn't have to be faked, did it?

Raina hunched her shoulders over the boy. She couldn't cry, but she could sob, keen, hold and rock him. Erica glided forward, tsking.

"He was nothing. No more than a bottom dweller. It's your

conscience bothering you, not a true caring for him. You'll soon lose that. Then we'll really have some fun together."

"You're a monster," Raina hissed, her voice shaking. She had her hand clasped on one of the bars for support, the other on Isaac. Erica wouldn't be able to help herself. She had to touch, and if she had to touch, she had to be real. Raina, flexing her fingers on the bars, imagined it as a Bruce Lee come-hither even as she shook, as if needing the support from something, anything. "I'll never serve you. I'll die before I do that again."

"I might not find one as noble as Isaac, true. But if I find less scrupulous sex demons, you'll favor your own life over theirs. Particularly if I suggest to them they might try feeding on you. You'll fight for your own life. I know it. You've always been a fighter. Poor baby."

Erica's talons overlapped hers. Letting go of Isaac, Raina whipped her other hand through the bars. Clutched in it was the six-inch length of steel Isaac had been concealing in the shadows, that he'd passed to her. Rebar from her destroyed fountain, just long enough to go all the way through that sharp-taloned female hand. She drove it through with everything she had.

You bet your ass I'm a fighter. The bars of the cage exploded outward as she channeled all that sexual energy into a blast too wild to be contained, even by that collar and cuffs. It broke their lock, made them drop free, though they took flesh with them. There was no time to shield herself, though, or poor Isaac. Rock rained down in the chamber, striking her shoulder, her back, leaving her with a dozen gashes. But Raina didn't let go.

Now she was airborne, the phase demon tossing her through the air to break her grip so she could pull that rebar out, phase out of range. Fifty years hadn't been long enough for Erica to hone her skills, to remember that staying a ghost was safest. She was going to have to cut off her own hand to free herself. She howled, becoming a whirling dervish. The world flashed by fast, and Raina grunted as she hit something hard, bounced off it, but it didn't alter her hold. A succubus could be strong as a fucking WWE wrestler, especially when motivated by pure, fury-driven vengeance.

Now there was heat, and a feeling of weightlessness, gravity clawing at her. They were suspended over the abyss, Erica trying to frighten her. The demon clawed at her, striking at her face, her knee hitting Raina's stomach. Raina used a few residual tendrils of that power surge to protect herself, but it wouldn't last long.

Erica had to be using some of her own magic to hold them both up, else that gravity pull would have been a hell of a lot stronger. The demoness wasn't ready to give up her half-breed prize. But if she let Raina go, Raina was ready. She'd put everything she had left into an anchor spell, drag them both down to hell. That abyss would take them both so deep into the fires of the Underworld, the center of the earth, that they'd be ashes instantly.

In her pain and fury, Erica had also given up one of her best advantages. With her suspended over the fire, her minions couldn't help her, though they were at the lip, poised and tense, eyes frantically shifting in those macabre faces. If they got hold of Raina, they'd break her arm to make her let go. Rip it off. Game over.

"Raina, let go. *Let go.*"

Mikhael's voice thundered through the chamber like the Old Testament God, raining fire and brimstone. It was so welcome she wanted to snarl in fierce triumph. *Yeah, that's my man.*

Seeing the flash of utter terror on Erica's face told Raina something else. Something she hadn't known. Erica was powerful, but she'd ambushed Mikhael the first time, which meant she *wasn't* more powerful than him. From her panic, it was possible she wasn't even *as* powerful as him.

Your ass is his, honey. We got her, Isaac.

Mikhael repeated the order. "Damn it, *let go.*"

They were whirling over an abyss. Had he noticed that?

"*Now*, Raina. Trust me. *Do it.*"

The command was sharp, absolute, and took over her senses as completely as it did when he took her body. She let go.

She'd expected a sudden platform to hold her up, something. Instead, her stomach flew up into her throat, choking off her cry as she plummeted, the cavern disappearing in a blink as she plunged toward that fiery pit miles below.

Mikhael charged forward. As he did, he snatched the soulkeeper from its perch, shattering the protections that held it with a sweep of fire that incinerated the nearest minion trying to rush him. These four had stronger protections, greater strength, but something far greater than Erica's magic, or even the combined magic of the entire Underworld, was fueling him. Mikhael didn't even pause. He snarled the words and became an agent of destruction, obliterating the next demon as he ran through him, the fire spell emanating from his very flesh.

As he emerged on the other side of it, the female demon spun toward him, pulling that steel from her hand. He launched himself over the abyss. She shrieked, began to dissipate—fuck, a phase demon—but he was faster. He might not have ever faced one, but a Dark Guardian was schooled in great detail about past battles fought by his kind. He plunged into her mind, plunged so deep she shrieked. Ripping out her real name, the one that called out the unique nature of her phasing so she couldn't hide from him, he bellowed it so it vibrated through the chamber.

She was caught in half illusion, half reality, but it was all he needed. With a vicious snarl, he impaled her on the soulkeeper, shoving it through her abdomen and activating its magic with the old language.

He called it straight from Lucifer's throat, that connection all Dark Guardians had with their liege lord. Somewhere deep in the Underworld, the dark angel spread his wings and thundered out the words. They resonated up through all the walls of the Underworld, into every cavern, every shadow, the depths of every mud pit, shimmering through every flickering flame. The Well exploded with gouts of fire.

Every creature that inhabited the Underworld quaked in frozen dread, for though Mikhael knew a different side of Lucifer, most creatures down here had good reason to fear the ruler of this world, as well as the legionnaires like Mikhael who served him.

Erica screamed her terror as those words gripped her. She struggled against him, her magic swelling from her in one last desperate attempt. His wings burst into flame, his flesh igniting, but Min hadn't known how right her tarot reading was. Explorer of Fire. He was a creature of the Underworld, a being of fire, and it couldn't harm him now. Nothing was making him let go until it was done. Nothing except one. He was counting the seconds since Raina had dropped. Five...four...three...two...

The demon gasped, her body going limp, a husk, and the soul-keeper glowed with its prize. He yanked it free, throwing her body to the lip of the abyss, leaving it hanging there like a rag doll. "Derek!"

The Light Guardian spun, an elegant follow-through as he decapitated the last of the four minions. His expression was as fierce as Mikhael's. Damn, Mikhael had actually missed the Boy Scout all these decades. Thank the Goddess there was no time to let the I-love-you-man sentiment overcome him.

He tossed the soulkeeper toward the sorcerer. Derek would catch it. Mikhael was already diving, streaking down into the fiery depths of the abyss.

～

It was a long way down, so protracted Raina had a surreal, fleeting thought of *Journey to the Center of the Earth*. The lackluster remake with the otherwise totally hot and appealing Brendan Fraser, the scene where he and his companions fell into the center of the earth. The fall took so long that eventually they stopped screaming and assumed casual, couch-lounging positions, even holding conversations. She wasn't entirely there, because unlike them, she could see what was at the end of her fall. Instead, she had time to think about the scientific principles that said the body would reach terminal velocity in so many seconds, but apparently that was for full-blooded humans, since she seemed to be staying fully conscious. The rate of her descent made it difficult to breathe, though.

She'd tried to summon some magic to slow her fall, and it had helped, but within thirty seconds it fizzled and she resumed the same rushing rate. She'd used all her energy holding on to the phase demon, and there was no time to recharge.

So she held on to the one magic she had, which had nothing to do with spells or charms. She'd told him she trusted him, and meant it. Even when her bones would turn to ash, she would trust him.

Then she'd haunt him for the rest of his life for not catching her. For giving her the utterly stupid order to let go.

She yelped as a gout of flame shot out just below her. She passed through it, and several others. They seared her flesh, but didn't burn, because she fell through too fast. She tried to maneuver her body

273

toward the walls, thinking she could grab on to a rocky protrusion, and instead ended up cutting her hand badly, bouncing against the rocks like a pin ball until she spun back to the center. Salamanders of flame passed through her fingertips, catching in her hair like pretty ribbons.

Falling, spinning, dropping toward the fires of the Underworld, the destruction of the body, leaving only the soul. It was getting closer, and now her heart thundered up in her throat again. It felt like a heart attack, like being on a roller coaster where she could tell the track was going to end and she would be launched into space...

But she trusted him. *Damn it, it makes no sense, but I do. I trust you, Mikhael.*

The walls shimmered with energy. A sonic-like boom made them quake, made bits of rock fall from them. Like pipes bursting, more flame shot out of the sides. The sound hurt her ears, stole more of her breath, compressed her lungs. But a smile stretched across her face and she spread out her arms, embracing whatever would happen. He was coming for her. No matter what.

It was like hitting a brick wall. An extremely hot brick wall, the inside of a pizza oven. It drove the breath from her for real, so she was gasping and nothing was coming in or going out, giving her air-hunger panic. But his arms closed around her, body fully against hers. When he righted them, no longer the horizontal mattress she'd landed against, the abrupt halt, the mind-numbing jar to the bones, gave her that dizzy near-nausea feeling. But it was all right.

He'd caught her in his arms, was taking her back up. The touch of flame was still there, the oppressive heat all around, but the heat that was him, that was the good kind of heat.

She'd closed her eyes when she'd realized she was about to hit that pool of flame. Since opening her eyes required energy, it took time to crack open her lids and see his determined, fierce warrior's face. A disgusting sort of slime was all over him, residue he was getting on her bare skin, but given the circumstances, and since it wasn't crawling or wiggling, she was okay with it.

He glanced down at her, and she saw his eyes were all dark, the way they apparently got when he was pretty worked up over something. If he stayed around her any length of time, she'd get to see that unusual trait quite often. That was okay, too.

"I trust you," she said. Though it came out a rasping whisper, she hoped he understood it was as important and significant to her as a declaration of something even bigger.

He held her gaze with that fathomless one. "I love you," he responded.

She fainted, mortifying herself.

CHAPTER TWENTY-ONE

*R*uby started up from the couch when Derek and Mikhael materialized right in Ramona's living room, Mikhael holding a naked and bloodstained Raina in his arms. Ramona came running in from the kitchen, where she'd been preparing another sedative potion for Cathair.

"She woke up long enough to protest. She told us to take her back to Sweet Dreams to check on things," Derek said grimly.

Ruby wanted to be relieved, thinking it was evidence that Raina was all right, but she looked far too pale and out of it in the Dark Guardian's arms. The one good thing about her being unconscious right now was they'd materialized in the room where Cathair was. The bird had worsened, and it had broken both her and Ramona's hearts when they realized the familiar was holding onto his life spark only for the chance of seeing his mistress once more.

Though he looked forbidding, Ruby laid a hand on Mikhael's arm, drawing his attention to the raven. Turning with his precious cargo, Mikhael brought the unconscious Raina to the table where Ramona had the bird nested in soft towels.

Towels spotted with blood. There was a bucket with more bloody pads on the floor. Mikhael met Ramona's gaze and the witch shook her head. She'd made him comfortable. That was all she could do.

Cathair saw his witch. *"Home,"* he croaked, weakly.

"We brought her home. Thanks to you. She's going to be okay."

276

Mikhael lowered her enough that Cathair didn't have to lift his weakened head far to rub his beak across Raina's ash and blood-crusted cheek.

Raina turned her face into the raven's feathers, her eyes still closed. "Go back to sleep, Cath," she muttered. "Not time to get up yet. Still...early."

Her familiar laid his head back down and Mikhael straightened, meeting Ramona's gaze. "Back bedroom," Ramona said thickly, swiping at the tears on her face. "You're sure she's all right? She looks..."

"It was a phase demon. She used torment spells on her, but the actual damage appears to be some bad cuts and burns, and exhaustion." Derek supplied that information as Mikhael strode toward the bedroom without comment. When Ramona followed, the Light Guardian turned to his wife. Ruby moved into his arms.

"Li told me he'd handle things at the house. He figured you'd bring her here, and they wanted Cathair to have all the help possible. I'm glad you're okay," she said into his chest, inhaling the harrowing scents of blood and fire. His boots were burned. Now that Derek took her with him on most of his assignments, she hadn't realized how it would tear her out of the frame, not being there to watch his back. After their baby was born, he wasn't doing it again, even if she had to take on an arrogant Dark Guardian or Lucifer himself.

"Go help them. I'll stay with Cathair." Derek pressed a kiss into her hair. "Mikhael won't want me in there with her naked like that."

"It's different with her. For him."

"Yeah. It is. I'll explain later. Go help your sisters."

When Ruby arrived in the room, she and Ramona did a full inspection. Her lips tightened with anger, seeing and knowing what the phase demon had done to Raina. Torment spells. They would exhaust the body, traumatize it and snap the mind. Raina was strong, though. The strongest of the three of them. Ruby knew Ramona would agree with her on that.

"Most of the cuts and bruises are from where she fought her," Mikhael said. His eyes never left Raina, marking every wound that Ramona discovered.

"She's in much better shape than I expected," Ramona said. The gentle witch had been thorough and proficient, though slow tears hadn't stopped rolling down her face throughout. Ruby knew Ramona was an emotional sponge, unable to withhold strong feelings when she had them. It just added to her appeal, because her quiet grief expressed it for all of them.

"The burns on her throat and breast will scar, but they'll never vanish. Unless she conceals them with magic."

Ruby stroked Raina's hair away from her drawn face. "Yeah, fat chance of that. She'll wear it as a badge of honor. *I kicked a phase demon's ass uptown and back.*" She glanced at Mikhael. "With help."

"No. The honor is hers. She was locked in combat with her when we arrived. She would have died killing her, but I have no doubt she would have done it." His onyx gaze flicked up to Ramona. "She is truly all right?"

Ramona nodded. "I'm going to give her a sleeping tonic to put her under pretty deep for the next twenty-four hours or so. While she's out, we'll clean out the cuts, tape up the ones that need that, and be sure she has no broken bones or internal bleeding. The succubus blood is resilient. Good healing properties. It will strengthen the human side."

"Very well." He rose from Raina's side. Ruby shifted as he leaned over her unconscious friend, cupping her face, his thumb sliding over the throat burn. He put his mouth on Raina's, a press of contact, and she heard his murmur as he allowed room enough to speak the words against her lips. "I will be back in only a few moments, witch. Behave yourself."

Raina's lashes fluttered. She wasn't awake enough to respond, but Ruby saw her gaze meet Mikhael's, and that was answer enough. Though she was still bemused and uncertain about the difference between this male and the cruel lover she'd experienced many months before when her life was plunged in darkness, she couldn't deny what she saw in Raina's gaze, something she'd never seen there before. Trust...need. Something that had the origins of love in it, the kind of love that was growing stronger between Ruby and Derek every day.

Turning on his heel, Mikhael strode from the room. Glancing at a bemused Ramona, Ruby followed him. In the living room, Mikhael had stopped in front of Cathair. Passing his hand over the bird without touching him, he registered the condition, the fading life energy. He looked over his shoulder at Derek, standing near. Nodded. Then he disappeared.

"Where is he going?" Ruby moved to Derek's side. "Does he have to go back to the Underworld? He said he'd return in just a moment."

"Step back." Derek drew her to the wall a blink before Mikhael returned. And he wasn't alone.

He tossed his bundle to the floor, a dazed-looking thirty-something male with shifty eyes and an aura so decayed and foul, Ruby knew instantly what he was. A drug dealer. He wore the bling that attracted young people to him, and she sensed the stench of his product. He'd also killed. She saw it in his eyes, because it was something any witch with enhanced senses could detect. She'd known Derek had taken lives when she met him, but the justice that pervaded his soul essence had told her the difference right away. What was in Ramona's house was something cold-blooded, something that took life without remorse, and profited on the misery and addiction of others.

"Mikhael—" She started forward, but Derek restrained her with a firm hand.

"Stay at my side." His jaw was tight, as if he didn't entirely approve of what Mikhael was doing, but he wasn't going to interfere. Something had shifted between them in rescuing Raina. A different understanding of one another. Since she herself had learned that there was a decided difference between Dark and evil in the past months, she stayed put, watching, though not without a measure of trepidation.

The male looked wildly around him. "What the fuck—"

Mikhael spoke several flat words in a language Ruby didn't recognize. Life vanished out of the human's gaze so immediately she would have missed it if she blinked. He dropped to the floor like a stone, nose and forehead first, the head toppling to the right so his cheek and lips pouched out in a lopsided way.

Spellwork usually required chants or tools. However, from working with Derek, she already knew a good sorcerer could accomplish it without either of those things. Now Mikhael stretched out his hand, eyes lasered on the dead drug dealer. He was poised in the manner of a pitcher watching for a line drive to come right at him, only he wasn't planning to duck. She caught the flash, the bluish light of the soul energy, and before it could escape, Mikhael spoke another sharp word. It sizzled across the room, telling her why

JOEY W. HILL

Derek had held her back. It was like the expulsion of a flamethrower, blinding her and leaving a streaked impression in the air in its wake.

Mikhael held the soul energy in his palm, then placed the two fingers of his other hand in its midst. Twisting them, almost like he was mixing the contents, he hummed a single syllable.

An energy expanded from Mikhael, an energy that pushed against the man-made structure around them. She felt the quiver in the walls, the floorboards. She didn't get to see the rest, for Derek turned her, pressing her and their unborn child against his body, shielding them. An abrupt, searing heat washed over her skin, a flash like a nuclear blast stiffening her.

She knew what Mikhael had done. Once she'd asked Derek if he had the ability to resurrect life. He'd said he did, but that it could only be done for very specific reasons, and there were always consequences. He couldn't give her back their first baby.

It was hard, but she turned. Derek briefly met her gaze. She could tell he was wondering if he should have sent her from the room for this, shielding her from painful memories. She placed her hand on his face, showing him the shadows of that grief that would always be with her, but also the love she held for him, which made all of it bearable.

He closed his hand on hers, so that when she turned fully toward Mikhael, she was still leaning against him, drawing strength. She would gaze upon this as a witch, marveling at the magic. She wouldn't allow herself to get trapped in the past. She'd done that once, and had learned her lesson.

The light in Mikhael's hand now had a trace of red through it, like blood. There was a cut on his forearm where he'd charged the magic. She could tell he was no longer aware of any of them, wrapped up in the concentration required. Bending over Cathair, he poured that light into Cathair's open beak so gently it made Ruby blink. The bird was weak, such that Mikhael had to cradle the head in three large fingers. The bird's chest rose and fell, rose and fell. It stopped. One beat, two beats...three.

Cathair took a deep, shuddering breath. Then another. A less deep one after that, his heartbeat evening out, then accelerating gradually, headed toward a bird's normal rate. His bright eye focused on Mikhael and they held that way, Mikhael obviously evaluating the bird's recov-

280

ery, his strength, so that when he finally pulled away, the bird was holding his own head up.

Mikhael stepped back, glanced at the empty body on the floor. It was gone in a blink, no evidence that it had been there other than some residue on the floor. He turned that to ash with another look, snapped his fingers, and even the ash disappeared.

Derek stepped to his side then, Ruby warily coming with him as they stared down at the spot. "Can you handle the cost of taking his soul?" Derek asked grimly.

"Offering to bear the burden, sorcerer?" Mikhael waved a hand before he could answer. "It's a cost I'm prepared to pay. She loves the bird. More importantly, he loves her. He was willing to give his life for her."

Derek nodded. Mikhael returned the gesture, then glanced at Ruby. His gaze stilled, measured. When he stepped closer, the memory of those wide shoulders, the powerful body, the things he'd torn from her in shame and pleasure at the darkest time of her life, came back to her, causing an unexpected tremor. She sensed Derek's tension, his shift to her line of sight, reassuring her. Then Mikhael spoke.

"Meet my gaze, Ruby."

"I don't answer to you anymore."

"No, you don't. You found your proper Master. And you found yourself." His voice lowered. "Meet my gaze, Ruby. Please."

The *please* lifted her lashes, and she looked up into the dark eyes. She'd very rarely met his gaze, she realized, and she saw a lot there now, things she hadn't expected.

He studied her a long moment. Derek didn't speak, but she knew his attention was locked on the Dark Guardian. While violence between them wasn't out of the question, different emotions were swirling in the air now. Mikhael lifted a hand, brushed a knuckle across her cheekbone. It instantly brought back their last meeting, when he'd struck her there, though his touch now was impossibly gentle.

"It was necessary," Mikhael said at last. "But I regret it, nonetheless."

Then he headed back into the room with Raina, leaving them to watch over Cathair.

Ruby let out a shaky breath. "I knew he was ruthless, but..." She shook her head. "You're right. He's absolutely made for her."

~

Twenty-four hours later, Raina surfaced. She wanted to go home. Ramona said she was a little too fragile to transport magically again, so Ruby volunteered to take her in her van. Mikhael had said little to her, understanding she needed some time. But he was by her side, so close. Raina had felt him even while she slept.

Now, he carried her out to the flower-painted vehicle, held her in his lap in the back as Derek and Ruby sat in front, Ruby driving the van along the winding road to Sweet Dreams. As the shadows of the ancient gray-beard trees passed over her face, alternating with the afternoon sun, Raina knew that fervent feeling that Dorothy had. There was no place like home. When she saw the house emerge, that ache in her throat nearly choked her.

She'd been trapped in Hell twice in her life, but both times, she'd ended up here. This was her sanctuary, just as Mikhael had said.

There were other forms of sanctuary, though. His heart was beating under her ear, his arms around her body. He'd rescued her. Stayed with her.

If something ever happened...I would come for you.

Once they got her settled inside, Derek and Ruby took their leave, knowing she needed to rest, though Ruby gave her a hug and the assurance she would be checking in on her daily. The head tilt toward Mikhael, followed by an amusingly intent look, was similar to the one Ramona had given her that day outside of her shop.

I expect deets, girlfriend. Lots of deets. Explicit deets.

Mikhael let her have some time in the parlor, accepting the hugs and touches of her succubi and incubi, reassuring them she was alive and well. Gina didn't want to let go of her, sitting at her feet to hug her knees, and Li and Saul draped protectively over the back of her chair while the others took every opportunity to press close, touch her hair, issue all sorts of promises about handling everything so she could just rest for the next few days, next few weeks, or they'd wait on her hand and foot forever if she needed it.

Raina hugged them all to her fiercely. Her babies were growing up, but not in the bad way for sex demons. Maybe her magic was helping them with that. The demolished fountain had been cleaned up, other sculpture pieces placed on the broken portions to make it look like a decorated ancient ruin, rather than the aftermath of a fight. She might just leave it that way for a while.

"Time for her to get some rest," Mikhael told them firmly, nudging Gina gently out of his path as he bent down, picked Raina up again. She could walk, but from his expression, she decided she'd wait to argue with him in private. Plus, it was three levels of stairs.

When they reached her room, she glanced toward the balcony, where Cathair was nested in leaves, shredded cardboard and down, arranged inside the cup of a thick *Baywatch* beach towel and a ragged box top. The ragged top suggested Cathair had added the shredded cardboard pieces to his nest. "Ramona's doing?" Raina asked.

"She said he won't be up to perching for a few days." The raven had his head under his wing, snoozing deep.

"I didn't think ravens could snore."

"Well, he's a badass. Taking out eagles and all."

"Ruby told me what you did." Her gaze turned to him. "You shouldn't have...but I'm glad you did. He means a lot to me."

"I know. Maybe next time, both he and his mistress will be a little less badass, live to fight another day. Let someone else do their fighting for them."

"You have any recommendations on that? My last protector got knocked out by lawn ornamentation. I need someone tougher."

"Keep it up," he warned. "You won't always be recuperating."

She smiled, closed her eyes. But her hand tightened on him and she couldn't help the tremor that ran through her arm. It was too close, all of it. Sensing it, he slid into the bed with her, holding her against his body. The shaking became worse, an ache that crashed over her, all of it coming together in one wave now that she was safe in her room, safe with him.

She was making noises against his chest that made her heart feel as if it were being shredded like that cardboard. Goddess, she wished she could cry.

"I'm here," he murmured. "I'm here, Raina. I'll always be here for you, no matter what. Sshh. You're breaking my heart. Please stop."

She nodded against him, but had to keep on for a while, until she exhausted herself. When she slowed down, he was rocking her. She liked the fact he didn't try to make her talk, didn't talk much himself. It made things easier, less complicated.

"Sleep, baby. When you wake, I'm going to show you an entirely different side of Hell. A much better one."

She wasn't sure if it was a good idea for her to return to the Underworld anytime this century, even if there was a part that looked like Wonka's chocolate factory. She didn't have the energy to argue, though. Ramona had slipped her one of those sleep tonics, saying it would make the trip easier. Plus she had more bruises and healing cuts than the loser of a prize fight. Only she'd won. In a lot of different ways. She hoped.

She slipped off into dreams with a vague protest. She felt his lips curve against her temple. That was all right. They weren't going to be able to tell her what to do forever. She'd let it go. For now.

Since she'd been wrapped up in something like a potato bag on her last trip into the Underworld, she wasn't entirely sure what to expect, but it turned out that Mikhael didn't take her down a long bumpy tunnel, through an ominous gateway or across the River Styx. He simply flew through the sky, then there was a shimmer of energy over them and they were somewhere else entirely. Below ground. Even trusting Mikhael, she was tense, but when they materialized, she was greeted by an image that was more out of Arthurian legend than Faustian. A crystal cave. Letting go of his hand, she slid her hand along walls glittering with stones the colors of flame, opal and fiery topaz. There were stalactites and stalagmites with rainbows of earthen colors. It was breathtaking. Light came from somewhere, a random dance of starlight in the room.

"The crystals have a variety of magical properties, and they're organic. Periodically they're harvested, used for different energy work, here and above."

There was heat here, but a heat that comforted and reassured, not the kind that burned flesh. When she put her hand to that burn on her throat, his overlaid it. He pressed his body up against her, providing reassurance, comfort.

"It's all right." She swallowed. "It's a reminder that I beat her."

"You had some help."

"A little bit." Then her voice softened, remembering Isaac. "A lot, actually."

He slid his arm around her waist. "He's in the Underworld now, going through Redemption. Tough, but not anywhere near as punitive as what he was originally facing, thanks to his sacrifice for you. You affected him, made him want to be something different. He'll have another chance, another life. I misjudged him."

"No, you didn't. But he overcame what he was, in a moment when it really mattered. I'll pray for him."

"Come with me." Taking her hand, he guided her onward, out of that chamber and through a couple more like it, and then into a cavern that opened up wide and tall, where the stalagmites and stalactites met like the pillars of an ancient temple. They were a clear quartz crystal, a constant flow of water down their surface making them glisten.

Water dripped from the walls as well, then down across the ground, over flat layered rocks and into a hot spring. Turning in a circle, taking in all angles of the chamber, something stirred deep inside Raina. That odd ache was in her throat, but there was something different about it. As she moved forward, Mikhael released her hand. She felt him watching her as she reached out, touched the walls.

She gasped, feeling a reaction to it, a reaction she'd never had before. When she touched her face, she came away with wetness. She turned to face Mikhael, emotions rolling through her chest, uncertain, vulnerable.

"This is where the tears of the tearless witches go," he said softly. He came to her, captured one as it came from her eye. "In this chamber, a tearless witch may cry."

She swallowed, gazed up at him. "Why?"

"Because I want to give you things no one else has. Now and always. I want you to heal from those things that have been done to you, to know that you can give your heart to me and I'll take care of it. I never want to cause a single tear of yours to come to this place."

She moved into his arms as those tears flowed. It was like it had been in her attic room, before she slept, only now it was even more powerful, the waves getting stronger and stronger. But it was okay. For the first time in her life, she experienced the catharsis of female weeping, of crying over her lost childhood, the things she'd seen done to her parents, to others of her kind. She cried for nearly losing Cathair, for what Mikhael and her friends had done for her.

And she cried for every time she'd watched *Titanic*, and Rose had told Jack she'd never let go. As well as when she'd told him she believed him innocent of stealing the blue diamond, not because she'd been given proof, but because she'd believed in him in her heart, above everything and everyone else.

Mikhael sat down on a rock near the edge of the pool, keeping her against his chest. While she cried, he patiently slid off her shoes and his own so they could put their feet into the salt water, and then he kept holding her until she ran out. For a long time, he didn't say anything, just let her gaze into that multifaceted pool, at all the tears of tearless witches. She wondered what they wished they could cry about.

Like the crystal caves, there was no evidence of a light source, but a dim glow made the water sparkle.

"Can we swim in it?" she asked at last.

"Only if you're naked. There are strict rules."

She smiled. "I would never doubt the word of a Dark Guardian, but since it's you, I think you're full of it, Mikhael Roman."

Nevertheless, she pushed away from him, rose and pulled her dress over her head, letting it drop to the side. She was wearing nothing under it, because he'd told her to wear only the velvet dress that clung to her curves. She liked pleasing him, liked the way he reacted when she did as he commanded. It made her react as well.

Stepping into the water, she followed the rock steps until the water lapped at her ribs, just under her breasts. Turning, she dropped beneath the water's surface, not at all surprised when he touched her, drew her up. He was naked, too.

"I think only witches are allowed in the tearless witch pool."

"Call a lifeguard."

She rested her hands on his hips, splaying her fingers over all the delicious muscle on his abdomen and chest until she reached his shoulders. When his fingers tangled in her heavy wet hair, she tilted her head at the pressure he exercised upon it, holding her captive as he bent and suckled the tears of witches off her throat.

"Will you say it again?" she whispered.

"What?" He murmured it against her skin.

"What you said...when you caught me."

He nodded against her collar bone, kept kissing her, making his way down to her breast. Tendrils of lust unfurled in lazy pleasure everywhere he touched, but she managed to give him a push.

"What?" he asked. "You meant now?"

This time she slipped from his grasp in truth, giving him a splash directly in the face. She evaded him for a solid three seconds before he caught her. He lifted her up against him, guiding her thighs around his hips, his arm banding around her back as he stroked into a deeper part of the pool, where her feet couldn't touch but his could, where she depended on him to keep her above the water. Or take her under, as their desire might dictate.

His cock slid against her sex. "Put me inside you," he said, low. "I want to feel your hands."

When she gave his testicles a little scrape with her nails, he bit her neck in response. She slid her fingers over him, her knuckles brushing her mound as she adjusted and he helped, shifting so she could angle him into her. The moment she was in the right position, he took over, tightening his arm around her back and hips, closing the distance and sliding in deep.

She hummed at the fullness, the near-painful stretch swiftly replaced with something else. He kissed her forever, taking a nip at her tongue as he withdrew, pushed back in.

He could get her aroused with only a look, but as hard as he was, as insistent, she was aware she could do the same, with no more than a lazy, hip-swinging walk into the water.

"Mikhael...please."

He lifted his head, those intriguing eyes studying her. So much unknown about him, but she had a feeling he'd open that treasure room for her now and again, whenever she desired, because she and she alone had that key. His mouth curved, and she liked the way it looked. It was pretty damn close to a smile. He had a sadistic side, but this wasn't that. It wasn't the torment of making her beg that turned him on. It was the fact that she would do it for him, that she trusted him with that side of herself. It flat-out turned him on when she begged, driven by raw need, lust...love.

"Please." She curved her arms around his shoulders, bringing her breasts up against his chest, pressing as close to him as she could get, one body, one heart, one shared soul. "Please. Tell me. I'm yours."

He shuddered. Exultation swept her, the knowledge that this ownership went two ways and would grow deeper and more binding with every passing moment.

"I love you, Raina. Always and forever. You have my heart. You'll have it long after you're gone and I've grieved you thousands of years."

The thought of him grieving made her heart hurt, and she locked her hands around his neck, pulling herself up to kiss him back fiercely. "I'll be such a pain in your ass, you'll be happy to be rid of me."

He touched her face, not smiling. Not saying anything. So she caught his hand, held it tightly. "I'll never be gone," she promised. "If Isaac can have another life, then so can I. I'll come back to you again and again."

When she saw raw emotion in those eyes, her heart cracked open entirely, giving him everything. "I love you, Mikhael. Always and forever. Through every life, now until eternity."

He shifted his hand to her nape, thrust, withdrew, took himself into her deep and slow, making her thighs tremble. She squeezed down on him, giving as good as she was getting, and was rewarded by the quiver in those powerful hands.

"Come with me," she said. "Together."

The climax made the water ripple all around them. Their cries echoed throughout the chamber, surrounding and reinforcing the pledges they'd made here. The pleasure of it brought tears to her eyes again. Unashamed, she baptized his shoulders with them, until he pulled her head back and kissed every one of them away.

They lay on that flat series of steps, half in and half out of the pool, the water lapping along their hips as she curved into the side of his body. He was stroking her hair.

Raina pressed a kiss into his chest, played with the silken line of hair down his abdomen. She wanted to swim some more, so she sat up, stretched, then stroked off into the water. It was shaped like a figure eight, so she made a couple passes, pausing under a waterfall to let the warm, salty water splash over her face, her breasts, before stroking his way again.

He was up on his elbows, watching her. He made quite a picture, sprawled out like that. His cock was stirring again, a wonderfully promising reaction. She didn't want to leave here until they'd done this at least two more times. After all, the law of three was very important to witches.

"I just had a thought."

"I bet." She gave him a sultry look. "Want to bring that impressive thought over here?"

"Nymphomaniac."

"Sex demon," she corrected.

"Same thing." But he slid fully into the water, lazy and dangerous as a crocodile. She held her ground until he was there in front of her, just his head above the surface of the water, for he stayed on his knees so he could wrap his arms around her hips.

"What was your thought?" she asked, watching his gaze course with heat over her breasts.

"If you come back to me in every lifetime, I'll have to court and romance you every time. That's a lot to ask of a man. It'll be like *Titanic*, times three hundred. No pussy is that good, even yours, and—"

She managed to push his head under. She was pretty sure he allowed it, but it was satisfying all the same. Then she shrieked as he came up under her like a swamp monster, carting her over his shoulder, suffering her pinches and slaps on his fine muscular ass until he sat her on a ledge along the water's edge. When he slipped back down to his knees, it put him at an ideal level, such that when he crowded himself between her thighs, his mouth ended up in a very strategic place. In no time she was gasping and writhing, arched back on that flat rock.

When she climaxed, her screams echoed off the walls again, and he left her limp, sated and tamed...for the moment. His capable hands brought her back into the water, letting her twine around him. They waltzed slow, languid circles together.

"You all right?" he said against her hair. She nodded. It touched her and made her smile, realizing he was worried he'd overdone it, because she was quivering. She definitely wasn't at full strength yet.

But when she was, she'd turn the tables and make him weak as a baby. She swore it to herself, but then the playfulness melted away before a stronger emotion.

"I would pursue you through any life," he said against her hair. "You'll never lose me."

She closed her eyes, held tighter and believed him with all of her woman's heart. A Dark Guardian didn't lie. Ever.

Especially *her* Dark Guardian.

* * *

WANT MORE? *Arcane Chaos* features Ramona and her Grim Reaper hero!

A Grim Reaper knows when every living thing will die. But Silas can't see Ramona's death. It's one of many reasons the Chaos witch intrigues him. She's the antithesis of order, but when a dire threat to a single soul reveals a deeper attempt to ruin the order of life and death in the world, her power might be the key to making things right.

If they survive the evil that wants to destroy everything that matters to them both, Ramona wonders if she's finally found the male who won't run from who and what she is. Suddenly the term "Death is the only certainty in life," isn't a threat—it might be a promise.

CLICK HERE TO READ NOW
ARCANE CHAOS

Reading this in print format?
Look for it at your favorite book vendor!

ABOUT THE AUTHOR

Having penned over fifty acclaimed BDSM contemporary and paranormal titles, which includes six award-winning series, *Joey W. Hill* has been awarded the RT Book Reviews Career Achievement Award for Erotic Romance. A submissive herself, Hill brings authenticity to her intensely emotional love stories.

She is grateful for the support of a wonderful and enthusiastic readership, which allows her to live on her beloved Carolina coast with her even more beloved husband and menagerie of animals.

- On the Web: https://storywitch.com
- Twitter: https://twitter.com/JoeyWHill
- Facebook: https://facebook.com/JoeyWHillAuthor
- Facebook Fan Forum: https://facebook.com/groups/ JWHMembersOnly
- MeWe: https://mewe.com/i/joeywhill
- GoodReads: https://www.goodreads.com/author/show/ 103359.Joey_W_Hill
- BookBub: https://bookbub.com/authors/joey-w-hill
- Amazon: https://amazon.com/Joey-W-Hill/e/B001JSCIW0

ALSO BY JOEY W. HILL

Mirror of My Soul

Mistress of Redemption

Rough Canvas

Branded Sanctuary

Divine Solace

Worth The Wait

Truly Helpless

In His Arms

Ignition Sequence

Naughty Bits Series

Naughty Bits

Naughty Wishes

Vampire Queen Series

Vampire Queen's Servant

Mark of the Vampire Queen

Vampire's Claim

Beloved Vampire

Vampire Mistress *(VQS: Club Atlantis)*

Vampire Trinity *(VQS: Club Atlantis)*

Vampire Instinct

Bound by the Vampire Queen

Taken by a Vampire

The Scientific Method

Nightfall

Elusive Hero

Night's Templar

Vampire's Soul

Vampire's Embrace

Vampire Master *(VQS: Club Atlantis)*

Vampire Guardian *(VQS: Club Atlantis)*

Vampire's Choice